Theater of Love

D.L. Drummond

1st edition 2024

ISBN 978-1-964588-02-5 (paperback)

ISBN 978-1-964588-00-1 (ebook)

Acknowledgements

To my dear family and friends, who dealt with my continual obsession for months, but also never stopped believing in me. I love you all.

Part One

Iyah

1

New York

He's late.

The fact that we're meeting on his home turf for this in-person chemistry read is mildly annoying, but I grudgingly acknowledge that the choice makes the most sense. Of the two of us, Julien Caffrey had the most easily recognized name. He has an established, successful modeling career *and* a personal agent. My resume, on the other hand, consists of a handful of local commercials and one non-speaking part in a film short.

I am the unknown here. Therefore, I must cater to his convenience. I get that completely. What I don't understand is how we are in *his* city, in *his* agent's office, yet *he* is the one who is late. I arrived on time, and I had to fly in from another state!

He staggers into the office ten minutes after the agreed upon time. When the bell above the swinging door jangles, I snap to attention…and immediately groan. He is scruffy, rumpled, and reeks faintly of cigarette smoke and cologne. His combat-style boots are black and scuffed, the perfect companion to his faded cargo pants and worn leather jacket. I wasn't expecting business attire, but this is almost *too* casual.

This is my first impression of Julien Caffrey.

The fact that he's a model made me skeptical about making a movie with him from the outset. I expect that he will be like most models turned actor: pretty to look at but severely lacking in substance. Now, it appears that he's inconsiderate of other people's time too. On sight, I make the immediate decision *not* to like him.

Although this is the first time that I've ever laid eyes on the man, I don't think I'm being harsh. My film director, Victor Marsden, has been wildly hyping this meeting for three days. "He's going to pull you in, Iyah," he promised, "This guy's a gem!" He was convinced that we would become "fast friends" too. This doesn't feel like a promising start.

I don't know why I'm so aggravated. I'm not usually such a stickler for punctuality. My own mother is known for being chronically and habitually late for *everything*. It's such a problem that my entire family has taken to lying to her about the timing of events just to make sure she arrives when she's supposed to. Having dealt with that headache for much of my life, taking someone to task over occasional tardiness is not a hill I choose to die on.

But what I won't make an exception for is being late to important events. And *this* is an important event. Or, at least, it is important to *me*.

It's debatable if Julien Caffrey has the same level of commitment to this project that I do. On the surface, he and I are in a similar situation. We're both young, inexperienced actors. While he might have a recognizable face here in New York, he's a nobody in Hollywood circles.

I'm accustomed to rejection, but I wonder how many times Julien Caffrey has heard "no." I recognize the incredible opportunity I've been handed. Does he?

How did this man get a callback, let alone a chemistry read? I don't doubt his pretty face has opened numerous doors. As far as those looks go, however, I find him rather basic.

Yes, he *is* good-looking, but he doesn't seem to embody the character at all. He is supposed to be portraying a young, rich socialite from an elitist family with an Ivy League education. Typical, standard, white boy, all-American cream of the crop. That is *not* the energy this man is giving.

There is something rugged and vaguely dangerous about Julien Caffrey. He strikes me as being more like a mysterious night-stalker than an Ivy League prep type with his closely cropped dark hair, beard stubble and the small, silver stud earring glinting in his right ear lobe. The only thing missing is a sleeve of obscene tattoos, which I'm certain he doesn't have because that would be a dealbreaker in modeling circles. Nothing about him screams wealthy law student with a promising future at all. He'd be a shoo-in for the part of "shady character" though.

Part of me knows that I'm stereotyping him without justification, and I'm not really proud of it. I try very hard not to get caught up in all that social justice nonsense because, at the end of the day, people are just people. My parents have drilled that into me all of my life. *Be cautious, Iyah*, my dad would always warn me, *but be open-minded too.* I generally try to give people an opportunity to disappoint me first before I write them off entirely. Unfortunately, I've yet to speak a single word to Julien Caffrey and he's already disappointed me.

I guess it's difficult for me to take the high road when I think about how hard I've worked to get to this point. The countless auditions, the long, grueling days of networking, the nights filled with frustrated tears. I've been so careful and deliberate with my look, my words, always mindful of inadvertently burning bridges. I've used every precious connection to my advantage, even for *this* part. I'm a young, black woman looking for a place in an industry that is more likely to typecast me than place me in a leading role. Additionally, I don't have that typical Hollywood look either.

I've often been described as "cute" or "simply adorable," but very rarely has anyone (besides my parents) dubbed me "beautiful." I have a round face with large, expressive, brown eyes, and lips that I sometimes wish weren't as full, but that others seem to envy. My favorite feature about myself is my wild, glorious cloud of natural curls. I jokingly refer to it as my "lion's mane," but I love that my bouncy, spiraled locks give me such character. So, while I probably won't stop traffic with my face, if you see me on the street, you definitely won't forget me either. The girl with the big hair.

But I know I'm at a disadvantage. Even the character I've auditioned for is described as having an "ordinary" appearance in the script, which I'm sure factored into me being considered for the part. I know what I'm working with, and I'm okay with that. I have to push myself hard to achieve my dreams. I caught a 5 a.m. flight from Detroit just to make it here this morning, and I arrived half an hour early. I wonder if Julien Caffrey possesses that same drive, if he even thinks he has to put forth the effort.

Truthfully, this industry was created and fostered by men who are exactly like him. Young, white men with the ability to command attention and amass heaps of praise while putting forth minimal effort. *He* can afford to stroll in here late looking as if he'd just rolled out of bed, and still get what he's after. I can't.

Even seated in the lavish lobby of a well-known New York agent, dressed in my most flattering sundress and designer heels, my make-up applied with stunning precision, my hair subdued with pins and clips,

I'm still afraid that this will be taken from me. That is the greatest irony. *I* have this part already. *He* remains the hopeful…at least for the moment. But I seriously doubt he's agonizing internally over whether he might not be good enough.

I've worked myself up into a righteous lather now. There's no doubt. I dislike him on pure principle. But he will not derail my future. His lazy entitlement will not dim my rising star. I *will* become a blinding force in this industry, and Julien Caffrey will not get in my way!

That steely determination must be stamped all over my face because when I shift to my feet, he scrambles backwards with stammered apologies. A short, stunned breath escapes me. The *last* thing I was expecting was an apology! I truly want to laugh at his terrified expression because the thought that *I* might intimidate *him* seems ludicrous.

He has, at least, four inches of height on me even with my heels on and probably outweighs me by a good 80 pounds. Yet, he's looking at me as if he expects me to dropkick him any second. In the power dynamic, he unquestionably has the upper hand. But he doesn't act like it.

That gets my attention. There's also the *way* he apologizes to me. He exudes humility.

"I'm sorry I kept you waiting." His tone is diffident. Embarrassed. Utterly sincere. He gestures towards his ridiculous attire. "I know I look like trash right now."

His contrition helps to diffuse my initial irritation. I'm not ready to change my mind about him, but I'm also not as committed to writing him off as before. And, because it seems rude to agree with his self-deprecating assessment of himself when we've been acquainted less than two minutes, I keep silent.

5

"I mean it. This isn't me," he continues, his brown eyes wide with emphasis. "I'm hardly ever late."

"If you say so…" I answer slowly.

"You're looking at me like you want to stomp me into the ground and, quite frankly, it's a little frightening."

A bubble of laughter rises with the visual he creates. I can almost hear my little brother making some wisecrack about my "resting bitch face," and I know I need to meet him halfway. The corners of my mouth curve into a strained smile.

"Sorry. That's just my face."

"I had every intention of being here on time!" He rushes to explain, "I'm in between auditions and photoshoots which is why I look like this. But when I ran home this afternoon to change, my dog had taken a massive dump all over the clothes I had laid out *and* my living room carpet!"

The snort that bursts from my lips is undignified, but I can't help it. "I'm sorry. What did you say?"

"He's a Yorkie. He has separation issues, and he's petty as hell." He thrust out his hand to me then, his face wreathed in a jovial smile. "Let's start over. I'm Julien Caffrey. You must be Aiona."

His friendliness disarms me, and the tension finally eases from my shoulders. I wasn't expecting him to be so nice, so affable. My opinion of him is already beginning to shift. I'm *almost* compelled to smile. The impulse is unexpected.

I hesitantly reach out to take hold of his hand. His grip is firm and committed. He looks at me directly, and I notice for the first time that his eyes aren't just brown. They have flecks of green in them too. Julien shakes my hand like we're already partners. I'm suddenly and surprisingly open to that idea.

6

"You can call me Iyah," I tell him, "Only my drama instructors call me Aiona, and none of them could pronounce it correctly anyway."

His grin widens, and I get a strange flutter in my chest. It is impossible to ignore how attractive he is when he smiles. It transforms his face entirely, elevating his "basic" handsome features into something radiant. I'm affected by that smile, and the realization causes me to recoil a bit. *What is happening right now?*

"How'd I do?"

The question takes me off guard because I haven't yet made sense of my incomprehensible reaction to him. "How did you do with what?"

"Your name. Did I butcher it?"

"No. You were surprisingly spot on. Very few people get it right on the first try."

"It's a very unique name."

I've heard some variation of that same comment all my life, enough times not to be easily offended by his unspoken implication that my name is odd. "I know it's different. It's like my parents had a contest for how many vowels they could pack into one name." To his credit, he tries to stifle his responding snicker of agreement as I add, "Meanwhile, my little brother got the name Ruben. Make it make sense."

"Aiona Grandberry is not a bad name. It has a regal quality to it. Very queenly."

I roll my eyes so hard I'm surprised they don't get lodged in my skull. "Now you're just kissing my ass."

"Whatever helps," he replies without an ounce of shame. "I'm trying to charm you here."

"Why?"

"This whole job is riding on a chem read between us. I wanna make a good first impression on you."

"Yeah…you're starting off great so far," I deadpan, tipping a glance down at my watch.

"Really? Are you gonna be one of *those* people?"

"*Those* people?"

He waves a tsking finger at me, his smile flashing again. "Don't be a clock-watcher, Iyah. They're no fun at all." I am two seconds away from rolling my eyes again when he adds in a superior tone, "Besides, if you consider what I went through to get here, ten minutes is not bad. Credit where credit is due."

"I'm not going to pat you on the back for being only 'slightly' late," I scoff, throwing the word "slightly" in sarcastic air quotes, "to a meeting *you* set. You agreed to the time! If that didn't work for you, then you should have picked something else. Besides, you *live* in this city!"

"I feel very attacked."

He's clearly joking. Julien Caffrey has a sense of humor. I'm not expecting that, and I find his cheeky sarcasm is somewhat refreshing. I suppose it's a good thing that he doesn't take himself too seriously. Sometimes, I'm much too critical and focused for my own good. One type A personality is quite enough. I like the idea of him being the jokester to my straight man.

I can feel it again. That stupid impulse to grin at him like a fool, and I don't understand it. Nothing significant has happened between us beyond a little banter, but there is something about Julien Caffrey that intrigues me. Now that we've had an actual conversation, I'm finding him extremely easy to like. The realization provokes a deep frown of self-annoyance, and it makes me a little desperate to ferret out some hidden flaw.

"Did you say that you were still auditioning?" The unspoken implication is that maybe he's not as serious about this film role as I am if he's scouting for other jobs, but Julien only shrugs.

"Why wouldn't I?" he asks, "Nothing's guaranteed, right?"

"I guess that's true."

I'm trying to remain neutral, but my opinion of him starts to shift even more. The longer we speak, the more I come to realize that he is not at all the conceited, pompous ass I had been expecting. It's possible that Julien Caffrey is as insecure about his place in this industry as I am, especially if he believes that *I* am the only thing standing between him and this part.

Maybe his looks are far from "basic" after all, I amend grudgingly to myself. He might just be perfect for this part. He can certainly clean up as an Ivy League type. Perhaps gorgeous isn't too lofty a description for him either because this man practically glows when he smiles. I've always thought it was a cliché when someone was described as having a smile that lit up their entire face, but Julien Caffrey's smile truly does.

He's not an especially tall guy, albeit he is much taller than me which isn't hard considering my meager 5 feet, 2 inches. He appears to be average height, probably 5'10 if I had to throw out a guess, with a slender to medium build and sharp, angular features. He has a symmetrical face which enhances his loveliness, but his best feature is his stunning smile. I'm sinking into that smile fast. Julien Caffrey has a way of smiling at you that *makes* you want to smile back at him.

I'm already concluding that this isn't going to work. Not because I find him unlikeable because that could have been a manageable situation. The danger is that he'll be *too* likeable.

This is no time for distractions. I have set a personal standard for myself. I will never date my co-star. *Ever.* I've seen too many relationships destroyed among my classmates to go there. Additionally, romance creates unneeded tension and often complicates whatever project you're working on together.

There is nothing wrong with Julien Caffrey being attractive. In fact, he *should* be. The entire film is going to revolve around his character. He needs to resonate with the audience, and his good looks will help accomplish that goal. It's practically a requirement for any leading man in this business. But just because Julien Caffrey is an attractive man that doesn't mean that *I* have to find him attractive. Nor do I *want* to find him attractive.

I have a career to establish. I don't have energy for schoolgirl crushes, especially on inaccessible white boys with whom I have nothing in common. Professionalism is key, and I'm determined to maintain it. If I can keep focused and driven, I know that I will be just fine. Julien and I will have a successful working relationship, and I will have a film credit added to my resume. The end.

"So, what's your dog's name?" I know the question is abrupt, but I'm determined to realign our conversation into more neutral territory.

"Scruff."

I can't quite stifle my disbelieving chortle. "You named your dog 'Scruff? For real?"

"When I got him, he was just this runty, scruffy little thing. The name kinda stuck. Now he's Scruff."

"No wonder he pooped on your clothes. I would too if you named me 'Scruff.'"

He laughs. Like a literal, full-throated laugh that makes his eyes sparkle with merriment, and suddenly I'm seriously questioning if I have this together after all. I think my earlier assumption about him was right. This guy *does* have the potential to derail my career if I let him, and not for the reasons I'd assumed. By this point, a chemistry read is hardly necessary. This five-minute conversation has confirmed for me that we have that in spades. That's not the problem.

The problem is that Julien Caffrey is, indeed, a gem. The problem is that my director was right. He *does* pull you in. We *will* become fast friends. But the biggest problem I foresee is the one I never expected, the one I didn't plan for.

I'm scared that I might end up liking him a little *too* much.

2

Los Angeles, California

"So…are you still going to claim us when you become rich and famous?"

My little brother Ruben offers me a cheeky grin through the phone screen. I know he's trying to goad me, but I'm way too tired to take the bait. The best response I can muster, while I balance my phone in one hand and my bag in the other, is a muttered insult under my breath as I shuffle inside my hotel room. My body hasn't grown used to California time yet. Then again, I've only been here for 36 hours so that's not entirely surprising. I've yet to shake off my jet lag from the flight.

Though the digital clock on the nightstand reads 6 p.m. and bright sunlight filters in through my open blinds, my internal clock screams at me that it's 9 p.m. I just want to crawl into bed. I'm in no mood to deal with Ruben needling me, especially when I made the effort to make this family Facetime call in the first place. Careful to stay in the camera frame, I throw my bag aside, kick off my shoes, and flop down onto my neatly made bed with a grateful sigh.

Any other time, I'd probably cut this call short because I'm in no mood to bicker with my brother. But my parents have been chomping at the bit for this conversation all day, and I don't want to disappoint them. I also can't start goading Ruben in return. I know that any attempt I make at a well-deserved comeback will only earn me a lecture from both my parents about tormenting my brother, followed by more admonishments on why I should "know better" because I'm the oldest. Oh, the perks of being the beloved baby and golden child of the family.

I suppose I should be grateful for the consistency, which has been severely lacking in my life for the past several weeks. I've been bouncing nonstop from one event to another, and this is the first real opportunity I've had to take a reflective breath. It will also probably be my last bit of respite before we start filming tomorrow morning.

The reality of this moment hits me anew. I am thousands of miles from home in a strange city surrounded by even stranger people, about to begin the biggest project of my limited acting career. I'm just a tiny bit overwhelmed. Excited, but scared too. The fact that my little brother can fall so easily into his pattern of teasing sarcasm even when we haven't seen one another in person in nearly a week is actually as refreshing as it is annoying. At least it is something familiar.

Despite my strict preparation for this role, including flying to New York for the chemistry read and then straight to California afterwards, I'm still uncertain about what comes next. I'm in free fall, but that's not a bad thing. I've never been the most meticulous planner anyway. I like to go with my gut. My father says that I do too much leaping and not enough looking. Maybe he's right but look where my leaping has landed me.

No one really expected me to get this part, least of all *me*, but I did it. I'm not even a local! Me…some unknown girl with barely any acting experience from a small township in metro Detroit actually beat out a hundred other young actresses, many of them native Californians, for this part.

That is an accomplishment. And yet, it doesn't *feel* like one. Not entirely. Perhaps because I know that my family, as supportive as they've been, doesn't view my decision to pursue acting as something wise or long-term.

They're waiting for me to decide that this is a transient phase. None of them believe that I will be catapulted into fame or that this career will be my final, decided path. It isn't because they think I'm untalented. My parents have been quite vocal about just how talented I am and have always encouraged my creativity. I express myself through music and words, but I've been known to change my mind.

At one time, I had an unparalleled passion for science and biology too. The human cell is a creative marvel, its own self-contained factory. Growing up with a trauma surgeon for a father and a registered nurse for a mother, it wasn't that difficult to become enamored with the mechanical and chemical processes of the human body.

My parents nurtured my interest. When I was fourteen, they enrolled me in a junior EMT course designed to prepare me for a career in trauma. I became BLS certified that same year. I've volunteered in the hospital every summer vacation since before I started high school. I've even had an opportunity to accompany my dad on continental healthcare related relief missions. The first time I saw an open fracture, I wasn't repulsed by the blood and torn flesh. I was fascinated.

But my passion for medicine is only surpassed by my passion for theater. Once I saw a production of *A Streetcar Named Desire* live on stage, I was hooked. The call of the stage was too strong. I decided to change my major from biology to drama in my sophomore year of college, and my parents didn't mask their disappointment.

My father took my decision the hardest, probably because medicine had been the thing we had bonded over the most. He'd been excited about the prospect of me following in his footsteps, filled with the burgeoning pride that came with telling his close friends that his daughter was bound for medical school. Struggling actress didn't hold that same prestige, especially one who stayed broke and out of work. The fact that this part has me playacting at being a nurse has probably added insult to injury.

To my father's credit, he's tried to be encouraging, but it's obvious he thinks I'm wasting my time, wasting my *real* talents. "A hobby is not a career, Iyah," he would lecture. His assessment hasn't changed much either. As far as he's concerned, acting is a frivolous pursuit. It's not a "sustainable career." His skepticism only makes me *more* determined to succeed. I *have* to prove him wrong.

All of those thoughts are banging around in my head when I shift upright and position myself cross-legged in the center of my bed. "I'm not getting ahead of myself," I reply, referencing Ruben's earlier teasing. "It's just one part. This is the chance to get my foot in the door."

"How long will you be out there?" Mom asks.

"Filming should take about six weeks. Maybe I'll be here two months at the most. I'll be home after that, but then I'll have to fly back out here before the film premiere for the promotion tour."

I start to fidget in the silence that ensues. Mom and Dad exchange furtive, obvious glances. Neither of them is thrilled to learn I'll be in L.A. for the next two months, especially when I don't have much money. I know my parents. They are both contemplating the most diplomatic way to address my current lack of funds. Mom chews thoughtfully on her lower lip. She's skirting the issue. Dad's forehead is creased with a familiar scowl. He doesn't seem to share Mom's hesitance.

"How much are they paying you for this thing?" he demands in a flat tone.

"Is the money really that important? Why do you lead with that?"

"So, next to nothing then? You've already spent hundreds of dollars on *two* plane tickets! Let's not even talk about how much those headshots cost you! And now you've got the added expense of an agent! It's like you're paying someone else for the privilege of working!"

"Dad, please. This is how it goes, and it's my first job. Everyone starts at the bottom."

"*Everyone* doesn't have thousands of dollars in student loan debt to pay off. *Everyone* doesn't live at home with their parents. *Everyone* doesn't have to live out of a cheap hotel for the next two months!"

"It's not cheap," I argue weakly, "This is actually a very nice place to stay, and the studio is paying for all of it. I get a stipend!"

"You mean, *you're* paying for it. Just not upfront. Best believe they are removing the cost of living from your final pay," he predicts darkly, "I can't understand why you couldn't do something else locally. Now you're in L.A. of all places! You don't even know your way around that city. I don't like it."

"Google is a thing. I can figure it out."

"You're going to spend every dime you make just trying to maintain your livelihood out there," Dad predicts. The unspoken crux of his argument is "Come home." I know it, and so does he. "What is the point of any of this if you won't have anything to show for it once it's over?"

"I can put this on my resume. My name will be out there. This role will solidify my credentials as an actress."

"You can do so much *more* than this, Iyah."

"Daddy, I don't want to fight with you. I'm tired, and I haven't eaten anything since breakfast."

Mom takes her cue at this point, indignant at the thought my nutrition might possibly be jeopardized. That is my mother's biggest peeve. She always says that no job is worth sacrificing one's health. Over the span of her nursing career, she has seen too many patients work themselves into literal sickness for businesses who had no interest in offering *them* aid once they were in the throes of a health crisis. It is a hill she will die on.

"Iyah, it's already after nine o'clock!" she admonishes, "You haven't eaten yet?"

"Don't start with me. I'm on Pacific time, remember?" I reply, wisely tamping down my sarcasm. "I'm going to get some In-n-Out and then head to bed."

My father's disapproving grunt follows. "I thought you had less than $500 in your account. Can you even afford that?"

"Oh my God, Dad!"

"Just use my credit card for whatever you need," he insists, "Don't worry about the expense. I want you to be taken care of. I want you to be safe."

"I'm not taking your money."

"If she won't use it, I will!" Ruben pipes in gamely, "I don't turn down free money!"

Dad makes a face at him before fixing me with a stern look. "Use the card, Iyah."

There's no point in arguing. I know he won't stop harping if I refuse, so I sigh in exhausted defeat, "I gotta go. I'll call you guys tomorrow."

I'm sad to tell them goodbye, but I'm also grateful when our call ends. The silence that follows settles like a weight, but also brings a strange relief. Sometimes, living up to their constant expectations of me is too much pressure. Or maybe I feel that way because I fear I'm failing them.

My parents are good people who have done their measured best to provide me with good things. After all they have given me, the *least* I can do is become the person they want me to be. So, why do I resent them so much for it? And why does that resentment make me feel like an even bigger failure?

I flop back into the bed. The last thing I want is to be sad and reflective. Not when I've just landed the biggest gig of my entire career! I'm not ready to come down from this high. Mom, Dad, and Ruben might not be proud of what I've accomplished out here, but I'm proud of myself. This is the first time I've truly been on my own, my first step towards making my dreams a reality. I want to celebrate that, even if that celebration comes in the form of a burger and fries from a famous fast-food establishment that I've always wondered about.

That enthusiasm dampens when I discover how much it will cost to have Uber Eats deliver my dinner to my doorstep. My father was spot on when he asked if I could afford it. A single meal will cost me almost as much as one night in my Los Angeles hotel. Thankfully, I don't have the cover the cost of staying here or the back-and-forth transportation to the movie studio or I would be completely out of money in less than a week.

The production company should provide us with a very small food stipend, but that's not even enough to cover the cost of one burger. Most meals and snacks will be served on site. If we want anything outside of what is provided (like In-n-Out burgers for dinner) we will have to pay for those expenses mostly out of pocket. Spending nearly a fifth of what's in my bank account for a burger seems like a ludicrous prospect but, at the same time, I'm not sure when I will have another chance to have this experience.

My purse mocks me from the nearby chair. I battle internally over swallowing my pride to use my dad's credit card or starving for my convictions. A sharp knock at my door saves me from the choice. A little leery, because I'm in a strange city and there is *no one* who should be visiting me, I cautiously scoot from the bed and pad over to the door to peer out of the peep hole. Julien Caffrey's grinning face greets me. I grunt under my breath and snatch open the door.

"Didn't we spend enough time together today?"

That is not an exaggeration. We've been practically glued to each other's sides since we landed. His hotel room is literally two doors down from mine. And while I don't find his company unpleasant, I can't afford to let this budding attraction I'm developing for him blossom any further.

Julien leans against my doorframe with a lopsided smile. "Hello to you too, Grumpy."

It's not a reprimand exactly, but I feel chastened. "I'm sorry. It's not you. It's me. I'm hangry."

"What a coincidence! I dropped by to see if you wanted to grab some dinner."

"I am going to have my dinner delivered."

I stifle a mortified groan because I sound pretentious even to myself, but Julien doesn't seem offended. The corners of his mouth turn up in an amused smirk instead. I hate that smirk. It makes him look unintentionally adorable. And that fact makes me want to kick him in the shin. I curl my bare toes into the plush carpet to squelch the impulse.

"You got money for delivery?"

I cast a woebegone glance back at my purse. "Not exactly."

Julien breaks into a wide grin. "You should come with me."

He barely gives me time to stuff my feet back into my shoes and grab my bag before he drags me out of my room and begins pulling me towards the main street. "Wait! Where are we going?"

19

I haven't learned very much about Julien Caffrey in the two days that I've been acquainted with him, but I am aware that he knows his way around Los Angeles just about as well as I do. Then again, he's a transplanted New Yorker, having originally hailed from mid-west Indiana. Perhaps stepping out into the unknown isn't a huge dilemma for him. As for me, I'm not big on roaming around in unfamiliar cities.

"Where are you taking me?" I ask again when we reach the sidewalk, and he still hasn't revealed his grand plan.

"A place called the Squealer."

That stops me dead in my tracks. "Tell me that's a joke."

"I found it online. The food looks good, and it's within walking distance. Just half a mile from here."

"No sir," I reply, crossing my arms in stubborn refusal. "I don't eat at places named after pig sounds. I must respectfully decline."

Julien cocks his head to one side and surveys me with a thoughtful expression. "Anyone ever tell you that you're kinda stuck up?"

Several people have told me that. In fact, their exact words were "high maintenance." I'm self-aware enough to realize that there is some truth to the charge, but that doesn't stop me from becoming offended. He's only known me for two seconds, so the assessment strikes me as a little audacious. It's the principle involved.

"Oh well," I say with a flippant shrug, "you enjoy your dinner alone then."

Before I can do an about face and leave him standing alone on the sidewalk, Julien briefly catches hold of my forearm and steps into my path to block me. "I was just teasing you. Don't be like that. Where is your sense of adventure? It's got 4 out of 5 stars!"

"Does it look like I care how many stars it has?"

"Give it a chance," he wheedles, "We're going to have loads of fun."

20

He's smiling at me again, that endearing, open, beautiful smile and I bite my lip when a reluctant twitch threatens. I am quickly growing to like this playful banter that is developing between us. It's easy. Natural. Effortless. The more I get to know him, the more I like him. But he doesn't need to know that.

Our easy camaraderie makes for compatible screen partners though. For our chemistry read, Julien and I had reenacted our characters' first encounter. We had naturally fed off of one another to build the emotionally charged scene in a way that felt authentic, like a volatile, awkward conversation between two antagonists meeting for the first time and not a manufactured performance.

It helped that Julien was truly a talented actor. I had worried about how he might be able to embody a character with whom he seemed to have very little in common, but when the time came, he slipped into the persona of Adam Sullivan with the same ease as someone slipping on a tailored jacket. I fully believed he was the resentful young man he portrayed, recently diagnosed with a mental illness that had derailed his entire life. And because I believed it, that made my response to him equally believable.

We are going to work very well together, which is both a good thing and a bad thing. Good because our chemistry will help to sell the love story between our characters. Bad because that same chemistry is only going to make it more difficult for me to get my burgeoning crush on him under control. I truly don't know how I'm going to make it through the next couple of months without making a complete fool of myself.

"Fine," I huff in answer to his cajoling. "I will eat at your pig place. But if I hate it, you will never hear the end of it."

"I'm sure I won't."

Once we arrive at the restaurant, Julien and I snag an unoccupied booth. I'm a little surprised by how busy the place is. It's a dank hole in the wall with scarred, wooden booths, lopsided tables, and grease-stained menus. The fastidious part of me wanted to wipe everything down before we took our seats.

But when our food is finally delivered to our table, I discover the reason that the place is so packed. The Squealer turns out to be worth every single one of its 4.5 stars. After Julien needles me about it, I finally offer him a begrudging thanks for the suggestion before we launch into thoughtful discussion about our characters and their motivations.

"Do you think he's unlikeable?" he asks.

Our characters don't share a promising start. In the scene, Julien's character Adam learns that his mother has hired a home health nurse to care for him without his input or consent. He isn't expecting Aubrey Lewis, nor does he want her to care for him. The character transfers his resentment towards his mother to the young woman hired to be his caregiver. As a result, Aubrey's first impression of Adam Sullivan is poor.

"He could have come across unlikeable, especially based on that first meeting but I liked what you did during the read," I reply, "It felt more like he was putting up a wall rather than being a jerk."

"That's what I was going for."

"But I think it's important that my character gives him pushback. She's not intimidated by him. I liked that she set her boundaries upfront."

"I liked that too. She let him know from the start that he couldn't bully her. I think that's what he needs."

I'm curious to know more about Julien Caffrey, especially if we're going to be jammed into each other's space for the next two months. "So…have you always wanted to be an actor?"

"Not really. I kinda fell into it the same way I did modeling."

"How's that?"

"I was something of a 'troubled' youth. Drama was supposed to help 'ground' me."

"Did it?"

He scratches his temple and then shrugs. "I guess it did. I'm here now. And I like becoming different people. It's an escape sometimes." I'm still trying to decipher what he means by that cryptic statement and if it's a good thing or a bad thing when he asks, "What about you? Have you always wanted to be an actress?"

"Yes. And an artist. And a writer. And a nurse. And a doctor. I have many aspirations."

"Multi-talented, I see."

"More like multiple interests. I didn't say I was good at all of them. I've just had a hard time nailing down what I want to do."

"And have you nailed it down now?"

"I hope so. I nearly emptied my bank account to get here."

"Same. Way to live up to that starving artist trope, huh? I'd probably be living in a cardboard box if it wasn't for Kate and her family."

The affectionate reverence in his tone is impossible to miss. "Kate? Who is Kate?"

He pulls out his phone and does a quick scroll through the electronic contents before passing the device across the table to me. Splashed across the screen is a picture of a pretty blond girl with a glowing smile and kind eyes. The lack of facial resemblance causes me to suspect the girl in the photo isn't a relative. My heart settles into the pit of my stomach when he confirms that suspicion a split second later.

"This is Kate Leland," he says with a proud, soft smile, "My fiancée."

3

The acrid aroma of burning tobacco combined with the damp chill of night air hits me in the face as soon as I exit my hotel room. It's four a.m. Artificial light from the overhang above streams down harshly, illuminating Julien Caffrey where he loiters on the sidewalk just outside his own room. He is already smoking. In the parking spot adjacent to where he stands, the white van that will transport us to the studio for our first day of filming idles. My breath hitches as I make my approach.

Noting the butts of several discarded cigarettes littered around his feet, I file away the observation as reason number 111 why this weird crush I'm developing on Julien Caffrey must die. As if it's not enough that he's distracting and capricious, he also chain-smokes. Delightful. And while that vice is definitely a turn-off, it is his romantic unavailability that is the biggest issue.

He spent nearly twenty minutes the night before regaling me with his fiancée's most winning attributes. His enthusiasm and devotion when he spoke about her was palpable. According to Julien, Katherine Leland had been one of the few people in his troubled existence to stick by his side through good times and bad. Their relationship sounded like the stuff marriage vows and forever were made of, which was likely the reason he'd asked her to marry him in the first place.

So, that was the end of it. He is off limits. Truthfully, he has never been *within* the limits because starting a romantic entanglement with a co-star is probably the stupidest thing an aspiring actor could do. I recognized that truth early on and was already staunchly against dipping my toe in that disaster from the start anyway. But the fact that he's practically married? That makes him untouchable.

After a restless night of trying to talk myself out of all the reasons I have for being drawn to him, I felt pretty confident that I had done a fairly decent job of reestablishing good ol' fashioned sense and rationale until I spotted him standing there. He's so full of nonchalance and is completely unaware of how off-balance he's thrown me. Even the sight of him pulling a long drag from his cigarette isn't enough to quell the reflexive flutter that unfurls in the pit of my stomach at the mere sight of him. I mask that response to him behind a deep frown, which he instantly misreads as disapproval.

As I close the distance between us, he puts out the cigarette on the sole of his shoe and offers me a sheepish smile. "Sorry. Nervous energy. I need to do something with my hands."

"Stress balls and fidget spinners *do* exist," I reply dryly before cutting in front of him to climb into the waiting van.

I know I'm not being fair to him. It's not like he led me on or anything. He was simply being friendly. I'm the one who got caught up just because he has a smile that could light up the night sky. *I* was the one who started reading more into his behavior than he intended. It's not his fault that I let myself become so attracted to him. It's *mine*.

The whole reason I'm feeling so foolish and embarrassed is because I forgot my sole objective for being here. It's not to fall in love. It isn't to make friends. It's not to take in all the sights L.A. has to offer.

The reason I'm here, the reason I need to *remember* above all else, is to establish my career as an actress. As long as I keep focused on that, everything will be fine. But then I watch him stoop down and diligently collect all his discarded butts before pitching them in the trash, and I experience a small burst of admiration for him over his conscientiousness that kicks up the butterflies all over again.

There is something about his self-awareness that is commendable and sweet. Perhaps because his personality is so inconsistent with his outward appearance. With his good looks, it wouldn't be surprising if Julien expected the world to cater to him. Most would readily make allowances for him because he's attractive. But he doesn't take advantage of that.

He climbs into the van a minute later and snaps into his seatbelt. I salute him with a dual thumbs up. "Good job not being a litter bug."

"You really hate it, huh?"

"Hate what?"

"The smoking. I won't do it around you if it's a problem."

"It's a health hazard."

An impatient snort follows my tart admonishment as the van rumbles into motion. "Yeah, yeah, I know. Lung cancer, blah, blah… I've heard it all before. You can save the lecture."

"Actually, smoking doesn't only put you at risk for lung cancer," I inform him rather haughtily, "Did you know that smoking also narrows your blood vessels and that can increase your risk for heart failure, stroke, and kidney failure? Not to mention the number it does on your skin and teeth! If you want to age ten times faster than normal, be my guest!"

He blinks at me in dumbfounded silence, as if he is trying to decide whether he should be offended by my tirade or amused. He must decide on the latter because a startled smile begins to slowly creep across his face. "You really did a deep dive into this RN role, didn't you?" he teases me.

I groan inwardly, considering for the first time how ridiculous I must sound to him. Of course, he would assume that I've learned these things as preparation for my part and likely thinks I've gone overboard. He probably thinks I'm an obsessive nut, which could possibly work in my favor given that I'm trying to actively kill my attraction to him, but... As much as I hate to admit it, even if it's only to myself, his opinion matters. I don't want him to have a negative impression of me.

"It's not research," I confess self-consciously, "My father is a trauma surgeon, and my mother is an emergency nurse."

"So that explains the aspiration to be a doctor or a nurse then."

"Yeah."

"So, why didn't you?"

"Why didn't I what?"

"Become a doctor or a nurse," he clarifies, "You seem pretty passionate about health."

"I am pretty passionate about it. But I'm more passionate about this."

He surveys me for a long moment, and I get the vague impression that he's trying to figure me out, as if what he assumed about me has been all wrong. I can empathize. I've been thrown for a similar loop with him. Finally, he settles back into his seat with a soft snort of laughter that sounds almost cynical.

"I guess you can afford to be a 'starving artist' then," he says, "Your family's rich."

The careless reflection causes me to stiffen in my seat. "Excuse me?"

"You're privileged." I sputter again, but this time with rising indignation. "It's not an accusation," he adds in response, "just an observation."

The strange irony of this abrupt turn in our dialogue is not lost upon me, and part of me wonders if he's doing it to deliberately get under my skin. Why else would a heterosexual, white male be lecturing me, a young, black woman, on privilege? Most especially, why would he lay down the unspoken implication that *I* had it…and *he* didn't? He must know that he's hit a nerve too, because he cuts a challenging glance over at me in response to my narrowed glare.

"Did I piss you off?"

"No. It was just a stupid thing to say."

"I don't think it was. I'm going to tell you something that no one else will, and you're probably going to get mad about it. But it's true. Privilege isn't about race. It's about power and wealth. It always has been. Whoever has the power and the money, has the privilege."

My stony rage must be evident despite my best efforts to keep my features passive because he adds, "Don't look at me like that. The truth is, *you* have more in common with my character than *I* do. You have a similar background to his. Where I come from, you'd have to travel 30 miles from your home just to see a doctor who specializes in *anything*, let alone have access to mental health resources! So, like I said before," he concludes triumphantly, "you're privileged."

Now I know for sure that I'm being baited. This is the primary reason I hate being drawn into these types of conversations. It becomes a circular argument and neither side seems to understand the other person's viewpoint. I know this, and yet I still find myself responding to his charge.

"Oh, please! You don't get to be downtrodden about anything! This country was built to benefit white males, tailor made for *your* success."

"Ah yes. *Rich*, white males," he counters, "That's not me. Therefore, *I* don't benefit from these so-called societal perks…not as much as *you* do."

Now he *is* touching a nerve. I clench my teeth so hard I'm surprised they don't disintegrate into dust. "How about we agree to disagree?"

"I'm trying to have an honest conversation here."

"No. You're trying to imply that I didn't work hard to get here, and that I somehow have it better than you," I snap back, "and I don't appreciate it!"

"Isn't that the same thing you think about me?" he asks quietly, "Why is that okay?"

My stinging retort becomes strangled in my throat as soon as he asks the question. His argument has some validity. I've been making assumptions about him since the moment we met. The same way he's making assumptions about me now. It's not acceptable in either circumstance. Perhaps we're *both* guilty of relating to one another based on stereotypes and faulty expectations rather than simply seeing one another as people. I concede his argument with a self-effacing eyeroll.

"It's not okay," I grumble finally, "Not for either of us."

"Agreed. I apologize for making a wrong assumption about you."

Once again, his apology doesn't strike me as pretentious, but earnest. It's not difficult for me to believe that his goal wasn't to offend, but to have "an honest conversation" just as he claimed. He wants to know the person who will be his screen partner for the next two months. That seems like a perfectly reasonable expectation to me.

The last of my irritation with him fizzles out and I ask, "Do you think we can start over?"

"I'd like that. I'm not a bad guy when you get to know me."

"If you say so."

"I do," he replies with a growing smile. "You're gonna love me."

God help me, I hope not! I know he's being facetious, but the potential would be disastrous. I cover my discomfiture with a tight smile. "Yeah, whatever…"

In the trailing silence, I lean back in my seat and close my eyes. We have roughly twenty minutes before we reach the studio. I'm hoping that we can continue the remainder of the ride in silence. It's not that Julien is getting on my nerves, because *he is*, but the reason for my agitation is not the one I was anticipating.

Julien Caffrey is far more than a charming, pretty face. While he seems so unserious about most subjects, I'm shocked to learn that he's enlightened too. I never expected him to be so philosophical and forthright, so willing to dive into uncomfortable conversations or call out hypocrisy where he sees it.

In my experience, people usually fall into two camps when it comes to social injustice. They either politely avoid the subject or they're belligerent. Julien Caffrey doesn't fit into either mold. He is his own entity. He's unwilling to shy away from controversial topics nor is he hesitant to speak his mind, but he's also not an aggressive jerk about it. Like most people, he wants his point of view to be heard. He's also open to listening to opposing viewpoints. The more time I spend in his company, the more intrigued I become.

"Hey, Grandberry? Are you sleeping?"

I crack open one eye and survey him with a sour expression. "What do you think? It's barely five o'clock!"

"Not a morning person, huh?"

"This isn't morning. Morning implies the presence of sun." I gesture towards the window and the twinkling city lights of a darkened L.A. beyond, "Do you see the sun out there, sir?" He emits a small grunt of laughter under his breath. When I look back at him, he's grinning at me. "What are you smiling about?"

"Nothing. Just wondering if you've always been this dramatic."

"Have you always talked so much?" I counter irritably.

His grin only widens, and I hate it. I hate it so much because all I want to do is grin back at him. *God, why must he be so beautiful?*

"I can't ride in silence," he explains, "Drives me crazy."

"You're kidding."

I'm surprised by his admission. The men in my life are not talkers at all. I've gone on extended car rides with my father and brother, and both of them could easily make the trip without exchanging a single word between them. Most often, the burden for carrying the conversation falls to me and my mom. I assumed Julien would be the same, *especially* at four o'clock in the morning. But as I survey his bright-eyed expression, I know I assumed wrong.

"I want to get to know you better," he says, confirming my earlier suspicion. "Tell me why you decided to audition for this part. Was it your way of becoming a nurse without actually becoming a nurse?"

"Not really. I was intrigued by the story, specifically how the script handles Adam's mental illness."

"How do you mean?"

"He's *more* than his schizophrenia. He's portrayed as an entire person. His illness isn't his defining characteristic. Instead, it's presented as a challenge he has to overcome."

"But he doesn't overcome it," Julien points out, "He kills himself in the end."

"Yeah…"

"Don't you think that's clichéd?" he wonders, "Wouldn't a better ending be for him to overcome, spend the rest of his life with the woman he loves?"

"That's a romanticized ending," I reply, "It doesn't always happen like that. People struggling with mental illness don't always overcome, and their partners don't always stay."

"The script is already full of stereotypes. What's one more?" When I squint at him for clarification, he provides it. "Ailing man falls in love with his caregiver? Typical Florence Nightingale effect. It's a common trope."

"Yes, but the script subverts the same 'love conquers all' theme that defines other stories. This feels more real, don't you think?"

"I guess if you don't consider the same old, tired 'poor minority from a broken home meets rich, privileged white person' theme, then I guess the storyline could be groundbreaking."

"That really bugs you, doesn't it?" I ask with some surprise, "Why?"

"Because the story is never flipped," he says, "Just look at you and me."

"What do you mean?"

"*I'm* Aubrey and *you're* Adam," he clarifies, "I didn't grow up with money. My dad left when I was six. My mom drank. I can remember days when school lunch was the only meal that I had to eat the whole day. This 'privileged' white life everyone talks about…it wasn't mine."

I'm not sure how to respond to this disclosure, or if there even is an appropriate response. He has a point. What he's describing is nothing remotely close to my upbringing. I grew up in a middle-class neighborhood with two stable and loving parents who met my every need. Up until the moment I decided to switch majors, my parents paid for all of my schooling.

I've never gone hungry, never been evicted from my home, never feared for my safety. Even my pursuit of acting hasn't left me without some sense of a safety net because I have no doubts if I fail, my parents will be there to catch me. I can't imagine how it must feel to live your entire life without that sort of security.

"I'm sorry," I say finally because I don't know what else *to* say.

"Don't pity me."

His eyes glitter with rebellious fire at me in the dim interior of the van and, for the first time, I sense the jaded cynicism beneath his affable exterior. This is yet another layer to Julien "the philosopher" and Julien "the theater nerd" that I did not anticipate, something fascinating and scary at the same time. I'm compelled by the desire to know him better too. But I also can't shake this gut premonition of looming disaster. Something about this man makes me suspect that he has the potential to turn my whole world upside down.

The thought leaves me so shaken that I sound aggravated when I ask, "Then why did you tell me all of that? Why did *you* audition for the part?"

"So that you get it," he says solemnly, "I'm not playing something I know."

"Neither am I," I reply with equal solemnity.

He transforms again before my eyes. The sullen anger darkening his features abruptly melts away as if it had never been there at all. His smile reemerges, easy, friendly, and open. "Alright then," he says, "We're in the same boat. You're going to be stepping outside of *your* comfort zone too."

Yeah, I am. And for more reasons than he could possibly imagine.

34

4

After one week of filming, my social life becomes nonexistent. Not that my lack of social life hasn't been a pervasive theme since I graduated from college and ended things with Devin in a laughably amicable breakup. Now, my world consists of this movie and the people involved in making it and nothing else.

I'm not unfamiliar with 10-to-12-hour workdays, but I had never in my life been subjected to a seven-day work week. There is very little down time to do anything outside of filmmaking. I work. I eat. I sleep. Then I get up the next morning to do it all over again.

It's been a grueling schedule thus far. On that first day, I didn't truly absorb the weight of this new reality. Everything was too surreal, too new. The endless rows of equipment and cameras. The numerous people flooding in and around the carefully constructed sets. I greedily drank it all in. I was in this heady place of relishing the excitement of being on an actual movie set, of knowing that *my* performance would be immortalized on film for a lifetime.

The pace is starting to catch up with me now. In order to push through, I constantly remind myself that this is the first step in defining my career as an actress. Besides, I've been able to carve out some downtime too. There are frequent enough breaks between scenes to afford me the time to read, scroll on my phone and chat with my co-stars.

My scenes are primarily with Julien and another actress, Kathleen Blanchard, who portrays his mother. She is well known and respected within the indie film circles and also the main reason for any media interest at all in this small, independent film featuring two very green, very unknown young actors. It has been a privilege and honor to be mentored by her.

Julien and I are both like sponges, ready to soak up whatever advice she dispenses because neither of us has done anything like this. The work we've had in the past doesn't compare. We're like newborns becoming acquainted with an intriguing, but strange, demanding, and overwhelming new environment together. It's been easy to grow closer under those circumstances.

My crush on him persists, but it's settled gradually into a place of admiration and respect rather than primal attraction. And, while that sounds like an improvement, it really isn't. If my interest in him had remained purely superficial, I might have had an easier time dismissing my attachment. Or, at least, I wouldn't have been concerned about my feelings deepening. He would be just another pretty face, and those were easy enough to get over. But I am drawn to him in countless ways, and his appearance happens to be the *least* of those reasons.

Julien Caffrey has many layers. He is more than what he seems. Whenever I think I've peeled back everything, I discover something new.

"Daydream on your own time, Grandberry!"

The sharp admonishment snaps me back into the present. I remember that I'm on set in between film takes with Julien, waiting with him for our marker to be called. I offer him a guilty smile.

"I did it again, didn't I?" My tendency to slip off into deep thought at random moments is a running joke between us. Julien likes to call it

36

"falling asleep with my eyes open." Which is a rather freaky concept when you consider it. "Are we up?"

"We've got two minutes. What were you thinking about just now?"

"That you're weird," I tell him, straight-faced.

He falls back with a sputtering smile. "*I'm* weird?"

"Why are you doing this? You already have a career," I point out, sounding more peevish than I intend. "You could ride that wave of fame and see where it takes you. Instead, you're starting at the bottom again. I don't get it."

"I want to do something that makes an impact," he replies, "Something that evokes powerful emotion." He is certainly evoking "powerful emotion" in me, but I keep that tidbit to myself.

"From what you've told me about your childhood, you've never had an issue with evoking 'powerful emotion,'" I tease him.

Julien smirks at me. "I mean something *other* than frustration and anger," he laughs.

While Julien hasn't been entirely forthcoming about his past beyond vague references and anecdotal stories, I suspect he spent most of his formative years as a human wrecking ball. I get the impression that he wants to create a substantial distance between the person he is now and the one he used to be. I'd like to probe him about it, but we're called to our marker, and the moment is gone.

And so, it goes with us day after day, snatches of meaningful conversation between film takes, during snack breaks, and on daily trips to and from the studio. Sometimes we talk about movies and poetry. Other times we argue about hot button political topics. We share similar Midwestern views, but very different perspectives on how we individually perceive the world.

We don't always agree, but his willingness to consider my thoughts with candid discussion is something I've come to deeply appreciate. Too many times he's come back to me after an impassioned disagreement with the statement, "So, I thought about what you said and..." And strangely enough, his inclination to listen has made *me* more open to listening too, even when I don't always like what I hear.

Julien and I gradually become unfiltered with one another, which is something unique that I've never shared with another person before. When we first met, my tendency to be brutally candid with him was a defense mechanism. I thought my brusque, direct nature might lessen his desire to be in my company. Instead, it's created a refreshing platform of honesty between us.

We don't wear masks around one another. We give voice to our emotions and the reasons behind those emotions. The lack of self-editing is freeing. I get to be myself in all my neurotic, high maintenance glory, and Julien seems to like me just as I am. I've come to value him as a close friend.

But it *is* difficult to be in his company almost nonstop. Not because I don't enjoy being around him, but because I *do*. I enjoy being around him *too* much. And, unfortunately, the nature of our jobs makes putting some necessary distance between us an impossible thing.

There's nowhere to go. It's like we're trapped in a box together. In essence, my nonexistent social life has come to center entirely around him...and it's beginning to break me down.

Two weeks into our filming schedule, the situation becomes more complicated. Julien and I begin shooting some of the most emotionally challenging scenes of the film, all of which revolve around his character's psychotic break. Due to Julien's hair being closely cropped, our director decides to film out of sequence because Julien's character shaves his head after a failed suicide attempt. It's a cost-saving move.

Unfortunately, the decision serves to ramp up my emotional investment in Julien Caffrey exponentially as well. The script involves such heavy content that our director even had the forethought to have a psychologist available on set to help us navigate our feelings about the material. How can I *not* feel closer to him after that?

I'm rationalizing my desire to be around him, but this growing attraction doesn't feel rational. I'm traversing uncharted territory here. While I don't have a great deal of relationship experience, having had a handful of random dates and *one* serious boyfriend since college, I have never been attracted to a man who wasn't also attracted to me, at least not beyond passing interest.

There is absolutely no chance of anything developing with Julien. Even if his fiancée *wasn't* in the picture, striking up a romance with a man who will be completely out of my life in a matter of weeks seems shortsighted and irresponsible. Our career paths are headed in diverging directions. Julien wants a future in television and film. While I, on the other hand, would prefer a career in theater. My ultimate dream is to one day write my own screenplay.

We are not in the same place professionally or personally. A relationship between us would never work even if the feelings were mutual. His fiancée only makes the circumstances all the more insurmountable. I tell myself all these things, but that doesn't soothe that funny little burn that quickens in my chest whenever he's around.

Unrequited feelings aren't fun.

My biggest frustration is that I can't escape them. I can't escape *him*. He's always there, and I can't push him out. I'm running away figuratively, but I'm physically stuck. The only boundary that I can truly put between us is in the evening when we return to our respective hotel rooms. I enforce that distance as much as I can.

But going into week four of filming, my standoffishness inevitably begins to bleed over into our working relationship. I'm missing cues, and so is he. Our chemistry is off. I'm mechanical and reserved in our scenes, and Julien is starting to feed off that energy. Our director understandably grows frustrated with us.

I know that I'm ruining this, but I don't know what else to do. I can't quit. I don't want to quit. But I also can't keep opening myself up this way either. I'm starting to have serious doubts that I'll be able to keep up with this constant inner tug-of-war for another four weeks.

I'm unceremoniously ripped from my private brooding when an unidentified something zings past my face and lands in my lap. I glance down with a muttered curse. A plastic wrapped coffee cake is cradled atop my thighs. When I look up again, I see Julien coming towards me. The expression on his face is determined, almost confrontational.

My heartbeat quickens, but I keep my expression bland when I gesture to the cake. "What's this for?"

Julien shrugs. "Peace offering," he says before he plops down into the empty chair beside me. "You ready to tell me what's been bugging you?"

"I don't know what you're talking about."

The denial is weak. I don't sound convincing even to myself so, I'm not surprised when Julien surveys me with squinted eyes full of skepticism. "You've been giving me the cold shoulder for five days!"

"I have not!"

"If I did something to offend you, just tell me so we can move on!"

"I never said you offended me."

"Then why are you freezing me out?"

"Why are you biting my head off?"

He closes his eyes for a beat, and I can practically hear him counting to ten in his mind. His expression gradually loses impatience. When he looks at me again, his dark, changeable eyes are full of silent entreaty.

"Whatever I did to tick you off, I'm sorry. Can we talk about it?"

Guilt settles in the pit of my stomach like a leaden ball. I can barely look at him. "Don't apologize. You didn't do anything."

"Then what's with the attitude? You're crankier than usual."

I can't rightly confess that I *like* him so, I go with a different truth instead. "It's not you. I'm tired. This schedule is ridiculous. I get grumpy when I'm sleep deprived."

"Yeah, I learned that about you on day one," he laughs, "But you need to suck it up, Buttercup. We have a job to do."

"Your sympathy is heartwarming."

"Look, I get it. Better than anyone. I'm exhausted too. But I've got your back. We can get through this."

It's actually irritating that he's *not* an ass. I almost wish that he was. While it is not a delight to work with someone you despise, the blessing of this industry is that the annoyance is usually temporary. Most often, you never cross paths with that person again.

Julien is the opposite. He's impossible to dislike. I would be genuinely interested in maintaining a friendship with him even after this project is done. Maybe that's not a realistic goal given my attachment for him, but I want that, nonetheless.

In the meantime, he's not wrong. We are professionals, and we have a job to do. This performance will reflect on my career either positively or negatively. I don't want to become known as a difficult actress or a "diva." But that is exactly what will happen if I continue allowing my personal feelings to interfere with this project.

That silent conclusion must be obvious on my face right then because Julien suddenly thrusts his hand out to me with an approving grin. "Does that mean we're good now?"

I shake his hand with a dramatic eyeroll. "We're good now."

Rather than releasing my hand, Julien hops from his chair and drags me with him. "Alright, come on then. Let's get to work."

That night after we've had a quick dinner together and outlined our plans for the following day of shooting, Julien sequesters himself in his room for his usual evening Facetime call with Kate, and I try to get some needed sleep. But it's impossible for me to relax. Every time I close my eyes, my mind invariably drifts back to Julien and his stupid smile.

I lie awake in bed, stewing and frustrated and staring up at the ceiling to contemplate whether the occasional spots I spy there are actual spots…or something alive. Around 11 p.m. I give up the pretense of trying to sleep altogether and decide to put in a desperate call to my best friend instead. Nicole finally answers on the fourth ring.

"Do you know what time it is?"

I'm not offended by the contentious greeting. This is Nicole Benson at her finest. Brash, blunt, and completely unapologetic about her hostility. That is exactly the reason she's been my best friend since high school. We have a similar crusty outer exterior. I haven't kept up with anyone else in our friend circle from those days, but she and I have somehow endured.

"Why are you always so crabby?"

"I'm not the one calling *you* at 2 a.m.! Did someone die?"

"No. Nobody died. Sorry. I keep forgetting about the time difference."

"Okay, well now that you've remembered, call me back tomorrow."

Before she can hang up, I exclaim, "Nicki, wait! I need to talk."

There is a long beat of silence before her weary grunt sounds in my ear. "Are you pregnant?"

I grimace at the phone. "No! What kind of question is *that*? When would I have time to get pregnant?"

"You have another fight with your dad?"

"We never ended the last one, but that's not it either."

"You hate your job?" she ventures next.

"I *love* my job and the people I work with. It's been great!"

"So, why am I awake?"

"I told you already. I love my job and I love the *people* I work with."

"Huh?" It takes her a few seconds to unpack my meaning and I can easily picture the look of dawned understanding that spreads across her face when she finally utters a deliberate, drawn out, "Oh."

"Yes, 'oh,'" I agree miserably.

She snorts a low laugh in response. "How hot is he?"

I don't bother to pretend I'm ignorant about her reference. "Very hot. I told you he was a model. But that's not the point."

"It's not? Is he a bad actor?"

"Surprisingly not. And I expected him to be trash because most models turned actor are."

"Okay, so he's good-looking, he's good at his job, *and* you like him. What's the dilemma here?"

"Julien is my co-star. He's not my type. We have wildly different backgrounds. He's a smoker. And we don't want the same things career-wise. Besides, it's tacky and unprofessional to date your co-star, don't you think?"

"Sounds like you have all the answers," she replies, "So, you don't need me. I'm gonna head off to bed now. Goodnight."

"I like him more than I should, Nicki," I blurt out quickly before she can end the call, "I like him *a lot. That's* the problem."

"Wait…are you…? Iyah, are you saying you want to know this guy

43

on a *naked level?*"

"Maybe…"

"For real? Ms. High Standards herself? I need to see a picture of him!" I can hear her rifling around, and I suspect she's put me on speaker so that she can go scouring the Internet for screenshots of Julien.

"Nicki, stop it! Don't you dare look him up!"

"Why not? You don't want me making fun of your swirl love?"

I absolutely know she will tease me mercilessly, but that isn't truly what makes me hesitant to be candid with her. I'm afraid that if I give an unfettered voice to what I am feeling, I am going to open up a floodgate of yearning for things I can't have. So, instead of going there, I tell her to "shut up."

"Fine. How does he feel about you?"

Here it is. The question I've been dreading this whole time. I push back the covers and prop myself up against my pillow. "Um…actually, it's not like that. He's engaged."

Nicole's response is swift and final. "Hard pass."

"I know."

"You say you know, but why are we talking about this?" I don't answer the question fast enough, which only provokes her righteous tirade. "Please don't be an idiot! If he's willing to cheat on his fiancée, then he'll cheat on you too. That's all you need to know. He's for the streets, Iyah."

"You're wrong. He is not cheating. He is not interested," I itemize briskly, "This argument is moot."

"So, why did you bring it up?" Before I can even begin to formulate an answer or quell her growing impatience with me, she groans, "Don't tell me you're out here making yourself look foolish, Aiona!"

I flinch in response to her succinct assessment. Nicole has a knack

44

for brutally snapping me back to reality. We've had multiple fights over her inability to incorporate tact, but that's what I need. Tactless or not, she's rarely wrong. Nicole Benson will always tell me what I *need* to hear as opposed to what I *want* to hear. And that is the mark of a true friend, I suppose, someone who isn't afraid to lose you if it also means they can protect you in the process.

"I'm not making a play for him, Nicki. It's only a crush."

"A crush?" I can picture the scrunched look of disdain on her face right then. "Iyah, you don't get crushes! You have *never* had a crush in the entire time I've known you."

"Don't be so dramatic. I've had crushes. I don't tell you everything."

"This is different! He. Is. Engaged," she enunciates flatly, "It's a 'no.' It is a HELL no!"

"Okay. I hear you. Stop yelling at me!"

"I'm sorry. I don't want you to do something stupid."

"I won't. It's fine. *I'm* fine. Everything is fine. I think I just needed to acknowledge what I was feeling out loud so, I could move on."

"There's nothing wrong with looking," she agrees, "as long as you're not really falling for this guy." She pauses for a moment as if she is waiting for me to jump in with a fierce denial. When I don't, she presses me with near screeching alarm. "You're not falling for him, right?"

The answer to that question doesn't come to me readily, mostly because I haven't made sense of my feelings yet. But I know what Nicki wants to hear, and I give her that. I'm not interested in having a fight.

"No, I'm not falling for him. I like him. I respect him as a fellow actor. He's attractive. That's all."

"Hallelujah. Can I go back to sleep now?"

"Yes!" I laugh, "Goodnight!"

After I end the call, I toss my phone back onto the nightstand and flop back into the mattress with a frustrated sigh. But I still can't sleep. I had hoped that my conversation with Nicki would finally shake me out of this lovesick stupor I've been in. Sadly, I'm more conflicted than ever.

I know it's wrong to lust after a man who is romantically unavailable. There is no debate about that. But *knowing* it's wrong doesn't alter my feelings. However, after Nicki's repulsed reaction, I am definitely more determined to hide them.

It's not that I blame her for reacting so strongly. She's been the "other woman" before, and the experience left her jaded. As far as Nicki is concerned, committed relationships are nothing more than an elaborate trap and the quickest way to lose pride and self-respect. She's given up on real, lasting companionship because, according to her, "all men are liars."

I don't know if I believe that. It's certainly not true in my father's case. He adores my mother. I'm waiting for someone who looks at me with the same devotion that my dad has for my mom. They have been together more than 25 years through a series of triumphs and failures, but they have weathered those trials together. I want that too. But I know I will never find that with Julien Caffrey. The knowledge doesn't dispel my feelings for him, but it *is* the wakeup call that I need.

The realization finally allows me to relax enough to close my eyes. But just as I start to drift off, my cell phone vibrates loudly on the nightstand. I flip up the screen to discover Nicki has sent a text through. In predictable fashion, she has done some Internet sleuthing since we spoke and has uncovered one of Julien's modeling photos. The screenshot is emblazoned across my phone.

He's dressed like a flamboyant runway model, gleaming from head to toe in pristine white slacks and an equally immaculate sweater. His dark hair is much longer than it is now and hangs in uneven waves over his hooded eyes. The corner of his mouth is turned up in a faint smirk, as if he's keeping a naughty secret that he's dying to share. I think he smolders for the camera lens, and Nicki clearly agrees. Beneath the photo she's typed a single word.

Damn.

Same, girl, I think to myself as I settle back beneath the covers, caught between a measure of girlish amusement and self-pity. *Same.*

5

I fully anticipated shooting a feature film would be a physically draining experience. The thing I had *not* expected was that the storyline would sap me emotionally and mentally as well. I won't go so far as to say I'm becoming depressed, but there have definitely been moments when I'm overwhelmed with hopelessness.

When our director informed me and Julien that he'd hired a psychologist to help us navigate our emotions during the course of filming, neither of us had known what to make of that. I think we were both wary of utilizing her expertise. I can't speak for Julien, but I had been so acutely focused on depicting the subject of mental health with the accuracy, grace, and dignity it deserved that I never gave a single thought to how this storyline might affect me personally.

Through my experience as a hospital volunteer, I've had limited interactions with mental health patients. While I sympathized with their struggle, I didn't get too deeply invested. I never thought I would be so profoundly affected by this script. I was wrong. Portraying someone who watches their loved one struggle with worsening mental illness can be emotionally taxing. It's impossible to remain detached.

Before I ever auditioned for this role, I believed that I already had a good grasp on the stigma surrounding mental health. The very nature of my parents' careers had put them on the forefront of those issues, giving them a ringside seat to the inadequacies that exist within American healthcare for those afflicted with mental illness. My mother has constantly lamented those inadequacies because she, much more than my father, saw to the core of the mental health crisis.

According to her, *all* patients are mental health patients. A diagnosis of schizophrenia or bipolar I disorder or even generalized anxiety and depression isn't a requirement. In her opinion, every human alive will eventually struggle through some sort of mental health crisis. I had once accused her of generalizing when she said that, but she's never once wavered in her stance.

"Iyah, at some point in their life, *everyone* is going to be confronted with mental health challenges," she would say, "It's inevitable given the world we live in. Despite that, most healthcare systems are ill-equipped to deal with those challenges. That is the sad reality."

I've reflected on her words often as we've filmed these scenes. Lack of adequate care and understanding is certainly a running theme in the script. Adam Sullivan is a young white male with a promising future and an affluent family. His caregivers are able to afford the best healthcare that money can buy, a personal psychologist, a nurse, and private treatment in the best mental health facilities available. Yet, his illness is still treated as a dirty, shameful secret. He is made to believe he is less than, something broken, and less valued, which further warps his self-perception and causes the character to spiral even further.

The character's experience is better than most who deal with mental illness in this country, but just because it's better that doesn't make it good. The scenario is difficult to explore and one from which I can't escape. I also have no context for navigating these complex emotions. I've never known anyone in my life who has grappled with serious mental illness or even clinical depression, nor have I ever personally experienced anything like that.

Even when Devin and I broke up after a two-year relationship, I wasn't left devastated in the aftermath. Though my family spent months tiptoeing around me as if I was nurturing some secret, soul-rending grief, I was okay. Rather than regret or heartbreak, I was relieved that it was over. I think we were both ready to walk away by that point.

Devin and I had been slowly drifting apart in the months that preceded our breakup. My decision to pursue acting had only deepened the wedge. He hadn't hesitated to call the move selfish and stupid (because his idea of a partnership wasn't financially supporting me while I pursued "nonsense."). He was entitled to feel that way, just as I was entitled to think that maybe he wasn't truly what I needed after all.

By the time we finally called time of death on our relationship, just shortly before he enrolled in medical school, it was an afterthought. I didn't grieve over the loss. I simply picked myself up and moved on.

If I'm honest, I've always been that way about everything. I try not to let myself get overly attached to anything or anyone. My brother likes to tease me about my reserved nature and often calls me "Bot." He thinks that I'm weird, but I don't find anything strange about how I operate. I might just be built differently. Besides, isn't it a good thing that I've found a healthy way of coping with loss?

And it's not like I haven't been driven to the depths of despair before. I have. When I was twelve years old, my favorite aunt, my mother's youngest sister, died in an automobile accident. Her sudden loss had been devastating. If I let myself think about it even now, the memory still has the power to utterly break me down. So, I don't think about it.

The space where she used to exist is still a gaping hole. I couldn't wrap my mind around how she had been so real and vibrant one moment, only to be cast into nonexistence the next. I still can't wrap my mind around it. I've been a devout churchgoer for most of my life, but nothing our pastor said could lessen the pain of her loss. There is no explanation for her death that will ever make sense.

After we lost her, there was a gnawing fear that took hold of me. It was like nothing I had ever experienced before. Suddenly, it occurred to me that it was possible that I could lose *everyone* I loved, and that felt like the most terrifying knowledge on the planet! I was overwhelmed with this irrational anxiety and reduced to a blubbering mess whenever my parents left the house because I couldn't be certain they would return.

I lived in that uneasy place filled with wild, invasive dread for almost a year. I was jumpy and obsessive and plagued by constant nightmares that left me sleep-deprived and moody. My parents had pushed me to speak to a child psychologist, but I was reticent about that. The problem was thinking about my aunt and talking about my aunt, and that was all my therapist had wanted to discuss. So, I found a way to cope with my fears on my own. I haven't gone back to that dark place since.

As a result, I *do* maintain a certain amount of emotional distance from people. It's nothing that I'm consciously aware of, more like an instinctual inclination instead. I have this secret habit of imagining how I would react if I lost my mother, father, or brother or suddenly found myself alone without anyone to support me. Then, I mentally plot out how I would persevere under such circumstances. On the surface, I know that must sound morbid and even a little callous, but *for me* I think it's the only way I could endure that kind of tragedy and *not* go crazy.

I think that might be the reason I'm struggling so much lately. My tendency to disengage doesn't work so well when I'm portraying someone else. I am beginning to internalize my character's feelings of helplessness, and I don't like feeling helpless. I'm not surprised when my mother picks up on that when I put in my weekly call to her.

"You seem blue," she notes after we've spoken for a few minutes. "Are you getting homesick?"

"Maybe a little bit."

She's perceptive enough to see past my hedging. "What else is going on?"

"Have you ever worked with a schizophrenic patient, Mom?"

"Yes, I have."

"Is it *really* like this?" I wonder thickly.

"Like what, baby?"

My throat aches with sudden tears. "So hopeless and depressing and brutal all the time. I just…I need a break."

She croons to me in motherly sympathy. "I'm sure much of what you're doing is dramatized for your role, but the struggles people face with that illness are lifelong. It's hard. Medication can manage the symptoms, but they don't make them go away."

This is not news to me, but the knowledge doesn't lessen the hollow sensation that lingers in my heart even after I say goodbye to her. I blame that entirely on Julien's gut-wrenching portrayal. It is too powerful. Every time we do a scene together, he puts me in that awful, emotional place. He channels his character's shame, fear and self-loathing in a way that is embodied, like a lived experience.

I've even cried myself to sleep thinking about it, and I don't know why. The character isn't real. The circumstances aren't real. But the struggles and the emotions, and the raw manner in which Julien is able to grasp them? That is very real.

I can't imagine how it must be for Julien to have to slog through those heavy sections of dialogue and physicality day in and day out. I would assume that it's an excruciating process, but Julien doesn't betray that at all. If he's wrestling with any inner demons, I certainly can't tell.

Julien Caffrey is probably one of the least temperamental people I've ever known. I have yet to see him legitimately angry with anyone. He has brief spurts of irritation and moodiness sometimes, but in general he's mostly easygoing.

His resilience is admirable. He refuses to wallow in self-pity, which I suspect drives his methodical efforts to be kind and patient to everyone. And while there are times when he is noticeably subdued after certain takes, he always bounces back and returns to being his affable, unserious self once again.

I envy that ability he has, especially because I'm very aware he didn't have the easiest childhood and probably harbors many unspoken traumas from it. I'm assuming, at least. Julien doesn't seem inclined to elaborate, and I don't push for details, though I am curious.

However, I know the salient bullet points. He grew up without a father. His mother was habitually in and out of rehab. He and his two older brothers spent some of their formative years in foster care.

Julien had a tough beginning, but he doesn't play the victim. He keeps focused on the good things. One of those "good things" is the reason he decided to pursue acting seriously in the first place. Julien says that he was headed down a "very bad road" until a court appointed psychologist literally swooped in, eventually became his foster father, and changed his life.

That man welcomed Julien into his home and family and later accepted Julien's request to marry his daughter. So much of who he is now is tied up in his future father-in-law and the compassion that was shown to him. It is clear that his gratitude towards the man is infinite. His is truly an underdog story.

Knowing all of those things about him makes me even more reluctant to make use of the on-set psychologist. Because honestly, if Julien doesn't need her to navigate this journey, then why the hell should I? I'm still asking myself that same question while filming the following day.

Julien plops down beside me in his designated chair. I barely acknowledge his arrival because my eyes are glued to my script. "Earth to Iyah. Earth to Iyah," he says, tapping my shoulder, "You're up in ten."

"Goodie," I reply with no real enthusiasm. An instant later, an individually wrapped Hostess cupcake appears beneath my nose. I look at Julien dolefully. "Is there a reason you're presenting this cupcake to me like a sacrificial offering?"

He grins and wiggles the package in what he *thinks* is an enticing manner. "Don't act like you don't want it."

"I do not, sir."

Julien laughs and rips open the package with a shrug. "More for me then," he says before polishing off the cake in three bites.

"Must be nice to be a man with all your easy, fat-burning capabilities," I grumble with a scowl.

"Don't be bitter."

I shake my head at him, caught somewhere between annoyance and bafflement at his lighthearted teasing. "I don't get you at all."

"Because I eat what I want?"

"Because you can shoot all these intense scenes and then shake them off right after like it's nothing. Tell me your secret."

His expression turns serious at the question, and empathy softens his expressive eyes causing them to appear greener than usual. "Are you having a hard time, Grandberry?"

"Not a hard time exactly," I reply evasively, "But this material is not easy."

54

Julien pauses to toss the cake wrapper into the nearest trash receptacle before facing me again. "You really wanna know how I do it?"

"Yes, please share, oh wise, acting guru," I reply with dry sarcasm, "Honor me with your abundant knowledge."

"It's cathartic," he says softly, "This role is incredibly cathartic. It allows me to say things I've never said out loud before."

This is my first indication that Julien might not be as unaffected by the material as I've assumed. There is something more beneath the surface. But he doesn't elaborate further, and I'm uncomfortable with the thought of prodding him.

Weirdly enough, I'm struck with the overwhelming need to hug him. It comes out of nowhere. I don't really know what to do with the inclination.

I stare down at my script again, trying to ignore the heavy thudding of my own heartbeat. The silence that stretches between us afterward is intense and uncomfortable. I quickly fill the space with distracting chatter.

"So, have you and Kate set a wedding date yet?"

"That's a random segue," he replies with a stunned laugh.

I shrug, trying not to analyze too closely why I chose that particular segue. "Well, you've mentioned that you're getting married, but you never said anything about *when*."

"We don't have a set date yet. I can only tackle one earth shattering life change at a time."

"Please elaborate."

"I didn't expect to land this role. And, when I did, I didn't want to split my attention between preparing for it *and* planning a wedding."

"Do you have any idea how self-centered that sounds? You must have the most understanding fiancée on the planet."

His answering laugh sounds mildly self-deprecating. "She's definitely better than I deserve."

"I don't know if I agree with that. You're a pretty good guy, even if you do say stupid things from time to time."

"Really? You think I'm a 'good guy?' That's funny because you looked like you wanted to throat punch me two seconds after we met."

"We've already gone over this a dozen times. You were late," I remind him with a theatrical eyeroll. "It is a peeve!"

"Yes. You have *a lot* of those," he wisecracks blandly, "That's not annoying in the least."

"Shut up." I trace the edges of my script, bracing myself inwardly for his answer to my next question. "You think she's going to come out here?"

"Who? Kate? No way in hell!"

I do a doubletake. I can't help it. That was the last response I was expecting. "Um…what? Why not?"

"Kate works for a very prestigious accounting firm in Manhattan," he replies, "She doesn't have time to fly out here to hold my hand, and I don't need her to. I'm a big boy."

"But don't you hate the distance?"

"I'm used to it. She works long hours, and so do I. Our time together is always limited. But quality over quantity, right? Isn't that what they always say?"

"Who is 'they?'"

"You know…the relationship experts," he says, "This sort of thing happens to all couples."

"What sort of thing?"

"Eventually you settle into a routine, and everything becomes mundane."

It *sounds* like a statement of contented acceptance, but the expression on his face says something else entirely. He looks disappointed by the reality, or at least, resistant to the idea. One thing that is abundantly clear to me, no matter how flippant he seems, Julien misses his fiancée. He wants her here with him, even if he won't say so out loud.

"You should ask her to come out," I advise, surprising myself and him with the suggestion. "She doesn't have to stay the entire time, just a few days."

"Why?"

"What do you mean 'why?' Spending time together is important," I tell him, "I don't care what the experts say. 'Quality over quantity' is a joke."

"Says who?"

"Says Regina Anita Grandberry, the smartest woman I know," I reply with a superior air, "She's been happily married to the same man for over 25 years so, I'm inclined to believe she knows her stuff."

"Oh really?" he replies with an amused, half-grin, "And what does your *mom* have to say about it?"

"Quality is important, but so is quantity. You and Kate need to prioritize your relationship above everything else, even your career," I tell him, "One day those good looks are going to fade, and the jobs will be gone. If you have children, they'll move away and start families of their own. It will just be you and her. Would you rather spend forever with your best friend, or a stranger?"

I'm not prepared for the moment when he reaches over to squeeze my hand in gratitude. Every nerve ending in my body comes alive. It takes me a split second to remember to breathe again.

"That's really solid advice. Thank you."

Deliberately, I remove my hand from his grasp but not in such a way to make him aware that his touch has sent inexplicable tingles shooting through my entire body. "Why do you sound so surprised? I *am* capable of profound wisdom."

"I think the precise word you're searching for is self-righteousness."

"Haha. You're hilarious, Caffrey."

"I'm teasing you. You make it so easy."

"Of course, you are. Because you never take anything seriously."

His smile wobbles a bit, becoming just the tiniest bit contemplative. "I take *you* seriously," he adds solemnly, "I mean that. You're a good friend. I'm glad you're my screen partner."

I want to echo those sentiments with the same ease. The words are there, but they are caught in my throat, which is suddenly tight and achy. Predictably, Julien teases me about my lack of response.

"And obviously that's not a mutual feeling," he laughs, "Way to level my ego."

"Oh, get over yourself," I reply gruffly, "You're an okay screen partner too."

He nudges me with his shoulder, that stupid, endearing smile of his on full display. "And a good friend too, right? Come on. You can say it."

"Yeah, yeah, yeah," I manage around the growing lump of emotion which almost strangles my reply, "You're a good friend."

6

"You look rundown."

I roll onto my side to tuck closer into my pillow while being careful to remain in my phone's camera frame. "Thank you, Mother. My self-esteem is soaring."

"I wasn't disparaging your looks, Aiona. I'm only saying you look tired."

She's not exaggerating. I caught a long look at myself in the mirror tonight while I readied myself for bed. Without the magic of movie make-up concealing the heavy bags and dark circles beneath my eyes, it's impossible to ignore how haggard I look…how haggard I *feel*. I had just enough energy to drag myself into a shower, wrestle my hair into two haphazard braids and pull on my pajamas before finally climbing into bed to Facetime my mother. Had I not made a promise to call her at least twice a week, I would have passed out as soon as my head hit the pillow.

Part of my sheer exhaustion is due to the crazy demands of making a feature film. Rising every day before dawn is taking its toll. The other part of my fatigue is due solely to how I've been occupying my time outside of work hours.

To my consternation and surprise, Julien enthusiastically followed my advice about Kate. After clearing the plan with our director and agreeing to spend extra time shooting to keep us on track, Julien arranged his schedule so that he could spend every free, available moment he had with his fiancée when she arrived on set. He created an entire itinerary with all the places he wanted to take her while she was in L.A. He planned an elaborate, romantic welcome brunch for her. And finally, he called her to ask if she would fly out to California to spend the next week with him.

She turned him down.

In her defense, her reasons for refusing him were very valid. As charming as his gesture had been, it was still short notice. Additionally, she was in the middle of a time sensitive work project and wasn't in a position to drop all her responsibilities without warning. She also needed to board their dog who, apparently, had been displaying quite a rebellious streak since Julien was gone. And though Kate reassured him that she might have more flexibility closer to our wrap date and Julien did his best to be mature and understanding, it was quite obvious that he was disappointed. He didn't betray his frustration to Kate, but he certainly didn't make any efforts to hide it from me.

"You set me up!" he accused me afterwards.

"I suggested that you ask her. I didn't guarantee she'd say yes!"

"It's still *your* fault!"

Though I accused him of acting like a spoiled child, I also couldn't ignore my part in his misery. I felt responsible since *I* was the one who got him hyped up in the first place. Consequently, in my efforts to cheer him up, we've become even more constant companions in these last few weeks of filming. The thin boundaries I had established in the beginning are nonexistent now.

I agreed to binge watch seasons one and two of *Stranger Things* with him on Netflix despite my leeriness about the show. I consented to become his running partner during his random late-night jogs even though I *despise* breaking a sweat for purposeless reasons. I patiently allowed him to teach me every annoying card trick he knew just because it made him happy. And it doesn't matter how much I complain and grumble or even fantasize aloud in excruciating detail about how I could cheerfully push him into oncoming traffic, he seems to enjoy my company regardless of my surface hostility.

It's a bit strange to me. All the traits about me that have been historically categorized as "problematic" by other men don't appear to be so with him. He seems to find me amusing rather than irritating. I think he might even get some perverse pleasure out of deliberately riling me. But despite my constant complaining, I really *do* like spending time with him.

Every day, I discover new reasons to like him, little idiosyncrasies and physical traits that become more noticeable the longer I'm in his company. He has the most gorgeous eyelashes that I've ever seen on anyone, male or female. They are lush and thick and ridiculously curly. And the reason I noticed them is because he has this adorable way of peeking up from beneath them whenever he is thinking or planning something mischievous. It's always a dead giveaway. The man has no chill.

I've also learned that he nibbles on his lower lip whenever he's anxious or very deep in thought. Additionally, he mumbles under his breath. Incessantly. Whenever he reviews the script, he always talks to himself as if he's having a full conversation with his character. It is a weird quirk that I find endearing and aggravating at the same time.

All of these charming factoids come together to shape this man that I've come to deeply admire and respect. They also, unfortunately, cause him to become even more deeply entrenched in my heart. I've forgotten all the reasons I should maintain my distance.

I recognize my misstep. I need to reestablish my boundaries. I shouldn't be hanging out with him in his hotel room late into the night, and he shouldn't be lounging around in mine after hours either. I shouldn't know that he watches scary movies with a pillow cradled to his chest and his head buried underneath a blanket. The fact that he has a weakness for dill pickle potato chips should largely be a mystery to me.

I've crossed over into risky terrain, far beyond attraction and shallow crushes. Somehow along this crazy journey, I've done the very thing I absolutely swore I would not do. I've fallen in love. I can't precisely pinpoint when it happened, but there's no doubt after spending nearly two months in Julien Caffrey's company, I am absolutely there.

This is bad. I'm in a very bad place and I know it. The quicksand is pulling me down fast, and I'm already up to my neck! Fortunately, I can take comfort in three irrefutable facts.

First, my desire for Julien is unreciprocated. He doesn't view me with any sort of romantic interest. And, if he did, I probably wouldn't be nearly as enamored with him. So, that's a win/win scenario either way.

The second and most important thing is that I will *never* act on my desire. It's not even a remote possibility I've entertained. He is ignorant of my feelings, and he will stay that way. As far as Julien is concerned, I am nothing more than his cranky co-star and friend.

Third, we'll soon say goodbye to each other. The filming is almost complete. In a little less than two weeks, we will both be on flights back to our respective homes. I will finally have the distance I need to gain some perspective. All I have to do now is hold it together for a little while longer.

It does help to remind myself that he is engaged. Julien has made it obvious that he adores his fiancée. He talks about Kate Leland like she

62

was personally sun-kissed by gods and dropped down directly from the heavens. That's not even a slight exaggeration. She gave him a chance when few people would. He has literally built her up in his mind as a savior. There's no way to compete with that!

I am *nowhere* on his radar romantically speaking, nor should I be.

That's probably why I continue to toe this line with him. There's no harm when the feelings are one-sided. Once I'm not continually in his orbit and he's not in mine, this private, internal battle I've been waging will become just an awkward memory. Afterwards, I will be left with an extraordinary friendship with an extraordinary man who I hope will stay in my life for an extraordinarily long time. No one will ever know.

The plan seems like a sound one and yet something remains restless in my spirit. There is a niggling voice in the back of my mind that whispers, "You're wrong. You know you're wrong." I try to ignore it, but it remains there, berating me for lusting after another woman's man.

I'm almost tempted to get my mother's thoughts. I would love to ask her opinion, but I don't dare to broach the subject. She already has a surplus of reasons to question my life choices. If I tell her that I think I've fallen for my *engaged* co-star, that will only feed my family's narrative that I am a directionless hot mess. I'm not eager to give my mother yet another reason to be disappointed in me.

"You're not going to say anything?" she prompts suddenly, reminding me that I still haven't responded to her earlier observation. Instead, I've been lying here in reflective silence for at least a full minute.

I shift upright in bed in the hope of keeping myself more focused on the conversation at hand. "What can I say?" I ask her, my tone mildly defensive. "You're right. I am tired. I can't argue with you."

"Are you sleeping enough?"

"Nope."

"What about your diet? How's your nutrition?"

"Nonexistent."

"For the love of God, Iyah!"

"Mom, I've been living in a hotel for the last six and a half weeks! It's not like I can have a home cooked meal every night!"

"There is more to life than burgers and fries." I stifle my long-suffering groan in anticipation of her looming lecture. She's made this speech so many times that I can practically recite the words with her. "Right now, you're still young, so you're not feeling the effects of these poor eating habits, but they will catch up to you eventually. Did you know that some studies have revealed that colon cancer can be attributed—,"

"—Mother," I interrupt tiredly before she can really pick up speed, "please, stop. If this is going to become an argument, I'd rather we end the conversation."

"I don't want that. But how am I supposed to be comfortable with the idea of you being on the other side of the country when you refuse to take care of yourself?"

It is the genuine worry in her voice, the tremor of concern I detect underneath her sprawling inclination to be a helicopter mom that helps to lessen my irritation with her. "I know. I'm sorry. I'll do better."

"Will you really?"

I duck my head shamefully at the skepticism she reflects back at me. She has good reason. I've made this promise to her dozens of times in the past too, only to work myself to the point of complete exhaustion. My dedication to my craft can become so obsessive that I'm rendered figuratively myopic in my pursuits. I can't see anything beyond my goal. It fuels my perfectionist spirit and drives me in my quest to continually improve myself. That single-minded focus is both a blessing and a curse.

So, rather than lie to her and give her the false hope that I'll actually re-prioritize this time, I tell her, "I'll try my best."

It's not what she wants to hear. That much is evident in her answering scowl, but she's gracious enough to let it go. Like me, I doubt she wants to spend this limited time we have together engaging in an argument with me that she can't win. Thankfully then, she changes the subject.

"How's the movie going?"

"Great. It looks like we'll wrap filming soon."

"And then you're coming home?" she asks, not bothering to mask her mounting excitement over the prospect.

"Yes, barring any catastrophes or delays, I'll fly home right after we wrap."

"Thank goodness!"

I don't share her same enthusiasm about returning home. While I have missed my family, I haven't really missed the cold, dreary gray of Michigan skies, and I'm not eager to return to braving salt encrusted roads and frigid temperatures. Besides that, these last seven weeks have been a beautiful glimpse into the future I want for myself.

Yes, the schedule has been demanding, and the work has been taxing, but I have never once regretted my choice to be here. The thought of returning to my life as a data entry clerk for a regional healthcare system doesn't seem like an incredibly exciting prospect after all that. Though, I guess I should be grateful that I've been such a model employee that they were willing to hold my spot for two whole months. At least I'll have a job to return to.

Though I leave these internal musings unspoken, the lack of eagerness has to be written all over my face because my mother says, "You can still get local work in commercials just like you were doing before."

"I know. But it's not the same."

"There will be other roles for you, Iyah. I don't doubt it."

I didn't recognize just how much I needed that verbal declaration of confidence until I heard her say the words. Grateful tears immediately well up in my eyes which I rapidly blink back into submission. "Thanks, Mom."

My mother understands how uncomfortable I am with displaying emotion, so she is ready to provide a needed segue while I compose myself. She asks me how I've enjoyed my time in California and if the weather really is as perfect as they claim. While it hasn't been perpetual sunny skies here, the moderate temperatures are definitely an improvement over Michigan's occasional arctic weather. My rosy report hardly inspires her enthusiasm, and she warns me not to get any ideas about relocating. When I reassure her that isn't the case, she changes the topic once again.

"Have you met any big-name celebrities out there? What about Idris Elba? Have you met Idris Elba?"

Her raging celebrity crush on the man is both adorable and embarrassing. I never know whether I should laugh over how openly she fangirls or cringe for eternity. "Mother, I have not met Idris Elba. I will *never* meet Idris Elba. Let it go."

"You never know. When you hit it big…" and I secretly thrill over the fact she says "when" and not "if." The distinction is telling. "…you might be cast in a movie with him. And, when that happens, I'm going to need you to introduce us. He's the only man I'd consider leaving your father for."

"I don't want to discuss your thirst for Idris Elba, Mom. This is uncomfortable for me. Please stop."

"Okay, fine," she consents with a laugh, "Are you doing better with the material now? I know you were struggling for a bit."

"I am. Talking with Julien helps. He's a good sounding board."

"Is he having a hard time too?"

"More or less. Ironically, he's better at detaching than I am."

"That's high praise from the Queen herself," she chuckles, "How have you liked working with him so far? I've heard that models can be temperamental. Is he professional?"

"Very professional. He did extensive research into schizophrenia and the latest treatment modalities after he got the role. I was surprised that he knew almost as much about the illness as I did. When it comes to this role, he's very focused."

When she asks about Julien's ability to portray his character in a believable manner, I'm much too eager to recount his brilliance. I go on eloquently for a full five minutes about his effortless ability to embody Adam Sullivan. There is one particular scene that is firmly embedded in my mind.

Julien's character is still coming to terms with the reality of his diagnosis. My character, who hasn't yet formed an emotional attachment to him, is reviewing the list of medications he will be taking and the associated side effects. During the scene, the script calls for Julien to be distracted and only half-listening to my character. Eventually, she notices that he's not engaged, and she asks him what's wrong. Specifically, she asks him to tell her what the voices are saying to him, and that instance signals the first glimpse of vulnerability from Adam Sullivan. Julien nailed the scene to perfection.

As I recount the story to my mother, I find myself crisply reliving every detail and how marvelously present I felt in that scene with him. "He didn't even have dialogue. He had to convey all of that emotion through his body language. Do you know how difficult that is? It was amazing," I finish with a wistful smile filled with unabashed pride. "*Julien* was amazing."

It's only after I'm done speaking that I realize my mother is staring at me with a stunned expression on her face. She is literally gaping at me. I immediately become self-conscious under her speechless scrutiny, because now I'm cognizant of how long I've been talking.

"What?"

"You like him."

"Yes, I do. I told you that already."

"No, Iyah. You *like* him," she emphasizes dramatically, "It's all over your face!"

"You're wrong. He is my friend," I declare implacably, and I'm secretly impressed with my ability to look her directly in the eye and lie with a straight face. "That is all, Mother. I admire him as an actor. There is nothing there."

"Right."

"Stop it! We're dealing with some very emotional material. It makes sense that we'd become close after that."

"I guess that sounds reasonable..."

"But?" I prompt when she still seems unconvinced.

"Something is off with you," she says, "I can tell. If it's not the work, and it's not your co-star, then what is it? And don't tell me 'nothing.' I've known you your entire life, and I know when you're lying to me."

The declaration causes me to squirm uncomfortably, mostly because I've done nothing except lie to her shamelessly for the last thirty seconds. If she can read me as easily as she claims, then this conversation is going to turn sour rather quickly. Wisely then, I don't dig in my heels and continue making useless denials. Instead, I settled on sharing a partial truth.

"I don't know how I'm supposed to leave this role behind when I'm done. This experience has been life changing."

"You've formed some close bonds, haven't you?"

"Yes, I have. I'm *really* going to miss him when I leave."

She doesn't ask me to elaborate on the identity of the "him" in question. I just finished delivering a sweeping monologue touting his unparalleled brilliance. At this point, it's obvious.

"There's no reason you can't keep in touch once you're done filming."

"He won't have time for me then," I argue sullenly, "Julien is getting married. He'll be busy with his own life."

"Ah," she replies in that annoying way she does whenever she thinks she's discerned something that I've left unspoken.

I make a face. "What does 'ah' mean?"

"There is more to life than chasing a career, Iyah."

"I know that."

"You could meet someone too if you put in more effort."

Only then does it dawn on me what conclusion she's drawn. "You think I'm jealous because Julien is getting married?" I balk in disbelief. The assumption is certainly true, but not for the reason she assumes. And because she's so astonishingly wrong, I can't help but laugh out loud. "Believe me, Mom," I chuckle with all sincerity, "Marriage is the *last* thing on my mind!"

"Why do you have to say it like that?" she grumbles in consternation, "You act as if it's some kind of disease! Nicki is a bad influence on you!"

"It's not Nicki. There are no viable candidates at the moment."

That's not untrue either. Julien is *not* a viable candidate no matter how much I wish otherwise. Further, I can barely let myself fantasize about the possibility of dating him, let alone imagine being *married* to him!

"I'm waiting for the right person," I sigh after a beat.

"Well, if you're looking, I know some eligible bach—,"

"—I said *I'm waiting*, Mom!" I interrupt stridently before she can really get going. "Not now! Good grief! I give you an inch and you take a mile!"

"I just want you to be happy."

"I am happy," I insist, "But I'm still trying to figure *me* out. You'll have to put away those dreams of having grandbabies anytime soon."

"But you're not ruling it out?"

"No, Mom," I answer, my thoughts invariably rolling back to Julien. "I'm not ruling it out."

7

"What are you going to do after we wrap?"

I cut a startled glance at Julien. We are enjoying a short break in between film takes while the crew reviews the latest footage we've shot. The set lights beam down on us, bathing us both in a baking heat that is made more oppressive by our heavy "winter" costumes. Though there are large, industrial fans blowing during the interim, they don't provide much relief. I'm ready to rip out of my coat and wig and, if the perspiration dampening Julien's forehead is any clue, he's feeling a similar discomfort. I'm not surprised he's trying to distract himself, but I wish he had chosen another subject.

"We have another ten days of filming. You're already thinking about that?"

"Ten days go by fast."

It does. But I've made a deliberate choice not to think about what happens after we wrap. I'm not eager to part with the mild California weather. I'm unexcited about returning to frigid Michigan temperatures and my tedious job. And I *especially* don't want to say goodbye to him. I'd rather avoid discussing it, but Julien seems determined.

"Do you have any plans for when you get back home?" he asks.

"You mean other than going back to my same old job, and living with my parents?" I reply in a dry tone, "Not really. What about you?"

"Same. It's back to modeling. Hoo-rah."

"You don't have to sound so enthused."

"I'm more than a pretty face."

"I don't know," I reply carelessly, waging a mighty struggle against grinning which would ruin the effect of my coming insult. "You've never struck me as being all that talented."

"You're right. I probably have no future after this." He looks so forlorn and defeated that I fear he's actually taken me seriously for a second, but then he smiles. "We should keep in touch."

Though I maintain a casual air, my heart is beating a wild, staccato rhythm in my chest. "Of course, we will."

"I mean it, Iyah," he insists with surprising intensity, "I don't want us to become strangers to each other after this. I would like us to stay friends."

"I would like that too."

I'm not being facetious, nor do I have an ulterior motive when I say that. Julien and I have shared many firsts during this filming process. When everything is stripped away, he is truly one of the best people I've ever known. I want to keep him in my life in whatever capacity I can.

Almost as if he's read my mind, a slow, satisfied grin forms across his mouth. "Excellent! It's decided. You'll come to New York, and we'll visit every restaurant named after an animal sound. Mark it on your calendar."

"Wait. What?"

"Michigan and New York aren't that far apart. We can still hang out and stuff."

"Won't you be planning a wedding, sir?"

"One thing does not preclude the other."

"Did you seriously use the word 'preclude' in a sentence just now? How pretentious."

"Oh, so *you're* the only one who can wave around ten-dollar words like a flag. Is that it?"

"I'm just saying, you'll have a lot to occupy your time once you get back home. I'm sure hanging out with me will be pretty low on your priority list."

His eyes flicker. "You'd be surprised."

The opportunity to investigate his cryptic remark further is lost. Our marker is called. For the remainder of the day, we're both focused on work. We don't have a spare moment to continue our earlier conversation.

By the time we're back in the transport van, Julien is clearly distracted. Asking him to elaborate on something he'd said hours earlier seems pointless. But I selfishly want to know what he meant by, "You'd be surprised."

Now, he's fidgety and agitated and doesn't appear to be in the mood to talk. He keeps clicking the locking mechanism up and down. Julien is normally a very tactile person, needing to flip and fiddle with buttons and latches to a near constant degree. I've threatened to tie his hands together more than once. This seems like more than his typical restlessness.

After the fifth click, I huff in exasperation, "What is wrong with you?"

He looks at me sharply. "Why do you ask?"

"You're driving me crazy! Do you need a cigarette?"

"Yeah…kinda."

"Go ahead then."

"And subject myself to a two-minute diatribe from you about the dangers of secondhand smoke?" he grunts with an eyeroll, "No, thank you."

"Oh, just roll down the window, drama king!"

A few seconds later, he fumbles around in his pocket for his pack and lights up before he's even finished lowering the window. The interior of the van is filled with a cacophony of sound from the incoming wind. I watch him soak in his hit of needed nicotine in silence. After five minutes, the cigarette is reduced to an unrecognizable stub, but Julien is noticeably calmer. He raises the van window and then favors me with a sheepish smile.

"Sorry about that."

"Don't apologize. Just know if I develop lung cancer later in life, I'm suing you for every dime you have."

He isn't alarmed by my threat. By now, Julien knows my bark is worse than my bite. Instead, he laughs, and I'm relieved to have diffused some of his tension.

Straight-faced, I reach into my purse and then wordlessly pass him a piece of gum, which he accepts with an ironic smirk. I watch as he takes meticulous care with rolling the remnants of his cigarette into the foil gum wrapper before tucking it away deep into his pocket. Conspicuously, he avoids looking at me the whole time.

"Sooo…" I drawl out in the awkward silence that ensues, "What's bothering you?" He swiftly denies being bothered at all, and I swiftly call him a liar.

Julien makes a sound, and I'm not sure if it's a sigh of exasperation or defeat. "We're filming the suicide scene tomorrow."

"I know. Are you nervous about it?"

"Not nervous. More like reluctant."

I don't blame him. There is an incredible weight on his shoulders. After all, this is the film's most climactic moment. We've been dreading it since we began filming. I'm ambivalent about the ending, mostly because it feels hopeless. Realistic, but very hopeless.

It would be great if this were a story of triumph where the character comes to accept his limitations and learns to function around them, but that is not the story our director wants to tell. For him, it is just as important to portray the tales of tragedy as it is to tell the ones of inspiring success. He says that there is nothing shameful about either ending, and both are heartbreaking in their own respects.

According to Vic, the ending is not about Adam giving up on life, but choosing his own terms and what kind of life he accepts for himself. His suicide is a release. I know that's the theme he's reaching for, but I'm not so sure an audience will grasp that concept easily. But it's *his* vision. Now, it is incumbent upon *Julien* to personify that intent onscreen, and that is a tall order. I'm not surprised he is anxious over the prospect, and I tell him so.

"I get what Vic is trying to accomplish," he says, "Adam's reality is never going to change. He is always going to struggle with his illness, and he will never be the person he wants to be. I can see why he would decide that he'd rather not be here at all than live like a shadow. It just feels too final."

There is a curious expression on his face, one that I've never seen before. It is a mixture of pain and empathy combined with shame. Seeing him so visibly distraught makes me sad. Before I'm even conscious of moving, I reach across the distance between us to place my hand against his. I'm not very good with comforting gestures. I'm often awkward and unnerved by other people's grief. But I'm compelled to do *something*, even if it's as simple as touching his hand.

"You're gonna be great."

He gives my fingers a gentle squeeze before pulling away. "Thanks. You gotta do what you gotta do, right?" he replies with almost forced dismissiveness, "It's just acting."

I'm not fooled by his cavalier response. "Is it just acting for you, Julien?"

He favors me with a careful side-eye. "Are you asking me if I've ever tried…" Julien makes a grotesque illusion to a noose around his neck, followed by a sound meant to mimic snapping bone.

"I don't think I would have phrased it quite that insensitively, but yes. Have you ever had personal experience with this kind of material?"

The possibility that this could be personal for him makes me flinch inwardly. I honestly can't imagine being in a headspace where I could believe being dead was better than living. But I recognize that there are plenty of people who can relate to that experience. It physically pains me to think that Julien Caffrey might be one of those people.

"Is it really insensitive if it's your lived experience?" he counters with an arch smile.

My heart contracts with the confirmation, but Julien is determined to make light of it all. I, on the other hand, suddenly feel like my throat is closing. "What…what happened?" I ask him thickly, "Do you want to talk about it?"

"It was a long time ago. I was a kid. As for what happened, obviously I didn't succeed. I'm sitting here talking to you."

I think I need that bit of sarcasm from him right then because it helps me to regain my slipping composure. "I can see that! I meant how did you recover?"

"Turns out ceiling fans aren't as sturdy as they look, which is lucky for me. I got a bruised trachea as a souvenir and bought myself a psych hold and brief stint in a juvenile mental facility."

76

"Oh my God, Julien!" I burst out before I can temper my response. "That's awful! Why would you even take this role at all?"

"I told you already. It's cathartic."

There is a lecture forming, but I swallow it back for fear of overstepping. I don't know if his choice is healthy or harmful. I'm leaning heavily towards the latter. I wonder if he might even be some kind of masochist, but I refrain from making the accusation out loud. Not because I'm afraid to call him out on what could very well be troubling behavior, but because I don't want my theory to be true.

My greatest concern is how casual he's been throughout our entire exchange. He recounts his past *suicide attempt* as if retelling the story of the first time he fell off his bike. I don't need him to dissolve into a blubbering mess or anything, but his general lack of sobriety is worrisome.

Finally, I ask him, "Does Kate know...I mean...is she aware that you...that you...?"

"It might help if you threw in a verb to complete the sentence," he replies dryly, "Yes. She knows."

"And how does she feel about it?" I press, "Specifically, how does she feel about you doing this movie?"

He turns his crumpled cigarette pack over in his hands as if it is the most fascinating thing he's ever seen. But I recognize the stall tactic. He doesn't want to answer. His hesitance speaks volumes. I can infer the rest. When he finally replies, my suspicions are confirmed.

"Kate wasn't thrilled. We fought before I flew out here."

"Is that the real reason she didn't come?"

"That's the real reason," he confirms softly.

"Don't be mad at her for caring about you. She doesn't want to see you hurt yourself."

"The same could be said about you and your folks, but you rant about how they don't respect your decisions all the time!"

"Not remotely comparable, Julien. I've never done…never tried…"

"…to unalive yourself?"

"Dude, you're way too glib about this!"

"I don't know how you want me to be. It happened. It's over. I learned from it. That one moment doesn't define who I am as a person."

I'm trying to school my features against betraying the yawning sadness I feel for him, but I don't think I do a very good job. He regards me with narrowed eyes, full of impatience and defiance. "Don't look at me like that," he mutters.

"Look at you like what?"

"Like I'm broken. I'm not."

"You know me better than that, Julien. I don't think that at all."

His eyes harden further, glittering in the lingering tendrils of cigarette smoke that hangs between us. "Well, don't feel sorry for me either."

"You're wrong about that too," I assure him quietly, "I just want you to be okay. Are you okay?"

"I am. I promise."

Once we reach the hotel, I am physically and emotionally spent. I don't have the reserves for any more naked soul-baring and neither does Julien. We keep our conversation lighthearted after that and cap off the evening with a little mindless entertainment. We retreat to my room with a bag of microwave popcorn to watch the television edit of *Nacho Libre*.

At the movie's halfway point, I become aware of Julien's constant shifting. He's folded on the floor at the foot of the bed. I crawl over to the edge to peer down at him.

"You look uncomfortable," I observe.

"I *am* uncomfortable."

"You wanna come up?"

He squints at me, his brow knit with indecision. "Are you sure?"

"My mattress is your mattress."

Julien vacillates briefly before accepting my invitation. After he settles in, I flick kernels of popcorn at his head, but miss him by several inches. He chides me for my terrible aim, which earns him yet another shower of popcorn.

"If you wanted to come up, why didn't you just ask me?"

"I didn't want to overstep your boundaries."

"But you have no problem forcing me to watch this god-awful movie!"

Julien falls back against the bed with a mock gasp. "How dare you speak such sacrilege? *Nacho Libre* is a classic! This is Jack Black at his funniest."

"If you say so."

He is right, though I hate to admit it. The movie is hilarious in a way that only farcical comedies can be. There are some parts where I have to stifle the urge to laugh out loud. I cover the impulse behind mocking commentary whenever possible. I refuse to give Julien the satisfaction. But I think he might know anyway. He has a stupid, endearing smirk on his face the entire movie.

Afterwards when the credits roll, as a gesture of goodwill, Julien agrees to watch *Keeping Up with the Kardashians* with me. Of course, he repays me for earlier by making sarcastic remarks during the entire show. I also won't admit that he's right in his assessment about that too.

Sometime during Kim's latest onscreen life crisis which I suspect is patently manufactured, I must fall asleep because when I open my eyes again, the show is over. I am drowsily aware that some infomercial for a "too good to be true" cookware is playing on the television screen.

What really captures my attention is that I'm surrounded by Julien's smell, the faint aroma of tobacco mixed with designer cologne. I'm cradled in his arms.

Julien's warm, lean body is spooned perfectly behind me, so close that there is literally no space between us. I can feel his breath stirring over my skin. But the thing that makes my heart quiver is the realization that his groin is pressed against my hip, and the ridge of his prominent arousal can't be ignored.

Every muscle in my body is frozen. I can't move. Can't breathe. My neurons are firing like mad, reaching Defcon 5 levels of sensitivity. My body tingles. There is an aching sensation that pulses between my legs. The most disturbing reality isn't that we're cuddled together this way, but that none of it feels foreign to me. It doesn't feel forbidden. It feels right. It feels *good*. I could happily stay pressed against him like this forever.

That secret acknowledgment belatedly triggers my sense of shame and rips open a tidal wave of guilt with it. Guilt that is only compounded when Julien moans in his sleep and lazily rolls his hips against me in drowsy overture. In that split second, I'm overwhelmed with the impulse to respond. Before I give in, I bolt out of the bed like someone electrified, violently jostling Julien awake in the process.

He rolls upright with a disoriented, mumbled curse, and I'm sure a confused frown, but I don't know for sure because I can't look at him. I'm too mortified, especially because my awakened desire has not subsided. I'm horrified by the unabated throbbing which provokes a sudden, overwhelming need to escape.

"I gotta go to the bathroom!" I blurt out wildly before making a mad dash towards the open door and slamming it behind me.

My fingers are trembling so violently that I can barely twist the lock into place. My face and ears are hot, almost feverish. My mouth is as arid as a desert. Driven by the instinctive need to make myself as small as possible, I climb into the bathtub and pull my knees close to my chest. The last several minutes tumbled through my head in a mortifying reel.

I don't know what happened. I can't even comprehend how I ended up in such a compromising position in the first place. It wasn't as if we had spent the evening flirting or making romantic overtures. There had been no underlying sexual tension. I've never allowed my conscious mind to go there. We were two friends hanging out, watching epically bad movies and TV shows. How we ended up spooning is a mystery.

And I could probably dismiss the entire moment as an embarrassing foible if desire for him hadn't been awakened in me. I *liked* how warm his body felt against my own. I *liked* the weight of his arm around my waist, and listening to the deep, even cadence of his breathing as he slept. Now that I know how good it feels, I'm not sure I'll ever forget. I'm not sure I'll be able to stop myself from wanting it to happen again…and that thought is terrifying to me.

There's no way I can face him now. Our friendship is going to be irrevocably altered. Our working relationship will be trashed beyond salvage. Everything is ruined and all because I couldn't control my stupid longing for him!

Halfway into my irrational plunge down the proverbial rabbit hole, I catch myself mid worst-case scenario. I'm overreacting. *Nothing* happened. Julien and I didn't have sex. We didn't even kiss. We fell asleep together, and we woke up together. The circumstances are far from disastrous. My mortification doesn't stem from what happened, but what I *wanted* to happen.

It's only when I recognize that truth that I'm able to uncurl myself from my protective ball and rise from the bathtub. I'm being ridiculous. As horrified as I am, this situation has an easy fix. I've become too lax with my boundaries, and they need to be reestablished.

Julien and I are friends. Surely, if I'm honest with him, he'll understand. He might even agree that some distance between us might be beneficial. There's no reason we can't have a healthy, mature discussion about it, especially when we've been so candid with each other about everything else. We *are* adults, after all.

Once I've finished constructing my carefully planned speech in my mind, I compose myself, square my shoulders and finally exit the bathroom. Unfortunately, it soon becomes apparent that my lofty plans for mature discussion were in vain. I step around the corner to discover the television is silent, and the bed is empty.

Julien is already gone.

8

The next morning when I climb into the transport van, I'm a little shocked to find Julien already strapped into his seat rather than chain smoking outside like usual. As soon as I note his posture, I know instantly that it's going to be a bad day. His headphones are on, and he is wearing a dark blue baseball cap that is pulled down low over his eyes. Only the lower half of his face is visible as he mouths the lyrics to whatever song he's currently listening to. He doesn't even look over to acknowledge me when I get inside.

It is a glaring indication that he does not want to be bothered. He's giving me the cold shoulder. Clearly, when he left last night without saying anything, that had been a deliberate choice on his part. And for some reason his attitude annoys me.

I wonder if he's somehow picked up on my secret longing for him. Maybe that's the reason he's being so standoffish now. I grit my teeth at the possibility. While his reaction would certainly be warranted given our circumstances, it still hurts. Besides, *I'm* the one with the unrequited feelings! *I* should be freezing *him* out, and not the other way around!

That mood sets the precedent for the entire day.

If we're not running dialogue or filming a scene, we're not talking. We avoid one another as much as possible. Our characteristic banter is nonexistent. We don't bicker. We don't share our snacks. We're politely civil to one another. The shift is excruciating.

The atmosphere between us is so uncharacteristically mechanical that even the crew begins to comment on our stiff exchanges. Some speculate that we might have had a falling out. And though both Julien and I deny that we're at odds with one another, our work screams otherwise. We miss our marks, flub lines and are embarrassingly leaden with one another in scenes that should be riveting and charged with emotion. When we ruin our fifth take of the day, Vic finally loses his patience with us.

"What the hell is wrong with you two?" he rails, impervious to surrounding gawkers. He's not assuaged by our mutual, but mumbled reassurance that, "Nothing is wrong." In fact, his scowl deepens. "I don't know if you're having a lover's spat or what, but this is unacceptable!"

He abruptly decides to wrap for the day because Julien and I are "useless," and, for a second, I think he might fire us on the spot. I can understand why Vic is livid. The scenes we've butchered happen to be some of the most pivotal scenes in the film, parts he had deliberately saved for the end because Julien and I should have internalized our characters by now. If there are any moments we must get right, these are the moments.

Before we leave the set, Vic pulls us aside to dispense another lecture, but with less hostility than earlier. "I don't want to know what this is," he says, "And, frankly, I don't give a damn! But when you're here, you're on my dime. Don't screw up tomorrow." The previous night notwithstanding, I can't remember the last time I had ever felt so mortified or disappointed in myself.

The worst part is knowing that, in my inability to display basic emotional maturity, I've put our filming behind schedule. Thankfully, it is not a significant delay, and we'll only have to tack on an extra day at most, but I still don't like being the reason for reshoots. Worse yet, tomorrow will undoubtedly become a dreadful repeat of today if Julien and I don't get ourselves together. I'm grateful that our director has already invested too much time and money in this project to find replacement actors, otherwise I'd be worried about losing my job. As it is, I don't doubt this delay will probably be docked from my already paltry final pay.

But, as chastened as I am, I'm still unable to swallow my pride and break the pervasive silence between me and Julien. Our ride back to the hotel is just as quiet and cold as it had been that morning. I know it's childish, but I refuse to talk to him, especially when he's the one who stopped talking to *me* first.

An hour later, however, I'm starting to rethink that petty stance. Pride aside, my career and reputation are on the line. We can't afford to have another day of filming like we had today. No director will ever want to work with us again if this is the legacy we create for ourselves. We need to be professionals and resolve our differences.

It's for the best anyway. Hadn't my original plan been to establish some much-needed boundaries between us? Does it really matter if Julien is the one to put them there? As long as they exist and enable us to maintain a certain degree of professionalism, why does it matter how they were established? In a practical sense, I know that's a reasonable decision. I just wish I didn't feel so rejected.

I'm in the middle of mentally planning my speech when I hear a knock on my door. I already know that it's Julien even before I roll from the bed. So, I'm not surprised when I pull open the door and I find him standing there dressed in a white cotton T-shirt and joggers. However, I *am* surprised that he appears apologetic.

"You wanna go for a run?" he asks as if we haven't spent literal hours ignoring one another. His audacity provokes my automatic refusal.

"Nope." But the response makes me feel childish, so I sigh and amend in weary annoyance, "Fine. Give me five minutes to change."

I don't really like running. There is nothing I find enjoyable about the pastime. It leaves you sweaty, tired, and out of breath. Most of all, it is physically painful. For the life of me, I don't understand how anyone does this activity out of pure enjoyment. Marathoners are an enigma to me.

And yet I can't deny that there is something revitalizing about running. No matter how tired and sore I am physically, I'm often in a better place mentally when it's over. Any problem that I was grappling with prior to my run seems infinitely smaller. Julien calls it an "endorphin high," and he swears that nothing on Earth can give you better mental clarity than that.

As the child of two healthcare professionals, I am fully aware of the positive benefits that exercise has on mental health. At least, I've always known about it in theory. I've never personally put it to the test. The occasional brisk walk has been the extent of my cardiovascular efforts, but that has never been purposeful.

Now that I've committed to a routine, I can attest from my own experience that the experts have been right all along. I still hate running, but I can't pretend that I don't like the way running makes me *feel*. I have Julien to thank for opening my eyes to that truth. Acknowledging that to myself helps to ease some of my aggravation.

We're about twenty minutes into our jog when I give him the universal sign for "time out" and stop on the sidewalk to double over. My chest is burning. Every breath is painful. I'm hunched over, panting heavily, and I can sense Julien's superior smirk as he observes my struggle.

"You're looking pretty winded, Grandberry. I thought *I* was the one with the 'compromised' lungs." I shoot him a death glare and, interspersed with noisy pants and heavy gulps of air, I tell him concisely and in graphic detail what he can do for me. His smirk only widens. "And you say *I've* got a potty mouth. That was positively shocking."

"Maybe you're a bad influence."

After I finally catch my breath, he asks, "You feel better now?"

"Yeah. But can we walk it out for a little bit?"

"Sure."

The atmosphere between us is much less tense than when we started. Almost companionable. We stroll together in a comfortable silence before Julien abruptly decides to shake things up again.

"So…we should talk about what happened last night."

My heart flutters. "Because you don't want to get fired?"

"Because I don't want it between us." I quickly glance away, tugging my lower lip between my teeth. He's not deterred. "Let's just get it over with."

"Do we have to?" I sigh plaintively, "Can't we just acknowledge it happened and move on? We don't have to have a whole conversation!"

"I *want* to have a whole conversation. Not talking about it is making things awkward between us. I don't want it to be awkward."

"I don't either," I mumble.

We exchange a telling look, our steps inevitably slowing as we regard one another. Julien inhales a shuddering breath. "So, last night when you—,"

"—Nothing really happened, you know?" I interrupt quickly, "It doesn't have to become a big deal unless we make it a big deal."

"But it *is* a big deal because I know you felt...um...I know that I was..."

He struggles to articulate himself for several seconds before I finally put him out of his misery. "It's really okay."

Julien clears his throat, his eyes skittering away as he contemplates the horizon ahead of us. "It's not okay. But I want you to know that it didn't *mean* anything. It was just a biological response! I wasn't trying to come on to you!"

Only then does it fully dawn on me why he's been so keen on avoiding me the entire day. He's clueless about my feelings! He stopped talking to me because he's ashamed and embarrassed. This entire time he's been under the mistaken impression that *he* offended *me*. No doubt my chilly attitude towards him only reinforced that assumption. Now I understand why he left so abruptly last night. He had been mortified, but not for the reason I thought.

"I never thought that you were coming on to me, Julien," I reassure him softly, "You were asleep."

"I wasn't sure. You weren't saying anything to me," he replies with equal softness.

"You weren't saying anything either!"

"How did you expect me to react, Iyah? Last night you shot out of the bed like I had set you on fire! Then you locked yourself in the bathroom for *ten minutes*! What the hell did you want me to do? Kick down the door?"

The expression on his face is priceless. It's a mixture of aggravation, incredulity, and general befuddlement. I almost want to laugh aloud at how silly our snippy behavior towards one another seems in hindsight.

"Was I really in the bathroom for ten minutes?" It hadn't seemed like that much time had passed at all, but I had been in the throes of introspective agony so I couldn't attest to it.

"Yes!" he cries, "It felt like fucking eternity!"

He must be truly flustered because he's dropping f-bombs with impunity now. This time, I actually burst out laughing at his reply. Thankfully, so does he. It helps to dispel the remaining tension that lingers between us.

"Oh my God," I manage between hysterical giggles. "I didn't realize I was in there that long."

"Yeah, you were. I tried to wait but then it started to feel like maybe you were trying to send me a message, so I left."

"I wasn't sending you a message."

"Then why were you in there so long? No one takes that long to pee."

I drop my face into my hands with an embarrassed groan. "God..."

"Did you think I...uh...I took advantage of you or something?"

"No!" I cry vehemently, a little saddened to know he jumped to that conclusion. "I didn't feel that way at all. It was just...strange waking up with you like that."

"Strange" isn't an accurate description. *Perfect. Wonderful. Right.* Everything I've secretly desired. So good I want to do it for the rest of my life. Those were all much better signifiers, but none of them are things I can say out loud. I hadn't barricaded myself in the bathroom for ten minutes because I'd been scandalized or offended. I did it because I wanted him. I'm in love with him, and I'm starting to think those feelings are not going to fade.

"I'm sorry," he whispers, "I never meant to make you uncomfortable."

"Will you please stop apologizing? You didn't do anything wrong. We can put it behind us."

"Really? We can do that?"

I shrug with a casual air I don't necessarily feel. "Is it really that big of a deal, Julien?"

"You woke up with my coc—,"

"—Let's not rehash the details, okay!" I interject a little wildly before he can conclude that crass statement.

"What's the point of sugarcoating it? We don't have any secrets between us, right?" *Other than the fact I'm stupidly in love with you.* "I promise it won't happen again."

"I appreciate the reassurance, but it's not necessary."

We walk together in silence for a few minutes, and I try to use that time to formulate my next words to him. I need to establish some measure of distance between us, but I don't know how to start. I don't *want* to start, but I can't put the discussion off any longer either.

Before I can open my mouth, Julien blurts out, "Be honest with me. Is it going to be weird between us from now on?"

"Weird how?"

"Weird like we won't hang out together with each other like we have been. Weird like you're going to avoid me. Weird like we're not going to be friends anymore."

"Julien…"

"I can count on one hand how many people truly know me," he says, "I don't have a close relationship with my family. I don't have a lot of friends, but the ones I *do* have are precious to me. You're one of them."

"But you barely know me."

"That's not true. I know your favorite flavor of ice cream. I know that you're always trying to prove yourself to your parents because you think you're a disappointment to them. I know that you have a hard time connecting with people emotionally, and that sometimes makes you seem cold when you're anything but. And I know that, even though you don't talk about her, you still dream about your aunt."

Though I don't respond to his quiet observations, a verbal response would be superfluous anyway. The way I start blinking rapidly against the sudden tears that come to my eyes is all the proof Julien needs that he's made his point. He takes advantage of my strangled silence to further drive home his argument.

"You and I connected with each other right from the start. You didn't feel that?"

I nod my head in solemn acknowledgment. "I felt that."

"I just...I don't want to lose that, Iyah."

I'm indecisive. A minute ago, I was ready to declare my need to step back, and now I'm not so sure. Or maybe I want to justify keeping him close. I could be mistaken. What if what I've been classifying as love is really the incredible connection and easy friendship that he and I have shared from the beginning? I've never experienced that sort of instant attachment with anyone before. Maybe that's normal. Julien clearly feels the same, and I know he's not in love with me. Perhaps this is the way a friendship like ours *should* be.

"I don't want to lose it either."

A wide grin of approval brightens his features. He makes a gesture like he means to grab me in a quick side hug, but I deftly dance out of his reach with a warning gesture before he can make contact. Julien blinks at me in mute surprise and confusion. "What?"

"We are *not* hugging. You're sweaty, Caffrey. And you stink." I thrust out my hand to him. "How about a handshake instead?" I note the devilish way he peers at me from beneath his eyelashes, and I know that he's up to no good. I take several tripping steps backward. "Don't you even think about it…"

"Come on," he cajoles, stalking me across the sidewalk. "We gotta hug this one out, Grandberry. It's the universal gesture of friendship…"

I squeal when he makes another unsuccessful lunge at me. "Don't touch me!"

We circle one another like children, literally engaging in a game of keep away right there. It's foolish and stupid, but I can't stop smiling. I can picture how we must look to others as they pass us by, two random joggers in the middle of a busy sidewalk, chasing one another around like kindergarteners.

When he finally catches hold of me, it's only because I've grown tired of trying to dodge him. He scoops me up in a massive bear hug, and I am strangely unbothered by his sweat or his smell, neither of which were ever truly a factor. I hang in his arms like a limp ragdoll and allow him to swing me around for two reasons.

It clearly makes him happy. And I like being close to him. I don't dwell too deeply on the possible meaning behind either of those facts.

"You really *are* one of my favorite people," he confesses when he finally sets me back on my feet. "I hope you know that."

I make a production of smoothing my t-shirt back into place. "As I should be. I am awesome. You're very lucky to know me, sir."

"Yeah," he agrees softly, his expression becoming inscrutable as we resume our walk. "I think I am."

9

"I'm going to quit smoking. I mean it this time."

I briefly glance at Julien as he exits the bathroom, fresh from his shower. To protect my modesty and his own, he's dressed in a pair of loose gray, cotton sweatpants and his usual white tee. His feet are bare. His hair, which he is still in the process of toweling dry, has grown considerably since we began filming, and is spiked adorably in all directions.

As has become our ritual in these last days of filming, we are camped out in his room. It's just after 8 p.m. Pacific time. We've already had our dinner and addressed our individual, personal correspondences with our loved ones, and have now reached the point in our routine where we're both ready to unwind. So, while Julien showered off the remnants of the day, I made myself comfortable on his bed and passed the time reading.

Before I made the trip to New York for our chemistry read, I purchased Michelle Obama's autobiography *Becoming* on Kindle. I've had few opportunities to get into the book. But, because I've learned through experience that Julien takes notoriously long showers (his water bill has to be outrageous), I decided to pull it up while I waited for him.

Though I had been fascinated by her husband's autobiographical account of his road to the presidency, I personally think Michelle's version of events is much more interesting. I enjoy her succinct, nononsense approach. She's definitely not as longwinded as our former president, which I appreciate. I am only a few chapters in, but it's already easy to grasp why this book has become so critically acclaimed.

I'm anxious to get through the current chapter. So, I don't really respond to Julien's grand declaration, especially because it's nothing that I haven't heard from him before. My disinterest evidently annoys him. A second later his bath towel comes flying across the room, missing my face by mere inches before disappearing on the other side of the bed. I glare at him in a mixture of disbelief and murderous intent.

"You *really* chose violence today, didn't you?"

"Did you hear what I just said?" he asks, not the least bit cowed by my implied threat. "I'm going to quit." My reaction to that grand proclamation is an unconvinced grunt before I redirect my attention back to my Kindle. "You don't believe me?"

Because he clearly has no intention of leaving me alone, I drop my head forward with a long-suffering groan and finally set aside the Kindle. "Julien, I've known you for two months…"

"Yes…"

"And in those two months, do you know how many times you've announced that you're going to quit smoking?"

He crosses his arms in a defensive posture. "I'm sure you've been keeping track."

"Five," I tell him, holding up my hand for emphasis, "You've said it five times. You wanna know how many times you've actually done it?" I make the universal gesture for a zero. "That's a goose egg, sir. At this point, it's become a running joke."

He grimaces at me, his expression filled with defiant hurt. "You don't think I can do it, do you?" His tone is vaguely insulted, almost belligerent.

"It's not about that. I know you can do it, but you also don't *want* to do it. That's the problem."

His expression flickers. The defiance melts away and is gradually replaced with self-recrimination. I know I've touched a nerve even *before* his pitiful denial. "That's not true."

"Yes, it is, and that's okay. You're not ready to quit."

I start to reach for my Kindle when his expression softens with relief. However, a second later, he's back to being a distraction. "But don't you think I should *want* to quit?"

I'm unsuccessful at stifling my groan of growing impatience. "Do *you* think you should want to quit?"

He responds with an irritated scowl. "Stop doing that."

"Doing what?"

"Answering my question with a question. I hate it when you do that."

I swing around on the bed to face him fully. "Then how should I respond?"

"Don't you want to launch into a whole lecture about the health risks and how I'm slowly killing myself, yadda, yadda, yadda? You've never pulled any punches before! Don't start now."

"Don't you already *know* all the health risks?"

"Yeah…"

"And they don't mean anything to you, do they? I can recount all the health statistics and data until I pass out, and it won't matter. You're still going to do what you want regardless of what I say!"

"Now you're making me sound like an asshole."

"Knowing the health risks isn't enough," I argue softly, "I'm not going to convince you with facts! You have to *want* to do it. Your reasons for quitting have to be *greater* than your reasons for smoking. Clearly, you aren't there yet."

"And you're okay with that?"

I shrug. "It's not my life."

"Wow. You're being really open-minded about this considering we had only known each other for *one whole day* before you were getting up on your soapbox about it!"

Belatedly, it occurs to me right then that he might be trying to pick a fight. The possibility stuns me. This isn't like Julien at all. He's always been straightforward, candid, and forthright to an almost mortifying degree. He says what is on his mind regardless of whether his message will be well received or not. So, the fact that he's trying to goad me rather than taking a more direct approach is puzzling.

"I can't *force* you to quit, Julien, even if I *want* you to do it." I study him for a moment, trying to discern the scattered thoughts going on behind his impenetrable expression. "Why are we really having this conversation?"

"What do you mean?" he brazens.

"You're being a jerk for no reason."

"I had a fight with Kate," he mumbles after a defeated sigh, "She says I'm being selfish because I don't consider how my decisions affect her."

As soon as he mentions his fiancée, I know I'm crossing over into dangerous territory. Unfortunately, it's too late to backpedal. But I'm the last person who should be handing him relationship advice. I'm hardly impartial. He shouldn't be confiding in me, especially because anything I say to him is going to come across as self-serving.

Truthfully, I don't agree with Kate's methods. I don't think she should try to guilt him into change. But I'm not sure if I believe that because I know Julien and his tendency towards self-recrimination or if it's because there is a part of me that wants him for myself and, therefore, is inclined to discredit Kate as a life partner for him. But when I take a moment to analyze, I'm certain it's the former. I honestly don't believe forcing him through coercion or guilt will work. That is due solely to human nature.

The fact is that every person has a specific motivation for their actions. There is often a reason behind what we do and why we do it, good or bad. In matters regarding addiction, that's doubly true. I saw that firsthand during my summers as a hospital volunteer. Unless you dive into the heart of a person's motivations and help them explore alternative methods to cope, they won't overcome their addiction. Friends and family often disregard that part and think that if they browbeat a person with enough hard facts and true tales of tragedy, it will serve as the motivation for change. But it never does.

Still, I know I have to tread carefully with this conversation, so I concentrate on the topic at hand. "Is that true?"

"Is what true?"

"Do you think about Kate when you make decisions? Do you think you're being selfish?"

"Just tell me what to do, Iyah!"

"No! *You* are the one who has to decide what's important to you, Julien! It's *your* life!"

He slumps forward again, the angry fire draining out of him just as quickly as it flared. "We were talking about kids," he confesses, "and what kind of future we want to have together."

"You guys are already talking about starting a family?"

I know I probably sound incredulous at the idea, but I can't help it. It's not that I think that Julien would make a terrible father. The image of him cradling a baby in his arms makes me smile. Fatherhood would suit him. But he's only twenty-four years old! He is still in the process of figuring himself out. His acting career has just begun. I'd assume planning for children was still a long way off for him and tell him so.

"You're not wrong," he says, "I don't know if I'm ready to be a father yet." I make a "then, what gives?" face at him. He sighs again. "Kate. She thinks I'm ready. She thinks *we're* ready."

Once again, I have to bite my tongue against commenting. Wisely, I wait in deliberate silence for him to elaborate, refraining from making any personal observations of my own. "She believes in me," he continues, "She has never discounted me, and her advice hasn't been wrong so far. I love her. I want to make her happy.

"I should *want* to do this for her." He pauses to exhale a trembling breath. "I should want to do a lot of things for her."

Hearing the quiet devotion and lamenting self-deprecation in Julien's tone as he speaks about the woman he loves has a needed grounding effect on me. This is his reality. And mine. I am not his girlfriend. I just playact being one in a film. What *is* true is that I'm supposed to be his friend. And, as his friend, I need to act in his best interest. I think about Nicki and what *she* would do in my place.

"Give me your cigarettes."

"Why?"

He's mistrustful of my abrupt turn around. It's written all over his face. Yet, in spite of his burgeoning suspicion, Julien complies with my demand. He dutifully grabs the pack off the bathroom vanity and passes it to me. Without a word, I immediately open the pack, remove the remaining cigarettes, and crumple them into unrecognizable bits of paper and tobacco into the trash can.

"Holy shit!" he cries in open-mouthed dismay, "What the hell did you just do?"

"You said you wanted to quit," I reply, dusting my hands free of debris. "Step one." He follows that explanation with a string of lurid f-bombs, and though it's a tiny bit heartless, I giggle helplessly at his overly dramatic reaction. My laughter only doubles when he stares down into the trashcan at his mutilated cigarettes and whimpers mournfully. "I thought this was what you wanted!"

"You could have warned me!"

"Sorry."

He glares at me darkly, which I'm probably not supposed to find endearing at all. But I do. I really do. "No, you're not sorry," he charges, "Not at all."

After making a Herculean effort to rein in my laughter because I know he's genuinely ticked off at me, I resume my perch on the edge of his bed and cross my legs primly. "Let's talk about your triggers."

"I *really* want to strangle you right now."

It's a struggle to keep a straight face, even when I know he's being deadly serious. He is *that* annoyed. "We need to explore the reasons why you smoke." He responds with yet another outburst of fervid curses. I'm practically choking on my own laughter. "Those reasons don't sound very valid to me at all."

"You're not funny."

"If we don't discuss the reasons *why* you smoke," I explain, "then we can't explore alternative measures for how you can *avoid* doing it."

"So, what are you asking me?" he bites out impatiently.

"Is it because you need to occupy your hands? Does it help you to relax? Does it curb your appetite? Is it a coping method for anxiety? Do you—,"

"—That last thing you said," he mumbles before I can finish the next question.

I nod sagely. "Yeah…that's what I thought." I noticed that quirk about him from the beginning. Julien smokes incessantly when he's nervous or anxious. "Okay, so now we need to consider another activity you can do to replace smoking when you feel anxious."

"I like running."

"Yeah, but you can't always do that as easily as you can reach for a cigarette. It needs to be something readily accessible to you."

"There's always food," he considers, "I could eat my anxiety, but I'd be over 300 pounds in a month."

"Duly noted." I tap my mouth and think for a moment before falling back on the tried and true for most individuals. "Have you considered prayer at all?"

"I'm an atheist. Next."

"Have you thought about journaling?"

"Not a writer. Try again."

He's doing it again, deliberately trying to goad me into a fight, but I won't let him shake my composure because this is important. I take a second to center myself, determined not to let his increasingly surly mood disrupt my focus. "What about talking to a trusted friend?" I suggest, "That's an option."

"What if that 'trusted friend' is the *source* of my anxiety?"

So much for keeping my composure! *Now,* I'm rankled because, even though he doesn't come right out and say it, I *know* that he's talking about me. Flames of seething affront burn in my chest.

"What are you trying to say?"

Of course, he immediately retreats as soon as he realizes I'm ruffled. "Nothing."

"Nope. You're the one who went there," I push stubbornly, "Say what you mean!"

I'm ready to tear into him as soon as he replies because I'm fully expecting him to say something accusatory. But his next words aren't what I expect. They shock me into momentary silence.

"We wrap in three days."

I blink at him in blank confusion. "And?"

"You're going to go home to Michigan, and I'm going to head back to New York."

"I think that's an expected conclusion of events, don't you?"

"What if I don't see you again?"

His quiet apprehension, the sheer vulnerability that is evident in his question further disarms me. "You'll see me again."

"That's easy to say right now. We're in a bubble. But what happens when we leave it?"

"If our friendship is genuine, it won't matter, will it?"

He throws back his head with an exaggerated groan. "That's such a cliché, and you know it! I'm being real with you."

I slowly relax my defensive posture and pat the empty space beside me on his bed. "Come here." Once he obeys, I take his hand and sandwich it between my own. "Listen here, friend. You're important to me. I am not going to leave here and forget about you. I need you to believe that."

"I'm not usually this clingy," he mumbles, half-joking, half-serious, "I guess I have some abandonment issues."

The look I give him is full of droll sarcasm. "I would have never guessed."

He responds with his typical two-word expletive and shoves me in the shoulder. I give the same right back. We engage in a bit of good-humored nudging, and the vulnerable moment we've been sharing is dispelled entirely. I'm actually glad the atmosphere lightens. It's easier to ignore my love for him when we aren't absorbed in profound conversation.

We're soon engaged in a spirited tussle that involves flying socks, hotel pillows, and threats of merciless tickling. We circle one another on our knees in the center of his bed, making a hopeless tangle of the bed linens as we duck and dodge each other's fluffy blows. I hold my pillow aloft in a defensive posture.

"Tickle me and die, Caffrey!"

Julien favors me with a wicked grin. "Why? Are you afraid I'm going to find out you squeal like a pig when you laugh? Trust me. It's already common knowledge."

"Liar! I do not squeal when I laugh!"

"Oh yeah? Watch me prove it in two seconds."

The instant he lunges at me, I try to take him out with the pillow but he's too fast for me. Somehow in the midst of our tussle, I end up twisted beneath him, my arms pinned above my head and his grinning face within inches of my own. We both realize that his hand is resting against my ribcage just millimeters below my breast and that he's inadvertently settled between my legs at the same time. As soon as he registers the intimacy of our position, Julien immediately jumps away from me as if he's been jolted with electricity.

He rolls onto his back, careful not to make any physical contact with me when he does. We lie there in silence for a moment, both contemplating the ceiling as if it is the most fascinating sight we've ever beheld. The entire time, however, I am vibrantly cognizant of his nearness. The harsh cadence of his breathing. The vaguely moist heat radiating from his skin. The tight expression on his face. All of it is magnified for me one hundred-fold.

The longer the silence persists between us, the more self-conscious I become. I am mentally searching for a way to relieve the sudden awkwardness when Julien announces rather curtly, "I'm tired. I think I'm going to go to bed now."

Still shaken but careful to mask my inner jitters, I turn my head to regard him with a wry expression and force a wobbly smile. "Is that your not-so-subtle way of asking me to get out of your room?"

He laughs, but the sound is curiously strangled, almost subdued. "Yes. That *is* my not-so-subtle way of asking you to get out," he confirms softly.

"Alright then," I agree, hopping from the bed to scoop up my fallen Kindle. "I will take myself off. I don't like to stay where I'm not wanted."

By the time I finish gathering up the remainder of my belongings and stuffing my feet back into my shoes, the growing tension has made me eager to get out of there. Julien watches me closely the entire time. When I reach for the door, his voice sounds behind me and stops me in my tracks.

"Goodnight, Iyah."

I glance back at him over my shoulder to find him propped up onto his elbow and staring at me with a shuttered expression. He doesn't smile at me, which is a puzzling change. Julien is always grinning at me for one reason or another, but at this second, he looks oddly thoughtful and…resigned. I'm unsettled by that look. It fuels the urgency I have to put some distance between us so I can collect myself.

"Goodnight, Julien."

I beat it out of his room quickly and, as I do, I feel his eyes on me the whole time.

10

"Can I get some space? We don't have to spend every waking moment together!"

Eight weeks ago, had Julien Caffrey dared to lash out towards me unprovoked, I would have promptly told him to go to hell. He would have been on my "nope" list for eternity. But now, I know him well enough to discern that this sort of blistering crankiness is atypical for him.

It's been *two* days, and nicotine withdrawal is kicking his ass.

I give him the space he demands because, while I understand the reason for his foul temper, it doesn't lessen my desire to throttle him. I also suspect his moodiness is due to something else. Yesterday morning, I overheard him on the phone with Kate. They were having a vehement disagreement over her refusal to fly out to California. I can still hear the desperate entreaty in his voice when he told her, "You don't get it, Kate. I *need* you here."

Having a front row seat to his need for her does break me a little, but I get it. He is on the cusp of finishing the biggest project of his career, and he wants to share that with the most important person in his life. Sometimes, I yearn for my family for the same reason.

Julien hasn't seen or held her in two months. It probably doesn't matter to him that he'll be back home in New York before the week's end because the only thing he can process is that he needs her now. I know the feeling.

So, I gave him a wide berth. It's a good idea to begin distancing myself anyway. Soon, I'm going to be faced with the prospect of saying goodbye to him, and I don't know if I'm ready. I try to keep myself distracted from the mounting dread by finalizing my plans for my own flight back home.

Ruben is unusually excited. "They're throwing you a party," he tells me, "But act like you're surprised, okay?"

"It's not in you to keep a secret, is it?"

"I'm just glad you're coming back! Maybe they'll leave *me* alone now."

It amuses me to learn that my absence has brought him the same critical scrutiny from our parents that I've endured for most of my life. You can only hear, "Iyah, you know better," or "Iyah, please think," so much before you start to believe that you're a hopeless screw-up. For the past eight weeks, I've been mostly insulated from their constant disapproval. It's been liberating to answer only to myself. I don't look forward to losing the relative freedom I've known while in L.A.

Then there is the looming goodbye with Julien. I hate thinking about it. I suppose he was right when he likened our time out here to "living in a bubble." It has been mostly the two of us in this small, manufactured world. After we leave, reality will inevitably seep in. And though I have every intention of keeping my word to him and staying in regular contact, I know things will change between us.

He will no longer be the beginning and end of my day. There will be no more evening jogs. No more late-night Netflix binging. No more running lines together after a sugar fueled breakfast. No more intimate, soul-baring conversations. We'll cease to be this single entity that we've become. Instead, we'll go back to being Aiona Grandberry and Julien Caffrey. Two actors who once starred in that small independent film together and now maintain a casual friendship in Hollywood circles.

The thought alone brings rueful tears, but I know it's for the best. Julien is getting married. If anyone should share that type of intimacy with him, it should be his future wife. It should have *always* been her. I know this. *I believe this.* But I can't quite banish the pangs of jealousy, this subtle resentment I harbor over the prospect of being replaced.

I am extremely cognizant of the limited time we have left to spend together, these dwindling, precious moments where I can still occupy this special place in his life. I don't want to squander that time, no matter how unbearable he's being. That need compels me to linger on set even after I resolved to give him space.

After he has finished reshooting his scenes with Kathleen, I make my approach. When he first catches a glimpse of me coming his way, he straightens and smiles. The reaction is fleeting though. He promptly scowls right after.

"I thought you went back to the hotel already."

"I wanted to hang out instead."

"Why?"

"Because tomorrow night is the wrap party. I go back to Michigan the morning after. I'm just checking to see if you want to keep this same energy before we say goodbye to each other."

I brace myself for further attitude, but he surprises me when he suddenly slumps forward with a contrite sigh. "I've been a jerk to you, haven't I?"

"You've been a jerk to *everyone*. But yeah, to me mostly."

"It's not you, Iyah. It's me."

106

"Oh, I know." I place a commiserating hand on his shoulder. "Nicotine withdrawal is no joke, huh?"

"No. It's not."

"It's okay," I murmur sympathetically, "I forgive you. I know you're having a hard time. It's the only reason I haven't kicked you in the kneecaps yet." My reply wrings a stunned laugh from him and as soon as he dissolves, I start laughing too. Two days of tension melts away as if they had never existed. My laughter eventually settles into a sentimental smile.

"I'm really going to miss you, Caffrey."

"Nope. Don't do that," he interrupts quickly, "Don't tell me goodbye yet. I'm not ready. We still have an entire day left."

"Who says I want to spend that day with you?" I tease him, "Quite honestly, I'm not so sure you'd make very good company after the last 36 hours."

"You have no room to talk, Ms. Perpetual Bad Mood."

"That is untrue, unfounded, and I am deeply offended!" I intone theatrically.

He laughs again, but this time it sounds vaguely bittersweet to my ears. "I'm going to miss you too. So much you don't even know."

"Is that right?"

"Yep. Especially your constant complaining. I love that you're always telling me what you're *not* going to do. It's only slightly annoying, but mostly cute."

I duck my head in response, suddenly nervous because I can't remember him being so unreserved with his compliments before. It's almost as if our impending separation has emboldened him, and now he's determined not to hold anything back. Then again, Julien has always said exactly what he's thinking. I could be reading things that aren't there. But I can't shake the sense that there is something significantly different about the way he is speaking and looking at me.

"What you call complaining, I call having standards. You should try it."

He chuckles softly. "Tomato, tomahto."

"Are you finally finished up for the day?"

"I've got one more take to do and then I'm done," he replies, "Will you hang out here until I'm finished?"

"Sure. We can grab some dinner afterwards. I'll even agree to The Squealer for old time's sake."

"Nah," he replies, shaking his head in disagreement, "Not tonight. Let's just hang out in your room instead."

Julien has made this same suggestion dozens of times in the past, but *this time* there is an undercurrent of something else. And then he does something unprecedented. He reaches over to take hold of my hand. My breath catches as he begins to stroke his thumb across the back of it. This is the first time he has ever touched me with such intimacy outside of his character.

"There's something important I want to talk to you about…and I want you to keep an open mind about it."

Transfixed, I watch mutely as his thumb slowly moves back and forth over my skin. It takes a while, but I eventually manage to unglue my tongue from the roof of my mouth. "Since when don't I keep an open mind about things?"

He squeezes my hand briefly for emphasis. "Just promise me you won't freak out. Okay?"

Julien has that look on his face again, that unwavering, deliberate expression that I haven't been able to put my finger on until this very moment. *Intent*. He is staring at me with pure intent. It's evident in his eyes, his posture, and even the gentle way he caresses my hand. He is sending a message without really saying anything at all. Something has shifted for him.

"Yeah…" I find myself responding in a daze as the realization slowly washes over me, "…okay."

It's only after I walk away from him that I begin to second guess my consent. There is *no way* that Julien Caffrey just made a pass at me. Just the other morning I overheard him on the phone making fervent declarations to his fiancée. He can't be genuinely interested in me at all and yet, that is the vibe he's giving. It's the equivalent of emotional whiplash.

I don't understand how he's gone from moody hostility to bedroom eyes and hand-stroking in the span of 48 hours. His sudden interest is out of left field. A theory for his possible motivation occurs to me with alarming swiftness.

He's feeling rejected. Obviously, Julien is hurt by Kate's refusal to fly out to California to be with him. Perhaps flirting with me is his unconscious way of getting back at her. And I need to believe that his actions are unconscious because I can't accept that my friend, *my* Julien, would use me so deliberately.

Though the realization does wound my pride, I also know that as his friend, I should call Julien out on his bad behavior and encourage him to correct it. As thrilling as it was to have him flirt with me, I recognize that none of it is real. Kate is the woman he loves, and she is the driving force behind his actions.

By the time we're on our way to the transport van an hour later, my mood has soured considerably. I speak in clipped sentences, my responses relegated to short, single word answers. Julien easily discerns the shift. As soon as we're buckled into our seatbelts, he starts interrogating me.

"What's up with you?"

"What's up with *you*?" I flare back.

He responds with a puzzled frown. "You're the one who's acting weird!"

"*I'm* acting weird?" I then proceed to destroy that charge, listing out my evidence on my fingers as I go. "What about you? Telling me that I'm 'cute.' Insisting on being alone with me, holding my hand! And what's with all the talk about me 'keeping an open mind' and the way you've been looking at me? It feels like you're flirting with me!"

Julien regards me with hooded eyes. "Maybe I am..."

"No. That's impossible because you are engaged!"

His gaze falters a bit with the reminder. "I...I know that."

"Then why are you playing this game with me?"

"I'm not playing a game," he replies earnestly, "We should talk. Don't you think?"

"Talk about what?"

"What's been happening between us," he says, quickly deflating the righteous indignation that's been building inside of me. "There *is* something happening. I feel it. I think you do too.

This is the worst-case scenario, but one I *never* envisioned. The possibility that his interest might be legitimate seemed an incomprehensible conclusion. I want to question his veracity, but it's pointless. I know Julien. He wouldn't be putting it out there if he wasn't ready to deal with the fallout. There's no use in backtracking. He's already ripped off the bandage.

"It doesn't matter what I feel. You're getting married!"

"I know that! You don't have to keep reminding me!"

"So, why are you doing this?"

"I don't freaking know, Iyah!" he suddenly explodes, stunning us both with his vehemence, "All I know is that every time I think about leaving you, I can't breathe!"

The avowal creeps into my bones, filling my nerve endings with overwhelming sensation. My entire body trembles. He is finally saying the words to me that I hadn't even allowed myself to dream were possible. It is everything I've been yearning to hear and yet…I can't give myself over completely.

"I heard you the other morning with Kate," I tell him, "You were practically *begging* her to come out here, Julien! Now you're trying to convince me that *I'm* the one you want! Don't use me to punish her! It's not fair!"

"I'm not doing that! Yes, I asked her to come out here, but not for the reason you think! I…I was hoping that if she came it would change things!"

"Change what things?"

"My feelings for you!"

I realized then that we're practically screaming at one another. Our driver has done an admirable job of maintaining his aloof demeanor, but I can tell from the way he keeps darting glances back at us from the rearview mirror that he's getting antsy. By now, he should be used to our back and forth, but we've never been like this. We both put forth a rigorous effort to calm ourselves. When Julien finally speaks again, his tone is lower and softer than before, but his expression is a mixture of shame and naked longing.

"You don't think I've been grappling with this for a while now?" he asks me earnestly, "I feel guilty as hell!"

"How long is a while?" I whisper.

He regards me with a fervent stare. "Since that night we fell asleep in your room. Maybe even before that. I don't know. It's taken me some time to stop lying to myself."

The confession is exactly what I want to hear, and at the same time, I don't want to hear it. This was a lot easier when I was only dealing with *my* secret crush. I don't even want to contemplate the proverbial Pandora's box that we are about to smash open. Once we do, there will be no containing the tide of emotion that rushes in.

"My God, Julien! Don't tell me that!"

"Why not?" he challenges, "There's no point in pretending anymore!"

"We can't have this conversation."

His features harden in an obstinate scowl, like he's past the point of treading cautiously. "Fine! You don't have to say anything. *I'll* do all the talking. You wanna know the real reason I've been such an ass to you these past two days—?"

"—I don't want to hear this!"

"The other night when we were in my room, I wanted to kiss you so much," he confesses softly, "I wanted to do *more* than kiss you…"

I catch my breath sharply following that heated admission. "Is that the reason you wanted to be alone tonight…because you thought—?"

"—No!" he bursts out before I can even complete the sentence. "I wasn't expecting anything, Iyah. I wanted to talk. Just talk."

"About what?"

"About what we can be together."

He is killing me. He is literally killing me in inches. His words are lovely, and it's even lovelier to hear him say them with such urgency, to have him look at me with brazen desire. But the reality of the road that we're traveling is cold and dark and filled with potential disaster. My "good girl," Christian values are too deeply inbred, and I can't easily yield to my yearning for him. I'm duty-bound to talk some sense into him and myself too.

"Julien, you're not being rational! This is a phase. You've been with Kate for more than two years! You've known me for *two months*! I don't want to be the reason your relationship falls apart!"

"Maybe it was falling apart long before this."

"Then why did you stay with her?"

"Because I hadn't met you yet."

I close my eyes briefly, beating back the wave of longing that threatens to engulf me following his heartfelt response. This situation is too delicate to go tripping headlong into foolish decisions. When I open my eyes again, I am careful to keep my expression unreadable.

"Does that mean you don't love her anymore?"

My heart shrivels a little when his bravado abruptly fizzles, and he drops his eyes. "It's complicated, Iyah."

"It's really not at all. Did you honestly think I would be with you when you have feelings for another woman?"

"You don't get it! I owe her *everything*. My entire existence is tied up with her!" He flops back into his seat with an aggravated groan. "I don't want to hurt her. And I don't want to hurt you."

"Then it seems like you have some stuff you need to figure out."

"What does that mean?"

"It means that this," I gesture wildly between us, "whatever's going on with us, it can't happen!"

He appears gutted over the pronouncement. "Are you saying you're done?"

I gape at him incredulously. "Julien, are you listening to yourself?"

It is no wonder that I've never let myself fantasize about the possibility of my feelings being reciprocated. Before this second, I thought I was sparing myself the inevitable heartbreak of yearning for a man who would never return my love, but the truth is…this is messy. Being in love with a man who belongs to another woman is messy. Having that man want you back and openly express that desire is even messier. But having him push for more than friendship even while his feelings for his fiancée remain unresolved? That is the messiest scenario of all.

Filled with disgust for him and for myself, I shake my head reproachfully. "*Nothing* is going to happen between us! Not ever!"

"That's not what I'm asking you! You're my best friend, Iyah! I don't want to lose you! I can't!"

He's never categorized me that way before, but I've always known that's what I've become. *His best friend.* We've bonded during this film in such a profound way that I can't contemplate a future without him in it. I know his darkest, most shameful secrets, and he knows mine. Our friendship has been characterized by a lack of boundaries, which might be the reason he's being so bold and careless now.

"I don't know how we can go back to being just friends after this," I whisper mournfully.

"We're not going *back* to anything. All we've ever been is friends."

"Have we?"

The question is still hanging between us when the van rumbles to a stop. Despite all the talking we've done, the unreserved honesty and the painful silence that follows, we still haven't come to an acceptable resolution about what's going to happen next. It seems impossible to go back to what we had before, to pretend that we hadn't confessed all the things we did.

At the same time, not having him in my life is an unbearable prospect. I don't want to cut him off. I'm not sure if I can. And though I know spending time alone with him now, when we're both so vulnerable and so raw, is an especially bad idea, I still want to. I want him.

Julien seems to sense that conflict in me. When he steps from the van, he comes around to the other side and waits for me to exit. Once I open the door, he holds out his hand to me with a patient, expectant expression as if he's accepted the inevitable, and he's giving me time to accept it too. He also seems to know that I'm going to take his hand even before I do.

We contemplate one another silently before we turn together in the mutual, tacit decision to head to my room. The van pulls away, revealing the unobstructed visage of our hotel. Our hands are clasped for a single moment when I spot her. The instant I do, I reflexively yank away from Julien's grasp.

There is a pretty blond woman dressed in tan slacks and a matching blazer loitering outside of his room. Her face brightens when she catches sight of Julien though his steps falter a little when he sees her. She requires no introduction. I know this woman at a glance. She's taller than I expected, her willowy frame the complete antithesis of my small, athletic build. She and I are nothing alike and yet, somehow, we've managed to attract the same man.

The realization leaves me so flustered that I barely register Julien blurting out her name in a rattled rush of breath.

Kate.

11

Life slows to a maddening crawl. Or, perhaps, I'm only hyperaware of my surroundings. Sound is magnified tenfold. The barking dogs in the distance. The melodic buzzing of nearby insects. My harsh breathing echoes like a hurricane in my ears.

I am most especially aware of how polished and elegant Kate Leland appears in her power suit and sleek blond bun in comparison to my comfy sweats and neatly braided hair. She is the perfect, delicate creature that Julien always described. While I am, in contrast, the despicable Jezebel…at least in my own mind.

Surprisingly, I recover from my shock faster than he does. I'm quick to plaster a smile on my face even if it is artificial. Julien, on the other hand, looks as if he's been sucker-punched. He acts like it too. When he approaches her, he doesn't present as a man eager to see his love again. Instead, his features are inert with shock and distress, his stiff movements reminiscent of the *Wizard of Oz's* iconic Tin Man. With noticeable reluctance, he staggers forward to embrace his fiancée.

Their hug is brief and perfunctory. She barely has the chance to return it before he steps back to regard her with the same wooden expression. "What are you doing here? I thought you weren't coming."

Beads of anxious sweat begin to form on my forehead. My breath quickens further with stirrings of panic. I fret over whether she noticed us holding hands before. Did she witness the earnest looks we exchanged? Did she know that I considered having sex with her fiancé tonight? I'm horrified that the answers to those questions are stamped all over me.

Thankfully, she appears oblivious. I don't know if I should be grateful or ashamed. Her hazel eyes are glued on Julien's face, almost as if she's silently pleading with him. When she reaches out to grab hold of his hand and press it between her own, I have to bite the inside of my cheek to keep from whimpering.

"I didn't like the way we left things yesterday," she tells him earnestly, "I think maybe you came away from that conversation believing something that wasn't true." Her voice is low, but not so much that I can't distinctly make out what she is saying to him. "I thought I would surprise you."

"I'm surprised."

There's no way to make a graceful exit. I want to slip away, but I'm terrified of drawing attention to myself. I don't want her to look at me. She hasn't acknowledged me yet, and I prefer to stay invisible. Julien ruins that plan.

He turns toward me, and I know before he even opens his mouth that he intends to introduce us. I give an imperceptible shake of my head, hoping he will yield to the unspoken cue and let me retreat into the shadows. He plows ahead defiantly.

"Kate, this is Iyah Grandberry. Iyah, this is Kate."

I am very aware of how he deliberately refrains from introducing her as his "fiancée." It feels like a purposeful choice for my benefit though it is possible that mortification and shame are causing me to read into his actions. Kate appears to notice his omission as well.

When she thrust her hand forward, her pretty features wreathed in an unguarded smile, she clarifies, "I'm his fiancée."

"She already knows, Kate," Julien mumbles irritably as I pump her hand.

"It's good to finally meet you. Julien talks about you all the time."

The admission pleases her. She favors Julien with an uncertain, entreating glance. "All good things, I hope."

"Very good things. He says you're the best thing that ever happened to him."

In those early days when I was first getting to know him, Julien had sung her praises endlessly. It is only now that it dawns on me how little he's spoken of her in these past few weeks. He and I have been steadily laying the groundwork for this horrifying moment, and we didn't even realize it.

I can't maintain eye contact with either of them. The guilt is suffocating. If I even *attempt* to meet Julien's eyes, I'm going to burst into tears. My throat burns. The mere thought of looking at him is agony.

"He talks about you too," Kate reveals, "He told me that you're a phenomenal actress, and that you've been a good friend."

I should hope that I am an incredible actress. Because this is nothing short of torture. "I'm sure I could be a better friend," I manage around my tightening throat, "but I appreciate the endorsement."

He is watching me. I don't have to look at him to know. The intensity of his stare is as heavy as the silent appeal rolling off of him in waves. I don't know what he wants from me. Or maybe I do, and I just don't want to deal with his distress. I have my own inner turmoil to navigate. But, more urgently than that, I need to get away from him and from *her*.

"I'm sure you guys have a lot to catch up on so..." I'm already waving them off and turning towards my own room as I make the statement. "It was nice to meet you, Kate." I force myself to meet Julien's eyes, but only briefly. "I'll see you in the morning."

His obstinate response stops me in my tracks. "I thought we were going to grab dinner, Iyah." And then he has the unbelievable boldness to suggest that we all go out together! It takes everything in me not to look at him like he's a complete lunatic. That he could even conceive that I would want to sit through a meal with him and *his fiancée* after everything we said and what we might have *done* if she had not shown up is both infuriating and horrifying.

Somehow, I mask my aggravation and manage a smile, but it feels like the effort will crack my face in half. "Don't worry about me. I'm a big girl. I'm covered for dinner. Spend time with your *fiancée*." He wants to argue with me, even with *her* standing right there, and his willingness to push the issue astounds me.

I do not have the reserves to do battle with him. Before he can blow everything to utter hell because he's clearly past giving a damn, I retreat hastily to my own room. As I shut my door behind me the last thing that I hear is Julien's voice. "I really wish you had called first…"

Once I've shut them out entirely, I collapse back against the door. Only when I'm alone does the gravity of the last half hour wash over me. Though I can no longer hear their conversation, I'm shaking uncontrollably just *imagining* what they might be saying. The possible scenarios are nauseating.

What if he breaks up with her? Could I really live with myself knowing that I was responsible for wrecking another woman's happiness? It's obvious that she loves him. She flew nearly 3,000 miles to be with him because salvaging their relationship was important to her. I can imagine that she'll be gutted and blindsided if he promptly trashes everything that they've shared together for a girl he just met.

But then there's the alternative. What if he *doesn't* break up with her? What if her spontaneous visit accomplishes exactly what Julien hoped for? What if he realizes that his feelings for me are nothing more than a fleeting crush? What if he's convinced that *she* is the one he truly wants after all? I'm not sure I'm ready to live with either outcome.

Only now do I fully understand what a fantastic mess I've made. In the beginning, when I was still trying to make sense of my feelings for him and they were largely unrequited, it hadn't seemed like an impending disaster. Back then I could justify the inordinate amount of time we spent together despite his engagement because the feelings weren't mutual. What was the harm when he didn't want me back?

Those thin excuses have been blown apart now. My feelings *are* reciprocated. It *does* matter that Julien is with someone else. We should never have allowed ourselves to grow so close to one another.

Kate Leland is no longer some high-resolution screenshot trapped in the electronic confines of Julien's iPhone to be swiped away and forgotten. I'm forced to face the woman I've been wronging so egregiously this entire time. And I have wronged her. I have assumed a place in Julien's heart that should have been rightfully and exclusively hers. The worst part is, I'm not completely sorry about that.

When I close my eyes, I can still hear his fervent confession in the van. *I wanted to kiss you so much…I wanted to do more than kiss you.* In the confines of my treacherous heart, I won't pretend to be unaffected by his words. If Kate hadn't shown up tonight, would I have been tempted to let him do what he wanted, *everything* he wanted? The answer terrifies me.

I'm already digging around in my pocket for my cell phone and pulling up Nicki's contact before I've even formulated what I plan to say to her. All I really know is that I need to talk to someone. I need her to tell me what to do.

"Why do you always call me when I'm in the middle of something?" she gripes at me when she answers, "You have the worst timing!"

"Can you talk?"

"I'm doing a season one rewatch of Scandal," she says, "Fritz and Olivia have got me in a chokehold!"

It's strange that she can be so invested in a fictional affair and even root for its success yet be equally and emphatically turned off by infidelity in real life. After I finish collapsing into the nearest chair because I don't think my wobbly knees will hold me up much longer, I tell her as much. She is quick to justify herself.

"This is pure, delicious guilty pleasure," she argues, "It's fantasy, Iyah. In real life, it's not fun."

"Yeah…tell me about it."

I don't elaborate further on that muttered reply, and Nicki doesn't need me to either. I can tell by the way she goes silent. She is quiet for so long that I start to wonder if she's ended the phone call on righteous principle but then she states in a tone tight with tension, "You slept with him, didn't you?"

"No, I didn't." Her audible sigh of relief resonates in my ear. However, a split second later she's positing yet another theory.

"You made out with him?"

"No."

"You kissed him?" she ventures a third time.

I can tell from the reservation in her voice that she is starting to second-guess her assumption that I'm a cheating heifer. Her accusations are starting to lose venom. But her softening doesn't bring me any sort of relief. If anything, my anxiety is heightened.

"You can relax, Nik," I sigh despondently, "Nothing happened between us." I am quick to add before she can commend me for not

121

doing anything foolish, "At least, nothing *physical* happened. But I want that. I want him."

"Don't do it!" she explodes, "Let me tell you how this will go. He won't leave her. He'll string you along until you end it, or he does, and then you'll hate yourself after it's over."

"Julien isn't like that," I argue tightly, "You don't know him."

"Do *you* know him? If he's moving in on you when he is engaged to another woman, he *is* like that!"

I'm not sure how I slide into the role of Devil's advocate, but suddenly I'm making the same excuses to her that Julien made to me. "It's not that simple, Nicki. Her family is all he has. He's estranged from his mom. He barely has a relationship with his brothers! It's not just a matter of leaving her!"

"Do you hear yourself?"

"I'm trying to give you context! The situation is complicated!"

"Sleeping with him is not going to make it less complicated!"

"I know that already!" My words are strangled with tears I refuse to shed. "But I'm in love with him. So, what am I supposed to do?"

Nicki is shocked into silence once more, but she recovers her power of speech much faster this time. "Are you sure it's love?" she asks me. "Maybe you just got too caught up in your character and now it's bleeding over into real life."

"That doesn't have anything to do with it. I've been drawn to him since before we even began filming."

"You said it was a crush," she reminds me, mildly critical.

"I thought it was a crush."

"And what about him? Is he in love with you?"

"I don't think Julien knows what he feels for me. He's still trying to figure it out. But I know he doesn't want to lose me. He told me so. I think he might love me. He acts like he does."

"Maybe you're only seeing what you want to see," she reasons, "Maybe he has some kind of swirl fetish, and this is his way of fulfilling a fantasy."

"You wanna know something? I would almost be relieved if that was it because then we wouldn't be having this conversation. But I don't think my race has ever factored for Julien. And his race doesn't factor for me either. I'm not into him because he's some novelty I've never experienced before. I'm into him because he's *Julien*. It's that simple."

"Oh, Iyah. You're on shaky ground…"

"I know that, Nicki! Tell me what to do."

"Well, don't sleep with him!"

"That's not going to happen. *She's* here now, and we wrap tomorrow. After that, I'll probably never see him again."

"Not exactly the reasoning I wanted to hear from you for not screwing him when he *has a fiancée*, but I'll take it. You need to stay away from him!"

"We work together."

"Yeah, for one more day, and then cut him off!"

The logical part of me can easily acknowledge her wisdom in this. Self-preservation alone should be enough to drive me into action. Even if Julien does choose to leave Kate, the emotional fallout from that decision is going to reverberate. He is going to wrestle with incredible guilt, not to mention fear and anxiety over losing the only stable family he's ever known. What if he grows to resent me for it?

We've never been tested outside of this sheltered world we've created for ourselves here while filming. Once we leave California, however, we'll be faced with long distance challenges, insecurities, and conflicting work schedules. Most relationships would be naturally strained under those circumstances, much less one that was built on shaky foundation to start.

Nicki isn't advising me to do anything I haven't already considered myself. I can clearly see the calamity laid out in front of me. Unfortunately, my sense of reason isn't prevailing at the moment. I'm being propelled by unfettered emotion. Part of me simply doesn't care about the probable fallout. I *want* to be with him.

When I consider the pain that I'll endure by keeping him in my life with the pain of walking away from him entirely, the former potential wins out every time. Without question. I suspect that unspoken determination must be abundantly clear to Nicki despite my resounding silence because she expels a heavy sigh filled with consternation.

"Did you say that she was there?"

"Yeah. She just showed up tonight without any warning. He's with her now."

"Is he breaking up with her?"

"I'm not sure."

"Is that what you want?" she presses me. I'm hesitant to answer that question because I know she'll judge me, and rightfully so. My silence is answer enough. Nicki grunts in disgust. "That *is* what you want. Oh God, Iyah, don't be so stupid! This isn't going to go the way you think!"

"You don't know that! You don't know him!"

"I've played this game before! Remember? You will lose! Men are liars. It's their nature."

"You're too cynical."

"I'm stating facts. Look at what your guy's doing to a woman he claimed to love! He can't keep his promises to her! What makes you think he'll keep the ones he makes to you? If you're going to go through with this, don't lie to yourself!"

"What are you saying? He should stay with her even if he's not in love with her anymore?" I challenge.

"Who says he isn't in love with her? Did he tell you that, or are you projecting?"

"I know him, Nik. He's obligated to her. He's grateful. I don't doubt that he cares about her very much. But I don't think she's the person he wants to spend his life with."

"And you think you're that person?" she scoffs, "He proposed to her, not you!"

"Would it kill you to be on my side in this? *I'm* your friend, but you're showing more loyalty to some chick you've never even met!"

"I *am* on your side! I'm trying to stop you from making a horrible mistake."

"We don't choose the people we fall in love with," I argue softly.

"Maybe not. But you can choose what kind of person you want to be…the reputation you want to have for yourself," she counters with the same softness, "Is this who you want to be, Iyah?"

Her question is still resounding in my brain long after our conversation has ended. Nicki gave me exactly what I asked. I have clear directions on what I should do next. Truthfully, I've known from the beginning. But I can admit in hindsight it hadn't been what I wanted to hear.

She knows better than anyone how closely I guard my heart in relationships. Even when Devin and I were together, I was reserved. Before I met Julien, I never questioned whether I had been in love with Devin. Now, I'm beginning to wonder. I kept my protective walls up the entire time I was with him. With Julien, I've been defenseless.

I've never been conflicted over a man this way before. I had hoped that Nicki would recognize that Julien was *different*, that what I felt for him was *different* and that would serve as an exception…or a justification. As ridiculous as it sounds, I had wanted her blessing to pursue him.

I wasn't prepared for her to be so unwilling to consider my viewpoint. As far as Nicki is concerned, there is no exception or justification. My need for Julien doesn't matter in the least. The choice is simple. I should walk away. Any other option is unacceptable and contemptible. I wish I felt the same.

My phone vibrates with a notification, and I glance down at the screen with a weary sigh, expecting to find a caustic "last word" text from Nicki. But it is not her name that appears briefly on my call screen. It is Julien's. His message consists of two words.

I'm sorry.

I stare at his text and wonder exactly what he's apologizing for. Is his remorse related to Kate's unexpected arrival which inevitably thwarted our plans together? Or is he expressing regret about his earlier confession to me? I'm not sure and, what's more, I find myself secretly hoping that it's the former even while I'm terrified it's the latter.

12

It's the former.

There is no doubt about that when Julien's second text message comes just after one o'clock in the morning. I am lying awake in bed obsessing over the deep, entangled mess I've created for myself when my phone flashes with the notification. I know it's him even before I shift upright to check the screen.

I need to see you.

Five innocuous words, so heavy with implication that I'm figuratively crushed under their weight. My chest burns with indecision and fear. It's possible that he wants to backtrack on everything and handwave it all away as a lapse in judgment, but I doubt it. He could have waited for an opportune time tomorrow to pull me aside and have that uncomfortable conversation. Texting me at 1 a.m. is a clandestine thing, a clear indicator that he's not interested in retracting anything. More than likely, he's trying to determine what can be salvaged between us.

This is the defining moment. I lie there for a long time and consider my next move, but a decision doesn't come easily. I should take Nicki's advice and ignore him altogether, but I know I won't do that. First, there is too much that is unresolved between us. I can't walk away when we've left so many things unsaid. Second, and quite honestly the most important reason, I don't *want* to walk away. I need to see him.

Though I've made up my mind to do the wrong thing, I keep my reply neutral when I answer him. *Where's Kate?*

His response comes quickly. *Asleep. Can I come over?*

Once again, I take my time answering him. That doesn't make my concession any less predictable. *I'll unlock the door.*

I click on the bedside lamp in anticipation of his arrival and rise to crack the door to my room. Afterwards, I pull on my robe, cinch the belt tight, and curl into the chair situated just beyond the door to wait for him. All the while I am hyper-focused on steadying my breathing and mentally willing my heart rate to slow down.

As much as I want this, want *him*, I don't want to betray the chaotic emotion grinding away inside of me. I may be lacking in self-control, but I don't have to make that obvious. I should put up some show of resistance, even if it's mostly manufactured. When he slips inside a few seconds later, I catch my breath at the sight of him but maintain my outward façade of stoicism.

He's wearing his pajamas, but it is evident from his haggard appearance that he hasn't slept any more than I have. He darts a careful glance at me before he slowly and deliberately closes the door behind him. Then we are alone, and the outside world is shut away just as it has been for the majority of our relationship. We regard one another in the pregnant silence that follows. Once that silence becomes unbearable, Julien fills it.

"You didn't answer my text from earlier."

"What exactly are you sorry for, Julien? Saying that you wanted me? Or because Kate showed up?"

I cringe inwardly at how angry and harsh I sound. Until this moment, I wasn't aware of the resentment that's been simmering beneath my reserved veneer until it comes spilling out. Suddenly I'm irrationally angry with him for opening this door at all. I've sat on my desire for him this entire time. Why couldn't *he* do the same?

There was no harm when it was only *my* feelings and *my* secret crush. Having Julien return those feelings is the most wonderful catastrophe ever. I resent him for going there when he was the one in a committed relationship.

"I didn't know she was going to come!"

"You asked her!" I remind him hotly.

"And she said 'no!'"

The absurdity of our argument smacks me hard. *I* am not the betrayed party here. *I* am not the person entitled to an explanation. That person is sleeping two doors down, unaware that her fiancé is in my hotel room and that he might be here for hours to come. This constant volleying between guilt and exhilaration is making me dizzy. I know that I should ask him to leave, but the longer he lingers, the less motivation I have to do so.

Julien continues to hover near the door, but the expression on his face is silently begging me for permission to come closer. When I don't give it to him, he asks, "So what happens now?"

"Shouldn't I be asking *you* that?"

"That depends."

"Depends on what?"

"On how you feel about me," he says, "I've been honest with you, but you haven't said a word. I don't know what you're thinking. So, tell me. Do you want me or not, Iyah?"

Rather than answering that directly and creating an even messier entanglement than we currently have, I respond to his question with a question of my own. "Does it bother you even a little that we're having this conversation while your fiancée is *sleeping in your bed*?"

"Do you want me to say that this whole thing is messed up?" he flares suddenly, "Okay! You're right! It's messed up!" He collapses back against the door with a strangled sound. "It's not like I planned to feel this way about you," he mumbles thickly, "I don't know what to do…"

"I don't either."

That admission seems to be the permission he's been waiting for, but when he pushes himself away from the door to close the distance between us, I hold out my hand to stave off his approach. "No, Julien! Don't!" I cry a little wildly, "If you touch me, then there will be no turning back! I'm going to end up hating myself and you!"

He stumbles to a halt, looking at me in a mixture of fear, longing, and regret. And then his expression crumples as he rapidly blinks back the welling tears in his eyes. The sight of them physically guts me. This moment isn't anything like what Nicki implied. We are not two selfish people set on a path to destroy everything and everyone just for our own personal gratification. Instead, we are two conflicted people in immense pain.

"Please, tell me I'm going to see you again," he pleads with me, "I don't want this to be the end for us."

Neither do I. The possibility that this might literally be the last conversation that I ever have with him is devastating. I've spent countless hours and nearly 70 days in continual proximity with this man. Now I can't even imagine how my life will look without him existing in my space. I don't know when that change happened, or how he became such an integral part of my being. I can't untangle him now. My need for him is incontrovertible, a tangible entity, something so real that denying him is denying myself. I can only hope that my longing will lessen with time and distance. Otherwise, I'm screwed.

"I don't know if it's a good idea for us to see each other anymore, Julien."

He glances away quickly, but not before I see a lone tear track down his cheek. "I never should have said anything to you," he mutters mostly to himself.

"I'm glad you did," I reply woodenly, "Now we can stop ourselves from making a huge mistake."

I'm reciting a script. The declaration is lukewarm. I am saying all of the right words, espousing the sentiments of some noble heroine filled with dedication for all things honorable and righteous. But none of what I say to him is sincere. None of it is what I want.

I'd prefer to bridge the distance between us and discover what it's like to kiss him as myself and not as my character. I would even take that kiss to its inevitable conclusion, let him take me to bed and explore every inch of my body while his fiancée sleeps two doors away. And that is *exactly* the reason that I need to end this before it goes any further.

"We should probably keep our distance from now on."

Julien cuts a startled look towards me. "Probably?"

"We should," I amend firmly because I don't want to give him any false hope. "We *should* keep our distance."

"Are you saying we can't be friends anymore because I told you—?"

"—We can't be friends anymore because we won't *stay* friends," I interject with quiet emphasis, "You know that already, don't you?"

He has no defense against that argument. I know it. He knows it. Thankfully, he doesn't even make the attempt. Instead, he asks me with stunning perception, "Is this what you really want?"

"What's the alternative? Are you going to break up with her, Julien? How are we supposed to make this work when we don't even live in the same state? Have you even thought that far ahead?" He doesn't answer, but the way he drops his head forward in tormented guilt is all the confirmation I need.

"Just go, please," I order him wearily.

After he's gone, I hope to feel some relief or, at the very least, some obscure sense of satisfaction for having made the right decision but I'm numb instead. I can't forget the look of pure anguish on his face as he turned to leave, or the hollow sensation I had in my chest as I watched him go. There is no inner peace that follows. All that remains is loneliness.

Technically, we didn't do anything wrong. We've never even touched. We're not cheaters, yet I still feel awful. Sleep eludes me. I only rest after my tears have left me exhausted.

The following day I drag myself through existence, mournful over wrapping the project that has been a substantial part of my life for two full months. The connotation attached to my relationship with Julien only makes it more unbearable. Further, seeing him with his arm looped around *her* waist while he introduces her to the cast and crew, even when I know his smiles are forced and I know he's as miserable as I am, only worsens the pain. I can't even bring myself to stay for the entire wrap party, and I leave after only an hour. Once I return to the hotel, I pack my belongings and prepare for the flight back home.

In the morning, I catch an Uber to LAX for my early flight without a single goodbye. And while that is probably the best course of action, especially when I'm still so raw over my last encounter with Julien, it *feels* horrible. I keep waiting for my aching for him to lessen the closer I get to the airport, but the opposite happens.

By the time I board my plane, I'm visibly distraught. For someone who doesn't like to cry at all, being reduced to broken sobs in public is

132

horrifying. The woman in the seat next to me offers her travel tissues and kindly hails the flight attendant on my behalf. And even though I tell her again and again that I'm "fine," the tears don't stop. When we land in Detroit four and a half hours later, I have no tears left.

Seeing my family again really tests my skills as an actress. When I greet them just outside of the terminal and bustle into the waiting car while my father loads my suitcase, I am all smiles and jabbering with excitement as I recount my first experience shooting an actual film.

Ruben drills me with a hundred questions about what the people in L.A. are like and which celebrities I spotted while I was there while my parents listen indulgently. Once we're finally home, I'm greeted with the proper hugs that we hadn't the time to exchange at the airport and welcomed with a surprise party that's not really a surprise. I plaster on a fake smile and muster through.

My entire family has come out to welcome me back home, grandparents, aunts, and uncles and so many freaking cousins that sometimes I struggle to remember how we're related. Even Nicki makes an appearance, and that's a feat because she hates attending my family gatherings. Inevitably, some well-meaning aunt or uncle tries to play matchmaker and pawn her off on their single son. She gets tired of dodging their continual efforts to fix her up.

The fact that she's here is a big deal, but I wish that she wasn't. I wish none of them were here. All I want to do is crawl into my bed, pull the covers over my head and sleep for eternity.

When I finally reach a point that putting on a constant happy face becomes an unsustainable task, I politely excuse myself from the group with a claim of jet lag. Only when I reach the refuge of my bedroom do I allow my carefully constructed mask to slip. After tucking my suitcase into a corner, I climb into my bed to contemplate the last few miserable hours of my life. I'm not even surprised, though I am deeply annoyed, when Nicki comes barging in two seconds later.

My best friend is what most on the Internet would refer to as a "baddie." Perfect hair, perfect make-up, perfect body. She commands attention and awe wherever she goes. It's hard not to feel a bit frumpy in comparison. And because she is so stunningly gorgeous and so very confident about it, Nicki is used to getting her way.

People, men in particular, rarely deny her requests. So, I know that the last thing she expects is for me to say "get out" the second she enters my room, but that is exactly what I do. Predictably, she ignores me and perches herself on the bed instead, which forces me to scoot aside to make room for her.

"Okay, you might have everyone out there fooled by your whole 'I had the time of my life' act, but I'm not buying it. What happened with the guy?"

Rather than answering, I snatch up my pillow to cover my head in an attempt to shut her out. My muffled reply follows, "I don't want to talk about it."

Nicki, being the bully that she is, shamelessly rips away my feather stuffed refuge and tosses it aside. "Did you sleep with him? Spill your guts."

"Nothing happened," I enunciate from between clenched teeth, "He stayed with his fiancée. I came home. End of story. Now leave me alone."

I hide beneath the pillow again, but it's not enough to drown her reply. "You did the right thing, Iyah. You'll thank yourself later."

"Great."

"Give it some time. You're going to forget about that guy in a week."

Needless to say, I don't forget about Julien in a week, though it isn't for lack of trying. I keep myself crazy busy. When I'm not working, I'm auditioning and when I'm not auditioning, I'm letting Nicki drag me to endless social functions, and when I'm not partying, I'm spending quality time with my family. I do everything possible to fill up every single second of every single day with every conceivable activity so that I don't have to think about Julien Caffrey or his amazing smile or how desperately I miss him.

But at night when it's quiet and still and I have nothing to keep me company except my own regrets, I think about him constantly. I check my phone in an obsessive ritual, secretly hoping that he will text me. He doesn't.

Another week goes by before bleeding into another and eventually an entire month passes without any contact. I still haven't forgotten him, even though it seems pretty evident that he's forgotten *me*. Because I'm pathetic, I've stalked his Instagram like a lunatic in the late hours of the night when I can't sleep. I know from the pictures that he posts that he's still modeling, but there is little on his page to indicate what's going on in his personal life. I don't know if I'm grateful for that or aggravated.

I work myself to the point of exhaustion trying to keep distracted and the pace inevitably takes a toll on my physical health. I'm bedridden with the flu and slightly delirious from all the over-the-counter medication my mother has pumped into me when my cell phone unexpectedly buzzes to life at 3 a.m. Half groggy, half irritated, I start to swipe left on the call because I'm convinced it's a spammer, but my intention is thwarted when I see Julien's name. My fingers are shaking so badly when I answer that I'm surprised I don't miss the call altogether.

"You sound like death," are the first words he says to me after a 4-week silence.

"I feel like death," I croak in agreement as I shift upright in my bed. "I have the flu."

"I didn't know you were sick."

"Why would you?" There's a beat of silence before I add somewhat ridiculously, "Julien, it's 3 a.m."

"I know."

"Why are you calling me at 3 a.m.?" While that is the question I ask, what I really want to know is why he didn't call me sooner.

"I needed to hear your voice."

The sentiment is very mutual. But I'm not ready to melt into a simpering puddle just yet. "I couldn't tell. I haven't heard from you in a month."

"You told me you wanted distance," he reminds me, and I almost smile at the irritation I hear in his voice. "I would have called sooner if I thought you'd answer."

"Then why did you call now?"

"You know why."

Three words. Free of accusation, and abundantly true. But I'm not emotionally ready to deal with those implications, especially when I feel so terrible, so I try to steer our conversation into more neutral territory. "How's it going?"

"I keep waiting for the moment when I'll stop missing you," he whispers, "Hasn't happened yet." Clearly, not neutral enough.

"Same," I mumble in commiseration, "Maybe we just got really used to each other."

"Right."

I pick at the loose threads on my duvet cover, forcing myself to voice the question that has been plaguing my thoughts the entire time we've been apart. I was too afraid to ask him in California because I wasn't ready to hear his answer. But I can't afford to skirt the issue any longer, not when he's making secret calls at 3 a.m. I need to know his intentions.

"Julien, do you still love her?"

"I don't know if I'm *in love* with her anymore."

It's an answer and yet not an answer at the same time. What he leaves unspoken is that he's still with her. I can easily make that conclusion without him saying a word. "Is that why you're staying?" I wonder aloud, "Because you *were* in love with her?"

"I owe it to her," he considers, "That's what commitment is, right? And I am committed to her."

"You don't sound convinced."

"Because there's *one* problem. No one has ever made me feel the way you do."

There is a part of my heart that is singing, but a bigger part is filled with jaded skepticism. This situation is far too complicated for me not to be cautious. "Isn't that what every guy trying to justify an affair says to the girl he's cheating with?" I quip lightly, "That's kind of cliché, don't you think?"

"We're not having an affair, and it's not a line," he replies almost angrily, "Falling for you was one of the easiest things I've ever done."

"You say that, but you're still with her. What am I supposed to think?" He doesn't have an impassioned response this time. I'm not surprised but I'm disappointed, nonetheless. I expel a tired sigh. "Why did you even call?"

"Because I'm weak, and I'm a coward." He'll get no argument out of me on that score because I wholeheartedly agree. Then again, I'm in no position to get on my soapbox about it because I'm equally weak and just as much a coward too. "I miss you, Iyah," he says after a long, quiet moment. "I miss you so much."

"I miss you too."

I imagine that something must shift for him after my admission because he laughs for the first time since our conversation began. It's a short, breathy chuckle filled with relief. When he speaks again his words and tone are free of timidity and tension.

"I had a dream about you the other night." I groan, instantly steeling myself against a lurid revelation that will benefit neither of us. But before I can cut him off from saying anything further, he adds wryly, "It wasn't *that* kind of dream, but I see where your mind is." I grunt two crisp words in response, Julien's own trademark response to nearly every disagreement, but he only laughs. "Apparently, you want to. Just own it, Grandberry."

"Shut up and tell me your dream. I have about five minutes of consciousness left!"

His teasing is instantly replaced by solicitousness. "Are you sure you don't need to rest? I can call you back tomorrow." I'm not sure if we should be planning for future conversations after this one. But instead of telling him that, I insist on him recounting his story instead.

"So, there's this Mexican restaurant here in New York called The Black Ant—,"

"—Why do I already hate this beginning?" I lament.

"Let me finish," he insists with a chuckle, "As soon as I saw it, I thought of you. And yeah, I dreamed that we had dinner there. But as soon as you found out they serve actual black ants in their dishes, you were out. When I woke up, I could practically hear you saying, 'I respectfully decline, sir. I don't eat insects.'"

138

His tonal impression of me complete with disdainful sniff is unbelievably spot on. I can easily visualize him mimicking my facial expressions to perfection, and I can't help but choke back my own laughter as a result. It's enough to cause me to temporarily forget how ill I am.

"I will admit that *does* sound like me."

"It made me smile. I woke up smiling. It was the first time I've felt happy in weeks."

"I don't know why taking me outside of my comfort zone amuses you so much. You get some kind of perverse joy out of it. It's very juvenile."

"I can't help it. You make me laugh. I love that." *I love you.*

The words seem to float between us unspoken. Or maybe it's because I really want to hear him say them to me. The sentiment is there, poised on the precipice of disclosure, but I don't think either of us is ready to deal with what will come after that. So, we say nothing. The resulting silence grows thicker until I finally force myself to say what I should have several minutes earlier.

"We shouldn't do this again, Julien."

"You're right," he agrees softly.

"The next time you call, I won't answer."

"That's fair."

"It's better that way."

"I know."

But he doesn't say goodbye and, more significantly, I don't hang up. Julien takes that as an opening. "Since this is going to be the last time we talk, there's really no rush for us to get off the phone, is there?"

This is the perfect time to remind him that it's after 3 a.m. In all likelihood he is probably sneaking this call while his unsuspecting wife-to-be sleeps in another room. We are doing a reckless thing. Maybe it's not cheating, but it's not completely innocent either.

But I make no mention of any of it. I don't even try. Instead, I whisper, "No. I guess there isn't."

13

Nicki takes it upon herself to get me "back in the saddle" as she calls it. She drops this bombshell on me over a late lunch and cocktails at a local sports bar. It's football season in Michigan. A plethora of mounted, flatscreen televisions simultaneously display the various NFL games taking place all over the country. The bar is predictably filled with raucous, shouting men thoroughly engrossed with each play by play.

I'm surprised that Nicki was agreeable to a booth in the bar at all given the noise, but she's a lot like me. She likes to people watch. I have zero interest in what's happening onscreen, but I find the passionate reactions from those who *are* interested rather fascinating.

"I'll be glad when it's over," Nicki says after yet another round of cheering and booing.

"At least you get a break. There's more of this waiting for me when I get back home." But when I imagine my dad and Ruben together screaming at the TV over sandwiches and pop, it makes me smile.

"You should think about getting your own place," Nicki advises.

"You mean like a shoebox? Because that's what I can afford."

She makes a face at me before taking a sip of her drink. I'm not sure what it's called, but I do know that it's fruity and boozy just the way she likes it. She studies me over the rim of her glass. "If you had a man, you could split the difference on a place," she tells me.

"That might work for you, Ms. Baddie, but I don't have a line of men fighting to pay my expenses for me. I have regular face."

Nicki stifles a snort of laughter. "You're beautiful, Iyah. The only person who doesn't see that is *you*."

"Uh-huh," I hum indulgently around a mouthful of chips and salsa.

"You might know that if you put yourself out there a little more."

I tense immediately at the segue because I already have a strong suspicion of where this conversation might be headed. After I dust my fingers free of tortilla crumbs and blot my mouth with my napkin, I lean back to regard her with a neutral expression. "How many times are we going to have this conversation before you let it go?"

"You haven't had a serious boyfriend since Devin."

"I'm focusing on my career."

"It's been over a year."

It's impossible to keep the surliness out of my tone when I retort, "And?"

"I know it's not because you still want him," she reasons, "I told you that he and Sheila got married, and you didn't even blink."

Sheila Weston and I had been college friends and study partners for two years. She was also majoring in biology when we met. We easily bonded over our similar career paths, particularly because young Black women who became medical doctors were a rarity. As we became closer so did our boyfriends. Eventually, the four of us were hanging out together on a regular basis.

Our dynamic shifted after Sheila's relationship fell apart. She began spending more time with me and Devin as we tried to comfort her following the breakup. But everything *really* changed shortly after I decided to switch majors. Once my personal interests started to diverge from hers and Devin's, they started to gravitate towards one another while he and I drifted apart. We weren't officially broken up a full day

142

before he started dating her.

"I'm happy for them. She's really good for him."

Nicki blinks at me in astonishment. "You actually mean that, don't you?"

"Of course I do."

"And what about that other guy?" she presses, the corner of her mouth tilting in a perceptive smirk. "Julien, right? Are you happy for him too?" I deliberately take a sip of my drink to avoid answering her, but Nicki doesn't miss the subtle tightening of my facial muscles. She crows triumphantly, as if she's just won the lottery. "I saw that."

"Saw what?" I ask in round-eyed innocence, but I'm not nearly casual enough to convince her.

"Your face! This is why I think you need a palate cleanser."

"A palate cleanser?" I echo dubiously, "What the hell is that?"

"You know…a transition guy to get you over the hump. Just some casual, harmless fun to get the other guy out of your system," she concludes sagely, "I don't care how much you smile and pretend with everyone else. I know you're not over him, Iyah."

She's right, of course. I'm not over Julien. And, if I'm honest, I haven't been trying very hard to *get over* him either.

We haven't really talked since that night he called at 3 in the morning, at least not an actual conversation anyway. It shouldn't count as conversation if you're only texting random emojis, memes and a handful of dialogue every few days, right? That's nothing compared to that night he called when we spent hours on the phone together engaged in flirty banter full of sexual innuendo.

In hindsight, I know I was freer with what I said and how I acted because I didn't anticipate that he and I would ever speak again. That night was going to be my last and only opportunity to give uncensored rein to our evolving attraction. It felt nice to flirt with him without agonizing over whether it could or would lead to something more. We haven't alluded to it since. It's almost as if it never happened.

An entire week passed before he contacted me again and, when he did, it was hardly anything groundbreaking. He texted me a smiley emoji. That's it. No context. No explanation. Just a simple smile. I sent one back. And so began this weird, but enjoyable exchange that we've kept up ever since.

What started with emojis gradually shifted to memes and silly jokes and, before I knew it, we began texting one another to say "good morning" and "good night." He's even become my Wordle buddy, even though he's barely consistent about solving the puzzles. Our interaction is fairly harmless.

It's not like we're engaging in any sort of lurid behavior or texting one another inappropriate things. We're trading jokes and playing games. None of it *feels* wrong. We are simply two friends who enjoy making each other laugh. Nothing to see here.

Besides that, Julien's arbitrary text messages are quickly becoming the highlight of my days. They break up the monotonous loop I've fallen into. But, more than that, they are the unspoken affirmation I need that he hasn't forgotten about me, that even though we haven't truly spoken to one another in weeks, I continue to occupy his thoughts in the same way he occupies mine.

I don't even realize I'm smiling to myself until Nicki calls me out on it, which causes me to stiffen self-consciously. "What? I can't smile?"

"You shouldn't fixate on a man that you know you can't have. Look around you," she says, gesturing towards the bevy of men of varying ages, sizes and race that surrounds us. "You can have your pick."

"I'm not interested in anyone else."

"Why? It doesn't have to be serious."

"I know what I want now, and I'm not going to settle for anything less."

"Then you're probably going to die alone, dry and shriveled and still living with your parents," Nicki predicts direly. I know that she's being completely serious, but I laugh anyway.

Later that night, however, I find myself solemnly considering her words as I study my reflection in the mirror. I am 23 years old. I'm an attractive woman. My brown skin is rich and smooth and relatively acne free. I could charm a man if I wanted. According to social media, I should be dating and partying non-stop anyway. Supposedly this is my prime.

And yet, the reality is that I have a low paying job that has nothing to do with my degree and is merely a means to an end. I live at home with my parents. I'm alone. And most distressing of all, I'm in love with a man I can't have.

Under the circumstances, I should be miserable. But I'm not. I don't feel deprived or stunted. In many ways, I'm fortunate and happy, and I can attribute that fully to Julien. Being in love with him, having him in my life in whatever capacity I can, *that* makes me happy. And perhaps that's been the secret all along.

I'm only further convinced of that when my cell phone vibrates on my nightstand, and I immediately break into a smile because I know it's Julien. He's feeling minimalistic tonight. His message is simple. He's texted "60 days no" followed by a little cigarette emoji, followed by a George Lopez meme with the caption "I got this!" He's so obviously proud of himself that I can't resist calling him directly.

I don't even stop to contemplate the wisdom of my actions. I've already hit the call button before I've formulated any sort of plan. He picks up on the first ring.

"You called me," he says, sounding both surprised and pleased.

"This is a milestone, Julien Caffrey! That deserves a phone call. I'm really proud of you."

"I wasn't sure I could do it, wasn't even sure I *wanted* to do it, but it feels good."

"Congratulations."

I carefully tiptoe over to my bedroom door to close it. From beyond the hallway, I can make out the faint sounds of my family moving about downstairs. I don't want to take the chance of being overheard. That might put me in the position of fielding questions later. For good measure, I also lock the door. After I'm done, I climb onto my bed and settle into a comfortable position because I intend to relish this call.

"Can you talk for a little bit?"

"Yep. Just me and the dog tonight."

"And how is Sir Scruffy Doo?"

He doesn't answer right away and I'm about to question if the call dropped when my phone abruptly buzzes against my cheek. I glance down at the screen to discover he's sent me a screenshot of his Yorkshire terrier curled up rather adorably in his lap. The shot also showcases Julien's hand. His tapered fingers are tunneled into Scruff's fur while he amiably scratches behind the dog's ear. It's a clear indication that he's quite amenable to being used as a human doggy bed.

"Doesn't he look spoiled and comfortable?" I laugh when I lift the phone back to my ear.

"Well, my lap is a very comfortable place," Julien murmurs, the suggestion in his tone rather obvious. I'm still in the middle of deciding whether I want to further that banter with an equally risqué reply or walk us back into more neutral territory when he notes, "Now that I think about it, you've never said one way or the other how you feel about dogs."

"I don't have an opinion about them because I've never had one."

Julien gasps theatrically, and I can envision him pressing his hand to his heart in mock affront. "You're kidding! You freak!"

"Kiss my ass, Caffrey."

His low chuckle rumbles in my ear. "Okay, what do you think about pets in general? Do you have any?"

"Does a betta fish when I was nine years old count?"

He clucks his tongue at me mournfully. "Oh, my sweet, Summer child," he laments in obvious teasing, "What will I do with you?"

"It's not like *you* made pet ownership sound all that wonderful with the many horror stories you told about that tiny terror sleeping in your lap! I don't do pet poop."

Julien dissolves into a fit of laughter, and I swear it's the most beautiful sound I've ever heard. "God, I miss that so much!"

"Miss what?"

"You and your 'standards.'"

I smile because the way he phrases it almost sounds like a compliment. He's never been repelled by my "high maintenance" persona at all, but rather filled with affection instead. That he freely admits to missing my little quirks endears him to me further.

"I don't think you should write off having a pet," he considers, abruptly shaking me from my thoughts. "Specifically, a dog. They are the best."

"I'll have to take your word for it."

"Don't let the Yorkie deter you. Scruff is an angel. You'll love him when you get to know him."

As occurs so often in relation to him, my heart begins thudding rapidly following that careless prediction. "You make it sound like I'm going to be around for that to happen."

"I hope you will be."

"As what? Your side piece?" I ask, only half-joking.

"As my friend," Julien clarifies softly, "My *best* friend."

"Yeah, the problem is that you and I feel *more* than friendly towards one another, Julien. It's messy."

"There is no law against being attracted to other people, Iyah," he reasons, "If that was the case, no one would ever be friends with anyone else! As long as we don't act on it, we're not doing anything wrong!"

"You're oversimplifying."

"I don't think I am. And quite honestly, I'm tired of punishing myself for something I haven't done, and I'm not *going* to do. Aren't you?"

On the surface, his argument sounds valid. Then again, Julien has a gift for making what seems absurd on its face hold some measure of reasonable plausibility. But there is one caveat in this particular circumstance. I love him. I'm in a place where I can admit that freely to myself even if I never dare to utter those words to him out loud. And the more time I spend with him, the more deeply I come to love him.

Julien's feelings for me are a bit murkier. While I know he's drawn to me and even profoundly attached, I'm not sure he's ready to label what he feels for me as love. It's very possible he's reached the point where he can definitively say that he will never cross a line with me, but I'm not sure if I'll reach a point where I'll stop wanting him to. But, at the same time, it's a little self-centered to say, "I can't be friends with you because you don't want me in the same way I want you." That is the odd predicament that I find myself in.

"Tell me what you're thinking," he prompts softly when I continue silent.

148

"Just wondering if we want the same things," I whisper.

"I think maybe we do," he whispers back, "but the timing is bad."

"That's one way to put it."

"So, why shouldn't we protect what we *do* have?" he reasons, "A friendship should be nurtured, Iyah."

"There you go oversimplifying again."

"I'm not," he insists, "I'd like to spend actual in-person time with the woman responsible for saving my life."

"And now you're being facetious. It's not cute."

"Were you or were you not the same girl who accused me of 'killing myself one cancer stick at a time,'" he counters in a mocking falsetto, "Did I get the exact quote?"

"That doesn't sound anything like me," I deadpan, but there is a distinct smile in my tone despite my best attempt at feigning offense. "Besides, I didn't do anything. You did all the work."

"A nicotine patch and some journaling helped with most of that. This girl I know said that might be a good idea."

"I thought you said you weren't a writer."

"I'm still not. But it turns out that I have a lot to say."

I hesitate to question him about what those things are because I suspect that conversation might take us somewhere neither of us is prepared to go. I'm aware that we've been talking for much too long already. We're starting to delve into that profound, soulful realm of emotional intimacy and that is where we usually get into trouble. When we keep our topics light and superficial, then this attraction between us is manageable. But when he allows me glimpses into his heart…that is something else.

Julien seems to sense I'm on the verge of ending the call because he suddenly exclaims, "I've got an acting gig coming up. Did I tell you that?"

Though I recognize his stall tactic, I indulge him for now. "This would be the first time you mentioned it. Congratulations."

"It's for a day part on a sitcom. I'm generic, good-looking guy. I'll have like two lines of dialogue."

"Deliver them with Shakespearean-like gravitas, my friend." We trade a spurt of laughter over that inside joke, and it helps to dispel some of the tension that has begun to balloon between us.

"The show is filmed in Atlanta. So, I'm going to fly out to Georgia to film and spend a few days exploring the city after I'm done."

"Sweet. I've never been to Atlanta," I muse aloud.

"Do you want to change that?"

I bite my lip in consideration. This is hardly an innocent inquiry. His unspoken invitation is evident. Once again, we're standing on tenuous ground. Even with all the thin justifications we've made for ourselves, Julien and I inevitably migrate right back to this same place. We both know very well that we're flirting with the prospect of blowing everything we know and cherish to absolute hell, and yet we seem helpless to stop ourselves. Even if we don't acknowledge the quiet part, we both know this won't be some harmless reunion where we catch up over drinks and then go our separate ways afterwards.

He makes no mention of Kate. That fact is telling and very likely deliberate on his part. I seriously doubt that she will be tagging along on this trip or that Julien is overly concerned with whether or not *she's* been to Atlanta before. If I'm being extended this tacit invitation, it is almost certain that she hasn't received the same courtesy.

I know I'm on track because Julien abruptly backpedals. "Just forget I said anything!"

"Why did you even go there?"

"For the same reason *you* called *me*," he retorts in mild accusation, "You wanted to talk to me. And I want to see you." He lets that admission sink in deep before he asks, "Do you want to see me?"

I groan aloud in frustration. "You already know the answer to that, Julien."

"Nope, I don't know the answer. Because I don't read minds."

"Fine, yes!" I sigh somewhat irritably, "I want to see you."

His amused grunt sounds in my ear. "Was that really so hard?"

"Yes! It was!"

"I'll make you a deal. If I promise you that things will stay completely platonic between us, will you come to Atlanta?"

"I have a better question. Will you tell Kate about this proposed meet up of ours?"

This is the ultimate test. If it's a secret, then it's wrong. He can't make excuses, and I can't let him. I prepare myself to counter his justification, but he actually surprises me with a different response altogether.

"What's to tell? I'm going to Atlanta to film a scene for a television show and hang out with some friends," he argues, "Yes, I'm going to tell her. Because that's what I'm doing. That's *all* I'm doing."

It's the truth, but also an obfuscation and we both know it. We keep dancing close to this flame, pretending there's absolutely no chance of either of us getting burned. The warning bells are clanging "danger, danger, danger" in my brain, but the desire to see him again is too strong. I've already begun imagining our imminent reunion and now that I've set my heart on it, I can't let it go. So, I concede to his proposal even when I know better because, in this moment, the benefits outweigh all possible risks.

"Okay. When do we leave?"

14

Any misgivings I might have had about flying to Atlanta are dispelled as soon as I spot him standing outside my gate. His own flight arrived half an hour prior to mine, but he made it clear before we both left that morning that he was going to wait for me after he landed. The sight of him fills me with simultaneous excitement and anxiety.

His appearance has changed from the last time we were together. When we were in L.A., he and I were at our most casual when we weren't filming, spending almost every day outside of work in sweatpants and T-shirts. We kept our appearances in line with our characters, so Julien had spent most of that time clean-shaven and his dark, wavy hair in a short, neat cut.

Now the beard stubble is back, but his hair is much longer. It falls in dark, unkempt waves over his brow line. The non-descript jogger attire that I'd grown used to has been replaced with loose-fitting, designer jeans and a blazer. Even the graphic T-shirt he wears is stylish and eye-catching. With his Versace sunglasses and Burberry sneakers, he looks every inch a fashion model. But when he smiles, he is just Julien.

He rushes towards me, and my mind races madly over how best to greet him. Do we embrace? Fist bump? Exchange awkward waves? Nod at one another meaningfully? How exactly does one welcome the man one loves when he is engaged to another woman?

Predictably, Julien takes all the guesswork out of my internal agonizing when he scoops me up in a tight hug that exudes only pure joy. It's impossible not to hug him back. He jokes about how it seems I've gotten shorter since he last saw me. I tell him that he can kiss the roundest part of my derriere. We laugh together the way we always do. The moment is over far too soon for my liking.

I reach up to touch his earlobe briefly, noting the silver stud that adorns his left ear in addition to his right. Normally, I don't find guys with pierced ears attractive, but somehow the look suits Julien perfectly. I'm certainly not repelled.

"You had to have them both pierced, huh?" I tease him, "I don't know…you might be too pretty for that." He grumbles his usual response as I continue, "What's next? A tongue stud?"

"Don't tempt me," he laughs, "Oh, the things I could do…but my agent would lose it."

He steps back from me with a wide grin and sweeps me with an appreciative once-over. "God, it's great to see you! You look incredible!" I'm positive that might be an overstatement given I'm dressed simply in black leggings and an oversized sweatshirt, but he seems sincere, so I accept the compliment with a demure smile. "How was your flight?"

"I guess it was alright. I slept through the whole thing."

"Good. Then you'll be refreshed for the evening I have planned for us."

I survey him through squinted, suspicious eyes. "Why don't I like the sound of that?"

He regards me from beneath his lashes with an expression that can only be described as devilish mischief before he reaches for my carry-on bag. After securing his own bag on top of it, he grins at me and then loops his free arm around my neck. "Just trust me."

"Famous last words," I mutter as we start from the terminal.

I don't know why I'm surprised that Julien has an entire agenda planned for us. When we were in L.A., he was always scouting new places for us to visit and explore on the altogether rare days we had actual downtime. Although we are staying in separate hotels, they are less than seven miles from each other, and both are just outside the Atlanta city limits. As much as I would have loved to stay in downtown Atlanta, there was no way I could have afforded the room rates there. Apparently, neither could Julien. His plan was to rent a car, commute into the city for filming, and then spend the remaining two days touring Atlanta with me.

After we stop at the baggage claim for my checked bag (a fact that Julien finds inexplicable because he can't understand who needs a checked bag for a 3-day trip even after I patiently explain to him the absolute necessity of a shoe bag), we head to the car rental place to pick up Julien's reserved vehicle. It occurs to me that this will be the first time I've ever been alone in a car with him before. Back in L.A. we were chauffeured almost everywhere we went. Even when our travel wasn't studio sponsored, we would often travel by Uber to get around the city. Given that he lives in New York and does most of his commuting via the subway system, I'm not even sure I knew if Julien had a driver's license before this moment.

"How many car accidents have you been in?" I ask, frowning over the consideration. Julien freezes in the process of packing away our bags in the trunk when I add, "Are there any traffic violations that I should be aware of?"

He favors me with a quizzical look that borders on outright laughter. "You're kidding, right?" I blink at him unsmiling, and he snorts in disbelief before closing the trunk. "You're not kidding."

"It's only that I'm unfamiliar with your driving record."

"My driving record?" he echoes.

"Are you safe on the road? Do you observe the speed limit? How many traffic citations have you received? I need to know these things."

His incredulous smirk becomes filled with unspoken challenge. "Alright then. You drive." Before I can prepare myself, he's already tossing the car keys my way. I'm genuinely surprised when I catch them because dexterity has never been my greatest strength. I can tell from Julien's astonished expression that he is too.

Skeptical, I glance from the keys to Julien and back again. "You're not serious, are you?"

"Go ahead," he invites, stepping around to the passenger's side of the car, "You obviously think you'll do a better job."

"Not better, per se, just more experienced. I'm used to driving every day, especially in heavy, inner-city traffic. You're not."

"Okay, Ms. More Experienced. Put your money where your mouth is!"

Forty-five minutes later I am whipping down I-285 like a true Atlanta native, weaving in and out of traffic with practiced ease. The drivers here are generally courteous and allow me to pass without much resistance. It's a sharp contrast to driving in Michigan. You learn to take the openings whenever and wherever you can because no one is going to leave you space to merge. At least here, I'm not constantly taking my life into my own hands. Even with thick rush hour traffic, I maneuver the sturdy, black SUV smoothly, unintimidated by the crush of cars that zip around us on all sides.

Julien, on the other hand, looks terrified. He keeps barking out orders for me to "slow down," "watch out," and "brake," as if I've suddenly lost the ability to see outside the windshield. When he's not questioning my driving skills outright, he's plastered back against the passenger seat. He white knuckles the armrest the whole time.

"What's up with you?"

"You're a menace, that's what! I thought you said you could drive! We're gonna die out here!"

I don't know whether to laugh at his alarmed expression or be insulted by his obvious lack of confidence in my driving skills, which I know makes me a hypocrite. Instead, I flip my hand at him with a superior, sideways smile. "Just admit it. I'm a boss."

"Don't look at me! Watch the road!"

We make it to my hotel in record time, just 22 minutes after leaving the airport. I'm rather proud of myself, but Julien acts as if he just spent the last half an hour on the Tilt-a-Whirl. Though I present a façade of annoyance on the outside over his theatrics and perpetual side-seat driving, I'm secretly amused by his dramatics. His flare for melodrama matches my own.

Before I exit the car, we finalize our plans to meet up again after he's done filming. I watch him drive out of the parking lot with a faint smile, noting that Julien does indeed obey the traffic laws after all. Only when he has disappeared from my line of sight, and I turn aside to enter the hotel do I begin to second-guess my actions once more.

What the hell am I doing? It is the refrain that has been playing in my head for the past week now, having grown louder when I stood in line that morning waiting to board Frontier flight 3017 from Detroit, Michigan to Atlanta, Georgia. There is no plausible reason why I should be here. Despite the impression I've given my family and friends, there is no big audition. I don't have any photographers interested in booking me for a shoot.

There is nothing remotely professional about this trip at all. It is purely personal. And that would all be very fine if that personal reason wasn't currently engaged to another woman.

I haven't forgotten that pertinent detail as much as I try to ignore it. From an outsider's perspective, what Julien and I are doing might seem very, very wrong. The strange part is that it doesn't *feel* that way. As soon as Julien hugged me in the airport, all awkwardness, tension, and hesitancy dissipated. Guilt became an alien thing. When I was in his arms everything made sense. My misgivings about whether I had made the right decision melted away in an instant. But now that he is no longer around to serve as a distraction, I'm back to overthinking everything.

It's very possible that I'm being too sensitive. He's not really acting any differently. In fact, he had the same relaxed air from when we were filming in L.A., back before he chose to confess his attraction to me. But even that makes me *more* uncertain. Is he acting that way because his feelings have changed or is he merely upholding his promise to keep things platonic between us? I'm not even sure if either scenario is an acceptable one. Frankly, I'm sick of going in circles about it.

By the time I reach my room, I make a resolution with myself to stop making things so complicated. I came out here to catch up with a friend. That's all. As long as I accomplish that goal, nothing else matters.

After I've placed a call to my family to let them know that I've landed safely, I twist up my hair and change into my workout gear before heading downstairs to check out the hotel's fitness center. Surprising my friends and my family, but most especially myself, I've kept up with the fitness routine I started in California with Julien. I'm still not a runner. That activity remains as unenjoyable as ever, but I do like the elliptical, speed walking on the treadmill and strength training with kettlebells. The lithe tone I've acquired has become quite addictive.

Fifty minutes later, I'm in a much better frame of mind than when I started the day, and I'm ready for a shower. Once I'm presentable, I settle down on the bed to order myself lunch and channel surf until Julien contacts me again. It's close to four p.m. when he finally calls and, by then, I'm somewhere between avidly watching an episode of *Real Housewives* and dozing.

"Were you asleep?" he asks, picking up on the gruffness in my voice.

"Nope. I was contemplating the back of my eyelids."

"Liar," he laughs, "I'll be finished up here in twenty minutes and then I'll pick you up for dinner. Be ready."

"Where are we going?" I insist, "I swear, if you take me someplace that serves bugs or where I have to slaughter and cook my own meal, it's your ass, Caffrey!"

"What are you talking about?"

"I'm being serious!" I say, but it's difficult to be indignant when he's laughing at me, and *I* want to laugh too. "I need to know what to wear tonight!"

"Wear something sexy," he replies.

I'm left gaping at the phone when he hangs up. *Wear something sexy? Is he serious?* Does this man have any idea what he's doing to me? Every time I think I have a firm handle of what's going on between us, he throws me right back into a tailspin again. I'm starting to think that maybe I shouldn't be the only one left perpetually off balance.

I have the perfect little black dress to wear. It's not the especially risqué style of strings, loops, lace, transparent mesh, or high-waisted splits that seem to be the fashionable trend these days, but it is rather elegant in its simplicity. The circular collar is wide and just low enough to reveal the barest hint of cleavage. The skirt of the dress, while only mid-thigh in length, is wide and flowy, much like the slightly, flared half-sleeves. However, the best feature of the garment is the open back which tapers down to just above the curve of my buttocks. It is one of those outfits that calls for a backless bra or nothing at all.

Afterwards, I accent the look with simple jewelry studded with rhinestones and a pair of black, strappy heels. Once I've finished carefully applying my makeup, I pull up YouTube on my phone for some inspiration on styling natural hair in an updo. When I'm done, I admire my reflection in the mirror, not only looking confident and beautiful but *feeling* that way as well.

When I meet Julien downstairs in the hotel lobby thirty minutes after I've finished putting myself together, he literally stops in his tracks when he sees me. "Wow."

It's a struggle to bite back my satisfied grin as I do a fashionable little twirl for him. "You like it?"

"You look stunning."

He also looks "stunning" in his tapered, black slacks and printed, silk button-down shirt. Then again, Julien could still be "stunning" even if he was wearing a burlap potato sack, but that has little to do with his classically handsome face. It has always been his incredible smile that adorns him, and that glamorous wonder is on full display.

I try to mask the incredible effect he has on me behind a droll reply, "You're only saying that because every other time you've seen me, I look like a hobo."

"You're always beautiful, Iyah," he whispers earnestly, "This is something else."

I'm shocked when he doesn't take me to some quirky dine in spot. Instead, he's reserved a place for us at a pricey, premiere restaurant in downtown Atlanta which I had only mentioned to him once in passing. I never expected him to take me there, especially because the eatery was located on the second level of the Ritz-Carlton. That was far too much to expect for a casual dinner with a "friend," especially when that "friend" insisted on paying for the entire meal.

"I think I should cover my own bill," I tell him after the server has finished taking our order.

"Why? It's my treat."

"Because if you pay then that would make this a date, Julien," I reply, "and this can't be a date because you're getting married." He winces at the reminder, but I force myself to push ahead. He's not the only one who needs to be reminded. "How is Kate, by the way?"

"Let's not talk about her."

"But we should talk about her, don't you think? That's a conversation *friends* would have, right?" He jerks a hesitant nod and I ask, "Have you set a date for the wedding yet?"

"Yeah. It's in 11 weeks. We're finalizing the details."

"So, you're going to go through with it then?" I conclude glumly, unable to keep disappointment from seeping into my every word.

"I've thought about *not* going through with it," he confesses, "But then how do you justify destroying a two-year relationship and an even longer friendship for a girl you've never even kissed?"

It's a salient argument, and because I can't truly refute it, I try to make light of the reality instead. "We've kissed before. Numerous times."

"No. *Adam* and *Aubrey* have kissed," he counters with a meaningful look, "but *Iyah* and *Julien* have not."

I carefully outline the edge of the cloth napkin folded in my lap, finding it difficult to meet his eyes in that moment. "Do you think it would change things if we did?"

"It would change *everything*."

Thankfully, the server arrives with our appetizer just then, which provides us both with an excuse to segue into a less profound topic of conversation. We scrupulously avoid discussing Kate, his wedding, or our increasing need to be together for the remainder of our meal. Instead, we cover every other inane subject possible from his experiences during that afternoon's shoot to the size of a blue whale's heart. We talk and linger over our meal and try to prolong it as long as we can because I think we've both come to accept that these three days might be all we have together. When the waiter comes to deliver our check after we've both declined desserts, I don't think either of us is eager for the night to end.

"How do you feel about dancing?" Julien asks suddenly.

"I think dancing is great," I reply in a dry tone, "I wish I could do it." My deadpan delivery incurs his stunned burst of laughter. "Don't laugh. It's a shameful secret. You have no idea what it's like to be Black and have no rhythm. Family functions are painful."

"I'm White and have no rhythm," he commiserates.

"Yeah, but that's expected."

"Shut up," he laughs good-naturedly, "I'm only saying I'm not ready for the night to end. Are you?"

Finding a nightclub in downtown Atlanta is not a challenge. We spend the next few hours dancing as close as we can and singing bad Karaoke together. When we're on the dance floor, crushed amidst a sea of people, Julien and I seem to have no trouble finding a natural rhythm.

It's easier to let him take small liberties in that environment and to take those liberties myself. His fingers strumming across my bare back, my hand on his chest. His hips circling against me, my thigh wedged between his legs. His hand cupping my bottom, my fingers sifting through his hair. Our inhibitions are further lowered by several cocktails. By the time we finally stumble back to my hotel room, I'm shoeless and tipsy and more than inclined to give into my mounting desire for him. He walks me to my door and the entire time I'm fully aware that we're about to do something stupid.

In the still functioning part of my brain, I know I need to put distance between us STAT, but when I turn to bid him goodnight, I find him standing impossibly close. His face is only millimeters from my own, his arm braced above my head. He leans in closer and drops a deliberate look to my lips before lifting his dark eyes to mine again.

"We could try it and see what happens," he suggests.

I don't need him to elaborate on what he means. He's making his intentions quite obvious, and he's close enough that I know the effect I'm having on him. If I make even a slight overture, we'll be kissing.

My legs are like jelly. I drop my head forward and lean into his body with a mournful groan. My self-control is slipping in millimeters. Truthfully, it started slipping months ago only to finally culminate in this moment. His scent and warmth engulf me. It's an intoxicating feeling, but dangerous too. Almost desperately, I make one final attempt to bring us both back to reality.

"I don't want to be your dirty secret, Julien. You can't be with me and be with her too."

That statement is enough to snap him back into sanity. He instantly straightens and takes a step backwards, nodding firmly. Julien stares at me for a long time, as if he's trying to decide what his next action should be.

Finally, he inhales a deep, shuddering breath and it sounds a great deal like resolve to my ears. And then he cradles my face between his hands and leans forward to press a tender kiss to the center of my forehead before whispering goodnight. My breath is suspended in my lungs as I watch him walk away and eventually disappear into the elevator at the end of the hall.

I'm expecting to be inundated with regret once I enter my room alone and contemplate the empty bed before me, but instead I am strangely relieved and vindicated. Not because we didn't give into the thing that we both obviously wanted, but because tonight we both proved to ourselves that it is possible not to. There's no reason for me to cut Julien out of my life or go to excessive lengths to keep my distance from him.

Despite the strong attraction between us, it's very clear that our friendship is much stronger. Julien made his choice, and I made mine. At the end of the day, he and I are still friends. Nothing has to change between us and, considering the circumstances, that is the best outcome that I could hope for. I think Julien must feel similarly because he texts me an hour later and doesn't make any reference to our near kiss in the hallway.

You asleep?

No. You?

I'm texting you right now, aren't I? The sarcastic retort is followed by a crazy-faced emoji.

Haha.

You were wrong, btw.

Never wrong about anything, I text back furiously, though I have no idea to what he's alluding. *But give it your best shot.*

163

You absolutely have rhythm. I like the way you move.

My stupid heart flutters yet again because I can easily imagine how he sounds saying those words in person, but I'm confident this effect he has on me will eventually pass with time. I'm so sure about this, so certain that we have this thing between us under control that I'm emboldened to reply, *I like the way you move too.*

It takes him quite a long time to respond after that, and I'm wondering if I've left him speechless for a change. I can see the three telltale dots indicating that he's in the process of making a reply, but nothing comes through. I'm about to send him a joking message about writing an entire dissertation when his text message finally pops up on my screen.

I'm glad you came. See you in the morning. Goodnight, Iyah.

I get the sense that wasn't what he'd wanted to say or what he'd originally typed. But I also get the sense that Julien thinks that whatever he meant to reply was better off left unsaid. And, because I suspect he's right about that, I don't press him about it.

Instead, I send him a smiling emoji and respond in kind. *Goodnight, Julien.*

15

Four days after I returned from Atlanta, I received an unexpected call from my agent. The independent film that Julien and I shot a little over two months ago has been given a premiere date. I'm expected to fly back to L.A. in two weeks for the promotional tour.

I'm stunned by the development. While I had known that promoting the film would become an eventual reality, I hadn't anticipated that happening any time soon. My agent informs me that while the cast and crew will be involved in some live press, most of the taped interviews and promo stills won't be released to the general public until closer to the film's premiere date.

The news is opportune. My father has been constantly harping about acting not being a "financially advantageous" career choice. Maybe having my film finally garner a bit of media buzz will be enough to convince him.

The possibility that this might amount to something leaves me dazed. I barely absorb the magnitude because, minutes after I hang up with my agent, Julien calls. His excited giddiness permeates the miles of distance between us.

"Can you believe this is happening?"

"It hasn't sunk in yet. The timing couldn't be better though. My dad is on the warpath about my recent unpaid gig."

"What unpaid gig?"

"I kinda told him that I flew to Atlanta for a photoshoot," I hedge sheepishly.

I'm not expecting Julien to let that admission go, and he doesn't disappoint me. "So, *I* had to tell Kate the truth about where I was going and why, but *you* could lie through your teeth to your parents?"

"It's not the same thing."

"I think the word you're searching for is hypocrite," he laughs.

Our relationship dynamic has evolved yet again since the three days we spent in Atlanta together. Or, more precisely, we've come full circle. After that first night, Julien finally did the thing I've been subtly pushing him to do since that day he confessed his feelings for me. He made a choice. And it wasn't me.

I can't pretend that it was the decision I wanted, but I also recognize there was no other alternative. On some level, I've always known he would not leave her. Part of the pain of this dance we've been doing for the past few months has been rooted in Julien's continual pursuit of me while still clinging to his relationship with Kate. He wanted me, but not enough to break his engagement. I wasn't too far off the mark when I implied that he was trying to have us both.

"You were right," he confessed to me the following morning when we met for breakfast. "I *have* been indecisive, trying to have you and Kate at the same time. That's not fair to her or you."

"Does that mean you know what you want?"

"I made a commitment to her, Iyah. I should honor that. She deserves that."

"What happens with you and me?"

"I hope you'll stay my friend."

Ironically, I'm back in the place I was at the start of this convoluted journey, tucked in the firm nook of unrequited feelings. But, strangely enough, I'm at peace with Julien's decision. At least we're no longer shackled by an agonizing emotional limbo. When we said goodbye to one another in Atlanta, I hadn't sensed any finality in our farewell even though I knew things would be different between us. Instead, it felt like we were forging a new beginning. I'm hopeful and excited for what the future holds.

I can barely contain that hopeful excitement during my short telephone call with Julien and then my subsequent call to Nicki. Unfortunately, the feeling doesn't last very long. As soon as I update my parents on my plan to fly out to California, all pandemonium breaks loose. They're not nearly as enthusiastic as Julien and Nicki had been. My father is especially livid.

"What about your responsibilities here?" he explodes, "You just took time off for the second time in less than three months! I'm surprised you haven't been fired yet!"

"Don't worry. They won't have to fire me," I consider with a shrug, "I'm going to hand in my notice tomorrow morning."

In hindsight, I have no idea why I thought that news would comfort him. He blinks at me like I've lost my mind. His brows practically shoot up into his hairline.

"You're going to quit? Just like that?"

"It's data entry, Dad. I wasn't changing the world or anything."

"You *were* getting a steady paycheck at least!"

Our argument only deteriorates further from there. Though I try to reason with him that I can't possibly keep my current job and do the promotional tour simultaneously, he won't listen. Any half-hearted attempt my father had ever made to be supportive of my dreams fizzles away like freshly fallen dew in the summer heat. He lays into me mercilessly, enumerating the various ways that I'm ruining my life *and* disappointing him in the process.

The diatribe has been brewing for a while too. He brings up long dead issues. He cites my "flighty" decision to switch majors, the various dead-end jobs I've had since graduation and even my failed relationship with Devin as evidence of my ongoing irresponsibility.

"If your plan is to sponge off me and your mother for the rest of your life, you're off to a great start!" he yells.

Needless to say, by the time I leave for L.A., my father and I are no longer on speaking terms. My mother graciously offers to drive me to the airport, but she volunteers as chauffeur for the sole purpose of playing mediator. She begs me to see my father's side in the argument and spends the entirety of the trip justifying his perspective.

I will hear none of it. The one bright spot I have in the entire debacle, besides the prospect of promoting a project I've worked so hard on, is the chance at seeing Julien again. We've only been apart two weeks, and I've missed him fiercely. Besides Nicki, he's the only person whose company I can tolerate.

After I land, I collect my luggage and loiter in the baggage claim to await Julien's arrival. He's due to land in half an hour. I snag a vacant bench and read my Kindle to pass the time. Forty-five minutes later, I spot him near the rotating carousel, waiting patiently for his bags to emerge from the tunnel. As soon as I call his name, he darts forward to greet me with a warm hug.

"Seems like we just did this," I tease him after we part.

"I'm good with making it a habit, Grandberry."

We wait together for his bags to emerge and discuss the latest developments with the movie. The filmmaker's marketing managers and producer have already lined up various local television and radio interviews for us, with the first of those starting in only a few hours. To everyone's shocked delight, the film has garnered a measure of critical buzz due to its sensitive handling of mental illness. There's even talk of film festivals and possible awards. We may even score a limited box office release. But even if nothing truly comes of it, the publicity we're getting is a good thing.

Everything moves at lightning speed after we leave the airport. Julien and I have only enough time to drop off our bags at our designated hotel and grab a quick bite before we're off to our first interview. Due to the hectic schedule, there isn't much time for us to have small talk because our producer is eager to review the promotional agenda with us.

As a result of the film's growing hype, the producers decided to extend the original 3 days of promotion to 2 weeks in order to capitalize on the interest. Julien and I can expect to spend the next 14 days here in L.A. doing multiple interviews, attending different red-carpet events, and taking hundreds of promotional shots. I'm anticipating nonstop activity from now until the day I fly back home, but I am not complaining.

It is nearly 8 o'clock in the evening when Julien and I finally make it back to our hotel. We've spent the entire day on the move, being shuttled to one venue after another, and we're both exhausted. It is only when everything has slowed down that I notice how unusually quiet Julien has been today. Granted, he's been animated and chatty during every interview we've had, charming most everyone we've spoken to with his quick wit and genial demeanor, but when he's not on camera or live on the radio, he is noticeably subdued. When he tries to slink off to his room with a mumbled "goodnight," I catch hold of his sleeve before he can disappear inside.

"Hey? What's going on with you?"

He bites his lip and glances away, a telltale sign that he's about to lie. His attempt to circumvent with a denial worries me more than his silence. I regard him skeptically, but he doesn't yield. Undeterred, I try a different tactic.

"How about I make a deal with you? I'll tell you what's bothering me if you tell me what's bothering you."

Julien doesn't argue with me after that, and I suspect that's because he's more concerned with discovering *my* dilemma than unburdening himself. He invites me into his room and gestures for me to take a seat in the empty chair. After I'm situated, he sits down across from me on the bed.

"Tell me what happened," he invites without preamble.

I recount the confrontation with my father. It's not surprising that he's sympathetic. Julien knows better than anyone the ebb and flow of this business. Acclaim must be seized when the opportunity arises because it's laughably fleeting in Hollywood.

"Doesn't he understand what an incredible opportunity this is for you? Your career could really take off after this."

"He doesn't care. This sort of career is meaningless to him. He doesn't view it as art. It's dress up."

Julien nods in commiseration. "He thinks you're wasting your time."

"He *thinks* I'm a freeloader and that I'm taking advantage of him and my mom. He came right out and accused me of 'sponging' off of them! I don't even know how I'm supposed to go back home after that."

"Did he ask you to leave?"

"No. But I don't want to stay there if he thinks I'm taking advantage of them. It's not going to work. I need to get my own place."

"Come to New York. We could get a place together."

"I'm sure Kate will be thrilled with that arrangement," I scoff.

"I don't really care what she thinks."

There is a harsh sincerity in his tone that puts me on notice. I don't think I've ever heard him speak about Kate that way in the entire time I've known him. The change is curious and mildly alarming.

"Trouble in Paradise?" I venture carefully.

"You could say that..." he hedges.

"What happened?"

"Do you remember when I told you that I was journaling?" he asks. After I nod, he lowers his voice an octave and confesses, "Well, I never told you what I was writing about in those journals."

"Was it something bad?"

"I was writing about you." The admission causes me to rear backwards in dismay. "It wasn't anything shocking or explicit," he rushes to explain, "Mostly, I was trying to make sense of this thing between us. I needed to put it on paper so that I could process everything. They were *my* private thoughts...things that I hadn't even told you."

"She read them, didn't she?"

He jerks a nod of confirmation, his features tightening with anger. "She wasn't even sorry! She said it was because I was being distant, and she was trying to understand what was going on with me," he scoffs in recollection, "And then she had the nerve to say it was *my* fault for lying to her!"

"Does she think something is going on between us?" I ask softly.

"I told her about Atlanta, and I told her we were just friends. But she's got it in her head that I've been going behind her back with you this entire time. She gave me an ultimatum about you! She said she couldn't marry me if she couldn't trust me!"

"She doesn't want us to be friends anymore, does she?"

The tightening of his jaw is answer enough. "She didn't even want me to come! I told her that this was about work, and she basically accused me of cheating on her!"

This is probably not the best time to point out that Kate isn't too far off the mark with her allegations. Maybe Julien and I haven't engaged in some torrid affair but when I think about all the hushed admissions, the growing intimacy between us and even the near kiss the other week, I think Julien absolving himself of all wrongdoing would probably be a stretch. At the very least, he's been emotionally unfaithful. I'm sure on some level Julien knows that too, but he's too infuriated to acknowledge the truth. His indignation blinds him.

"That's not the point, Iyah," he says, as if he's somehow read my thoughts. "We both agreed nothing could happen! We didn't even *do* anything! I tried to do the right thing, and it got trashed anyway!"

"The 'right' thing?" I echo, frowning. "But that was what you *wanted*…right?"

"No. It wasn't," he whispers, scooting closer. His expression begins to transform in that moment, from frustrated and outraged into something earnest and fervent. His dark eyes are turbulent and intense as he regards me. "It was *never* what I wanted."

A subtle tingling starts in my chest. "Julien, what are you saying?"

I'm not prepared for his kiss even though I absolutely know it's coming. One moment he's on the bed and the next he is leaning in to press his lips to mine. I think we're both shocked by the contact. He doesn't move for a full second and neither do I. We're locked together, breaths suspended, but I don't push him away. Instead, I part my lips for the tentative exploration of his tongue and when I do everything changes.

That sweet, hesitant kiss transforms into something primal and desperate. It's unlike any kiss we've shared before. His hands are everywhere, cradling my face, sweeping my collarbone, pressing into my back. This is unrehearsed, unscripted. There is no direction on where to place our hands or position our heads, no half dozen pairs of eyes watching intently to guarantee that we stay within the camera's frame. There is only us and our hunger and need and longing, and that fuels our desire.

I'm not even sure when we stumble to our feet, but we never break contact with one another when we tumble back onto the bed together. My senses are overwhelmed with his taste and warmth and smell. I can't get close enough, can't kiss deep enough. I can't get enough of him.

Our bodies twist together as one sensuous entity, nimble fingers tearing away layers of clothing in a feverish need to be skin to skin. He drags avid, open-mouthed kisses across every inch of my naked flesh. When he finally sinks inside of me it feels like fulfillment, the completion of something that has been building for centuries, and I have no remorse. I ride out those rough crests of fierce passion with him, straining and greedy, until we both reach the finish with broken cries of release.

Clarity returns the instant the last remaining currents of my orgasm ebb away. I'm acutely aware of the weight of Julien's body against my own, the sensation of him slick and hot between my legs. I clasp him close to me, counting the steady beats of his thudding heart.

Finally, he rolls away, and a pervasive chill comes with the loss of his body heat that is as metaphorical as it is physical. I wonder if he's grappling with the sheer magnitude of what we've just done. But when I turn my head to glance over at him, his mercurial eyes are not filled with confusion or regret. Instead, Julien is regarding me with a drowsy smile filled with contentment. He reaches over to fiddle with the fluffy ends of my hair.

"What are you thinking?" I whisper.

"I'm thinking we should do that again," he says, pulling me against him once more. "But slower this time."

And so, we do. We spend a leisurely amount of time acquainting ourselves with each other's bodies. Then we sleep afterwards.

When I'm awakened a few hours later, it is to Julien's cell phone buzzing incessantly on the nightstand. I'm still a bit groggy when he reaches across me to silence the call but when I catch a glimpse of the picture displayed across his caller i.d. screen I am abruptly wide awake. It's Kate, and I am suddenly very aware that I am in bed with her fiancé.

A quick glance at the clock reveals that it is 2 a.m. Even with the three-hour time difference, that is an early hour to call. My mind inevitably begins racing with all the possible reasons. By Julien's own admission, he and Kate have left things unresolved between them. Perhaps she was calling with the hope of hashing out their issues. And, if so, would Julien be receptive to the idea?

But while I'm obsessing over all the possibilities and unspoken meanings, Julien is unbothered. He snuggles back against me as if the call never happened. His nonchalance surprises and alarms me.

"You're not going to call her back?" I ask after a beat of silence.

"No," he mumbles, "It's 2 a.m. I'll call her back tomorrow."

"What if something's wrong?"

"Trust me. It's not."

"Don't you think you should talk to her?"

"Yeah, I do…but not right now. All I want is to snuggle with you. Is that alright?"

It's not a bad answer. Under more ideal circumstances, it would be an absolutely perfect answer, but unfortunately what should be a sweet admission sounds like avoidance to me instead. I'm not so naive that I can't recognize how complicated our situation has become. Despite our earlier lovemaking, Julien and I haven't actually discussed a path forward for us or our relationship. Furthermore, he hasn't formally ended his engagement to Kate. We are now, *officially*, cheating.

It's true that he's infuriated with her, and he may even believe that he can no longer trust her after what happened with the journals. But that doesn't necessarily translate into him being done with her either. That is my biggest fear.

What if he isn't ready? What if this night between us, which has marked a significant turning point in our relationship for me, doesn't change anything for him? It's a conversation that I don't want to have because I'm so uncertain of his answer and because I don't want to ruin this wonderful night we've shared. But I also know that I'm never going to sleep if I don't get some straight answers from him.

"Julien?" He hums sleepily in response. "What exactly are we doing?"

"*I'm* trying to sleep," he mutters grumpily, "*You're* having an existential crisis."

I kick him in the shin just hard enough to make him grunt. "You know what I'm asking you."

"Will you relax? I'm going to tell her about us, Iyah." He punctuates that promise with a warm kiss against my shoulder. "This isn't just sex for me, okay?"

Relief floods through me, coursing down through my limbs and I melt back into the circle of his arms with a small sigh. "It isn't just sex for me either."

175

"Good. We're on the same page. Can I sleep now, or do you want to kick me some more?"

"Fine, Julien," I laugh, satiated exhaustion finally overtaking me, "Go to sleep."

16

I tiptoe from Julien's room just before dawn breaks.

Waking up next to him felt perfect and surreal at the same time. For those first few minutes, I watched him sleep. He's even more ridiculously beautiful when he's unguarded and peaceful, or it could be that the way I look at him is colored by how hopelessly in love I am. Either way, fawning over how perfectly gorgeous he looked with his tousled hair and flushed skin made me very cognizant of my own appearance, which I couldn't imagine was nearly as lovely.

Julien has seen me at my least glamorous on multiple occasions. I'm talking clay face mask, silk bonnet, and fluffy socks. We became very comfortable with one another when we were filming. But there's something intensely more vulnerable about waking up next to the man you love when your make-up is smeared, your face is puffy, your eyes are crusty, your hair looks like a bird's nest, *and* your breath isn't necessarily the freshest.

And, what's more, I hadn't planned on spending the night in his room. So, I'm without the resources necessary to fix those horrifying realities. Additionally, because I'd been forced to forgo my usual bedtime routine, my hair is a tangled mess and needs to be wrestled into some semblance of order. The lack of ready access to my electric toothbrush only adds insult to injury. There's no way in hell I'm letting him wake up to all that!

Of course, I am back in my own room less than twenty minutes before he tracks me down. A quick glance through the peephole reveals a half drowsy Julien. He looks like he just rolled out of bed and pulled on the most comfortable clothing he had, the all-too-familiar combination of cotton tee and sweatpants. He still has the pillow imprint on one side of his face. An armful of various toiletry items is clutched against his chest. Evidently, he plans to complete his morning routine with me.

As soon as I open the door for him, Julien shoulders past me with a mumbled "good morning" as if we've done this same routine a dozen times in the past. "I woke up in bed alone," he declares with a sullen pout, "You didn't even say you were leaving." He makes the declaration as if I've committed the most egregious sin imaginable, and he legitimately expects an apology over it. I can't help but smile over his petulance.

"Sorry about that. I needed to get ready. We have another interview in less than three hours."

"We can get ready together."

Even after all we've done and experienced, sharing a bathroom counter with Julien Caffrey feels more intimate than making love. He is literally in my sacred space. His personal items are scattered among my face creams and hair moisturizers. The sheer domesticity of this moment fills me with an odd, contented giddiness.

I watch him go through his morning routine of primping, inspecting, and shaving, and it's all ridiculously fascinating to me. But I can't understand why. It isn't as if I've never shared a bathroom with a guy before because I have. Yet, even when I was with Devin, I don't recall ever wanting to do this for a lifetime.

Back then, it was just a routine, a necessary part of the day that was pleasant to share, but nothing too profound. This moment with Julien feels like a milestone in coupledom in comparison, a steppingstone towards something deeper, something with potential longevity. We're not just two people engaging in casual sex. I can see myself building a future with him. I *want* to build a future with him. The realization is thrilling.

"Why are you looking at me like that?" he asks around a mouthful of toothpaste foam.

I bite back the impulse to say, "I love you," but the words are there pounding in my heart, pressing at my lips, threatening to burst right out of me. I don't say them because it's too soon, too foolish to make avowals of love after one night of inarguably exquisite sex. Instead, I shrug and go back to applying my make-up.

"No reason."

He spits into the sink, quickly rinses his mouth, and then turns to face me with a superior smile. "If you want me, Grandberry, you should just say so."

My resulting rant on his sheer arrogance and unmitigated gall is subsequently ruined because five minutes later I am pressed between his thrusting hips and the bathroom counter. There is something incredibly erotic about watching your lover's face in the mirror while he makes love to you. I'm profoundly aware of every moan, every caress, and every flicker of arousal that flashes across his face. What's more incredible is that *I* am the one evoking all of that. It's definitely intense.

We showered together afterwards, an amusing experience for me because Julien complains like an old lady the entire time. We can't agree about the water temperature and consequently, bicker like children about who should stand beneath the spray. I can't risk ruining my hair, and Julien refuses to "freeze his ass off." It also doesn't help that we have a wildly difficult time keeping our hands to ourselves. The fact that we're late to our first venue isn't shocking.

Our second day of promotion is just as chaotic as day one. In addition to several cast interviews and panels, Julien and I are also booked for a photoshoot in the afternoon. A number of commentators have noted the extraordinary screen chemistry that Julien and I share and that has been fully ramped up in our interviews together. We already possess a natural tendency towards playful banter, but that has developed an undercurrent of flirtation now which certainly doesn't escape the interviewers' or our producers' notice.

The journalists and hosts feed into the obvious attraction between us and, predictably, try to pry more out of us while the producers encourage us to play up the flirtatious angle as much as possible. I think Julien must get a kick out of being facetious and insisting with a straight face that we are merely good friends and how working on the film has "bonded us for a lifetime." I'd like to think our "lifetime bond" has very little to do with that.

When they ask if we are dating each other, we tell them no. When they ask if we are dating at all that answer becomes a bit stickier. Julien reluctantly admits that he is currently in a relationship but that he prefers to keep his private life separate from his professional life. That answer seems to be enough to shut down even the most tenacious host, but it is an unwelcome reminder for me that he has yet to have "the conversation" with Kate. I'm eager for him to get it over with, but I also realize that he is dreading it just as much. I haven't pushed him about it, but I want to.

We finish up around 6 p.m. and our driver arrives to take us back to the hotel. Instead of making a straight shot back, however, Julien convinces him to take a detour to the local supermarket because he needs to "grab a few things." I frown, curious over his intentional ambiguity.

"What did you forget?"

He mouths the answer back at me, clearly not wanting to be overheard by our driver. "Condoms." I choke back a self-conscious cough as he continues in a regular tone, "We should probably start using them, don't you think?"

I can't believe I hadn't considered that before now, and I'm a little dumbfounded by my own carelessness. We've had sex several times, and we've never discussed protection even once. Truthfully, it never crossed my mind.

I'm not especially worried about pregnancy since I've been using birth control faithfully since I was thirteen to regulate my heavy menstrual flow. STDs are something else. I've thankfully never had any experience with one, but I don't know the extent of Julien's sexual history with that. What I do know is that, while I've been practicing abstinence for more than a year now, Julien can't say the same. I wonder if this is something typical for him, or merely a lapse in judgment as far as I'm concerned. Because we've done a fairly good job of being direct and honest with one another, I ask him outright.

"It's the second thing," he says, "I'm usually very careful. It's not like I was planning for last night to happen."

"Right."

He nibbles his lip in thoughtful silence. "What about the other thing?"

"You mean pregnancy? You can relax. I have an IUD. No babies for us."

I could almost swear the corner of his mouth turns up in a thoughtful smile. "For now, anyway."

Walking through the store with him hand in hand makes me stupidly giddy. We make a huge production of placing snacks and random toiletry items in our handheld basket to cover for the actual item we came in to purchase. It's such a juvenile thing to do, and yet there is something about being with Julien Caffrey that makes me feel like I'm a sixteen-year-old girl again experiencing my first crush. There is a heady fluttering in the pit of my stomach that intensifies with his every touch.

I like being close to him this way, walking hip to hip and nudging one another with our shoulders. I like the way he swings me forward so that he can hug me from behind, and the way he whispers naughty things against my ear as we walk in step. I even like the small, sideways smiles that we receive from passersby when we are being cutesy with one another. I honestly can't imagine being any happier than I am right this second.

By the time we make it back to the hotel, it is well after 8 o'clock. We retire to my room to share a non-nutritious dinner consisting of pizza and chips. Afterwards, we make love, once on the floor and then again in my bed. I would expect after so much constant activity that I would doze off immediately. But oddly enough, I can't sleep. Neither can Julien.

We lie on our sides facing one another in the low lamplight. Julien traces his fingers across my mouth and kisses me softly, gently, as if he can't quite believe I'm real. The infatuated way he's looking at me, I don't think I've ever felt more beautiful in my life.

"Tell me something about you that I don't know," he whispers.

"You know everything already," I whisper back.

That's not too much of an exaggeration either. He has seen the best and worst of me and witnessed my highs and my lows. He knows my secrets and my greatest fears and the unique, little quirks that make me who I am. He's also quickly familiarizing himself with my body and all the ways I like to be kissed and touched. The only thing he doesn't know yet is how hopelessly in love with him I am, and even that won't be a secret from him for long. It is both rattling and exhilarating to know that everything about me has been laid out so openly for his scrutiny.

"I don't think I have anything new for you," I sigh after a thoughtful beat.

"Impossible. There has to be one thing."

I consider his argument for a minute longer, combing my brain for some tidbit I haven't yet shared with him. When it comes to me, I almost want to cringe in laughing embarrassment because it's so utterly stupid. It's not even something that is widely known outside of my immediate family, and they tease me about it every chance they get. But I know instinctively that Julien will appreciate it.

"There is one thing."

He scoots closer, his smile filled with sweet, boyish interest. "What?"

"I can pick things up with my feet."

His reaction to my disclosure is exactly what I expect. I can't keep myself from giggling at his baffled expression. "You can do what now?"

Rather than wasting time unsuccessfully describing my strange talent to him, I crawl from the bed to provide him with a demonstration instead. The sheer absurdity of this moment, especially because I'm totally naked, has me laughing uncontrollably and him too. "May I borrow your wallet, good sir?" I ask with exaggerated courtesy.

"What are you doing?" he chuckles in exasperation.

"Just trust me."

As soon as he passes me his wallet, I drop it to the floor. And then with nimble ease I pluck it from the carpet using only my toes and place it neatly beside him on the bed. When I'm done, I throw open my arms with dramatic flourish.

"Taa daa! Pretty impressive, huh?"

Julien can't suppress his answering snicker though he struggles to keep a straight face. "That's great," he says, "If you're ever in an accident and both your arms are severed, you'll at least have the comfort of knowing your life can go on like normal."

I cheerfully smack him in the face with a nearby pillow. "Fine! Laugh at me. Do you have something better?"

"Something like what?" he asks, pulling me down on top of him.

"It's your turn now. Tell me something I don't know about you."

"It's nothing as amazing as your foot thing but…" He emits a laughing grunt when I tweak his flank for that wisecrack, "…I like to paint."

I rear back in surprise. I've long suspected he might have an artistic side, but Julien never confirmed. He and I have spoken about *my* love of art at length. I appreciated how genuinely interested he seemed in the subject, and knowledgeable too. Now, I know the reason.

"Why didn't you say anything?" He shrugs in response. "What do you like to paint?"

"Everything. But mostly I stick to landscapes. I can show you some of my work."

After I nod eagerly in agreement, he gently shifts me aside to reach for his cell phone. He has carefully avoided looking at it all day. There is a brief flicker of guilt across his features when he unlocks his screen. I assumed that's because he has several missed calls from Kate. But he ignores them for the time being and concentrates on scrolling through his various apps until he finally finds what he is searching for. Once he does, he passes his phone to me.

"Most of these are a few years old," he explains, "I don't do it much now, but I've been into it since I was twelve years old."

There are dozens of thumbnails in his gallery depicting various forest scenes and rolling valleys and breathtaking waterfalls that look so realistic I'm almost convinced they are photographs and not paintings. Each canvas is splashed with vibrant colors and hues. I click on one particular painting of a cascading basin of stair-step falls that are partially hidden behind a copse of verdant Evergreen trees. The attention to detail is incredible.

I regard him in gaping wonder. "Where is this place?"

"In my head," he replies, retrieving the phone from my loosened grip. "I made it up."

"You made it up? That's insane! Do you have any idea how talented you are?"

Julien ducks his head in response, his cheeks pinkening with a self-conscious blush. "I wouldn't go that far."

"You could sell these!" I insist, "Have you ever tried?"

"Never," he replies almost as if the suggestion is the most ridiculous thing he's ever heard, "It's just a hobby, Iyah. I'm not that good."

"Who the hell gave you that idea?" I demand, incensed and ready to do battle with whoever dared to kill his self-confidence so cruelly.

"My mother."

His answer deflates me for multiple reasons. One, because I'm crushed to learn his own mother would discourage him that way. Two, because he has very obviously internalized every criticism she gave. I am overwhelmed with pity and fury at the same time. But I know Julien well enough by now to recognize he won't be receptive to my sympathy.

That is the quickest way to shut him down. He doesn't like to dwell on his past. And because I know encouraging him to talk about his feelings will likely lead nowhere, I take refuge in my fury instead.

"With all due respect, Julien, your mother is a mentally and emotionally abusive drunk! You should take anything she tells you with a grain of salt."

"My mother may be a drunk, but she's an honest one. I was never going to make a name for myself as an artist. There are plenty of people out there way more talented than me. Painting is just an outlet. I like doing it."

I'm saddened by his answer, but I don't push him further. "More catharsis?"

"Exactly."

"I still don't agree with what she said," I tell him, "You're very good. You shouldn't let her get in your head."

"She's not in my head," he denies softly, "I think my biggest fear is that I'm just like her, and I don't want that to be true."

"I don't think you need to worry about that."

His answering grunt is self-effacing. "You don't know me well enough yet. I am a master at screwing things up, Iyah."

"Is that what you think you're doing with me?" I ask a little sorrowfully, "Do you feel like you're 'screwing things up?'"

He reaches out to pull me back into his arms, reassuring me first with his touch and then with his words. "I'm happy. You make me really happy," he confesses fervently, "I hope I make you happy too."

"You do."

It's the closest we've come to exchanging declarations of love, and it feels right to affirm that poignant exchange with more lovemaking. I fall asleep in his arms with the unshakeable certainty that I am right where I belong. My world is perfectly perfect.

When I awaken later, the room is awash in murky darkness, and I am alone in bed. As I shake off my grogginess, I gradually become aware of Julien pacing the floor just beyond the bed. He is on the phone, carrying on a hushed, but very intense argument with the person on the other side of the line. It doesn't require a lot of deductive reasoning to figure out that person is Kate. I lie there, perfectly still, and strain to catch snippets of Julien's responses to her.

"…what do you want me to say?" he mutters sorrowfully, "…It just happened. I tried to stay away from her, Kate! I really did! I've tried to fight what I was feeling every day!" I can't discern her reply, but I have to imagine it's not good because Julien sounds like he's about to start sobbing. "I'm sorry. I'm trying to be honest with you." Again, I can't hear her exact response, but her muffled weeping is quite detectable as is Julien's anguished expression. My throat aches with guilt.

Finally, Julien drops his head forward and mutters, defeated and clearly broken, "If you really feel that way then maybe it's a good thing that we're calling it off."

Her reaction must be devastating because Julien looks positively stricken when the phone call ends. He glances over at me, and I immediately feign sleep, not wanting to reveal to him that I've been eavesdropping the entire time. When he's reassured that he hasn't disturbed me, he makes another phone call.

"…Yeah, I know it's late," he says to the person on the line, "Sorry. Can you check on Katie for me? Nothing. We had a fight. Good. Thanks." Once he ends the call, he stoops down to rifle around in his suitcase before disappearing out onto the balcony. I stay huddled beneath the blanket for a long time afterward, until I finally muster the courage to slip from the bed.

I pull on his wrinkled t-shirt and open the sliding glass door to join him outside. The bitter odor of tobacco immediately assaults my nose. Julien angles a guilty look at me over his shoulder as I step closer. He doesn't put out the cigarette though and, instead, takes another deep drag.

"Don't give me a hard time about it," he mutters irritably, "I'm not in the mood."

"I heard you on the phone," I reveal in a quiet tone, "Is it over?"

"Yep."

"How do you feel?"

"Like shit!" I start forward with some half-formed intention to comfort him, but he staves me off with an anguished expression. "I broke her tonight. She was nothing but good to me. She didn't deserve it."

"Julien…"

"And I can't figure out *why* I did it," he says mournfully, "It's not her. It's *me*. *I'm* the one who's screwed up, you know?"

I'm helpless to comfort him, helpless to ease his guilt and self-hatred especially because I understand that *I* am the source of that guilt and self-hatred. "You can't help how you feel."

He rejects that argument with a disbelieving snort and takes another puff, his mouth hardened in an embittered line. "I didn't even try. I didn't try hard enough to stay away from you."

"What are you saying?"

"I don't know…maybe this was a mistake." He can hardly look me in the eye as he continues, "Maybe what we're doing together is a mistake."

It feels like I've been punched in the chest. I knew breaking things off with Kate would be difficult for him, but I never imagined it would make him second-guess being with me. Only a few hours ago he was proclaiming how happy I made him, and now he's filled with doubts.

I'm not sure how to respond. I don't know if this is some guilt-induced reaction or if he's feeling genuine reservations. He looks like he wants to cry so, I'm inclined to believe it's the former. Then again, maybe that's what I *want* to believe. I certainly don't want to contemplate the possibility that he might regret being with me.

"Do you want to be alone?" I hate how timid and needy the question makes me sound.

"I don't know," he hedges, "I just feel like…maybe you and I should back things up a little."

"Back things up?" I parrot dumbly.

"I was with her for 2 years, Iyah! I asked her to marry me! I thought we were going to be together for the rest of our lives. I wanted that. I don't know where that feeling went."

"Do you want to get it back?" It physically pains me to ask him that question, but I force myself to do it despite the torment the effort causes.

"Don't I owe it to her to try and make things work?"

"And what exactly is that going to mean for us, Julien?" I feel like a simpering idiot for even asking because a blind man could see where this whole thing is going. But I want to force him to acknowledge it out loud. I want him to say the words. "Are you breaking up with me?"

His answer to that is a helpless shrug. "I don't know…maybe it's not a good idea for us to be together."

A slow, definitive chill creeps through my entire body after he says that before I abruptly go numb. My throat starts to burn and constrict, and I know that I'm seconds away from bursting into tears. But I refuse to cry in front of him. I won't beg him to change his mind either. He's compromised enough of my pride already. Instead, there is a cold fury that overwhelms me with the realization, and I lean into that. I channel every ounce of anguish coursing through me into hot, burning anger.

"You selfish asshole! You couldn't figure that out *before* you slept with me?"

"I wasn't trying to use you."

"But you did, and I was stupid enough to let you!"

I don't linger long enough to listen to his apologies or weak justifications. I go charging back into the main part of my hotel room in a righteous fury and begin yanking up his discarded clothing from the floor. I shove the bundle along with his shoes into his arms as soon as he materializes from the balcony. Before he can say a word, I rip off his t-shirt and toss that at him as well. In that moment, I'm too infuriated to care that I'm standing there in front of him stark naked.

"You can get out now," I order him coldly.

He has the nerve to plead with me. "Iyah, please don't hate me..."

I'm about a hairsbreadth from losing it. My anger is fuel, pumping me full of righteous adrenaline, but it is burning out quickly. My chest is aching with the effort it takes to hold back my sobs. I concentrate on yanking on my clothing to cover my slipping composure but everything around me is starting to blur. When he dares to touch my shoulder, I lash out.

"Don't touch me!" I scream, "Just get the hell out!"

Thankfully, he does. He doesn't try to argue with me or make excuses for himself. He just slinks away quietly. Honestly, it's a blessing too, because he barely clears the door before I start to break down.

17

The next twelve days are literal hell and the longest of my life. I seesaw wildly between intense anger and crushing despair. Sometimes I hate Julien so much I'm afraid I'll choke on my own bitterness, and other times I cry until I become physically ill. I have had some very rough days, but I have learned something vital about myself during this experience. I am a consummate actress. I could have never made it through the two weeks of film promotion otherwise.

That isn't to say that seeing Julien's face day after day didn't take a heavy toll on my mental health because it did. I was barely able to muster the energy to drag myself out of bed, let alone muscle my way through hours and hours of interviews. Any excitement I had initially over the tour and the buzz and the potential acclaim for the film quickly died after that second night. All I wanted, more than anything, was for it to be over.

I suppose Julien felt bad about breaking my heart because he made multiple attempts to explain himself to me, but I either ignored him or avoided him entirely. If we weren't on camera or live radio, then he was dead to me. But when we were on, I went through all the motions, and I gave the interviewers and producers what they wanted.

There were days when I hovered like a hapless shadow in my own life. I did my part in crafting the narrative that Julien and I were inseparable partners on and offscreen, but inside I was dead. I smiled and flirted and laughed and played all the ridiculous games they wanted me to play. I treated it like any other part. I pretended I was the girl who really *did* have "happily ever after" with her co-star. But she was only a caricature, and when the cameras stopped rolling, the character faded away as did my reasons for joy.

I could navigate the interviews fairly well. I could laugh and pretend and keep my sanity. The photoshoots, on the other hand, were pure torture. Those involved long hours of touching and repositioning, hours of intimate poses where I was forced to be in close proximity to Julien. Having him invade my personal space over and over again understandably left me uptight and anxious. No matter how many times I was admonished by the photographers to "relax" and "be natural" I simply could not do it.

When a crew member suggested that I try a glass of wine to "calm my nerves," I was eager to take her suggestion. I never did another photoshoot or interview with Julien sober after that. The alcohol helped to ease my tension, but it also kept me numb. It lessened my inhibitions, made me more inclined to initiate friendships with the male models who sometimes served as background "props."

I made a habit of partying with them after hours as a way of avoiding the ride back to the hotel with Julien. At times I would even flirt with different ones right in front of him, just for pure spite, not that he cared either way. He had chosen his precious Kate, and I wasn't a factor any longer.

Keeping myself functionally intoxicated seemed like a workable solution. The more I drank, the less I cared, and the less I cared, the more I drank. But, of course, Julien eventually felt entitled to offer his unsolicited advice about it. Three days before the film promotion was due to end, he cornered me as I was leaving my hotel room for yet another party.

The sight of him standing outside my door had been enough to momentarily shock me into paralysis. My body still reacted to him as it always did, heart pounding and breath catching. It was my anger and self-hatred that finally propelled me into shouldering past him without a word. But he wasn't deterred by my silent dismissal and moved to block my path. The memory of that exchange still fills me with humiliation and shame.

"Can we have a discussion, please?" he'd asked in that soft, unassuming way he had.

Verbal disarmament, I often called it. In the past, he had managed to successfully diffuse my irritation with him on countless occasions by using that gentle, beguiling tone, even when I was determined to stay angry. That night, I was immune, and what I really wanted to do was punch him.

"No, we can't. Get out of my way."

"I'm worried about you."

"Don't bother. Move." But no matter how many times I had tried to sidestep him, he kept stubbornly blocking me, determined to make me hear him whether I wanted to or not.

"Iyah, I wasn't trying to hurt you. I want what's best for you. I want you to be happy."

I had wanted to scream at him then. I couldn't understand how he could ever imagine that what he had done could possibly lead to my happiness. Either he was delusional, or I was! But though I had to clench my hands against the impulse to slap him, I kept my indifferent veneer. I never revealed how deeply he had gutted me. I would *never* make myself vulnerable to him again.

"If you have a point, Julien, make it, and then move," I had told him instead.

"You're drinking too much."

"I don't remember asking your opinion about it."

"Go right ahead and hate me. I deserve it. I know that. But don't hurt yourself."

I hadn't realized at the time how prophetic those words would prove to be, or perhaps I had and that was the reason they had made me so angry. That night I dismissed his warning and dismissed him too. I told him that I could take care of myself and that he should worry about his future wife. *I* was no longer his concern. We were *not* friends.

He left to fly back to New York on a Tuesday, and I can remember how much the thought of him leaving me behind hurt so much. And I hated myself for that. I hated myself for still wanting him even after he had made it so abundantly clear that he didn't want me back. I hated myself because I honestly didn't know what I was going to do without him.

I couldn't go back home. My relationship with my father was too strained. I couldn't talk to my mother, and I couldn't admit that I had been foolish enough to fall for a man who was unavailable from the start. I'd never felt lonelier in my life. And that day that Julien left, it had felt to me like I would always be alone. I wanted the pain to go away, or to become something that didn't have the potential of swallowing me whole.

So, while Julien was on his way to LAX to catch his flight home, I accepted an invitation to join a group of young models for a boat party off the coast. When Julien was in the air, I was having cocktail after cocktail and flirting with every man that showed me interest. And as Julien was most likely hailing a taxi to take him back to the apartment he shared with Kate, I was below deck having sex with a man I barely even knew.

An unexpected reprieve from returning home came in the form of a photographer who was interested in using my likeness for several local print ads. It was a chance for some extra money and a way to delay returning to Michigan so, I jumped at the opportunity. I spent an additional two weeks in L.A., sleeping on the couches of various acquaintances, partying as late as I wanted, drinking how much I wanted and having sex with whomever I wanted.

Nicki laughingly dubbed it "the great THOT tour of L.A." In her estimation, I was "living my best life," and I let her believe that. I *wanted* to give her the impression that I was having the greatest time ever because, in those moments when I was free of reticence and fear, I almost believed that I was. I didn't think about Julien. I didn't think about my parents. I lived in the moment. I lived for *me*.

The shedding of my inhibitions was empowering. But in the silence, when things stopped moving and I was alone, my permeating emotions were shame and sadness. After waking up one morning naked and hungover in a strange bed with a strange man and no memory of how I had gotten there or what I had done the previous night, I knew something had to change. I called my mother and tearfully asked her if I could come home.

And that's where I've been for the past three weeks, but I can't leave my room. I can't get out of bed, not even to take a shower or fix my hair. I can't make the effort. I don't care. Sleeping is my only interest.

My behavior is starting to raise concerns from my family. I'm provoking questions that I can't answer but I can't make myself move. Sometimes I think I would be perfectly alright with closing my eyes and never opening them again. Even as I try to rationalize that such thoughts are too dramatic for a simple broken heart, they don't *feel* dramatic. I'd much rather be dead than hurt like this. Not even the news that my film will have a limited box office release is enough to rouse me from my bed. At that point, I think my parents truly start to worry.

When my mother creeps into my room later that night, I barely even acknowledge her, not even when she scoots down next to me on my bed. But I can feel her staring at me in the darkness before she reaches over to click on my bedside lamp. I recoil from the sudden flood of brightness and reflexively bury my head beneath my blanket to block it out.

"Did something happen in L.A.?" Mom asks gently.

"No."

"Iyah, you've been locked in this room for three weeks. You don't talk. You don't eat." She falls silent, as if she expects me to chime in and fill in the gap for her. When I don't, she continues. "At first, I thought this might be some residual resentment towards your father, but now you're scaring me."

"I'm fine."

"You're not," she insists, "Did someone...?" She goes silent once again and I suspect that she's trying to find a careful way of phrasing her next question to me. Finally, she asks, "Were you assaulted while you were in L.A.? Is that why you're acting this way?"

That ludicrous conclusion is enough to make me flip up my blanket to peek out at her. "Are you asking me if I was raped?" I bleat incredulously. She jerks a nod and I scoff before retreating back beneath the blanket. "No, Mom! I wasn't raped. *God!*"

"Well, what else are we supposed to think?" she cries, "Something obviously happened! And if it wasn't that, then what was it?"

With a frustrated grunt, I flop onto my back to glare at her mutinously. "Will you please leave me alone?"

"I can't do that. Tell me what's wrong."

"Nothing is wrong."

"Iyah…"

Her image shimmers and blurs before me. The tremor of worry in her voice when she says my name beckons the tears. "Mom, please don't make me talk about it…" I beg miserably.

"You might feel better if you do." I shake my head in avid denial. "If you state your fear out loud then it loses its power over you. Just tell me. I won't judge you."

I turn my face aside so she can't see the tears tracking my cheeks. "Yes, you will," I tell her hoarsely, "because *I* judge me."

The soothing touch of her hand skims warmly against my face. She silently coaxes me to look at her again and, when I do, begins gently wiping away my tears. "You are my daughter. There is nothing you can do or say that will make me love you any less."

It is the combination of her touch, her tone and her pleading expression that make it impossible for me to disbelieve her. Before I've even decided what to say, everything comes spilling out of me. My friendship with Julien that turned out not to be a friendship at all, how I fell so blindly in love with him that I missed all the red flags and finally the details of my own self-destructive spiral. I tell her all of it, and when I'm done, I'm as empty and as numb as I was before I said anything. Nothing changes, and I think that must be the most disheartening realization of all.

To her credit, Mom absorbs my story with stoic calm. Her silence strikes me as thoughtful and tentative. I wonder if she's scared that one wrong word might send me sailing straight over the edge. She's not wrong in that assumption.

Finally, she takes my hand and sandwiches it gently between her own. "Iyah, I'm going to ask you some questions, and I need you to be very honest with me. These last few weeks…have you been using any protection with your sexual partners?"

Under normal circumstances, that question would have caused me to sink into the depths of my mattress out of pure mortification. I could have never imagined having this type of conversation with my mother in any capacity, not even under the threat of death. But at this second, I don't really care. And so, I answer her honestly and matter-of-factly.

"No. Not always. I don't really remember."

Again, she accepts my answer with remarkable composure. "Okay. The first thing we need to do is get you tested for STIs," she says.

"Does it matter?"

"Right now, you *think* it doesn't, but it will, Iyah. Eventually, it will."

"If you say so."

"What about drugs?"

I'm a little reluctant to admit the truth about that, and my answer comes slowly. "Some."

Her expression flickers, almost like she's physically pained. She swallows heavily. "Intravenous?"

"No, Mom. I'm not *that* stupid."

I'm sure she would heartily refute that statement if she weren't so busy slumping forward in exploding relief. "Thank God!"

"Hoo-Rah." She ignores my sarcasm and instead bends forward to scoop me up into an upright position. I'm not exactly thrilled about it, but I'm also not very motivated to fight her off either. "What are you doing?"

"Come on," she urges, quite literally manipulating my body so that I'm perched on the edge of my bed. "We need to get you cleaned up."

"Why?"

"I'm taking you to the hospital."

It's ten o'clock at night. I don't understand why an STD panel would necessitate a trip to the emergency department, which is the excuse she gives for dragging me out of bed. What she doesn't tell me is that she plans to have me petitioned and certified for a 24-hour hold pending a psychiatric evaluation. I find that out when I arrive, and the hospital staff confiscates all of my clothing and appoints me with a designated "sitter" while my mother explains to my father why she's decided to have me "committed."

I'm enraged over the deception, and that fury only grows when Dad and Ruben rally around her for "support." There is talk of four-point restraints and sedation before I finally calm down, but even when the screaming and kicking has mostly subsided, I'm still crying furious tears. The glare I give my mother is full of blazing hatred.

"I don't know why you're doing this! I'm not suicidal!"

"That's not what you told your nurse."

I told my nurse that I didn't care if I died, not that I had thoughts of harming myself or even had a plan for doing so. "That's a HIPAA violation!" I explode, "I want to talk to the hospital administrator now!"

"Iyah, calm down."

"I'm an adult! I did not consent! I want to leave!"

Before I can escalate further, my father is there beside me. I'm ready to attack him for the blustering lecture about "respecting my mother" that I know is coming. But he doesn't yell at me. Instead, he cradles my face in his large hands and for the first time I see the tears welling in his eyes. The realization that I've made my father cry subdues me in a way that nothing else has. The shame is overwhelming.

"Please don't fight us," he pleads with me, "We love you, Iyah. We want to help you."

"I don't need help."

"You do, sweetie. You *do*."

Another three weeks pass before I get to a place where I can admit that I *do* need help, first to myself and then to my family. The road to recovery involves counseling and prescription medication, a combination I am initially very resistant to trying. I thought that it would be enough that I was willing to rehabilitate myself into the land of the living again and that, thankfully, there were no lasting consequences from my last six months of stupid mistakes. No physical consequences anyway. Emotionally, though, I am wrecked.

That was the crux of my mother's argument for therapy in the first place, the reason she advocated for it so strongly. In the beginning, I was convinced that she was pushing an agenda. She was on another mental health crusade, and I wasn't going to be her guinea pig. I was dumped, and I was understandably sad about that, but it didn't warrant psychological counseling or medication. It never once occurred to me that I might be going through depression until I had my first therapy session. I thought I was just heartbroken.

I endure two months of twice weekly therapy, but it doesn't seem to fix much. I've yet to regain any true interest in anything, most especially acting. On the surface I've progressed since the days when I would vegetate in my bed for hours at a time. I have a job now as a checkout clerk at a local food market chain. I get up daily and shower and eat and go through the routine of the day. But nothing I do is motivated by actual desire.

"You should call Nicki," Mom suggests, "She stopped by to see you again."

"I'm not in the mood to socialize," I reply, "I'll call her later."

"What about auditions? Do you have any prospects?"

"No time," I tell her, "Too busy with work."

Sometimes when I want to torment myself (and that happens frequently these days), I'll scroll through Julien's Instagram page just to see what he's been up to. He is still beautiful. He's cut his hair again, but it isn't as short as when we first met. But his smile doesn't seem the same to me. It strikes me as very artificial now. Maybe his smile was always artificial, and I could never see it before.

Our film's debut has given him a modicum of public recognition and his follower count has increased dramatically over the past few months. I'm sure it's done the same for me, but I'm not nearly as interested in my own social media status as I am in his. Julien's career has been steadily advancing since we parted ways as he has multiple stills from recent jobs posted to his Instagram. But everything on his page is purely professional. There is nothing at all that hints about his private life. Based on the timeline, I suspect that he's likely married by now.

That hurts to think about, but I can't stop myself from Internet stalking him or scrolling through the dozens of selfies we took together while filming and during our trip to Atlanta...back when I was convinced that he was in love with me. It's borderline pathetic. And while I readily confess my secret shame to my therapist, I don't dare tell my family about this self-loathing little habit of mine. They already walk on eggshells around me. Even Ruben is uncharacteristically gentle in his approach, like he believes I'm so fragile that I'll fall to pieces if he even *looks* at me with aggravation.

I suppose to the outsider, I am barely holding it together. I would step carefully around me too. Then again, I've always been too impulsive and headstrong, but I used to think that was a strength. But after Julien, I'm not so keen on trusting my gut anymore.

My therapist suggests that I might want to stay away from Julien's social media page. Her theory is that I follow him out of some masochistic need to punish myself, but also because I want to be close to him. According to her, I can't truly begin to heal emotionally until I completely sever my unhealthy ties and move on from them. But I'm not ready to detach.

A turning point comes when I finally yield to my agent's incessant pestering, and I audition for a local commercial advertisement. I land the spot, and only then do I rediscover my love for being in front of the camera. It's slow and painful, but I get there in small, stumbling steps.

Before I know it, I have a part in a small theater production as an understudy for one of the supporting actresses. It is only a two-week gig, but it is enough to reignite my desire for the stage. That first part leads to more auditions until, remarkably, 2 days before my 24th birthday I'm given the most amazing career opportunity to date...a chance to play the role of Beneatha Younger in *A Raisin in the Sun*. The production is set to run for six full months. The only caveat is that it will premiere at the Gershwin Theater...in New York City.

My initial hesitancy to take the part has little to do with disinterest and everything to do with my irrational fear that I'll cross paths with Julien and Kate while I'm there. I'll need to relocate for the part, but the prospect of seeing Julien again paralyzes me with fear. Although I'm in a much better mental space, I am nowhere near ready to live in the same city as he does, let alone risk the chance of bumping into him on the street. It all seems too daunting. And, if that were not enough, my parents hate the idea.

"I don't think you should consider it at all," Dad advises me over breakfast, "There will be plenty of other opportunities for you."

"But don't you think I should try?"

Dad and Mom exchange an uncomfortable glance, and it makes me suspect that they have already been privately discussing this matter for a while now, long before they decided to broach the subject with me. My mother's next words confirm that suspicion. "I'm not sure if you're ready to be on your own just yet, Iyah. You don't want to move too fast."

Four months ago, even the mildest whisper that they sensed instability would have sent me flying into a rage, but today I accept their apprehension with a reticent sigh. "You're worried about me seeing him again, aren't you?" Neither of them nods in confirmation, but the answer is plain on both their faces. "I'm worried about that too."

My mother sags in relief. "Then don't go," she pleads.

Despite my own misgivings, I surprise myself by playing Devil's advocate. "It's a big city. Do you think he's letting *me* dictate his career choices?"

Dad responds with a dismissive grunt. "I don't care what *he* does. I care about *you*. I want you to stay happy and secure."

I lean over to press an affectionate kiss against his cheek. "Then let me figure out what I need to make that happen."

After I leave my parents in the kitchen to agonize over my latest life choices, I finally find the courage to call Nicki and explain myself. She is angry with me for shutting her out, but mostly relieved that I didn't ghost her permanently. She also admonishes me for giving her the impression I was having fun when I was really dying inside.

We talk for hours, and I deliberately refrain from asking her advice about my potential move to New York. After dodging her for months, petitioning her guidance now feels a little self-serving. I invite her to my birthday celebration happening later that evening instead. In the end, however, Nicki gives me good counsel even when I don't ask for it.

"People screw up, Iyah," she tells me, "You're human. Learn from your mistakes and keep trying anyway."

I know what I'm going to do after that conversation is over. I'm ready to put in the call to my agent but when I look at my phone, I notice a missed text message. It is from Julien.

My hands start to shake as I'm suddenly gripped by crippling anxiety. Months of absolute silence and *now* he reaches out. Not with an explanation. Not with an actual phone call either. He sends an emoji. A stupid, innocent birthday cake emoji. It seems like a simple gesture, but it's so full of unspoken implications that I can't even breathe.

He remembered my birthday. Even after so much time apart, he's thinking about me. That has to mean something, right? Without warning, I'm caught up again in that swirling vortex of need and yearning for him. Every bit of control that I've fought so hard to regain is beginning to slip from my grasp. I'm spiraling back into that dark, lonely place...

And then I catch myself. No. I can't let this happen again. I loved him. I still love him, but he isn't good for me. He was *never* good for me. And while he might be thinking about me now, he is undoubtedly married to someone else while he's doing it. That is the reality, and I can't afford to let myself forget that a second time.

Just that morning, I told my father that I needed to figure out for myself how to be happy. I know that being honest with myself is the first step. Reopening my heart to Julien won't allow me to accomplish that goal. He will stifle my growth. I have to shake him off for good.

I delete the text message and then I go even further by deleting the entire thread of messages from my phone. One by one, I go through the photos in my gallery, and I purge his images from there as well. I'm crying as I do it, but I'm also freed.

18

New York is a big city. Sometimes it feels like the narrow walkways overflowing with stone-faced pedestrians will swallow me up. A literal sea threatens to engulf me each time I take the subway. I never see the same faces twice, so it's only in hindsight that I realize the fear I held about crossing paths with Julien again was a little irrational.

My first two months in the city I was a nervous wreck. Every time I spotted a dark-haired white boy in my peripheral vision, I recoiled like a scalded cat. I constantly recited different scenarios in my head for how I would react if I found myself face to face with him again. Even my choice of residence was dictated by the rampant paranoia that I might see him. Not that I could ever afford to stay somewhere as pricey as Manhattan even *with* roommates, but at least Brooklyn felt far enough away to dramatically reduce the probability of running into him.

It was bad enough that I would occasionally see his likeness splashed across a random billboard ad or whenever I was casually flipping through a magazine while on the subway. The last thing I wanted was to deal with the living, breathing version of Julien Caffrey. However, about four months into my run as Beneatha Younger, my feelings about seeing him again shifted dramatically.

The critics lauded my performance. I was touted in the media as the newcomer who was taking New York's Broadway stage by storm. Suddenly, I wanted Julien to know I was there more than anything. I wanted him to know that I was *thriving* without him. I wanted him to know that I had shaken him off just as easily as he had shaken me off.

By my sixth month in New York, when my time as Beneatha was drawing to a close and the accolades had faded and I didn't have another acting gig in the works, I stopped thinking about Julien altogether. The competition for acting parts in New York was stiff. The initial buzz from my film with Julien had been the push I needed to land the part of Beneatha Younger, but it wasn't enough to maintain the momentum needed for an upward career trajectory. I wasn't the standard and not many acting parts were written with people who looked like me in mind. The reality was simple. I was going to have to keep proving myself over and over.

To my parents' disappointment, I decided to remain in New York to build my acting portfolio. Once I determined that was the long-term plan, my next order of business was to find a job to bridge the gap between bookings. I quickly found work as a barista with a local coffee house chain. Suffice it to say, that my father bemoaned "coffee shop girl" being the best I could do with a bachelor's degree, but I knew it would be much easier to maneuver time off from selling coffee than it would if I worked a traditional nine to five.

In the meantime, I worked occasionally as a photo double and background performer in a handful of productions. I no longer worried about Julien or kept myself preoccupied with what he might be doing. It was enough to worry about paying my bills. Life eventually settled into a predictable sort of monotony that I grew to appreciate. My day-to-day was manageable without surprises. I liked knowing what would happen next, which is precisely the reason I was so unprepared when my world turned sideways yet again.

There is no glory in customer service. Patrons are rude, impatient, and downright obnoxious most days. It is aggravating but that is the nature of my work, day after day, week after week. Until one day when a middle-aged woman three customers deep in the line at *my* register decided to go into cardiac arrest and collapse to the floor.

Being the child of two healthcare professionals who made sure both their children earned certifications in CPR for occasions just like this, as soon as the woman goes down, I dive over the counter to provide aid. My adrenaline is pumping as I begin compressions. I bark out orders to the gathering crowd around me, reciting the script that has been drilled into my head since I was fourteen years old. I'm on a strange sort of autopilot.

"You, in the purple sweater, call 911! You, near the swinging doors, find me an AED!"

It's like I'm in a movie, but every moment is crisp and real. The rigidity of the woman's chest wall creates a subtle resistance with each compression. Every awareness is amplified. The bluish gray tint to the woman's skin. The beads of sweat that trickle down my back from the effort it takes to deliver good, quality CPR. The mechanized voice of the AED repeating every two minutes, "No shock advised. Continue compressions." I hum the beat of the BeeGees' *Staying Alive* under my breath to maintain my rhythm and try not to think about how tired I am.

My arms feel like spaghetti. My back is on fire. There are gawkers pressing all around us, filming every second, but not a single one of them steps forward to help. I'm losing steam. This is a literal workout. I'm not sure I'll be able to keep this up much longer, but I'm terrified that this woman will die if I don't. But just when the last of my energy begins to ebb, blessed assistance comes in the form of two capable paramedics. I've never felt such relief in my life!

I briefly make eye contact with the most striking pair of green eyes I've ever seen before I'm shouldered aside with an authoritative, "We've got this now."

I'm good with being dismissed from my post. With grateful pants, I stumble back obediently and stagger to my feet, sweaty and exhausted. When I hobble back behind the counter my co-workers and several patrons welcome me with stunned applause, which I find mildly embarrassing given the paramedics are still actively working on the woman less than twenty feet away. I brace myself against the counter and struggle to catch my breath while they work, dimly aware that my co-worker, Gia, has moved to stand beside me.

"That was awesome!" she exclaims, "You saved that lady's life!" I'm not so sure about that assessment, but I *do* make the 6 o'clock evening news.

The next afternoon I arrive at work and discover my manager has my picture posted on the wall with the caption "local hero" underneath. I don't think I've ever experienced anything so cringeworthy in my life, and that's *before* he begins recounting my "feats of heroism" to every single patron who walks through the door. Unsurprisingly, I spend most of my shift awkward and self-conscious. I can't imagine the day can get any more embarrassing, but then I raise my head to greet my next customer in line and come face to face with a familiar pair of intense green eyes. I snap to instant attention.

"You're one of the medics from last night," I say, praying devoutly that he won't notice my picture on the wall. "How's that lady?"

"She's going to live thanks to you." He hitches his thumb towards my photo and my hope that he hadn't noticed dies a swift, ignominious death. "That was very quick thinking."

I would sink into the floor, but this is the first time that I'm really looking at the guy. His eyes are extraordinary, made even more so because the color is uncommon for someone with such dark skin. He is very tall, probably several inches over six feet, which only makes him seem like a giant in comparison to me. I hadn't noticed last night because we were both kneeling but now, I'm cognizant of how far back I must cock my head to maintain eye contact with him.

He's also unbelievably good-looking, almost too good-looking. I'm immediately repelled. My track record with "too good-looking" men is not the greatest. I'd rather not fall into that pretty boy trap again.

He has a smooth, even complexion with perfectly sculpted features, a neatly trimmed goatee, and beautifully full lips. Some might even describe his lips as kissable, but I'm too cognizant of his cocky smirk to pay much notice. It's clear to me that he is very aware of his own beauty and expects others to take notice as well. Very likely, he's used to women fawning all over him. He probably expects the same reaction from me. If he does, he picked the wrong girl.

"I didn't really do anything other than buy her some time," I reply, dismissing his earlier assertion. "But I'm glad she's going to be alright. That was scary!"

"You handled yourself like a pro. It's not every day a barista administers good quality CPR," he praises me with a smile. "Where did you learn that..." He leans in dramatically to read my name tag, "...Iyah?"

It takes every ounce of willpower I have not to roll my eyes into eternity. "From a class..." I reply, sarcastically leaning forward to read his name tag in a similar manner, "*Hez*. I get recertified every 2 years. Did you want to order something or what? I have a line."

He seems a little surprised when a quick glance over his shoulder validates the veracity of my claim. But after he rattles off an order for a black coffee and a pastry, he continues to chat me up as if the growing line behind him doesn't exist. I mask my annoyance behind a polite smile.

"So, what's your deal?" he asks when I'm done ringing him up, "Do you have a medical background? Most civilians don't take CPR classes for the hell of it."

I step away from the register to put together his order, aware that the crowd behind him is starting to grow impatient. Mindful, I keep my answer brusque and to the point. "My parents are in healthcare."

"That explains it then," he says when I pass him the coffee and pastry. However, he doesn't move away from the counter after that. Instead, he lingers as does his grin. I stare at him impatiently, but his smile only widens. "Thank you for the coffee and danish, *Iyah*," he says meaningfully.

The way he keeps placing special emphasis on my name is getting on my nerves, and I manifest that aggravation when I reply, "You're welcome, *Hez*."

Gia is quick to sidle up against me after he finally departs just before I greet my next customer. "I think he likes you," she giggles.

"I couldn't care less."

Six hours later when I'm finished with my shift and locking up the coffee shop, I spot him loitering on the sidewalk next to his emergency vehicle. I stop short and tense at the sight of him, my fingers curling reflexively around the small can of pepper spray I keep in my jacket pocket. If this guy has it in his mind that he's going to snatch me tonight, he's going to work hard for this kidnapping.

"Can I help you?" I demand rather aggressively.

"I was hoping we could talk."

"Why?"

He emits a stunned laugh, as if he's thrown off balance by my surly response. "What do you mean 'why?' That's what people do when they want to get to know someone better."

"Again...*why*?"

"At the risk of turning you off, I thought maybe we could get a coffee to—,"

I'm already shaking my head in refusal before he can finish making the offer. "No."

"Slice of pizza?"

"Also no. Have a good night."

As I start to walk past him, he stares down at me with a puzzled look. "Did I do something to offend you?"

"Other than thinking you're God's gift to women? No. Not at all," I reply flippantly, not even breaking my stride. I don't know why I'm surprised when he falls into step next to me. "And what kind of name is 'Hez,' anyway? Am I supposed to be impressed?"

"I can't tell you what it's short for. You'll judge me."

"Doubtful."

"It's Hezekiah. My name is Hezekiah."

His doleful tone stops me in my tracks and almost makes me smile. *Almost.* "Tell me your mom is religious without telling me your mom is religious," I tease him.

"Or tell me you paid attention in Sunday school without telling me you paid attention," he counters with a smile, "And my *grandmother* is the religious one. Unfortunately, I'm a junior. My dad had to carry this name first."

"He was a good king and was favored by God," I remind him, "You should be honored."

I don't know how I've gone from annoyed and aggressive to tolerant and almost smiling, but here I am, and I don't really like it either. This was how it started with Julien too and look how well that ended. The last thing that I want is to get involved in another romantic entanglement. I'm still trying to regain my lost dignity from the last one. I'm not interested in dating, possibly never again for the rest of my life! I make that perfectly clear to Hezekiah Dennis from the outset.

But no matter how many times I turn the man down or reject his numerous requests to join him for coffee, pizza, a walk in the park, a movie, he keeps coming back for more. Part of me wonders if he's intrigued by the challenge, the idea that there is a woman in existence who isn't instantly charmed by him. He obviously likes the chase and, if I'm being honest, I like being chased for a change. I like the harmless flirtation that develops between us strictly because of its superficial nature. It's fun without sacrifice.

I would have gladly played our little game indefinitely, but one day everything inexplicably changes. I'm not sure when things start to become serious for Hez, but once it happens, I'm not really prepared for the shift from him. I'm not ready for how vulnerable his interest makes me feel.

"When are you going to let me take you out?" he asks me after I close up the coffee shop for the night.

"On the 32nd of Nevuary. Put it in your phone." I laugh at my own joke.

But he doesn't. He doesn't smile either. Instead, he comes to stand behind me while I sweep the floor. He plucks the broom from my fingers, giving me few options except to turn and face him.

"I'm not playing around, Iyah. I want us to be something more."

"I already told you that I can't."

"Why not?"

"Did you ever consider that maybe I'm not into you?"

"That's a lie," he refutes in a superior tone, "You've wanted me since day one."

I roll my eyes and snatch back the broom. "Boy, bye."

"Go out on one date with me," he insists, green eyes beseeching. "Just one. If it's a disaster, I'll never ask you again."

Against my better judgment, I yield to his coaxing…and, unfortunately, it is *not* a disaster. I can't rightly say that I fall in love with him. There isn't an electric moment of instant connection, no constant yearning simmering beneath the surface.

It's nothing like what I felt for Julien. The attachment I develop for Hez is quiet and gradual, like the slow, inevitable erosion of rock by the trickling stream over time. He progressively shifts from someone I share casual laughs with to someone who makes me laugh, from someone I occasionally hang out with to pass the time to someone I want to be with all the time.

It is the first time since Julien that I've felt anything close to romantic desire, the first time I've *wanted* to have it again. I'm relieved to learn that I'm still capable of that depth of emotion because, for a long while, the inclination was dead. I had started to believe it would never be resurrected, but Hez has woken something up in me. And I might have been able to grow into that realization if Hez and I continued progressing at that slow, steady trickle but, as is quickly becoming the standard with us, he is ready to move forward much sooner than I am.

"We should live together."

Hez and I are snuggled together under a fleece blanket, curled up on his living room couch, half asleep, our naked skin bathed in ethereal blue light from his television screen. We have been dating for four and a half months, but we've only recently become lovers. Lately, I've begun toying with the idea of taking him home to meet my parents. I'm getting there at my own pace, but then he asks me to move in with him and it's like being doused with cold water.

All drowsiness is chased away in that instant, and I twist around to face him with a deep scowl. "Where did *that* come from?"

"Your roommates drive you crazy. You're here practically every night," he argues, "Half your stuff is here. It makes sense."

I pull the blanket more securely around me and scoot to the opposite side of the sofa to regard him warily. "I don't know if we're ready for that."

"We've been together almost five months."

"That's not a long time, Hez."

"It's long enough to know I love you."

To hear him say the words out loud freaks me out though I can't put my finger on the reason. But it's something that I never wanted or asked for. The avowal flips a switch inside of me, and I'm struck with the sudden impulse to run. I'm already scrambling off of the sofa and wiggling back into my clothes before I've even put a name on what I'm feeling. Panic. Pure, unrestrained panic. Hez watches me dress in speechless confusion.

"What are you doing?"

"I'm going home."

"Because I said 'I love you'?" he bursts out incredulously.

"Because you're always pushing," I retort, snatching up my coat and shrugging into it. "You do too much! You can't leave well enough alone!"

"I'm not always pushing, Iyah," he replies very quietly and sadly, "*You're* always running."

Two days go by without seeing or speaking to Hez. The enforced reprieve affords me plenty of time to think about his accusation. I've recently landed a supporting role in a small musical production and, though I've been busy with show rehearsals and nightly performances, my fight with Hez has me moody and distracted. Is he right? Am I running from love?

I've never told him about Julien, and that was a deliberate choice on my part. Some of that silence is due to shame. Who wants to admit to falling for a guy who was unavailable from the start? But part of it is because I still haven't resolved my feelings for him.

There was a time when I obsessed over Julien every day. He invaded my every waking thought and plagued my dreams. I've reached a point now where he hardly enters my mind anymore, where the sight of his face in a magazine doesn't make me catch my breath. But the ache in my heart over him remains. It's not nearly as fierce as it once was. After all, I haven't seen him in close to two years, but I'm not over him. And, because I know that, I'm hesitant to commit to someone else when my feelings for Julien are still so muddy.

But, at the same time, it seems ridiculous to rob myself of possible happiness for a man I will likely never cross paths with again in my life. I'm endangering a good thing now, a *stable* relationship and for what? Regret? Penance?

Hez is exactly the sort of young man my parents would approve of. He's a "good, God-fearing boy" as my father would say. Husband material. I have no doubts that my parents will love him when they meet him. He and Ruben will become fast friends too. Hez is supportive and devoted, and he loves me. What more could I want?

That night, after my performance is over, I'm prepared to call him and grovel for his forgiveness, but he's already waiting for me. He's congregated with the crowd of fans milling about for after show autographs and pictures. I indulge a few of them before I make my way over to him though I barely process a single second because I'm too focused on Hez. When I finally close the distance between us my palms are clammy.

"Hey," I greet inanely, "I thought you were working tonight."

"I'm on call."

"I...overreacted the other night," I begin in tentative apology. He merely grunts his agreement to that, but nods for me to continue. "I have a fear of commitment."

"You think?"

"I've made very bad choices in the past. I don't want to make any more mistakes."

"Do you think I'm a mistake?"

"No," I tell him thickly, "You're not a mistake. And that's the problem."

"Why is that a problem?"

"Because you might be *more* than I deserve."

The rigidity finally eases from his shoulders, and he draws me into his arms for a kiss that is both reassuring and fervent. Security and comfort envelop me. It's the first time in a very long while that I'm not seized by panic or dread. This thing I have with him might be alright after all. Maybe I might be alright too. Hez's next words to me solidify that budding hope.

"You don't have to be afraid. I'm not going to hurt you," he whispers against my lips, "You believe me, don't you?"

"I'm getting there."

My preference is to go back to his place and spend the rest of the night in his arms, but Hez yields to my castmates' insistence that we all go out for pizza and beer instead. He's a social butterfly by nature and constantly encourages me to broaden my friend circle. It helps that I've grown very fond of my castmates on this production which makes building friendships easier. They have also grown fond of Hez.

It's a blustery night in New York City with windy gusts and intermittent bursts of snow flurries. Being from Michigan, I'm used to bitter cold, but I'm still a bit daunted when I step out into the artic night. My chosen attire of black leggings, oversized sweater, boots, and leather jacket are a meager barrier against the frigid temperatures.

Hez admonishes me for being underdressed, especially because I've also chosen to go without a hat. He doesn't seem to buy my argument that my hair, in all its natural, fluffy glory, is warmth enough. And so, I indulge him when he insists that I take his scarf and his gloves.

"But then what are *you* going to do?" I argue as he secures his scarf around my neck between sweet, nibbling kisses. "You're going to get frostbite."

"I'll be fine," he whispers against my mouth, "I gotta keep my girl warm."

"You guys should really get a room," one of my castmate's jokes from behind us.

I'm just about to deliver a sassy retort when a sudden burst of wind abruptly snatches one of Hez's gloves out of my hand and sends it tumbling down the sidewalk into a sea of pedestrians. "Damn it!"

I dive for the glove as it goes tumbling down the walkway. I'm like a lone salmon fighting to swim upstream while the glove is knocked and tossed haplessly across the feet of impatient passersby. I'm vaguely aware of Hez behind me, but I'm so focused on not losing the glove that I don't give heed to his calls to "let it go."

In hindsight, I truly wish that I had. Because when that soft scrap of leather finally comes to a halt against the ankle of a men's designer boot, it is quickly retrieved by the owner of that boot just as I make one, last desperate grab for it. As soon as I look up, however, every coherent thought scatters from my brain. My breathless "thank you" and my thudding heart simultaneously lodge in my throat when I come face to face with my unlikely savior. I don't doubt my shock and panic are plainly visible.

Standing less than two feet in front of me and smiling as if no time, regret, or bitterness has passed between us at all, is Julien Caffrey.

Part Two

Julien

19

Eighteen and a half months earlier

I'm in love with her.

I've been coming to the realization for a while now, though I can't really pinpoint when things started to change. Maybe that night in her room when we watched *Nacho Libre*. Or maybe it was when her long list of peeves stopped being mildly annoying and became amusing and endearing instead. It could have happened even before that, back during the late nights when we would lie out on the poolside beach chairs and tell each other our darkest secrets.

Not that Iyah's secrets are all that dark. In fact, they are rather tame compared to my own. Her biggest problem is that she places too much pressure on herself. She works too hard to live up to other people's expectations of her, and often feels like a failure when she doesn't.

She rarely relinquishes that tight band of control that she holds over herself…except with me. When she's with me, Iyah is free to be as insecure and indecisive as she wants. I love that I have the privilege of witnessing that vulnerability about her. It's not that I celebrate her perceived weaknesses, but I value granting her the autonomy to say her quiet parts out loud. She knows I won't judge her. I won't try to silence her either. It's not surprising that she became my best friend long before I ever realized I was attracted to her.

Iyah is a beautiful, contradictory mix of innocence and fire, sweetness and spark. Sometimes she displays sage-like wisdom. And other times, she can be the pettiest person I've ever known. She's quick to argue, but not above admitting when she's wrong too. Iyah was easy to like from the beginning, even with her enduring crankiness. I recognized the protective shell she'd built around herself early on. Once I was able to burrow past her gruff exterior, she was even easier to love.

Having her nestled against me and watching her sleep feels like a rare privilege. I try to make a list in my head of all the reasons I adore her, and I can't. I can't spell out a single thing because it is *everything* about her. It's just Iyah.

Because she lectures me. Because she's passionate about everything she does. Because she can be both mature and childish at the same time. Because she does that haughty head tilt when she's about to put me in my place. We are compatible in all the ways that are meaningful. Artistically, emotionally, and now sexually.

With Kate, my reasons for loving her have always been logical, reasonable. There is a sensible foundation for why I should love her…why I still *do* love her. When we met, she was kind and considerate and thoughtful. She welcomed me, an outsider, into her home and family without resentment. She befriended me when I didn't have a single friend in the world.

I am grateful to her. I will always be grateful to her. But it is only now that I recognize that the gratitude I feel is not love. At least, it's not what I feel for Iyah. Not even close.

As much as I dread it, I know I can't put off the conversation with Kate any longer. She deserves better than to be treated like an afterthought. And Iyah deserves more than to be treated like a secret. By delaying the inevitable, I'm doing a disservice to them both.

But *knowing* what I have to do and *doing* what I have to do are two very different animals. My feelings aren't ambiguous. I'm not undecided. It's the execution that makes me hesitant. I'm not only breaking ties with Kate. I will be breaking ties with her family. *My* family. The only stable household that I've ever known.

The Lelands took me in when I was a truant runaway with a sketchy past. They sheltered me. I can't fully expect them to continue sheltering me after I've shattered their youngest daughter's heart. It's going to be messy. I'm not ready for the mess.

I need a cigarette. Just to calm my nerves. Just to think rationally. I've been sneaking them for the past week already. The tumble off the proverbial wagon happened right after Kate confronted me about those journals.

I'm infuriated that she read them, and I've mostly leaned into that anger because it distracts me from the guilt. When I close my eyes though, I can picture the anguish on Kate's face clearly. Nicotine helps to manage the guilt and shame that come with the memory. I'm disappointed in myself. But my greatest concern is that Iyah doesn't know. She's proud of me, and I don't want to disillusion her too. I've already failed her enough.

Iyah is one of the strongest, bravest people I know. She's not afraid to make her own rules, even when met with disapproval and resistance. Her decision to pursue acting rather than a more lucrative career is testimony to that. She doesn't fear the wreckage she might leave behind her, at least not enough to dissuade her from her goals. I'm not sure if that's an admirable trait, or a selfish one, but I need to embody that same spirit now. Regardless of the consequences, I know I can't marry Kate.

Once I've managed to tamp down my craving for nicotine, I finally roll from the bed and pull on my jeans. It seems mildly disrespectful to end my engagement in the nude. It's bad enough that I'm doing it over the phone with Iyah sleeping less than six feet away from me.

With that harsh reminder of what an *awful* person I am, I almost talk myself out of it. Before I lose my nerve, I snatch up my phone from the nightstand and scroll through my favorites for Kate's contact. She answers immediately. I wonder if she's been sitting there with her cell phone in hand just waiting for my call. The thought makes me sick with guilt.

"Hey," I say because I can't think of any other greeting to befit this moment.

"Hey," she replies. Her voice is shaky and hoarse. It sounds like she's been crying. I know that's because of me. "I was beginning to think I wasn't going to hear from you."

"I've been putting this off."

She sighs my name. Her tone is earnest and weary when she says, "I think we both said things we didn't mean."

"Did we?"

"If you say you're not sleeping with her, then I believe you, Julien."

"Kate, please..." I can't let her absolve me when I've proven that claim a total lie. If I'm honest, it was a lie before I ever touched Iyah. Because I wanted it. In my heart, I've always wanted it.

She immediately begins justifying her actions, and I don't say a word. What can I say? I don't have a leg to stand on here.

"You have to put yourself in my shoes!" she cries, her voice breaking with emotion, "All those things you wrote about her... I felt blindsided! Obviously, you feel *something*."

"You're right," I whisper, "I do feel something."

"So, what is it? Is...is it lust? Is this a physical thing or...is it something else?"

222

"It's something else." My throat suddenly feels constricted and dry, and my words catch there as I continue to explain. "I think…um, I *know* that I want to be with her. I *am* with her, Kate."

"You're with her?" she echoes woodenly.

"Yes. I thought you should know."

She becomes very quiet after that. I can almost hear her thoughts processing the magnitude of what I've just admitted. I know the exact moment when it all comes together for her. There is an audible hitch in her breathing, a subtle quickening as she slowly begins to see the whole picture.

"You slept with her, didn't you?" Her delivery is matter of fact, almost eerily calm. "Is that what you're telling me? Did you sleep with her, Julien?"

"Yeah. Yeah, I did."

Only then does she explode, and when she does it is like a wild, wounded animal lashing out. She's screaming and cursing and crying all at once, her words so garbled that I can barely understand them. "You liar!" she weeps hysterically, "You lying son of a bitch! You looked me in the face and said you were friends and that was all! You said that you were just 'mixed up' about your feelings! And this entire time I've been blaming myself because I thought *I* was the wrong one! *I* was the one being ridiculous! My God, Julien! *Why are you doing this to me?*"

"I don't know…I wasn't planning for it to happen…"

"You weren't *planning* it?" she scoffs tearfully, "That's your excuse?"

"I was being honest with you when I said that nothing had happened between us before!" I insist vehemently, "That wasn't a lie! There was nothing going on! Not until last night."

"So, basically I gave you an excuse to do what you wanted to do the whole time."

She's drilled straight to the center of truth, but I don't want to acknowledge it. "That's not what happened."

"Like hell it isn't! It's been *two* days! You couldn't even wait! I read your journals, remember! I *saw* the text messages on your phone! You've been cheating with her since the beginning!"

"No…"

"How long?" she snaps, "How long have you been screwing her? Just be honest with me!"

"I already told you," I insist quietly, "I didn't do this to punish you, Kate. It's not you. It's me."

"I know damn well it's not me! I can't believe you!" she sobs, "I can't believe you would do this to me! We're supposed to get married! *God*!"

"I don't know what you want me to say."

"Tell me why? What did I do wrong? I don't understand!"

"You didn't do anything wrong. It just happened. I tried to stay away from her, Kate! I really did! I've tried to fight what I was feeling every day!"

"No, you didn't! You fed those feelings! Don't think for a moment that you didn't feed them, Julien!"

"I'm sorry. I'm trying to be honest with you."

"Stop saying that! You're a liar and you're a cheater, and I hate you! I hate you so much right now!"

The words hurt more than I care to admit, particularly because I know she means them. "If you really feel that way then maybe it's a good thing that we're calling it off."

"And maybe *you* should try being honest with yourself for a change," she sniffles tersely, "I know what you're doing. You're blowing it all to hell because you're scared. You *always* do this. For as long as I've known you. I understand that about you. Does she?"

The accusation chips away at my fragile outer shell and causes me to question myself though I say nothing. My silence is hardly a deterrent. Kate does not relent.

"We've been together for more than two years. I know you inside and out. You've known her less than six months! If you can't make it work with me, do you honestly think you can make it work with her?"

She ends the call after that, and I'm not surprised. It's her "gotcha" moment, and there's nothing I can say to refute her. After all, she's right. She *does* know me inside and out, just like she knows her words have homed in on every secret insecurity I have.

I am a perpetual screw-up. This is a fact I've long known about myself. I do it well. I do it without even half trying. And I especially manage to screw up the things I happen to cherish the most...like my relationship with Kate.

When I made the decision to propose to her, it felt like taking my first legitimate steps towards manhood. It was the first time in my life when I felt stable and accomplished, like an actual adult capable of making good decisions. Kate was a good decision. She felt inevitable. That she and I would eventually tie the knot was always a foregone conclusion. We've been inseparable since the moment her father brought me into their home. We were Julien and Kate, Kate and Julien, one single, breathing entity almost from our inception.

Kate became an ally, then a true friend, then my lover. The first time I experienced sex that wasn't purely transactional was with her. She made me feel shiny and new and clean. The natural progression towards matrimony seemed fated. I never once questioned it or questioned us and our future together until I met Iyah.

I do try a few times to call Kate back, but the effort is half-hearted at best. I have no idea what I'm going to say even if she does answer my call. My decision won't change. We are over. I can't go back. Not after Iyah.

Left with few options then, I reluctantly put in a call to her older brother instead. Ted will rightly want to kick my ass when he finds out what I've done. I'm not keen on confessing though. I'll leave it to Kate to paint me as the heartless, cheating liar that she believes I am. Maybe she's right.

When he answers, he sounds groggy, like I woke him out of a dead sleep. I don't realize how late it is. It's close to 2 a.m. where he is right now. I definitely woke him after all.

He's not angry when he greets me, only alarmed and frantic. Somehow his worry makes everything worse. "Julien? Everything okay? It's 2 o'clock."

"Yeah. I know it's late. Sorry."

"No. It's fine. I know you wouldn't call unless it was important. What's up?"

"Can you check on Katie for me?"

Ted is a bit slower to answer this time. When he does, he sounds much more alert. "What happened?"

"Nothing. We had a fight."

"Another one?" he groans in consternation, "Look, you guys are going to have to learn how to compromise with each other. That doesn't mean that you're going to do everything Katie wants you to do or vice versa. I can't keep playing mediator!"

"I get it."

"But I'll check on her…make sure she hasn't done something foolish."

"Good. Thanks."

When I end the call, I'm saddened because I'm pretty sure that was the last decent conversation I'm going to have with Theodore Leland. He's going to hate my guts before the night is through. I don't blame him either. I'm also filled with self-disgust over my actions. It's been a very long time since I've felt this revolted to be in my own skin. After the Lelands took me in, I almost believed I would never feel this way again. But you can never fully escape your roots, can you?

I look over at Iyah. She's slept through it all, sweet and oblivious. She has no idea what she's signed herself up for. I've done a superb job of concealing from her just how screwed up I truly am.

It's funny because she knows everything, the darkest, most twisted parts of my past, things I've never shared with anyone, not even Kate. And it was easy to share those things because I knew that Iyah would hear me without judgment. For all her lofty "standards," Iyah Grandberry is one of the least judgmental people I know. It's an admirable quality and the thing that made me so determined not to weigh her down with my emotional baggage.

I know it annoys her when I'm glib about my past, but that has always been a deliberate choice on my part. I refuse to wallow. But my dismissive attitude is also born out of self-preservation. I must constantly strip off the shame that follows me like a shroud. There's the Julien I used to be and the Julien I am now, and I never want those two personas to touch at all. But then there are times like this, like now when old Julien and new Julien feel exactly the same.

As soon as my thoughts start rolling down that dark, winding road I know I've got to get out of there. I need some distance. I need to think. I need time to convince myself that I'm not about to lose everything in the world that matters to me, most importantly the girl sleeping so

227

soundly only a few feet away. I take advantage of that naïve slumber and slip out onto the balcony for a few hits of nicotine and clarity.

I'm going to mess this up. Kate's words are clanging around in my head non-stop. *If you can't make it work with me, do you honestly think you can make it work with her?* Do I? Look how reckless I've been already! Kate called out my actions squarely. I have pushed and pushed, whether subtly or outright, until I had what I wanted all along…Iyah in my bed.

Kate's perception was spot on when she said she had provided me with an excuse. I knew I was going to sleep with Iyah from the moment I boarded the plane for L.A. I hadn't known it would be last night, but I'd made up my mind that I was going to have her and screw the consequences.

And I don't regret it. Being with Iyah does *not* feel wrong. It never has. Then again, it hadn't felt wrong to be with Kate either. At one point, I had been sure *she* was what I wanted too, *all* I wanted. Now I've taken a torch to everything we had without even blinking. I've proven to myself that I'm capable of that type of destruction. Clearly, I'm incapable of loyalty. Do I really want to risk doing the same thing to Iyah?

I'm terrified of finding myself back in this same place again. There will be other movies and more co-stars and grueling schedules that stretch on for weeks or even months at a time. We won't be in the same place. We might even end up on different continents depending on the job. Is that constant distance going to break Iyah and me the same way it broke me and Kate?

I remind myself that it hasn't happened yet. In the last six months, Iyah and I have only spent a handful of times together in person. Our relationship has largely persevered through phone calls and text messages. Until very recently, we hadn't even kissed. Despite all of that, my love for her has remained like a fire. It burned white hot, powerful and electric. It still burns.

Because I fed it. That's what Kate said. And it's true. I've nurtured what I created with Iyah as opposed to cherishing what I had with Kate. So, what kind of man does that make me…is it the kind of man I want to be? Is that even the type of man that Iyah deserves? I'm still pondering all of those questions when she steps out onto the balcony to join me.

By then I'm already on my third cigarette, and I don't bother to hide that from her. "Don't give me a hard time about it. I'm not in the mood."

My tone is needlessly combative, and I know it. She doesn't deserve my attitude. This isn't her mess. It's mine. She's just the innocent bystander being dragged along for the ride. And maybe that's why I'm so abrupt with her. Maybe I want to provoke a fight. Maybe then she'll leave me because I sure as hell don't have the strength to leave her.

"I heard you on the phone," she whispers, and I cringe inwardly to know she was cognizant of any of it. I know what her next question will be even before the hesitant delivery. "Is it over?"

I blink away the sudden tears that blur my vision. "Yep."

"How do you feel?"

The fact that she's asking after *me* when I was the one to blow someone else's life apart feels ironic. The concern is certainly undeserved. "Like shit!" I tell her forthrightly.

From the corner of my eye, I see her move closer and I reflexively dance out of her reach. I can't let her touch me. I don't deserve her comfort, but I'm greedy and I know I'll take it. I'll let her kiss me and hold me. I'll have her right here on this balcony because I want to feel the good that only *she* makes me feel. It's a selfish inclination. *I'm* selfish.

And suddenly I need Iyah to see that. I need her to know that I'm no good for her. I'm no good for anyone. "I broke her tonight. She was nothing but good to me. She didn't deserve it." She whispers my name in that soft, chiding way that she does when she thinks I'm being ridiculous, but I can't let her absolve me anymore than I could allow Kate.

"And I can't figure out *why* I did it," I lament out loud, more to myself than to Iyah, "It's not her. It's *me*. *I'm* the one who's screwed up, you know?"

"You can't help how you feel."

I don't think I even realize how trivial and weak that argument sounds until I hear her make it on my behalf. "I didn't even try. I didn't try hard enough to stay away from you."

Her expression changes, becoming perceptive and wary. It's like she can sense my intention to pull away from her even before I've completely made up my mind to do it. She takes a step backwards, a small frown forming.

"What are you saying?"

"I don't know…maybe this was a mistake."

That is a lie. The words taste like ash in my mouth. Even now, in the aftermath of all this chaos, we don't feel like a mistake. Not to me. Most certainly for her though. *She's* the one being shortchanged in this scenario, and she doesn't even know it. But she won't see it. I have to *make* her see it. Still, I can't look her in the eye while I say these things because none of it is true. It will *never* be true.

"Maybe what we're doing together is a mistake."

To her credit, Iyah doesn't snap right away. She grants me patience and grace in this moment. But I know her. The fire leaping behind her eyes is imminent. This is only the calm before the storm. I'm about to blow her world apart too.

"Do you want to be alone?" she asks softly, as if retreat at this point will fix anything.

I answer her as honestly as I can. "I don't know. I just feel like…maybe you and I should back things up a little."

She blinks at me like I've just spoken another language. "Back things up?"

"I was with her for 2 years, Iyah! I asked her to marry me! I thought we were going to be together for the rest of our lives. I wanted that. I don't know where that feeling went."

"Do you want to get it back?"

The conversation goes downhill quickly from there. When she asks me if I want to break up with her, I tell her that it's what I want. I give her the impression that I mean to go back to Kate and make it work with her when all I really want is for Iyah to find someone better than me. And it's awful to watch her fall apart only to become reserved and cold because she believes it's all been a lie. Because she doesn't think I love her when the truth is so much more complicated than that.

Because it's very possible, I'm going to love her for the rest of my life.

20

There's no one to pick me up from the airport when I arrive home. This does not come as an unexpected surprise. In the last twelve days, I've accumulated about 50 missed calls and over a dozen voicemails and unread text messages from various members of the Leland clan. I've allowed them to accumulate on purpose. Every single person is, no doubt, eager to tell me what a worthless human being I am. They should have saved themselves the effort. I'm already painfully aware.

By chance, I glanced at one message from Ted purely by accident. Several harsh expletives jumped out at me before I swiped it away. Maybe I'm a coward, but I don't want to know how much the Leland clan hates me. I don't want to imagine the discussion between Kate and her parents when she told them that, not only had I cheated on her, but I had also called off the wedding...a wedding that was less than 7 weeks away.

Kate settled on her wedding dress months ago, but now her aunt is hand-stitching her veil. The venue has been chosen. All the necessary deposits to the various vendors have been paid. 75% of our guest list has already RSVP'd. As far as everyone else is concerned, it's a done deal. I am the lone dissenter. I'm the one who's caused this mayhem.

Under the circumstances, I have no reason to expect any sort of warm welcome upon my return. That doesn't stop me from hoping for a little grace. The best-case scenario is that I'll be able to grab my stuff and my dog from our Manhattan apartment and creep out of sight without further incident. That's unlikely to happen. The worst-case scenario (and the outcome I'm expecting) is that her entire family will be there waiting when I arrive. An hour-long free-for-all drama fest most certainly awaits me. I'm fresh out of emotional stamina for that, especially after the last confrontation I had with Iyah.

I can't believe that she and I were in Atlanta together a little less than a month ago. They were the most perfect three days imaginable, second only to those first two days of our film promotion. I never anticipated that it would go to hell so quickly and irreversibly. That was all *my* fault of course. I have to live with that.

Her constant drinking worried me. It was too reminiscent of my mother. She had used alcohol to cope with her emotional pain too, and that had resulted in a living hell for me. I hadn't wanted to see Iyah follow that same path.

I've seen Iyah drunk on several occasions. Those were carefree incidences when she had just a little too much to the point of giggling intoxication. Her recent drinking was nothing like that. She spent practically every day of our last week together with a glass in her hand. And while that might not be something completely out of the ordinary given that she's in her early twenties, it was impossible to ignore the reason *why* she was drinking. She wasn't having fun. She was numbing herself.

That killed me. As remote as she'd been, I didn't doubt that I'd hurt her. But when I tried to address it, hell, when I wanted to take it all back, she had blown me off. I know I have no right to be bothered by her dismissal. I lost the moral ground to be jealous or angry because she threw herself at every guy who wandered across her path that last week of the promotional tour. But it *did* piss me off. It was one thing to be hurt, but quite another to act as if we hadn't been insatiable for one another those first two days. The sharp turnaround was a little disorienting.

Maybe it's childish and irrational, but…I'm aggravated by her indifference. I wouldn't have welcomed tears and confrontation, but I'd have preferred that to glacial detachment. As hot and greedy as she had been for my touch before, Iyah was equally repulsed to be near me afterwards.

I get it. The thing my girl hates more than anything is being vulnerable, especially with someone she doesn't believe is worthy of her tears or time. And she's decided that I don't deserve either. I'm nothing to her now. If she had been torn up with anguished misery that would have broken me, but at least I'd know she gave an actual fuck.

Quite frankly, I don't have the reserves for going through something similar with Kate. I'd rather not face her at all. That might be selfish and entitled of me, but I have nothing left to give her or anyone else for that matter.

In the taxi on my way to the apartment, I make plans to crash with a friend until I can figure out my next move. Once that's done, I rehearse what I plan to say to Kate when I see her again. Or rather, I rehearse how I'm going to listen. There's nothing I can really say at this point. I fell in love with Iyah. I broke every promise I ever made to Kate when I slept with her. There's no erasing that.

Even if Kate and I were somehow able to move beyond that massive betrayal, there is no reconciling the fact that I want to be with someone else. Iyah and I might not ever lay eyes on one another again, but I know without question that I will always want her. I've come to terms with that truth for myself. I'm dreading the prospect of making Kate understand it.

234

Although the trip from La Guardia Airport to Midtown takes close to 50 minutes in rush hour traffic, it feels as if it goes by in a blink. I'm not anywhere near to having myself together when the taxi comes to a stop. There is a small part of me, the reckless, irresponsible part that just wants to say, "screw it," and disappear into the ether. It wouldn't be the first time I've ghosted people who love me. But there is a larger part of me, the responsible adult part that recognizes that I need to accept the consequences of my actions.

Once I exit the cab, I stand there on the sidewalk for a long time and contemplate the high-rise apartment that I've called home for more than a year now. This is the first place Kate and I purchased together. It will also be the last.

I can still remember how excited we were when we found it. A 740 square ft apartment that offered such amenities as a game room, in-house fitness center, indoor pool and rooftop terrace was a good deal for a young couple starting out. We didn't even have to pay an additional deposit for Scruff. A single bedroom had been all we needed because we weren't planning on having children together for some years to come. At least that had been the plan until Kate decided to revise it.

There was a time when I believed that was the thing that started this whole spiral. Disagreements about kids. Disagreements about careers. Disagreements about personal choices. It seemed that Kate was going in one direction, and I was going in another. Back then, it never crossed my mind that we wouldn't eventually find our way back to the same place. I never anticipated that one day I wouldn't even want to.

It takes me a few minutes to finally propel my legs into movement. I buzz past the doorman and begin the long, lonely ascent towards the 25th floor. Once I'm just outside of our unit, I pause and take a deep breath before letting myself inside.

Before I even clear the door, Scruff begins a frenzied barking. I vaguely note the two pieces of luggage and single duffel bag lined up neatly against the foyer wall as he comes skidding across the polished hardwood floors to greet me. His tail is wagging exuberantly while I scratch his belly and ears. I tolerate the enthusiastic flicks of his tongue, but if I'm honest the attention I give him is half-hearted. I'm too aware of a pale-faced Kate huddled in her mother's arms on the living room sofa while her older sister stands vigil over them both.

As soon as Kate spots me, she bolts off the sofa and goes sprinting towards the bedroom. "I don't want to see him!"

Her mother spares me a sorrowful, disappointed look before she goes after her and the bedroom door slams, muffling Kate's miserable sobs. Kate's sister, however, remains behind. The look she gives me could easily pulverize a concrete slab into dust.

Elizabeth Leland-Garrison, or "Bethie" as she is affectionately known to her closest friends, is everything you would expect a New York socialite to be. She is poised, cultured, sophisticated…and all too aware of her own superiority. She has never liked me. The feeling is mutual. Albert, Ted, and Kate have always been the three I was closest to in the Leland household. I think Amelie, Kate's mother, eventually came to accept me as a son after a few years, but Beth has only ever tolerated me.

From the beginning, when her father first welcomed me into their home, she considered me an unwanted interloper. Out of respect for her father she never vocalized her withering dislike for me, but her feelings weren't a secret. She, at least, had the good manners to mask them in polite company. But that is over now. There is nothing holding her back from making her disdain known.

"You have some nerve showing your face here after what you did," she sneers.

I pause to scoop a wiggling Scruff into my arms before addressing her. "I'm only here to get my stuff and my dog. That's it."

"Eager to scamper back to your little tramp, are you?"

My jaw tightens with the tacit reference to Iyah. I'm willing to endure whatever insults they have to throw out. I know that I deserve them and more, but I won't allow them to disparage Iyah. She's been gutted in this whole mess too.

"Listen, if you want to lay into me, go right ahead," I invite Beth, "But leave Iyah out of it, please."

"*You* brought her into it when you slept with her!"

I give her a warning look. "Beth, stop."

"Aww, so protective of your mistress! How adorable. If only you'd shown the same consideration for my sister, then maybe we wouldn't be in this mess!"

"I am not having this fight with you," I tell her calmly, "This is between Kate and me."

"This involves our entire family! She's my little sister! You *destroyed* her! Do you not get that?"

"Of course, I do! Give me a break!"

"No, I won't give you a break, Julien! What do you have to say for yourself?"

My only response is a helpless shrug. "I'm sorry."

"That's it?" she scoffs. I grit my teeth against the impulse to justify myself. There is really no justification that I can make, at least not one that won't wound Kate further. My silence only makes Beth angrier. "You didn't just hurt and disappoint Katie. You hurt and disappointed us all!"

"Let's be real, Beth. I lived *down* to your expectations, and we both know it! Congratulations! You get to be right about me!"

"I wanted to give you the benefit of the doubt. You made her happy. I thought she meant something to you. I *thought* you would treasure her." She sounds genuinely disillusioned when she asks, "How could you do something like this?"

"There's nothing I can say to make you understand," I acknowledge gruffly, "All I can do is leave before I hurt her anymore. Just let me get some stuff for the dog and you never have to see my face again."

"If only it were that easy."

Ignoring her, I head over to the kitchen with the intention of grabbing a trash bag so I can start collecting Scruff's toys and food bowl when I hear the bedroom door creak open. I turn around to find Kate listing against the doorjamb looking more haggard than I've ever seen her. Her face is swollen and splotchy from tears. Her long, blond hair, which she typically keeps in a neat bun, is pulled back in a dull, haphazard ponytail that appears matted. There are dark circles beneath her eyes, as if she hasn't slept in weeks. That's probably not too far off the mark.

I wait for her to speak because I have no idea what to say to her. I'm prepared for ranting and cursing. I wouldn't even be surprised if she bounded forward and slapped the hell out of me. I'm waiting for all of it, but what she says instead is the last thing I expect.

"We already sent out all the wedding invitations," she frets in a pitiable tone, her words hoarse with tears. "I put the deposit in for the caterer. What am I supposed to tell people, Ju?"

"Tell them whatever you want," I whisper gently, "You don't have to protect me."

Her eyes flash defiantly. "I wasn't planning to protect you!" The anger is coming now. I can sense it. I stand there suspended, wanting like hell to get out of there but also feeling like I shouldn't leave, *can't* leave, until she dismisses me. "I called you," she says after a deafening silence, "Over and over again. All week long. I guess you were too busy screwing your new girlfriend to answer the phone."

Amelie's and Beth's accusing glares bore into me like hot firebrands. If I could physically sink through the floor, I would. Shame blisters, hot and painful.

"Kate, don't," I protest weakly, "Let's not do this in front of your mom and sister."

"Why not? They already know everything. I can't be any more humiliated than I already am!"

"I wasn't trying to humiliate you."

"Yes, I know. You think you're in love," she scoffs derisively, "You don't even know what love is, Julien! You don't have a clue!"

"I'm sorry I hurt you."

"Stop saying that! Your apologies mean *nothing* to me!" She suddenly pushes herself away from the doorjamb to begin a frenetic pacing. "Tell me something…were you having sex with her when I came to see you in L.A.? Is that why you were so pissed off when I showed up?"

"I wasn't pissed off."

"Yes, you were," she argues, "And you were both guilty as sin too! Did you have a quickie in the car? Was that the reason you were both so tense when you saw me?"

"You're imagining things that never happened!"

"And then you put me off that night…because you were tired," she recounts bitterly, "You didn't even want to touch me! I can't believe I didn't see it then! I missed all the signs! I'm so stupid!"

"You weren't stupid. You trusted me, and I didn't deserve it." She looks at me in pure anguish. "I don't want to make things harder for you, Katie. I really don't. I'm going to grab some things for Scruff and then I'm going to—,"

"—You're not taking him," she snaps before I can finish, "You're not taking the dog."

I may not have any moral ground to stand on, but that declaration infuriates me. Of all the scenarios that I've prepared myself for, not once did it occur to me that she might want to keep Scruff. She loves him, but I also know that he's more responsibility than she cares to handle. Besides, he's mine. I'm the one who chose him from the litter. Getting a dog was *my* idea. So, her sudden insistence on keeping him seems suspect to me...and spiteful.

"He's *mine*. Scruff is my dog! He's coming with me."

"No! He's *my* dog! You're never here, Julien! I'm the one who walks him, who feeds him and who takes him to the vet! All you do is visit!"

"Don't do this. Don't use him to punish me!"

"Get over yourself," she retorts scornfully.

She approaches me for the first time since I arrived, but it's not to knock me senseless. Instead, she holds out her hands to Scruff. He leaps into her arms without reserve, tail wagging happily as he licks at the salty tears that have collected on her face. Kate levels me with a glacial glare that is filled with superiority.

"I packed your things," she announces, nodding towards the three bags near the door, "That's *all* you're taking. My dog stays here with me."

"You've got to be fuc—,"

Her mother steps between us before I can finish the rant and addresses me directly for the first time. "Are you really going to fight her on this after what you did?" she demands softly, "Haven't you taken enough from her, Julien?"

It's impossible to argue with the brutality of that question no matter how indignant I am. I don't want to back down, but I also can't drag Kate through another emotional battle either. Her mom has a point. I've taken enough. So, in the end, I left without the dog, the last worthwhile thing I had ripped away with everything else.

To add insult to injury, I also encounter Ted and Albert on my way down to the lobby. Other than a few muttered words of disapproval, neither man acknowledges my existence as they step around me and onto the elevator. I may as well be dead to them.

By the time I reach my friend's place nearly two hours later, I'm exhausted. My nerves are frayed to such a degree that I suspect it will only take the smallest provocation to set me off. It doesn't help when my buddy takes one look at all the bags that I have with me and bursts out incredulously, "Dude! Exactly how freaking long do you plan on staying?"

He offers to put me up for three days on his living room sofa. For the time being, his couch is my couch…though I do share it with several empty beer cans and some long-forgotten Fritos. I have no idea what I'm going to do once the three days are up though. There's no way I can afford an apartment in New York on my own, not without blowing through every dime I've managed to save in the last six months. I do have a few modeling jobs lined up, but that will cover me for a month's rent tops…maybe two.

And there's no one I can call either. There is no one to come to my rescue. Unfortunately, I've managed to alienate nearly every single person who's ever cared about me.

I'm sitting there on the sofa, watching my buddy play *Call of Duty* and feeling quite sorry for myself when my cell phone vibrates in my back pocket. For a split second, I'm hopeful it's Iyah. I'm prepared to take back every word I said to her about being apart. I'm even prepared to fly out to meet her wherever she is right then. I just want to be with her.

But it's not Iyah calling, and when I recognize that, I'm disappointed but also a little relieved. I have nothing to give her. While I miss her to the point of aching, I don't want to drag her into the middle of my mess. It's not her responsibility to sift through the wreckage I've left. It's mine. I want to be able to give her better than what I've become.

The realization that it's not Iyah calling doesn't bring total relief, however. The caller is not unknown to me. I vaguely recognize the area code and the location associated with it, but it's also a number that I haven't seen in a very long time. So long that I don't even have the caller saved as a contact in my phone anymore. I'm filled with an odd mixture of curiosity and dread when I answer the call with a tentative, "Hello."

"Julien? This is Jacob Dylan Caffrey. Your older brother."

I roll my eyes at the ridiculously formal greeting that is somehow so on brand with my eldest brother. Granted, he and I haven't spoken to one another in close to four years but addressing me with his full name seems a little over the top. Then again, no one is better at serving drama than a Caffrey.

"I know who the hell you are, Jake!" I sigh brusquely, "Why are you calling me?"

"I wasn't sure," he says, "It's been a while. You went to New York and forgot all about where you came from."

"It's not like I came here for a day trip! I came to find our dad, remember?"

"Yeah. I do. But you didn't find him. So, why'd you stay?"

"I'm not going to get into this same tired argument with you again. What do you want?"

"You need to come back home, Julien."

"You're nuts! Why in the hell would I *ever* do that?"

"Because…our mom's dying, and she wants to see you."

21

"You look like hell."

It's not the most loving observation a son can make to his mother, particularly a mother who happens to be dying from late-stage pancreatic cancer, but I'm not feeling particularly loving towards Lucille Caffrey. I'm apathetic towards the woman, at best. Besides, the critique is not an exaggeration. She looks awful.

Not surprisingly though, she takes the remark in stride. In fact, she shrugs and cackles. "Yeah, well…dying's not a good look on anyone, kiddo."

In her case, truer words have never been spoken. She has to have lost at least half her body weight since the last time I saw her, which was nearly a decade ago. My mother has never been an especially large woman to begin with, but now she looks extremely frail and far older than her 52 years. While her constant drinking had unquestionably aged her before her time, the cancer has effectively ravaged what was left of her youthful vigor.

Her skin, which is a pallid, sickly yellow hue, hangs loosely from her gaunt frame. Her long, dark hair, which was once her crowning glory and greatest asset, has thinned considerably and is heavily streaked through with gray. But her eyes are the most unrecognizable feature about her. They have become dull and sunken deep into her skull, the whites the same ghastly yellow as her skin. The only large part of her is her abdomen, which appears so rounded that she almost looks pregnant.

Jake told me that it's due to a buildup of fluid. The doctors have to "tap" her almost every week just so she can breathe comfortably. I look down at her propped up against a mountain of pillows, looking so helpless and small in her sickbed in the back of my brother's small, three-bedroom house and I don't want to feel pity for her…but I do.

This dying woman has caused me more misery than any person alive. And not because she was a cruel, verbally abusive, negligent mother. She was all of those things. But sometimes she wasn't. Sometimes I caught rare glimpses of the kind, considerate mother that she could be. I spent most of my childhood chasing that phantom woman, waiting for her to come back and always hoping she would stay. But she never did. The bottle always chased her away. Eventually, I grew to hate her for it.

I'm not really sure why I'm here. When I left Beckston, Indiana on a bus just shy of my 16th birthday, I had vowed in my heart that I would never return. By then, I was in the foster system again. Jake had declined to take guardianship of me. He had been fairly young himself and not financially stable enough to take me in, not when he had a wife and two kids of his own to support. At least, that had been the excuse he'd given to the social worker assigned to my case. I've always suspected that his wife Dina didn't want the added responsibility of caring for an unruly teenaged boy, and her will prevailed over family loyalty.

My middle brother, Johnny, was already doing his first stint in prison for drug possession and grand larceny when the state took custody of me. So, he wasn't an option for guardian either. I'd been largely on my own. It felt like the only choice I had back then was to strike out and find my father, a man who left our family when I was barely six years old.

And now I'm here, back in this small, dusty town where no one goes anywhere, and nothing ever happens. A pathetic full circle. And for what? To fulfill the dying request of a woman I hardly even know, and I don't particularly like.

"You can come in and sit," she invites me when I continue to hover near the doorjamb.

Reluctantly, I push away from the frame and venture deeper into the bedroom. There's not much too it at all. The furnishings consist of a single twin bed with a faded, quilted bedspread and a scarred chest that looks antiquated. I suspect the chest is solid wood, good quality despite its ravaged appearance. An equally battered desk and matching desk chair are situated against the adjacent wall. I pull up the rickety, wooden chair closer to the bedside and take a seat.

Lucy studies me with a faint, fond smile. "I'm glad you came. You look good. Being out in New York must agree with you."

"I guess."

"Your brother says they print your pictures in all the fashion magazines. I'm not surprised. You've always been such a pretty boy."

"Thanks," I reply with no real enthusiasm.

"All my boys are handsome, but you were the heartbreaker."

"Is there a point to all of this, Lucy?" I sigh tiredly, "Why did you ask me to come here?"

"I want to make things right with you."

I choke back a snort of sarcastic laughter. "You're about two decades too late on that!"

"You came, didn't you?" she reasons, "Maybe you want to make things right too."

That's hardly what motivated me to travel all this way, but I don't bother to correct her. I came because I had no place else to go, and because Jake practically badgered me into it. He and Dina have been acting as our mother's primary caregivers ever since she was diagnosed. The expense and travel involved in taking her back and forth for her chemotherapy treatments has taken a financial toll on Jake's family. After several discussions with Lucy's healthcare team, he and Dina finally came to the painful decision to place Lucy in hospice, but they were still desperate for assistance with her day-to-day care. Even after that heartfelt explanation, it still took me another two months before I finally broke down and made the trip to Indiana.

"We need help," Jake had pleaded with me, "I got a nurse coming out here once a week, but it's not enough. I'm not asking you for money, Julien. Just be a decent human being."

I'm no caregiver, and I'm not even sure if I'm motivated to try. But I feel obligated. Regardless of what I think about this dying woman, she *is* my mother. She gave birth to me. Sitting vigil at her deathbed is the *least* that I can do. Besides, I'm determined not to turn my back on Jake the way he turned his back on me. I want to be better than him.

"Jake said you needed help," I tell her, "So, I'm here to help."

She emits a small, disbelieving grunt under her breath. "You could have just sent money," she argues, "Isn't that what you always do?"

"You *do* understand that I'm not made of cash, right?"

"That's not what Jake says. He says you live in a big, fancy place out in New York...that you got taken in by some well to do family out there." I know she's trying to goad me and, when I don't rise to the bait, she adds, "I saw a commercial for that movie of yours, the one you made with that black girl. I guess you're finally putting your name out there. Remember how you used to always talk about how you wanted to be famous?"

"Yeah. I also remember how you used to tell me to get my head out of my ass because it was never going to happen. Good times, Lucy."

"Well, I guess you showed me," she huffs, "Now you're a movie star."

I don't know if I'm more amused that she thinks her stamp of approval matters an iota to me, or I'm appalled to know that she's aware of the film at all. The fact that it's the story of a young man struggling with crippling mental illness probably didn't register for her. But I can imagine how the depiction of an interracial relationship in that same movie especially threw her into a righteous tizzy. Not surprising given that she grew up in one of the whitest counties in southeast Indiana. I don't think my mother has had a single non-white friend in her entire life. That being the case, I hang back in silence and wait for her to make some sort of offhand comment about it. She does not disappoint me.

"I guess that's the trend now," she considers aloud, "to have all the races mixing like that." I groan her name, aggravated by the pure ignorance of that statement. "Don't take that tone with me, Julien David Caffrey! I don't have nothing against those people, but I don't see anything wrong with sticking with your own kind."

"We're all the same kind," I tell her flatly, "The *human* kind. Race is only skin deep."

I want to tell her about my relationship with Iyah just to watch her head explode, but I bite down against the impulse. It won't serve me to be spiteful and throw my past love affair in her face. I'll only end up hurting myself instead of her. Besides that, I'm not interested in wielding my feelings for Iyah like a weapon.

"You should broaden your horizons, learn about different cultures and customs. Life isn't everything you see on the news."

"I'd expect you to say something like that living out in New York City."

"What's that supposed to mean?"

"Well, you know. You live there. That city is full of homosexuals and transvestites."

She makes the statement authoritatively, as if she has firsthand knowledge which I know she does not. Lucille Butler Caffrey has never traveled outside of the Indiana state lines as far as I know. She's never even been beyond the neighboring towns of Beckston. That hardly makes her an expert on any geographical region beyond her own small corner of the country, and I tell her that. The admonishment doesn't go over well.

Her narrowed eyes linger on the small, silver loops that adorn both my earlobes. I'd probably be pierced all over if I wasn't sure that my agent would have a stroke if I even dared. As it is, I was subjected to an hour-long rant from him just for piercing my other ear. He wasn't thrilled about it. Lucy doesn't appear too thrilled at the moment either, not that her opinion matters to me.

I'm waiting for her to voice her disapproval and preparing my own comeback when she says, "You're mighty touchy about it. Are you one of them?"

"Am I one of what?"

"A homosexual," she clarifies.

For an instant, I'm almost tempted to say "yes" because I know it will get her riled up with indignation. The way she's staring at me with vague disgust, I'm sure she'd believe it too. But I also consider the fact that she's dying and deliberately upsetting her for my perverse enjoyment seems like an especially cruel thing to do…even if she partly deserves it.

"No. I'm not a homosexual. I like women. I identify as a man. My pronouns are he/him. Is there anything else you want to know?"

"Are you married?"

"Nope."

"Got any kids?"

"No, I don't," I answer impatiently, "Why are you so interested in my personal life?"

"It's been a long time. I want to know how you're doing and what you've been up to."

"Since when do you care?"

She shrinks back into the bed at my sharp retort and her dark eyes suddenly fill with tears. "I know I wasn't a good mother to you," she sniffles pitifully, "and I'm sorry, Julien. I'm so sorry. I want to make it up to you."

"You can't fix it, Lucy," I reply, abruptly pushing to my feet. "The damage has been done. Now we both have to live with it."

I'm quick to step out of the room before I say something I'll truly regret. But rather than going back towards the front of the house, where I know my brother and sister-in-law are waiting, I make my way out onto the back porch for some air. The house is situated far off the main road, so the backyard spills right into the dense forest of oak and elm beyond.

Like the rest of the house, the back porch is decorated sparsely. There are two vinyl lawn chairs and a single grungy table between them that looks like it's seen better days. A garish, hand-made ashtray sits in the center of it already overflowing with old cigarette butts. Apparently, I'm not the only person to find this to be a good smoking spot. I stare out at the natural canopy overhead and pull out a cigarette while I admire the glow of the setting sun filtering through the tree leaves.

"Good place to hide a body."

I take another pull off of my cigarette as my brother comes up behind me. "Not quite what I was thinking, but I'll file that information away just in case I decide to become a homicidal lunatic."

"What were you thinking?" he asks, coming to stand beside me near the wooden railing that edges his back porch.

"It's quiet here. A good quiet. I can hear myself think. Not like back home at all."

"You forget. Indiana is your home."

"It never felt that way," I tell him after a puff.

"You shouldn't be so hard on Mama," Jake advises after a beat of silence, "She's not the same woman she was before."

"Sure."

"She hasn't had a drink in three years, Julien!"

"Sorry. I'm fresh out of medals for that."

"Would it kill you *not* to be a jackass for once?"

I whip to face him with a deep scowl. "*I'm* the jackass? Really, Jake? Everyone else in this family gets the privilege of not giving a damn, but when *I* don't, it's a crisis!"

"You still haven't let it go, have you?"

"Let what go?"

"The fact that Dina and I didn't take you in all those years ago!" he fires back in accusation, "It had nothing to do with not caring about you! I *cared*, but I was 23 years old! I had a wife and family, and you were out of control! John was already in jail, and you were headed that way too! I couldn't handle you on top of everything else! Goddamn it, Julien! Cut me some slack!"

The last thing he probably expects from me is a snort of self-deprecating laughter, but that is exactly what he gets, and it surprises us both. Jake scowls at me. "Did I say something hilarious to you?"

"I was just thinking about when I was younger, and every time I did something to drive you crazy, you'd shout, '*Goddamn it, Julien!*' For a while, I thought that was my actual name."

His frown gradually gives way to a wry chuckle. "You were such a hellraiser back then."

"I know that." The acknowledgement is quiet, free from the anger and judgment that hardened my words minutes earlier. "I felt so unwanted by everyone. It hurt that you felt the same way, you know?"

"It's not that I didn't want you," Jake confesses with a deep, rueful sigh, "You were a lot. I didn't know how to deal with you." He appraises me with a thoughtful glance. "Maybe it's a good thing you went up to New York and remade yourself," he considers, "Now look at you. Big time model and movie star. You've got it all figured out."

I take another puff off my dwindling cigarette and laugh. "Yeah, that's an overstatement for sure."

"I've seen that trailer for your movie. Folks in town can't stop talking about it."

"I'll bet."

"Looks like it's going to be pretty intense." Jake's tone is speciously casual, but I can tell from the canny expression on his face that he's about to start prying. "So, what does your fancy, high society family in New York think of your newfound fame?"

The last time Jake and I had an actual conversation, we had fought over my refusal to return to Indiana and visit my "real" family. At the time, the expectation had sounded ludicrous to me. What "real" family? Dad was long out of the picture, most likely dead! Lucy had always cared more about her liquor than she did about us. And Johnny was doing 15 years in the state penitentiary for a surplus of crimes I could barely list! We had no family!

But Jake had meant him, Dina, and the girls. He probably felt like I was rejecting him. Truthfully, I was.

I had wanted so much to wash away the dirty remnants of my past, to forget where I had come from and the struggles that had resulted and start over with the Lelands. Jake had been a part of that past, and I had wanted to get rid of him too. I told myself that it was because *he* rejected *me* first, because *he* had turned away. But I hadn't wanted him in my life. I was too ashamed.

"You won't be surprised to learn, given my history," I reply with a hint of humorless irony, "that I've screwed that up. They don't want anything to do with me."

My brother groans my name, as if the news truly disappoints him. "What did you do this time?"

"I asked their daughter to marry me and then I cheated on her, and I left."

Jake emits a low whistle which is code for "that's messed up" in these parts. "Wow…"

"Yeah," I agree.

"Maybe you weren't ready to get married," he considers diplomatically.

"I think you might be on to something there, Sherlock."

That earns me a playful, but solid punch in the shoulder. "You're still the same old smart ass."

He says that as if he's surprised that part of me is still recognizable to him. I understood then that I've become as much a stranger to Jake as he's become to me. It's an odd thing to consider because we come

253

from the same place. We share DNA. I look at his face and I literally see an older version of my own. There should be no one on the planet who knows me better. And for the first time in a long time, I'm saddened because he doesn't.

"What are you going to do now?" he asks.

"I don't know. My agent's been hounding me to keep the momentum going for my career, but I'm not feeling it." I flick the butt of my cigarette into the nearby ashtray. "I'm not feeling much of anything."

"You could stay here in Indiana."

The hopeful edge in his words is easily detectable, but I'm already shaking my head before he's finished. "Maybe you're finally in a place where you can be in the same room with her and not want to scream, but I'm not," I say, "Being back here is stirring up too many bad memories for me."

"Stick around and make some good ones then!" I snort in disbelief at the suggestion because I can hardly believe he's being serious. But he is. He is deadly serious. I blink at him like he's lost his mind, but Jake just plows on like it's the most brilliant idea he's ever had. "Forget about Mama for a second," he argues, "What about my family? Don't you want to stay and get to know your nieces?"

Chelsea and Carrie Ann are 11 and 9 years old respectively and are freckled, mini productions of my older brother. It's as if their mother hadn't contributed to their genetic makeup at all. The Caffrey genes are definitely strong in them both. I wonder briefly if my kids with Iyah would look more like her or like me. But as soon as that random thought surfaces, I quickly drown it. Not only because it comes from out of nowhere, but because the possibility of Iyah and me ever having kids together is nil.

Very deliberately, I turn my thoughts back to my nieces. They've been acquainted with me for less than two full days and, already, they think I'm one of the most interesting people on the planet. Their admiration would probably be more flattering if I didn't know they'd been surrounded by farmers and blue-collar workers all of their lives. Anyone who doesn't fit into that mold is going to be fascinating to them by default.

I think that was what initially attracted me to Kate. She was so different from every other girl I had known growing up. She seemed so cultured and sophisticated and world-weary. And, most surprisingly of all, she had wanted *me*. Not to use me or exploit me or even sleep with me. She had only wanted to know me. I wonder, yet again, how I managed to screw up something so fundamentally good. Clearly, it's *my* defect. There's no doubt that Iyah dodged a bullet.

I'm aware that my brother is waiting for me to answer, and I shake an admonishing finger at him before lighting another cigarette. "That's a cheap move, using your adorable kids to manipulate me. It's not cool, bro."

"What else are you going to do?"

He has a point. It isn't like I'm eager to get back to New York anyway. Other than my career, I have nothing waiting for me there. I'm not ready to contemplate what that new reality means for me now. But I'm not confessing any of that to Jake. I can barely deal with being truthful with myself.

Instead, I say, "I'll stay a week, and that's it. No promises after that."

22

How one week becomes four weeks instead baffles me.

I've been so preoccupied with taking care of Lucy and doubling as a human pony for Chelsea and Carrie Ann that I can't even pinpoint what changed or when. Now, here I am 21 days later helping Lucy get situated more comfortably in her bed. I've tidied her room. I've brushed her hair. And I'm wondering the whole time how the hell I got to this moment. I don't even *like* this woman!

It isn't like I made a conscious decision to become her caregiver either. There hasn't been any sort of verbal agreement that's passed between Jake and me. Yet gradually, I've been molded into the role without even being aware.

An unspoken routine has been established. Jake works. Dina looks after the girls. And I, by default, look after Lucy. I haven't made a fuss about it because I'm only here a few hours out of the day. I can sacrifice that time. It isn't like I'm occupied with anything else. I tell myself that I'm motivated purely by some vague sense of familial obligation towards my brother, but it *feels* like something else...even if I don't want to admit it.

Lucy's ascites (the fluid collecting in her abdomen) has gotten worse over the course of the last few days. It's causing her to have increasing difficulty with breathing, especially at night. She's been forced to sleep at a near 90-degree angle just to breathe comfortably.

And so, this has quickly become our routine before I leave for the night. I prop her up against a mountain of pillows and build a makeshift fort of blankets all around her to keep her from slipping off to the side while she sleeps. Then I have dinner with my brother's family and return to my motel room. Lather, rinse, repeat.

In the meantime, she's obviously miserable, but she is refusing to go to the hospital to have the fluid drained. She claims it's because she doesn't want to risk being kept there overnight. She cites her mounting medical bills which amount to a waste of money when they "can't do a damned thing for her anyway."

It's a good show of bravado, but I think her resistance is due to something else. She's secretly hoping she'll die in her sleep. Lucy Caffrey is a virtual stranger to me, but I can easily recognize the telltale signs of someone who has given up. I know what that looks like. I've *had* that look. She's ready for it to be over. So am I.

Her home health nurse just left a few minutes earlier. I didn't realize how much she had been carrying the conversation between Lucy and me until this second. The bedroom is silent now. She had done her best to convince Lucy to take a trip to the hospital that night but hadn't been any more successful in changing her mind than Jake or Dina had been.

In the end, she settled on giving Lucy a dose of morphine to reduce her pain and help her rest. She had given me clear instructions on what signs to look for in the event Lucy worsened overnight and what to do if she required immediate medical attention. I refrained from mentioning that I had zero intentions of staying the night.

The morphine has eased some of Lucy's discomfort. She's less restless. Her breathing is no longer rough and labored. She's lethargic and pliable now that the narcotic she was given has begun to take effect. It has also relaxed her inhibitions enough to speak more freely with me.

Her words are slow, slurred, and unfiltered as she crosses the clear, but implicit boundary between us.

"I think she likes you," she tells me after I finish tucking her blanket.

I straighten and regard her wearily. "What are you talking about?"

"My nurse. I see the way she looks at you," she rambles with a small smile, "Always finding reasons to get close to you and talk to you. I can tell she likes you, and she's a pretty girl. You could do worse."

"And that matters because?"

"You need a wife."

"Who says I want one?"

"Maybe you should want one," she considers, her eyelids beginning to droop heavily as she speaks. "Maybe you ought to start thinking about settling down and getting yourself right."

I don't ask her what she means by that comment. Frankly, I'm not interested in going down that convoluted road with her about what she constitutes as "getting right." I'm more interested in why she's suddenly so wildly preoccupied with my personal life.

"What's this obsession you have with who I may or may not be dating?" I ask, "Why does that concern you?"

"Maybe I like the idea of you giving me grandbabies," she mumbles tiredly, "Even if I'm not around to meet them when they're born, it's nice to imagine."

My thoughts automatically veer to Iyah and the babies I would have loved to have made with her. The bitterness that accompanies that sudden yearning has me retorting before I've even finished mentally filtering my response, "I seriously doubt you'd like any grandbabies I gave you, Lucy, even if you *were* around to meet them!"

She flinches in response and looks at me with those dull, sunken eyes filled with hurt. "That wasn't a nice thing to say."

"Why the hell do I need to be nice?" I ask brusquely, "You were *never* going to meet my children. Your dying doesn't change that."

"How can you be so hateful?"

"I can't believe you asked me that with a straight face!"

"I'm the only one who's trying!" she cries, "But you won't let me know you!"

"What you're *trying* to do is mother me!"

"Well, I *am* your mother," she sighs plaintively.

"Not in any way that counts."

She drops her head forward with a mournful grunt. "You're fighting so hard, Julien, and it's not helping you or me. We don't have much time to fix it. Why won't you give me a chance?"

"I have given you chances," I remind her, "And you disappointed me every time."

"I disappointed myself too. I can't change the past though. I can only try to be better now. Let me be a mother to you," she pleads, "I won't disappoint you again."

I honestly don't know whether I should laugh over how completely ridiculous it is that we're even having this conversation when I stopped needing a mother years ago or feel annoyed that she thinks a few trivial platitudes can erase the past entirely. It is absurd that she thinks finding me a wife will somehow make up for all the years she was a negligent mother. I almost wonder if this is her warped attempt at securing her legacy through me because she's been confronted with her own mortality.

Objectively speaking, I guess I can understand why she might be overly concerned with that given the community she had grown up in. My 25th birthday has come and gone. That is well past the marrying age in these parts. Most young men in Beckston already have a wife *and* a family by this point. Even Lucy was married at the age of 18 and became a mother by the time she was 19. That was the life cycle here in Beckston, Indiana. You married and you had kids so those same kids could grow up, get married and have kids of their own.

It was no wonder then that Lucy was so preoccupied with my personal life. But, at the same time, her constant obsession with marrying me off is beginning to aggravate me. No, her behavior has worn on my nerves from the start because she doesn't have the right to share any sort of intimacy with me. Beyond DNA, we have nothing in common. She's a stranger who happens to have given birth to me. And that's all she will ever be. I pull up the desk chair, sit down, and lay that out to her in the plainest terms I can manage.

"I'm here to help Jake and that's it," I finish curtly, "You shouldn't get the wrong idea here. You and I are *nothing* to each other."

"Why are you trying so hard to hate me? Aren't you tired of being angry yet?"

"I've got news for you. I don't have to try!"

"Is it really so hard for you to believe that I might care about you...that I really want what's best for you?"

"Yeah, it is! Because you never have, not in my whole life!"

"That's not true," she laments wearily, "I wanted to be better for you boys. I tried and tried until I eventually gave up because I figured a drunk was all I was ever gonna be."

Something cold and awful runs through my veins with that muttered revelation. How many times have I echoed those same sentiments in my own head? I've spent most of my life with those same inclinations towards self-loathing. I've also been perched on that same lonely precipice of hopelessness where I feel like I'm never going to amount to anything. My latest mistakes with Kate and Iyah have only reinforced that sense of hopelessness. But I'm disgusted by the notion that I should have anything in common with this woman, let alone that disappointing character flaw. It makes me fearful of what other characteristics we might share.

I don't want to empathize with her on any level, not when she is the source of every festering insecurity I have. Every childhood trauma and awful memory is tied up firmly with her. If I even begin to see myself in her even a little bit, then what does that say about what kind of person I am? Maybe I'm not any better. Or worse, maybe I'll be inclined to make excuses for her past behavior. Maybe I'll be compelled to forgive her. I'm not ready to do either thing.

"So, I suppose that excuse lets you off the hook for being a crappy mother then."

She is surprisingly clear-eyed when she meets my sullen glower. "I never said it did."

"You don't have to! You want me to absolve you!"

"I want you to understand!" she explodes forcefully. Her vehemence is enough to momentarily shock me into silence, but not without obstinate resentment. "Your worthless father left me alone with three children to raise by myself! I was 33 years old! I didn't have a job. I had no skills. I had no money and no family to support me!

"I had to make very hard decisions to take care of all of you...decisions that made me hate myself," she weeps softly, "And I drank to cope. But I did my best for you and your brothers. I really did! I just didn't have anything more to give you back then!"

She is so heartfelt, dripping in sincerity, her words garbled with tears and regret. But I don't feel anything besides anger. I must be the most heartless person alive. She is sobbing raggedly in front of me. This wasted, broken woman riddled with remorse is practically begging me to forgive her and I...can't. All I can feel is fury because...*that* was her best?

Leaving us alone for days at a time with no food and no money was her *best*? Calling us "stupid" and "worthless" and "useless" was her *best*? Bringing strangers into our home, men who routinely treated me and my brothers like filth was her *best*? I can't even fathom what her *worst* would have been! What the hell would have become of us if she truly hadn't tried at all?

Besides that, it is all a fantastic lie. I know very well she could have been a better mother to us if she had tried harder. I can recall foggy snatches of that mother, tender touches when I was sick, gentle kisses on my forehead with whispered goodnights, Saturday mornings at the local park. When she was sober, she was everything. But as time went on, she was sober less and less.

I can distinctly remember the last time too. She had risen early that morning to make us all pancakes for breakfast before school. Afterwards, she walked me and Johnny to the bus stop. She waved us off like a real mother, and I truly believed that day that things would be different when we returned home from school. We didn't see her for three whole days after that.

She claims she did her best, but she didn't. I know she could have been better. I have seen glimpses of her best. But we hadn't meant enough to her to keep trying. And now she's tired and old and dying and demanding something from me that she does not deserve. To her credit, when I tell her all of that, she doesn't try to deny any of it.

"You're right," she whispers, "I hated your father so much. He ran away and left me with all the problems. I couldn't make him pay for what he did, so I took it out on you boys. I punished you because I couldn't punish him."

An acrid lump of tears forms in my throat, but I don't know if it's due to anger or anguish. "And you want me to forgive you after all of that?" I utter incredulously.

"I wasn't a good mother to you! Is that what you need to hear? I admit it! I didn't do right by you…by any of you! But I barely loved myself, Julien! How was I supposed to love you?"

I shrug helplessly in response. "What do you want from me? You want me to say that it's water under the bridge? Should I just pretend like none of it ever happened?"

She suddenly reaches out to grab my hand in a remarkably strong grip. I stare down at her bony fingers clutched around my own, but don't immediately yank from her grasp. "I don't want to die with you hating me," she pleads hoarsely, "*Please*. You're my baby. I'm begging you."

I continue to stare down at her fingers until the image begins to waver and blur and then I pull away. My entire body is shaking when I push to my feet. "I'm sorry, Lucy. You don't get to saddle me with your guilty conscience."

I'm quick to turn on my heel and get out of there just as she starts to break down. I need to get out of that house. Despite Jake and Dina's insistence that I stay for dinner and the girls pleading for me to spend the night, I hop in my rental car and speed back to my motel room instead. As soon as I clear the door, I start packing my bags with the full intention of leaving on the first flight out of Indiana the next morning. I won't stay here another second.

I knew that being around my mother again would be difficult. There were too many bad memories, too much unresolved trauma for me to forge even a modicum of a familial bond with that woman. Just being in the same room with her fills me with rage. My hatred eats away at me like acid.

But I hadn't known that it would be *this* hard. I was ready for her to be the same thoughtless, heartless person that I remembered. She's by no means perfect, but she's clearly not what she used to be either. That is where there's a disconnect. I can handle a drunken, loud Lucille. I've been handling that version of her for most of my life. This soft, penitent version of her, however, is starting to get to me.

It's impossible not to empathize with her. I don't have to try too hard to imagine the challenges she faced after my father walked out on us. *I had to make hard decisions…decisions that made me hate myself.* I'm sick inside when I think about what those decisions might have been and how similar they could have been to my own, decisions I made as a teenage boy living on the streets of New York.

But that was *her* fault! I suffered those things because of her negligence! If she had been an actual mother to me, if she had tried harder to be what I needed, I would have never gone chasing a ghost halfway across the country! That was the very reason that I hadn't wanted to come back here. I didn't want to find myself back in this self-pitying space again, wallowing in every terrible memory I had. I would have much rather left the past unacknowledged, unreferenced and something I barely ever thought about at all. Now, it's consuming me all over again. I'm reliving every painful moment, and she has the audacity to ask me not to hate her?

I wish so much that I could talk to Iyah. The thought comes unbidden, but once it surfaces my heart and mind run the gambit. I need to hear her voice. I need the grounding presence that she brings into my life. But mostly, I just need *her*. I miss her.

With a small, shuddering breath, I drop down onto my bed and scroll through my phone to my list of favorites to find her contact. For a long time, I studied the photo that serves as her screenshot. It was a selfie we snapped together when we were still in L.A., just outside of the film studio. I cropped myself out of the picture so that only her lovely face and that amazing hair that frames everything are on full display. Her eyes are hidden behind big, round sunglasses but her smile is incredible, almost like I caught her mid-laugh. She looks so happy and looking at her awakens stirrings of happiness in me too.

It's my favorite picture of her. The sun is setting in the background, bathing her bronze skin in a radiant, golden hue. She's beautiful. There are times when I've stared at this screenshot for hours, wrestling with myself against calling her up and ending the stalemate of silence between us. I often imagine what would happen if I worked up the courage to do it. Would she talk to me, or would she hang up as soon as she heard my voice? I honestly don't know. I'm afraid to find out.

Or maybe I know exactly how she'll react, and I simply don't want confirmation that we're truly over. I'd like to believe that I could call her up and she would be open to conversation, that we could talk for hours. She would probably dispense her trademark practicality too. Iyah had little patience for tolerating negative influences. While others might encourage me to forgive Lucy for the sake of family or even because it was the "right" thing to do, Iyah was unlikely to fall into that camp.

She'd probably ask me to consider what was best for *me* and *not* my dying mother. She would say that if forgiving Lucy didn't result in some personal benefit then I shouldn't waste my time. I'm inclined to agree. Lucy lost her right to be my mother a long time ago. For my own sanity, I should leave this place and never look back.

But I can't do it.

Every time I contemplate leaving or executing the actual follow through, I manage to talk myself out of it. My conscience whispers for me to stay. I'm conflicted. When I close my eyes, I can still hear my mother's tearful pleading and the sincere fear that she will go to her grave with me hating her. That fear robs her of peace, and I can't pretend I'm immune to her pain no matter how much I wish otherwise.

I know the reason why. I've been where she is. I'm standing in that same place.

Iyah decided she was done with me too. I hurt her just like Lucy hurt me and my beautiful, smart girl does not suffer fools. From her standpoint, I've lied to her, used her, and betrayed her trust. For all her admirable qualities, Iyah Grandberry can be a callous bitch when she's crossed. There's no question that she's done with me.

I sincerely doubt she's been obsessing over me the way I've been obsessing over her. She cast me out of her life, and she didn't look back. But I've been wishing every day since that she would. Because no matter how deserving I am of her hatred and disgust, I don't want to be dead to her. It is an awful, eviscerating existence.

And I can't help but wonder if my mother feels the same way about me.

23

That night, my plan to leave is derailed. Jake calls shortly before 4 a.m. to tell me that Lucy's health has taken a turn, and she is declining fast. They are rushing her to the nearest medical center, which is twenty minutes away. I roll out of bed, throw on my clothes and drive out to meet them.

I'm not sure that I grasp just how serious the situation is until I arrive in the ER. Alarms are clanging. Staff are running back and forth, dragging heavy pieces of complicated machinery behind them. The scene I walk into is nothing less than pandemonium.

Jake and Dina are huddled together in the small alcove just outside the makeshift trauma bay comforting their hysterically weeping daughters. I know it's not a good thing that they are congregated outside rather than at Lucy's bedside. I jog up to Jake to press him for answers.

"She started saying she couldn't breathe," he recounts woodenly, "And then she…" He pauses to swallow and quickly composes himself. "They're trying to stabilize her now. She stopped breathing in the ambulance. If she pulls through, we'll have to transfer her to another hospital that's better equipped to take care of her."

It's clear that the situation is dire, but I also know this outcome is not unexpected. The plan to stabilize her and move her seems odd to me. "Shouldn't we just…uh…let nature take its course?" I ask him in a low tone so as not to be overheard by the girls. "This is what we knew would happen, right?"

"She's not ready yet, Julien!" he snaps furiously, "Don't you get that?"

"She's not ready or *you're* not ready?" I counter.

"Both, goddamn it!"

I refrain from pushing him further about it. I'm honestly not trying to come across as an unfeeling jackass, but I don't see any value in prolonging the inevitable. Lucy's ready, and I know that I sure as hell am too. But she keeps holding on in spite of her obvious misery. She won't let go.

I have a fairly good idea why she won't. So does Jake. I can read the blame plainly in his eyes, and I don't want to deal with it.

"You want me to take the girls for a while?" I offer, hoping to give him a reprieve and myself as well.

He knows that I'm just using them as an excuse to make myself scarce. It's written all over his face and stamped into his body language. Thankfully, he doesn't call me out on it or argue with me. To my eternal relief, he agrees to the request with a terse nod.

"Don't take them too far," he warns me, "Just in case…"

Neither Chelsea nor Carrie Ann is particularly eager to leave their parents' side but when I promise them a waffle breakfast at the local Waffle House, they are persuaded. I'd forgotten how ridiculously easy to please children can be at this age. A dinner plate sized waffle and a side of semi-crisp bacon, and I'm a hero in both their eyes.

I can remember Waffle House being a rare treat for me when I wasn't much older than Carrie Ann. The place doesn't hold the same thrill for me now as an adult with its cramped booths, sticky tabletops, and warped silverware, but being there still provokes a measure of nostalgia.

I'm surprised by the flood of fondness. Not *all* my memories of this place are bad ones.

"Hey, Uncle Julien?" Carrie Ann pipes up around a mouthful, "How come you don't like Grandma?"

Leave it to a nine-year-old to come at you with no filter whatsoever. She's so direct in her approach that it's hard not to feel flustered, especially when she blinks at me with her big, round innocent eyes. "I never said I don't like Grandma."

Chelsea interjects her own brand of verbal brutality then. "You sure act like it," she says matter-of-factly, "Do you want Grandma to die?"

"I don't want Grandma to die," Carrie Ann mumbles, eyes watering. "She's the best grandma I got."

"Better than Granny Marie for sure," Chelsea agrees, "She always swats us for stealing her cookies. We can't ever have any until after supper, but Grandma Lucy always lets us sneak a few." She draws into herself with a small, introspective frown. "I'm going to miss her cookies."

I blink at her a little incredulously. "Lucy bakes for you?"

Carrie Ann confirms with a proud nod. "You should ask her to make you brownies when she's feeling better. If you say 'please,' I bet she will."

It's like I've been ejected into some alternate dimension. Since when does Lucy bake anything? In all the time I've known her, the woman barely cooked for us, let alone *baked*! And yet Chelsea and Carrie Ann are talking about her like she's Martha freaking Stewart! It's too surreal. Either they are referring to someone else, or this is one hell of a joke!

Both the girls seem oblivious to my dumbfounded reaction. Carrie Ann continues to munch happily, chatting incessantly about her grandmother's numerous baked creations while ignoring her sister's irritated admonishments not to talk with her mouth full. Finally, she asks me between gulps of food, "Uncle Julien, how come you call Grandma 'Lucy' stead of 'Mama'?"

"That's her name, isn't it?"

"My daddy calls her 'mama.'"

Well, I'm not your daddy, kid. I narrowly miss making the retort out loud, but I catch myself at the last second. Instead, I tell her, "She's always been Lucy to me, even when I was young."

Chelsea takes a sip of her cola and regards me almost speculatively. "Daddy said that you're mad at Grandma because she made a lot of mistakes when you were little and now you can't forgive her."

"Oh yeah? What else did your daddy tell you?"

"You should try to be nicer to her, Uncle Julien," Chelsea advises me with a wisdom that seems far beyond her eleven years, "She'll be gone soon, and then you'll be sad. You'll wish you tried harder, but it'll be too late to do anything about it."

"Don't say that!" Carrie Ann cries plaintively, "I don't want Grandma to die, Chelsea!"

"But she is going to die, Carrie," Chelsea replies, her solemn, too old eyes boring into me the entire time. "She is."

It's almost portentous when Jake calls just as I'm paying the check. The ride back to the hospital is somber, without all the excited, girlish chatter that had dominated when we left it. Upon arriving, I see that the chaos from earlier has settled. The endless, hurried line of hospital personnel rushing back and forth has subsided.

Lucy is stabilized for the time being, but her doctors have come to the grim consensus that she only has a matter of days left. She has two choices before her. She can live out the remainder of that time at a larger medical facility in Indianapolis that provides hospice services for dying patients, or she can return home with her family and die there. It's a weighty decision, both for her and for Jake. I'm hardly qualified to add my thoughts at all, so I hang back with the girls and do my best to comfort them while Jake and Lucy discuss what comes next with Lucy's attending physicians.

She's in bad shape. That much is evident. There are various tubes and drains snaking out from her wasted body now. Her face is half covered by an oxygen mask which effectively muffles her already faint responses. From where I stand, it's impossible to make out a word she says, but I can easily guess based on how Jake responds. He keeps shaking his head at her and biting his lip as if he's struggling not to break down in front of her.

"…listen to me, listen to me," he pleads with her, "That doesn't matter, Mama. It's the past. We put that behind us, remember?" Whatever she says in response to him only makes Jake more adamant. "…no, no, you're not a burden. You're my family. You're my mother. I'm taking you home with me."

I don't think I've ever felt like more of an outsider than I do this second. This is my family. My blood. Yet, I'm so far removed from them that it's almost frightening.

Jake, Dina, and the girls are all grieving. They can feel Lucy's impending loss viscerally. All I can feel is unnerved and awkward. For the first time ever, I envy Jake's remarkable ability to brush aside Lucy's past sins and just be her son again. Before this moment, I always thought that his willingness to forgive her made him a fool. But now I can clearly see how that forgiveness has freed him instead.

Now he can grieve for his dying mother. He can hold onto her and cry and tell her how much he loves her. He's not separated by some

271

unscalable, emotional wall that compels him to hold himself apart. *His* heart isn't like a stone in *his* chest.

Jealousy prickles. I can't comprehend how he's made it to that inexplicable place of unreserved forgiveness. Once upon a time, he harbored the same resentment towards Lucy that Johnny and I did. But, unlike us, he eventually let it go. Maybe it's because he's the oldest and wisest of the three of us. Or maybe it's because he can remember when she was an actual mother. He has more good memories of her than bad ones.

By the time Lucy went off the rails completely, Jake was 14 years old. He had known years of stability with her and was just entering that age where a boy didn't rely on his mother quite as much. Johnny and I, on the other hand, were 10 and 6 years old. We hadn't yet reached that point. We were still young enough to yearn for her protection. We needed her to make us feel safe. The irony is that, out of us three, Jake is the one who should have harbored the most bitterness…because when she stopped being all of those things, he was the one who had to step up and fill the void she left.

But as I watch him now, there are no traces of bitterness that I can see. There are no undercurrents of animosity as he beckons his girls closer to embrace their dying grandmother. There is nothing but sadness and grief, especially when he looks up at me and clearly wishes that I could do the same. I shake my head at his silent entreaty.

I don't move at all. I'm rooted in place. And it's not because I want to punish Lucy by being aloof. It's because I don't know how to feel. I'm waiting for this flood of anguish to sweep through me and there's nothing. Not for her at least. I'm saddened for my brother. Seeing him cry makes me want to cry too, but I don't know this woman. I can't be sad over the loss of someone I don't know, someone I've *never* known.

The only question left is do I want to know her? Is that even possible now?

Eventually, the doctors and nurses begin to file out. The plan is to admit Lucy to the hospital overnight, give her fluids and pain medication and then discharge her the next day. After that, she'll go home to die surrounded by her loved ones.

Dina and the girls whisper their goodbyes and kiss Lucy goodnight before finally stepping away from her bedside. I'm aware of the cautious sideways glances the three give me as they usher past. I pretend not to notice their scrutiny.

Jake is the last to leave. Lucy must ask after me because he suddenly points over in my direction and assures her that I've been there the entire time. She glances over at me then and I tip my head to her in acknowledgment. The relief on her face is apparent even with the distance that separates us. At Jake's gentle urging, she relaxes back against her cot. He reassures her that he will return the next morning when she is ready to be discharged.

After he kisses her goodnight, he starts over towards me. I already know what's coming before he even says a word. His features are stony with resolve. "Go say something to her!" he hisses at me angrily.

"What do you want me to say?" I hiss back.

"Hold her hand. She's dying, Julien!"

"Stop saying that like it's supposed to magically fix things!"

"She might not be the mother you wanted, but she's the only one you have," he tells me gruffly, "That won't be for long. Is this really how you want to leave it?"

Once he's gone, it is just Lucy and me in the room. I can no longer put off the inevitable. I approach her cot on stilted legs. She pulls her mask aside as I come closer and favors me with a tired smile.

"…you…stayed…" she whispers. Her voice is reedy and thin, her words pushed out between labored breaths. "I'm…glad…"

"How are you feeling?" The question is perfunctory, but it fills the silence.

"…tired… Your brother…he's a good…boy…"

"He is." I mean that sincerely too. Jake is the best of us. I've always known that, even when I was angry and determined to cut him out of my life. Perhaps that's the reason I found it so difficult to forgive him. He had never disappointed me before.

"…don't deserve him…" Lucy rasps, "…or you…"

"Let's not get into that," I interrupt her quickly. I'm not ready to hear her heartfelt deathbed confession. I have nothing to give her in return. "Save your energy. Rest."

"…get what…you wanted…"

The accusation, though made without any real acrimony, still offends me. "You think I want you to die?" Lucy rolls her eyes at my indignant response and repositions her mask. It's clear from her reaction that she thinks I'm lying. "Give me a break! You're not my favorite person, but I have never once wished you dead!"

Her eyes flare wide with surprised interest and something else too, something that looks almost like hope which is a strange thing to see from a dying woman. "…no…?" she asks, her disbelief muffled beneath the steady whoosh of compressed oxygen.

"Of course not!" I huff impatiently, "I'm not a goddamn sociopath!"

She seems to consider that reply for a long time before she finally says, "…start over…?"

"Who? Us?" She nods. "Why?"

"…wanna know you…before I die…"

"There's nothing to know, Lucy."

"…want you…to know me…then…" she counters breathlessly, "…*please*…"

The prospect is vaguely intriguing, but unrealistic. Yet, I think about Grandma Lucy who bakes cookies and has the abiding affection of her granddaughters. This Lucy who is so obviously adored by her entire family, a family that will be devastated when she's gone. I'm curious about *that* Lucy. There is an undeniable part of me that is interested in learning more. And an unacknowledged part of me that is hopeful.

"Okay. I'll think about it."

I'm still thinking about it two days later when I go to visit her again after she's been discharged from the hospital. The back bedroom has been transformed in the interim. Her old bed has now been replaced with a fully automated hospital bed. There is a bedside commode situated within reach, so she doesn't have to exert herself getting to the hall bathroom. There is also a large oxygen compressor emblazoned with a glaring caution sign that prohibits smoking due to the risk of explosion. I make a point of removing my package of cigarettes from the breast pocket of my shirt and cram it into my back pocket instead. The thought is that if I keep them out of sight, I won't be tempted to light one up.

Lucy smirks at me as I sit down at her bedside. "Planning to blow us all to kingdom come, are you?"

She's in much better spirits since her brief stint in the hospital. While she still looks like general hell and her color is abysmal, she seems to be rallying since her discharge rather than deteriorating. She has graduated from her oxygen mask to a simple nasal cannula since her discharge. It is much easier to hear her now, even with the compressor whirring constantly in the background.

"I wasn't going to smoke in the house anyway," I tell her, "Jake has a rule against that."

"Never took you for a rule follower."

"I'm not. But I also don't want to be the lead story on the six o'clock news. You gotta pick your battles."

She grunts a little laugh at that and so do I. It's probably the most relaxed exchange we've had since I arrived here. For that reason, I should have known that it was destined not to last. As soon as I start to let my guard slip around her, she says something to make me regret it.

"You didn't come by yesterday," she notes in a tone she means to sound indifferent, but that rings with disapproval. "We were starting to think you might have left town."

"I was on the phone haggling with my agent all day. He's got a few jobs lined up for me, but the timing isn't the best."

"Sorry I couldn't help you out by dying sooner, kiddo."

It takes me a second to recognize that she's being facetious and not self-pitying at all. And, once I do, I returned her droll sarcasm with equal flare. "Yeah. That's a real selfish move on your part. Do better."

Her answering laugh is short-lived though. She studies me with a serious, almost mournful expression and then she remarks, "I know how your agent feels about you being out here so long, but what does your girlfriend say?"

Tension stiffens my frame with the abrupt mention of my personal life. "Who says I have a girlfriend?"

"Jake said you were engaged, but it fell through because you cheated on her. I figured there had to be a girlfriend somewhere."

That explanation aggravates me even further. "You guys just sit around and gossip about me?" I demand angrily, "That's how you pass the time?"

"It's not gossip!" she flares back, "We're trying to understand you! It's not like *you* tell us anything!"

276

I don't know what compels me to confess it all to her then. Maybe it's because I want to get it all out in the open so that she will finally shut the hell up about it. Or maybe it's because I desperately need someone to talk to.

The unique thing about Lucy is that I know I can unburden myself to her without any consequences. I'm not dreading her rejection. There's nothing to lose. It's like confessing your sins to a perfect stranger. I can do so without fear of judgment or reprisal. And so, I do it. I finally answer the question she's been badgering me about since I arrived here.

"You know that girl…the one I did the movie with?" I wait for her to process her astonishment over my surprising willingness to talk and don't continue until she nods. "You want to know who I cheated with? She's the one. We were together." I let that bombshell settle down on her a bit and prepared myself for her possible horrified response.

She is clearly flustered by the admission but doesn't say anything right away. Her silence hardly matters though. I can easily read the gambit of emotions that chase their way across her face. Dismay. Confusion. Curiosity. She wants to ask me a dozen questions, but strangely enough she seems to be holding herself in check. I prod her a little.

"Does that shock you?"

"Have you…have you always dated Black girls?" she asks me finally. She seems simultaneously fascinated and repulsed by the idea.

"No. She was the first."

Lucy appears thoughtful for a second and I almost get the impression that she is trying to be careful with her response. The idea is surreal because she's never bothered filtering herself with me before. This woman has literally hurled every insult imaginable at me. Why she would choose to censor herself now is both peculiar and perplexing.

Finally, she speaks again, and of all the questions she chooses to ask me, it is the one I don't see coming. "Well…what's she like?"

"Bossy," I laugh, "She is the bossiest woman I've ever come across. She has an opinion about *everything*. She's super smart and very funny. She makes me laugh more than anyone I've ever met."

"You sound like you love her."

"I *do* love her," I confirm softly.

"What happened?"

"I'm not a good person," I reply simply, "She would have figured that out eventually and she would have left me. It seemed like the more noble thing to save her the stress and keep my distance instead."

"Is that what you think I should have done with you?" she counters in a quiet tone, "Should I have been noble and stayed away?" I say nothing, and I suppose that's answer enough for her. "I did try that at first," she says, "It took me 6 years of trying to get sober before I was able to stay that way. I promised myself that I wouldn't contact you until after I had my life together."

"Jake said that you haven't had a drink in three years. Why did you wait?"

"Would you have wanted to hear from me, Julie?"

I'm neutralized by her candor as much as the use of the affectionate childhood nickname that I haven't heard since I was a small boy. "Not at all."

"Then you have your answer," she grunts humorlessly, "I figured you had a good life, and there was no room for me anymore." And then she laughs again as if a sudden thought occurred to her. It's a deep, wry bark of pure amusement that sounds vaguely ironic. "It's crazy. You might look like your daddy, but you are all *me*." I imagine my reaction to that observation must convey dubious skepticism because she chuckles again. "I'm serious. We are two peas in a pod."

"How do you figure that, Lucy?"

"Because you and I are masters at self-preservation."

"I'm not following you."

"You don't even know that you do it," she murmurs in a sorrowful tone that is a stark contrast with her earlier laughter. "You can't see it. But I do."

"What do you think you see?"

"I see myself. I see this scared, little kid who would sooner burn everything down to the ground with his own two hands rather than wait for someone to come along and take it from him."

24

Lucy dies on a Saturday afternoon, and it feels like it comes from out of nowhere.

She lived for nearly a month after her final prognosis, much longer than the doctors initially predicted. I had actually started to believe that maybe they were wrong, and she was going to surprise us all by beating the odds. In the time we were waiting for nature to take its course, however, something unexpected happened. I started to wish she wasn't dying at all.

Surprisingly, Lucy wasn't being presumptive when she claimed that she and I were alike. I inherited my sense of humor from her and my natural inclination towards sarcasm. I also discovered that I wasn't the only amateur artist in my family. Lucy was a painter too when she was younger.

I began to understand the motive for her cruel discouragement back then. Those demoralizing critiques hadn't been born out of brutal, drunken honesty, but jealousy and envy instead. If she couldn't realize her dreams, then I sure as hell wouldn't realize mine either.

Somehow the revelation of her profound pettiness didn't increase my hatred. Her actions humanized her in a way that nothing else had, perhaps because I can see glimpses of Iyah in her. The realization opens my eyes to the impossible standards I'd held Lucy to all of these years. She was never superhuman or infallible. She was a frightened, single mother of three wrestling with her inner demons the same way I've been wrestling with my own. And while I doubted that I would ever get to a place of unencumbered forgiveness where she was concerned, I was finally able to extend her some grace.

By doing that, I also granted myself the freedom to come to know the woman she had become, a woman who was curious and insightful, but also forthright and tenacious. We didn't always agree, but she was never averse to listening. When I finally let myself stop being so angry with her, those last few weeks were like a revelation.

She wasn't the callous, self-centered monster that I had built up in my mind for so many years, but she also wasn't the mother I had yearned for either. I came to like her as a person. I started to wonder if one day I might even grow to love her.

But then one ordinary Saturday afternoon filled with ordinary things, Lucy decided to take a short nap after lunch. I pulled up her blanket, assured her that I would be there when she awakened, and left the bedroom. She never woke up. I wasn't completely prepared for the paralyzing sorrow that followed her death. I'm not sure what to do with the emotion.

It sounds cliché to say it was unexpected given the circumstances, but none of us saw it coming. I had spent that morning teasing her about her limited experience with social media. She always insisted on referring to the various platforms with a definitive article whenever she referenced them. I grew so used to correcting her that it became a running joke between us. But that morning I had said, "It's not 'the' YouTube, Mama. It's just YouTube."

I hadn't even fully processed what I had said until I noticed her stricken expression afterward. Even Jake and Dina had been shocked into silence. But Lucy had made the deliberate choice not to make a big deal out of it. She hadn't brought attention to it at all, didn't even acknowledge that I had called her "mama" even though I suspected the moment had been profound for her. I hadn't acknowledged it either.

At the time, I hadn't even come to terms with what it meant or what had compelled me in the first place. We moved on from the incident like it never happened. I thought we would have plenty of time to hash it out between us later without an audience. But later never came.

I've been holed up in my motel room since that day, strictly avoiding Jake and the family. I'm flirting heavily with the idea of cutting out of here before the funeral. Running is a cowardly choice, but I'm in a precarious mental state. It doesn't feel like it will take very much to break me. I need a distraction.

Work would be the perfect medium. My agent has a list of jobs and auditions lined up for me, and he's been hounding me for weeks to take advantage. I just need to purchase a plane ticket and leave.

It's only when I'm scrolling through Trip Advisor for available flights out of Indiana to New York that I become aware of the date. Today is Iyah's 24th birthday. I don't realize just how much time has passed since I last saw her until this very second.

It's been more than four months. I can't believe how quickly the weeks have been eaten away, particularly because they've progressed in a tortuous crawl for me. I think about her daily. And thinking about her always brings with it a desire to talk to her too. And, in my current vulnerable state, I'm motivated to indulge that impulse.

I almost call her directly, but then lose my nerve at the last second. A random phone call is too forward after nearly five months of silence. It's an especially bad idea because I know as soon as I hear her voice, I'm likely to break down and unload all of my emotional baggage on her. That is not how I want the conversation to go. This is *her* birthday after all. This day should be about her and not my unresolved conflict over my dead mother.

So, I start very simply. I send her an emoji. Just a single, innocuous emoji of a birthday cake. I send it to her, and then I wait.

Seconds pass and blend into minutes but the time feels infinite. I must check my phone messages at least a dozen times while I wait for her to respond. Meanwhile, I ignore the dozens of texts, voicemails and missed calls from everyone else. I keep myself focused on Iyah and being prepared for her call. I know if I do that, I won't think about my mother. And if I don't think about my mother, I won't dwell on the grief I feel over her death. And if I don't dwell on that grief then I won't splinter into pieces.

I wait an entire hour before I lose my resolve against calling Iyah directly. The phone rings once and then goes straight to voicemail. I don't make up my mind to leave her a message until I am literally speaking at the prompt. The words simply tumble out of me without thought.

"Hey, it's me. I know you probably don't want to hear from me. I don't blame you. I just wanted to wish you a happy birthday and to tell you that I miss you. I miss you so much, Iyah. And I love you. I never told you that before and I should have. I should have said the words and… My mom died yesterday, and I don't really know how to feel about it. I wish I could talk to you. Please call me back."

The regret that overwhelms me when I end the call is instantaneous. In that single message, I did everything I promised myself that I wouldn't do. I feel pathetic and stupid, but it's too late to undo the damage. All I can hope for now is that she'll listen and be moved to call me back. And if she doesn't respond, then at least I'll know for sure that she is permanently done with me. Maybe then I can begin the process of finally moving on from her...

I stare at my phone and wait impatiently for it to vibrate to life. I smoke almost an entire pack of Camels while I do. But she doesn't call back. Not even a text.

And it hurts like hell.

After that, I crawl into bed because my interest in anything besides sleeping dwindles down to nothing. While Iyah clearly isn't inclined to reach out to me, my brother, on the other hand, has called me no less than six times in the past hour. I'm not in the mood to talk to him. I'm not motivated to move from the bed or have a meal or even shower. Not even my craving for nicotine is enough to rouse me. Instead, I lie in the dark and scroll indifferently through TikToks.

I'm not really sure how much time passes. Minutes? Hours? Who knows? The seconds blend together. But I think I must fall asleep because the next thing I know I'm being jarred into keen alertness by a fierce round of pounding on my motel door. Disoriented and a little alarmed, I rolled out of bed to stagger over to answer it. I yank the door open just as Jake is about to begin another round of violent banging.

"What the hell is your problem?" I demand harshly.

"What the hell is *your* problem?" he counters with equal harshness, shouldering past me in a fit of anxious temper. "I've been calling you all day, Julien! Are you drunk?"

I survey him with a withering glare. "I was asleep!"

Jake scrutinizes my rumpled appearance with narrowed eyes. "Have you been in bed all day long?"

"Yep," I confirm, "and I'm going back to bed."

"You couldn't answer your phone at all?"

"Didn't feel like talking."

"How about, at least, letting me know you were alive?" he snaps.

"I'm alive." I gesture towards the door and then climb back into bed to burrow myself deep under the blankets. "You can go now."

He doesn't go. Instead, I hear him move closer and then he's standing over me. I can picture him in my mind, glowering down at me with that familiar disapproving frown, his arms crossed like a thunderous, judgmental god. It's a stance that I've come to know well.

"You really are a selfish son of a bitch sometimes," he mutters, "Do you know that?"

"No one's forcing you to stay here."

"Goddamn it, Julien! You're not 15 anymore! Grow the hell up!"

I whip back the covers and rear upright with an aggravated snarl. "What do you want?" I grate from between clenched teeth.

"I'm trying to plan our mother's funeral! It would be nice if you could contribute!"

"I can't do that."

"Why the hell not?"

Over the course of my lifetime, I have crafted a variety of flippant responses to avoid dealing with my feelings. Whether it's anger, fear, heartbreak, or betrayal, I have become quite accomplished at brushing them off by way of joking, derision, or outright indifference. And that has worked brilliantly for me for many years now.

But when I open my mouth to fire off my usual sarcastic retort what comes out instead is this odd, choking sound, almost like the whimper of a wounded animal. The wave of overwhelming emotion comes from out of nowhere. I realize with dawning horror that I'm about to start sobbing uncontrollably, and there's not a damned thing I can do to stop it.

I am only half aware of Jake putting his arms around me while I dissolve. It all rushes out of me in a gasping torrent, losing Kate, losing my mother, losing Iyah, losing everything, and I'm swept away in that sorrow. But I only allow myself those few, fleeting minutes of weakness before I stiffen and push him away. I can't even make eye contact with him at all as I say over and over again, "I'm fine. I'm fine. Leave me alone. I'm fine." Thankfully, he refrains from trying to comfort me further while I struggle to pull myself together.

When my tears have dried and my composure has been restored, Jake says softly, "You don't have to do this by yourself, Julien. You have a family. I'm not going to write you off no matter how many times you screw up."

It is still very difficult to meet his eyes right then, but I do manage a grateful nod as I mumble, "Thanks."

"You should come stay at the house. It makes sense. You're having your mail forwarded there already." He looks around my dank motel room with a grimace of distaste. "Besides, this place is a hellhole."

"I'm not trying to impose upon you and your family," I tell him gruffly, "I can't stay with you indefinitely, Jake."

"It's not an indefinite offer," he says, "Just until you figure out what you're going to do next."

I simply nod in concession because, at this point, I'm too tired to fight. "Okay."

Once Jake and I get back to the house, he convinces me that a shower and a hot meal are just what I need to feel human again. I'm a bit skeptical about the advice but he turns out to be right. I don't know if I necessarily feel better afterwards but I do feel more in control. At least, mentally I'm in a better place. I can discuss my mother's funeral arrangements without a sense of impending doom. Jake and I also talk about making the drive to Westville Correctional Facility to deliver the news about mom to Johnny in person. Neither of us is looking forward to that task.

Afterwards, I bunk out on the pull-out sofa in the living room (because I refuse to sleep in that back bedroom) and go through the stack of missed calls and text messages that have collected over the past two days. Most of them are from my agent demanding to know where I am and why I keep dodging him. There are more than a few calls from acquaintances back in New York wondering if I have any intentions of returning any time soon. A handful are from various members of Kate's family expressing shock and disappointment over our aborted wedding. And at least one comes from one of Kate's former bridesmaids expressing her desire to "hook-up" now that I'm a "free man."

Most surprisingly, however, I have three missed calls from Kate herself. I ignore those for the time being and return my agent's call instead. We're on the phone for more than twenty minutes. Though he does an admirable job of trying to be sympathetic and commiserative in the wake of my mother's death, I can tell that his primary objective is to put me back to work as soon as possible.

"Two weeks," I tell him, "Give me two weeks, and then I'll be back at it."

When that's over, I shoot off a couple of cursory texts to several friends to reassure them that I am still alive and then delete the rest. I deliberately save addressing Kate's calls for last because I can't imagine that her reasons for reaching out are positive at all. That suspicion is confirmed when I'm thumbing through my mail and find a very official-looking, very certified letter from the Department of Justice. When I ask Jake about it, he confirms that it was hand delivered earlier that afternoon.

I know what it is before I even open the letter and scan the contents. Kate is suing me for "breach of contract" and "emotional damages" related to our canceled nuptials to the tune of half a million dollars! At first, I don't really react because the amount seems fairly ludicrous. It's as if someone is playing a very bad joke on me, one that is not at all funny.

But the longer I stare at the summons, the more real it becomes. The official letterhead and seal make it clear that this is no joke. That's the moment my shock and disbelief finally give way to fury. I snatch up my cell phone to call her with no regard for how late it is.

"You're suing me?" I explode as soon as she answers.

"You *do* remember how to operate your phone," she replies tartly, "I was beginning to wonder."

"Half a million dollars, Kate? Really? What the hell? You can't be serious!"

"I'm not joking either."

"This is ridiculous."

"Is it? The total cost of our wedding was nearly $55,000, Julien! Most of the deposits were non-refundable. Who do you think was left recouping all of those expenses? Not to mention the humiliation I've had to endure when I explain that you left me for a girl you met while *filming a movie*! Half a million dollars is fairly light!"

"You want me to pay you back? Fine! I can do that. But you know I don't have $500,000! Come on!"

"That's not my problem!"

"Please, Katie, listen to me," I plead with her as the bluster abruptly drains out of me and all that's left is battered weariness, "I can't do this with you. I know I don't deserve it, but I need you to cut me some slack. This is a bad time."

"Why? Am I putting a damper on your romp fest with your new girlfriend?" she sneers.

"I'm not with Iyah. I'm in Beckston. My mom just died."

As soon as I tell her the news, I instantly wish that I hadn't because I'm sure she'll only see it as a manipulative tactic on my part. And perhaps it is. I need her to back off and nothing subdues people faster than a dead mommy. But I know that's not fair to her. The truth is that I screwed up. I broke her heart, and then I left her holding the bag. Literally. It wasn't that I didn't have the full intention of reimbursing her financially for the wedding, but that has been inarguably low on my priority list.

"You know what?" I sigh after a beat, taking advantage of her stunned silence. "It doesn't matter. You're right. It's not your problem. I owe you the money, and I should pay. I'll see you in court."

I hang up quickly before she can reply, and I have a chance to lose it all over again.

25

"Where are you staying?"

I squint groggily at the time in the top corner of my phone and then back at the picture splashed across my screen. I think I'm dreaming. It's 9:25 a.m. Not an ungodly hour, but still too early for an inquisition especially from my ex-fiancée who is currently suing me for half a million dollars. I croak out her name in bleary confusion, still half convinced I *am* dreaming.

"What's going on? Why are you calling me?"

"I need the address where you're staying so I can tell my Uber driver," she says.

"Your Uber driver?"

"Yes! My Uber driver," she insists, sounding somewhat impatient. "I'm in Beckston. Tell me where to find you."

The words sluice over me like frigid water, and I'm promptly awake. "I'm sorry. What did you say?"

"My flight landed twenty minutes ago."

There are a hundred thoughts running through my mind and not a single one of them is coherent. I'm slow to process the reality that Kate is in Beckston, Indiana because I can't understand at all *why* she would be. Our last conversation was hardly civil or pleasant. There is enough resentment and tension between us to suffocate a rhinoceros. I'm pretty sure that Kate hates my guts, and with good reason. But I can't fathom that hatred is what compelled her to fly halfway across the country on a moment's notice.

"Are you going to tell me or what?" she presses me anxiously when I continue silent. I'm still a bit dazed when I rattle off my brother's address.

I am propped on the edge of the pull-out bed trying to make sense of the last five minutes when Dina pops her dark blond head around the corner. "Hey? Who was on the phone?" she asks.

"Um…my ex."

"Oh," she says, her curious frown becoming commiserative. "Did you get some bad news?"

"I don't know… She's on her way."

"On her way? You mean *here*?" she bleats in disbelief.

"Yeah. Here."

"Then you might want to get yourself together," Dina advises, "You look like crap."

As I study my reflection in the mirror after I finish brushing my teeth, I have to admit that Dina's candid assessment was fair. The lower half of my face is covered with at least three days' worth of unshaven beard stubble. But that, at least, does a fair job of concealing the gaunt hollowing of my cheeks. There is no concealing the dark circles and sagging puffiness underneath my eyes. After I've shaved, I feel a little bit more like myself, but I still look far older than my 25 years. Pretty appropriate since I feel like I've aged an entire century in the past five months.

After I'm dressed, I go out on the front porch and sit in one of the dilapidated rocking chairs situated there to await Kate's arrival. While I wait, I mentally rehearse what I'm going to say when she does. I doubt she came all this way to fight with me. I know her pretty well. Kate is a very compassionate person. Likely she came here because she sensed that I was emotional, and she still cares about me. But I don't deserve her kindness. And so, my plan is to simply tell her "thank you" and then gently send her on her way.

She arrives forty minutes later, and when she steps from the car, I feel a little unnerved. The last time I saw her she was in ratty sweatpants, a T-shirt and she looked haggard and broken in spirit. Now, our roles are reversed. She's poised and put together in a crisp black pants suit and black stiletto heels, and I'm the one who is broken and looks that way too.

"Hi," she says as her driver busies himself by pulling her bag from the trunk. "Long time no see."

"Yeah," I agree. I wait for her to finish tipping her driver and watch him drive off before I ask the question that has been burning in my mind ever since she called. "What are you doing here?"

Kate appears just as flustered by the question as I feel. "You know what? I really can't tell you what I'm doing here," she laughs after a few flailing attempts to explain herself. "All I know is that, after you hung up last night, I couldn't stop thinking about you. I booked the first flight to Indiana, and now here I am."

"Why?"

She shrugs noncommittally. The answer she offers is simple and, somehow, not simple at all. "Because you sounded like you needed a friend."

While I ponder why she's made the choice to volunteer as that friend, Kate looks around at the house and yard, taking in her surroundings for the first time. I can tell she's a bit put off by the ramshackle house and barren front yard complete with the proverbial broken down, rusted out pick-up truck. It's definitely not reminiscent of the urbane, city living she's used to.

She has never been to Beckston before. That is no accident either. I had absolutely no intention of ever bringing her here. She knew very well that I had grown up in rural, mid-west America, but she had no tangible evidence to connect with that knowledge. Now she does. She can see with her own two eyes exactly what sort of place I've come from, and I can tell she's a little appalled by the reality. But strangely enough, I don't feel any shame.

"So...this is where you've been staying all this time?" she asks finally.

"Yep."

"I'm surprised. I assumed you'd be with her," she says softly, quietly. And then she demands in seething indignation, "Why isn't she here with you, Julien?"

"Why do you sound angry about it?" I counter in an incredulous tone.

"Are you really asking me that? It's because of *her* that we're not together anymore!"

"That's not true," I deny before she can really settle into that self-righteous rant, "It's because of *me* that we're not together."

Her cheeks become red with mutinous anger. It's obvious that she's itching to refute my argument. After all, it's much easier to lay all the blame at Iyah's feet and paint her as some predatory seductress who "stole" me away rather than admit the truth to herself...that the flaw was mine. I wasn't brainwashed. I wasn't seduced. I did what I wanted. I chose someone else.

Maybe her pride won't let her accept that truth just yet. I watch her jaw flex in her effort to bite back her answering retort. In the end, her self-control wins out. She doesn't engage me further.

Instead, she mutters, "I didn't fly over 700 miles on 3 hours of sleep

293

to fight with you, Julien."

"Then why *did* you fly over 700 miles on 3 hours of sleep, Kate? Tell me the truth."

"To talk," she sighs, "I think we should talk. Don't you?"

"Yeah. We should."

I notice then how she keeps directing distracted glances at something just beyond my shoulder. When I swivel around to see what has her attention, I catch the surreptitious stir of the kitchen curtain as Dina ducks out of sight. I shake my head in amused disgust over her obvious prying. If I have any hopes of having a private conversation with Kate, it won't happen at the house.

"That's Dina," I reply in answer to her unspoken question, "My brother's wife. I think if you and I are going to talk, we probably need to go someplace else."

I'm expecting some pushback over the implied prospect of being alone with me, but Kate is surprisingly agreeable to the suggestion. "Where can we go?"

"There's a walking trail not too far from here. Let's take your bag inside first."

Dina does an admirable job of pretending to be casual while simultaneously being nosy as hell. She basically launches a mini-inquisition, mining for details on Kate's past, present and future. But as soon as she learns that Kate dropped everything to come to my side after hearing about Lucy, Dina becomes an unapologetic Kate Leland fangirl.

She is beyond warm and welcoming to Kate, and I have to admit that I'm secretly happy to see them get along despite their vastly different backgrounds. Dina covertly mouths things to me like, "She's pretty," and "I like her" when Kate's attention is diverted. It's as if she thinks Kate's being here means that she and I have a second chance. I don't know where Dina gets that idea though. That's not a thought in my head, and I seriously doubt Kate is interested either.

After Kate changes her shoes, because stilettos are hardly sensible walking wear, we make our way to the trail together. At first, we mostly engage in awkward small talk while tacitly avoiding the subject that is festering between us. Am I still running? What's the weather like in New York? How's the canine? Is her family doing well? She laments the fact I've shaved off my hair once again, and I comment on how long hers has grown since I last saw her.

We talk about her work and the new projects she's been spearheading and discuss my upcoming movie premiere and the film's limited release in theaters. She chides me on resuming my smoking habit and reminds me of all the health benefits of quitting. I promise her that I'll do better at making my health a priority.

For the most part, it feels like polite conversation between polite acquaintances. We tiptoe around the unspoken parts. But then, very gradually, it begins to grow serious, and we finally start to address the matters that remain unresolved between us. Kate is the first one to break the dam wide open.

"I'm sorry to hear about your mother," she whispers.

I swallow hard past the sudden lump that rises in my throat. "Me too."

"Were you finally able to make peace with her at least?"

"I don't know." My words become hoarse with emotion when I add, "I didn't hate her so much at the end though."

"Good. That's good." There's another awkward pause before she notes gruffly, "You look like you've lost weight. Are you okay?"

I come to an abrupt standstill and turn to face her. "Why do you care?" I challenge, "Why are we doing this, Katie?" It's not an accusation at all. I am sincerely baffled by her motives. I can't understand why my pain would give her any pause whatsoever. If I was in her shoes, I doubt I'd be so sympathetic. If she had wronged *me* like I wronged *her*, I'd tell her to go to hell.

"Do you think I stopped loving you when you left, Julien? If only it were that easy." She regards me mournfully. "When did you stop loving me?"

"I didn't stop loving you, Kate. I still love you."

In hindsight I realize I should have prefaced those words with an explanation. But at that moment, I could never have anticipated that she was going to kiss me. I'm not prepared at all. At first, I'm too stunned to push her away.

Her kiss feels familiar. Pleasant. Safe. And for a fleeting second, I allow myself to yield to it. I let her kiss me, and I kissed her back. Only when I feel the timid dart of her tongue do I regain my head and gently push her away. It's difficult to meet her bewildered gaze in the uncomfortable silence that follows.

"I don't understand," she whispers, "You...you just said that you still love me..."

"I do, Kate...but not the way you want."

It's taken me a while to come to that understanding and really grasp what it means. When my feelings for Iyah first began to develop, I couldn't comprehend how I could risk compromising something so perfect. And when I ended our engagement, the guilt felt immense. Was it fear of commitment like Kate theorized? Was I simply blowing our relationship to pieces because I harbored some secret fear that I would lose it in the end?

At the time, I couldn't be sure. My own ingratitude and unworthiness berated me. I couldn't trust my own judgment or feelings. Surely, there was something wrong with *me* because I had failed to treasure this beautiful, perfect woman who absolutely adored me.

But eventually I came to realize that I had wanted Kate mostly because that was the expectation. How many times had I heard from her family and my friends that I was "lucky" to have her? I was "lucky" that she loved me. And I felt lucky too. I was a homeless runaway who had come from nothing, and she had chosen me. She could have had any man she wanted, but it was *my* love she wanted, *my* ring. That was a heady awareness.

These last, agonizing months, I've turned my feelings for Kate over and over again in my mind, and I've come to a different conclusion altogether. I'm not in love with her...and I don't know that I ever was. She was all of the things that I *should* have wanted and yet, not the thing I wanted at all. But I do love her as a person and a friend. Even now, I love her deeply. She is someone I greatly admire and respect. That will never change.

She is a force in my life. She made me feel safe once, a safety that I hadn't found in my childhood. She made me feel worthy and needed back when I had seen very little value in myself. And I liked feeling those things. I liked who I became when I was with her, and I thought that was what it meant to be in love. That was the way love was *supposed* to feel. And I guess that is true. That sort of love is the foundation for an enduring friendship. But for a marriage? I'm not so sure.

When I tell her all of that, she buries her face in her hands and begins to cry. "Oh my God...I feel so stupid..." she sobs.

"Why do you feel stupid?"

"I thought if I came here that you might want to...because you weren't with her...and..." She steps away and swipes at the tears steadily tracking her cheeks in a bid for composure. "I made a fool of myself," she says again.

"You didn't. It means so much to me that you came here. Your incredible capacity for compassion is just one of the reasons I love you."

"Please don't tell me that, Julien," she groans, "You're not making it easier."

"Our friendship means so much to me."

"Friendship!" she scoffs tearfully, "That's all? I wanted to have children with you. I wanted to grow old with you! This wasn't what I thought we'd become."

I wish I could go back in time and make different choices. It's not as simple as establishing personal boundaries with Iyah early on, though I can see how my inability to do that compounded this mess. But if I'm honest, there were doubts about my relationship with Kate fermenting long before I met Iyah Grandberry. Iyah only forced me to confront those doubts. I should have been honest with Kate as soon as they surfaced. Maybe if I'd had the courage to address them when they began, she and I wouldn't be having this painful conversation now. Maybe Iyah and I would still be together.

"I don't want you to feel like you wasted a trip here."

"But I did, didn't I?" she counters, mildly embittered, "I came here thinking that we might reconcile—,"

"—That would have been a mistake," I interrupt her softly, "You deserve someone who is every bit as good for you as you were for me."

She slumps forward with a tearful grunt. "I don't have it in me to keep on hating you, Julien. It takes too much energy." I step forward instinctively, driven by the need to comfort her, but she sidesteps my reach with a quick shake of her head. "But I can't be your friend either. It's too soon. It hurts too much."

"What do you want me to do?"

"I want you to be in love with me," she replies, "But since that's obviously not an option, maybe we just need to go our separate ways."

I'm truly heartbroken at the thought. "Forever?"

"For now," she relents softly, "At least until I can see you in the same way you see me."

26

I remain in Indiana just one week more following my mother's funeral. Unlike the last time I left the state, this goodbye is bittersweet. This time it actually feels like I'm leaving my family behind. I've built surprising bonds while I've been here, but none more surprising than the close relationship I've developed with my sister-in-law. I might even go so far as to say that Dina and I have become friends.

She is genuinely disappointed that there will be no wedding bells for me in the near future. Dina, like everyone else in my life, is adamant in her belief that Kate is my perfect love match. According to her, if Kate is willing to forgive me for my "indiscretion" and move on from it, then I should also be willing to forgive myself.

Dina believes that I'm being self-flagellating. She doesn't seem to understand that the reason Kate and I aren't together has nothing to do with guilt or self-hatred. Further, I don't view my relationship with Iyah as an "indiscretion" at all. It was messy and heartbreaking and probably ill-advised, but I will never view it as something shameful.

In the meantime, I've decided to refocus on my career. For the past several months, I've been languishing both personally and professionally and that is something that can't continue. Primarily because I've nearly exhausted all my savings, but also because I need to feel productive again.

I have a handful of photoshoots lined up over the next several weeks and my agent is also pushing me to audition for a new pilot series being pitched to one of the major television networks. It's a remake of a popular science fiction show from the 80's with a new modern twist. The script is a classic retelling of aliens assimilating into a hostile society that resents their presence on earth. My agent seems confident that it will be picked up while I have my doubts. The script sounds interesting but in this volatile political climate, I'm not sure the show's premise will be well received.

Then again, I like that the script seems to challenge prevailing stereotypes and has the potential for a diverse cast. That's not difficult to accomplish when most of the main characters aren't human. Besides that, it will be nice to jump back into a familiar routine. Maybe eventually I'll stop feeling so dead inside.

While reuniting with my family has been a good experience for the most part, it has also forced me to confront some aspects of my past that I'd prefer not to address. Aside from my complicated feelings for my mother, my older brother Johnny is also one of those difficult aspects. But unlike with Lucy, I never struggled with the question of loving him or wanting to support him. I think part of my problem is that I love him too much, and there's really nothing I can do to help him now.

Only a select few individuals know that I have a brother who is incarcerated. My agent, Kate, and Iyah. It has been a well-guarded secret, like it would be for most people who have a family member serving time. On the scale of crime, I don't think that being a thief and a conman are the worst offenses a person can commit, but it's challenging to justify that argument in polite company.

I can't really say that I've kept Johnny a secret for the sake of my career either. I'm a relative unknown. Beyond the New York city limits,

I'm not recognizable at all. While I've enjoyed a sizeable bump in my social media presence and some increased job opportunities since making the film, I am never recognized on the street. Even referring to myself as a D-list actor, which is a notoriety on its own, would be grandiose. No one in the general public cares if I have a brother doing time in an Indiana state penitentiary. But *I* care, and I feel guilty and ashamed.

My feelings don't spring from the fact that Johnny is in prison, though that reality does bring a stigma that can't be ignored. The larger truth is that he and I are no different. If it were not for a few incidental life choices, I would be right where he is now. But due to a slight divergence in our comparable paths, I've remade myself entirely and I am free while he is not.

When I think about him in that prison jumpsuit, shackled at the wrists and ankles, it makes me sad but also relieved that I escaped that same fate. Johnny, on the other hand, seemed unbothered. Even in chains, he was proud and nonchalant.

He's always been the most resilient of all the Caffrey brothers, though if anyone ever asked which of us had rebounded the most Johnny and Jake would swear it was me. But that's not true at all. Prison would have finished me off. I have no doubts. In contrast, the experience appeared to have strengthened my brother.

He took Lucy's death surprisingly well, probably the way I would have taken it had I never come to Indiana in the first place. He doesn't weep, and he isn't shocked. Instead, he seemed comforted by the assurance that she had achieved some semblance of peace before she died. But he didn't particularly react as if he had suffered a great loss with her passing either.

I suspect the thing that made him emotional was seeing me and Jake again. The last time we had all been together was in a courtroom just before his sentencing. It wasn't a good memory. Maybe he had that in mind when he saw us because he kept going on and on about how glad he was that we had made better choices. He expressed pride and happiness that we had "made something of ourselves," and seemed very insistent that he didn't want his mistakes to "taint" what we had built. But that's not how I want Johnny to view himself, and that's not how I want to see him either.

Johnny was my idol when we were growing up, my favorite brother. Jake was the disciplinarian, but Johnny was my best friend. He was the person in my life who let me be my most imperfect self without judgment, and he always told me the truth. As I reflect on that, I realize that many of the qualities that attracted me to Iyah in the first place were also traits in my brother that I valued and admired. It's little wonder that my friendship with her came so easily. She filled the void that Johnny left. I didn't even realize it until now.

It was impossible to quantify how much I had missed him until I was sitting across from him with a stone-faced, armed guard towering over us. We weren't able to have any real, deep conversation, not in an open room with other people keenly listening to every word we said, but I was able to tell him a little about my life and what I was doing. He definitely had a great time teasing me about making a living off of my "pretty face."

"Don't ever get yourself locked up, baby brother," he'd laughed, "You'll end up somebody's girlfriend for sure."

We only had an hour with him, and it felt much too short. As Jake and I were leaving the premises, I was very aware that I would probably not see Johnny again for a very long time. The thought saddened me, and if I regret leaving anything behind in Indiana, I will regret leaving him behind.

I am thinking about all of that as I pack up the last of my luggage. There is a heavy sensation in my chest that feels very much like sorrow. That surprises me. I thought when the time finally came to leave this place, I'd leave burning skid marks in my haste to get out of here. I wasn't anticipating this devastating sense of loss and sadness, and I don't really know how to compartmentalize those feelings. I'm emotionally adrift, and I have no idea how to get myself back to stable ground.

"Is this going to be the last time I see you?" Jake asks me plainly on the drive to the airport.

Up until the moment he spoke, we had been riding in silence. I was lost in my thoughts, and he was lost in his. But his question is a stark reminder to us both that we're about to say goodbye to one another and that this might possibly be the last time too.

I know that I could probably be polite and make promises to Jake that I'm not sure I have any intention of keeping, but I choose to be candid instead. "I don't know," I sigh, "Part of me never wants to see this place again as long as I live."

"And the other part?" he prompts.

"The other part is going to miss you."

"You can come back whenever you want," he says, "You have a home here. The girls love you. Dina loves you. And I love you too."

I squirm a little with his admission. This is a new thing for us. The Caffrey family has never been known for emotional sentiment. We don't do touchy-feely. We're much better at leaving things unsaid. I understand that Jake is trying to change that. I appreciate his efforts, and I want to meet him half-way.

The words are there, but I can't voice them out loud. I can only mumble, "Thanks," because I haven't yet reached that place where I can be emotionally vulnerable with him. That time in my motel room doesn't count. That was completely involuntary. To this day, we've never discussed my breakdown or why it happened. I wonder if that's primarily due to my own reluctance or his.

If Jake is aware of my current internal struggle, he doesn't comment on it. Instead, he regards me with a thoughtful, sideways glance, splitting his attention between me and the highway. "I'm serious, Julien. Don't just drop out of sight again. You'll devastate the girls if you do that."

"Do you think you could layer the guilt on just a little thicker, Jake?"

"I'm just saying that your decisions don't only impact you. If you disappear again, I won't be the only one who gets hurt."

"Got it."

I expect him to lean deeper into his lecture despite my compliance because Jake likes to beat the proverbial dead horse until he gets his point across. I'm mentally rolling my eyes in preparation as I scroll through my phone. But he abruptly segues into a totally different subject matter, and it takes me off guard.

"Are you thinking about patching up things with your ex?"

The question is so random that I snort with laughter. "Uh no. That ship has sailed."

"That's not what Dina thinks. She says there's something still there between you."

"Oh, I know. She told me. Multiple times."

"Maybe you ought to think about it," Jake advises.

That comment earns my undivided attention and is enough to prompt me to set aside my cell phone. "I have thought about it. It won't work. I can't give Kate what she needs, and she can't give me what I need."

"What do you think you need?"

Iyah. The answer is automatic and instinctive, but I don't say that part out loud. She remains at the heart of everything that I want. But that is the simplest answer and far from being the big picture. Her absence from my life is only a small piece of the problem. Finding value in myself is the more pertinent issue, and that's where I need the most work.

"I think I need to figure out who I am," I tell Jake after some thought, "and how to like myself for a change."

The journey to get to that place proves to be a laborious one. It's not a linear path at all. What makes it even more challenging is that I make the figurative journey largely on my own.

Upon my return to New York, I keep myself solely focused on work because that is something I can control. I become a virtual machine about "go sees" and auditions, rarely refusing any opportunity my agent presents to me. He, of course, is giddy with that arrangement because more work for me means more money for him. But his satisfaction isn't what motivates me.

I work incessantly because it keeps me preoccupied. I don't have time to think or dwell on how lonely I actually am. I push myself to the point of exhaustion so that the only thing I have energy for is sleep at the end of the day. Then I get up again and do it all over. That remains a manageable arrangement for many weeks until it finally becomes not so manageable anymore.

It takes one comment from me about life being meaningless to kick my family into meddling overdrive. There is a growing consensus among them and even some casual friends that my unhappiness stems from loneliness. Everyone has an opinion, and they all seem to think that I need to get back into the dating scene. According to Dina in particular, my constant isolation is the thing that's causing me to feel so dissatisfied and unfulfilled. A girlfriend, it seems, is supposed to fix everything.

I'm highly skeptical of her theory for many reasons. But the true source of my reluctance is that I find the idea of dating again distasteful for two very important reasons. First and foremost, there is only one woman I want that way and anyone I date will only be a placeholder in my heart. I can't see myself committing to anyone else until I can say unequivocally that I'm over Iyah. And I'm not.

Secondly, even if I *wanted* to date, I've been out of that game so long that I wouldn't even know where to start. If I'm honest, I've never truly *been* in the dating game in the first place. I know how to hook-up, but the idea of asking a woman out feels a little daunting. I've only had two serious relationships in my entire life and neither of them began with traditional dating. The mechanics involved in wooing a woman are foreign to me.

My intrepid sister-in-law gamely decides to take matters into her own hands and volunteers to set me up on the latest dating app, which feels slightly pathetic if I'm honest. But, after weeks of enduring her constant badgering about it, I finally relented and allowed her to create a profile page for me. She was very confident that I was going to generate a lot of interest, especially because she strategically used my professional photos as a lure. I wasn't worried about that part.

That's not a flex. I've always known that women (and some men too) find me attractive. I've literally made an entire living off my face. In my past, I've also used my good looks to leverage for things that I wanted.

So, it's no great surprise that winning the genetic lottery works in my favor dating wise. The issue (if you could really consider it an issue) is that most of the interest generated is superficial and meaningless.

While the women I meet are intrigued enough to go out with me, and sometimes on several dates, they aren't usually invested beyond casual sex. These women are rarely looking for anything long-term. Quite frankly, that suits me fine because I'm not either. Those women who *are* interested in something more meaningful, I tend to give a wide berth.

But it doesn't take long for me to become soured on shallow, no strings sex. That's not to say I don't enjoy it. Sex is a pleasurable distraction from the mundane void my existence has become. But that ecstasy is fleeting and once the euphoria fades, I'm not fulfilled afterwards. I want something else, *someone* else.

But she isn't an option any longer. At this point I would be grateful just for the chance of forming a genuine connection with someone who stimulates me mentally as well as sexually. Unfortunately, the bar has been set ridiculously high.

I need to get out of New York. I am certain of that fact just two months after I return. I'm beginning to feel trapped, and when I feel trapped, I do very stupid things. It's very fortuitous that I get news from my agent that the obscure pilot I auditioned for months earlier has been picked up.

The first season has been greenlit. Even more surprising is that the casting director was so impressed with my audition that, rather than awarding me the recurring part that I tried out for, he decided to offer me one of the supporting roles instead. The show is also set to be filmed in Atlanta, Georgia, which means I will have to relocate. After literal months of aimless couch surfing, it is just the shake-up I need.

Unfortunately, I'm still not financially solvent enough to rent an apartment on my own. Atlanta real estate isn't as pricey as New York, but it's not cheap either. I'll need a roommate.

I pull up an internet search for "roommates needed in Atlanta, Georgia" and start from there. I'm surprised to discover that there is an actual website dedicated to Atlanta residents looking for compatible cotenants. The adverts include abbreviated bios of the person advertising as well as pictures of the place being offered and expectations for rent.

The list is substantial, consisting mostly of couples looking to supplement their incomes by renting out space in their homes. I'm leery of that set-up. I've rented space from couples in the past. It's always turned out to be more than I bargained for. I swipe left for most before finally narrowing my search to singles.

That yields better results. The first person to catch my attention is a 27-year-old guy named Travis. I don't know if it's the crazy colorful outfit he's wearing in his profile picture or the fact he looks stoned out of his mind, but I'm intrigued enough to read his bio. He exudes an "I don't have a care in the world" persona that appeals to me.

His blurb is unintentionally hilarious. Travis describes himself as an "entrepreneur," a "visionary," and a "professional gamer." I have zero idea what a "visionary" does, but it immediately makes me want him for a roommate. I'm already half on board even before I start scrolling through the immaculate photos he's posted of his condo. Being a "visionary" obviously pays well.

His two-bedroom condo in Fulton County, Georgia is nothing short of luxurious. The place is equipped with an outdoor swimming pool and a private fitness center all housed within a gated community. The condo even has two full bathrooms, so we won't be forced to share our space.

And it's dog friendly too. In the event Kate ever relents and allows me to see Scruff again, I won't have to smuggle him in. At $1300 per month, the place seems almost too good to be true. The only requirement is that I submit to a background check. Without even thinking about it, I send Travis a quick message to let him know that I'm interested.

More than a week goes by before he finally responds. After some back-and-forth messages via the app, we cleared up a few misconceptions about where I currently reside and how soon I expect to be in Atlanta. Since Travis' previous roommate is still in the process of moving out, I have a little time before we make the official transition. Travis eventually suggests that we exchange phone numbers so that we can have a live conversation.

The first time we talked on the phone was an experience. I knew two minutes into the phone call that my initial assumptions about him were correct. Travis *is* an avid weed smoker. He is ridiculously chill about everything, and I suspect he might be a little crazy.

That's not a dealbreaker at all.

27

Travis Lorenzo has only two rules.

"Pay your rent on time. Don't eat my food." I follow them both religiously and, unsurprisingly, we have no problems.

My new roommate is everything I expected him to be and more. Standing at only 5 foot 9 with a lean, wiry frame, long, Rastafarian-like dreadlocks, and the scraggliest beard I've ever laid eyes on, Travis possesses a surprisingly commanding presence. He exudes charisma in everything he does. He speaks persuasively, dresses outlandishly and practically struts when he walks. Even his gestures and facial expressions are dramatic and filled with flourish. He is also an unapologetic womanizer. Women stream in and out of our condo on a constant basis.

I'd probably peg him for an actor based on his personality alone, so it's not astonishing to learn he's an aspiring musician and songwriter. He is the walking, talking embodiment of "go big or go home." According to Travis, if it's not a challenge then it's not worth his time. He is what Iyah would label as "extra." Beyond our creative interests, he and I have very little in common. It's a bit incongruent that we get along so well.

Despite my being a stranger, Travis welcomes me into his social circle without reserve, and that circle is equally welcoming of me. It's the first time since I was a teenager that I've cultivated friendships with people outside of my profession. Travis runs with a crowd characterized by wildly diverse interests, and he exposes me to all of that.

While he's curious about my work as an actor, he doesn't badger me with questions like everyone else. Instead of probing me about show business contacts, he introduces *me* to *his* world. Traveling from club to club with him night after night, I learn my way around Atlanta's congested highways and crowded streets in a short time.

We lived together for two months before he pressed me for any details about my private life. It seems appropriate that our first truly personal exchange happens when we are both high. Our loosened inhibitions easily contributed to what could be constituted as an "overshare." It isn't the first time I've smoked marijuana, but it's not something I do often.

I'm not even sure what sparks the conversation between us except that we were discussing our taste in women. We're at some random music studio listening to a demo tape and surrounded by acquaintances of Travis who are, incidentally, just as stoned as we are. But, unlike the main group, Travis and I are seated on the outer perimeter of the compact room nearest to the exit. We're somewhat isolated from everyone else. I'm a week away from wrapping filming for the first season of my television show and this latest "adventure" was Travis' idea of celebrating.

"So…" he drawls after blowing out a perfect ring of smoke. "Who's that girl in your phone?"

I squint at him blearily. "What girl in my phone?"

His bleary eyes gleam with amusement. "You know the one I'm talking about. The one whose screenshot you're always caressing."

He has the nerve to reenact the description complete with a dramatically sappy expression. I reward him for the effort with a one

312

finger salute. He only laughs at my wordless insult, and so do I. But that laughter is short-lived when I consider answering his question.

Travis and I have a good, easygoing camaraderie, but I'm not sure I'm ready to divulge this part of myself. I realize he's probably curious because I'm a young, white guy with an obvious affinity for a non-white girl, but the question still feels too personal. Iyah isn't just any random, non-white girl. She is *the* girl.

"Her name is Iyah," I confess after a vacillating silence. "I met her when we were filming a movie."

"And?"

"Blew it all to hell. Now she hates me."

Travis tsks me in commiseration. I'm not surprised that his reaction is non-judgmental. Travis rarely gets stressed about anything. Instead, he dispenses sympathy and advice.

"That's a rough spot, bro. But I gotta tell you, if you mess up with a black woman, that's over for life. She ain't coming back."

I don't doubt his wisdom. I'm sure he would know that truth better than anyone. After all, that's how I ended up as his roommate in the first place. He takes another puff of the joint before he passes it back to me. His vacant expression looks almost introspective, and I'm expecting him to respond with his usual comeback for everything. "Plenty of trash in the can, my brother."

But he shocks me when he advises with the utmost sincerity, "If you love her, don't give up though. For real."

However, in typical Travis fashion, after that night he makes it his mission in life to fix me up with someone else. Though I warn him that others have tried and failed because I am *not* interested, Travis is confident that he'll meet with success because he, unlike the rest, knows my type now. When I jokingly challenged what he thought that type might be, he had retorted with a toothy smile, "You know what they say. Once you go Black, you never go back."

He offers to fix me up with a friend of his named Cassandra. I agree to the blind date mostly to get him off of my back. But I'm also a little intrigued to see if his theory has merit. Never once had I considered I might be drawn towards a certain "type" now. Though I keep my expectations low for that first date, Cassandra and I hit it off. Our surprising chemistry shocks us both. For nearly three months she and I had a very good thing going.

I enjoyed dating her. I remembered how to have fun and flirt. I remembered how to laugh. We had incredible sex, but I had difficulty committing. I wanted to. I tried, but it never felt organic. After Kate, I wanted to avoid the trap of forcing something because it "made sense." Once Cassandra began wanting things I couldn't give her, I ended it quickly.

"Is there someone else?" she'd asked me.

It was a loaded question. Even after so much time, Iyah remained a specter. We were over but I hadn't stopped wanting her. I doubt I ever will.

"Yes and no."

"Which is it, Julien?"

"I'm not over her yet. I don't want to give you false hope, Cass."

We were able to part on amicable terms and remain friends, but I'm disappointed that I couldn't make it work. I'm tired of living in limbo. While I still miss Iyah, the pain over losing her has become a distant ache. It's receded into the background like white noise. I still think about her sometimes, but I'm no longer resistant to the idea of moving on from her. In fact, I'm ready to be over her entirely.

In the meantime, I keep focused on things I can control. After a decade's long struggle, I'm close to kicking my smoking addiction for good. Instead of reducing the number of cigarettes I smoke per day, I decide to quit cold turkey. I refuse to indulge myself with even one.

I'm proud of how far I've come. And while I can't claim that I'm the most pleasant individual during the transition (Travis has been very vocal about that), I'm certain that after this rough patch is through, I'll be able to put the habit behind me for good. Thankfully, I have other things to keep me distracted.

I am managing the new challenges that come with budding fame. I'm a long way from being hounded by paparazzi or being accosted in the streets by fans, but the show is starting to get some national media attention. The cast is now in full promotion mode for our upcoming series premiere and the interviews, photoshoots, and different sci-fi conventions have been endless. I still maintain a fair bit of anonymity since my character is an alien, and I'm mostly in makeup, but I wonder how long that will last once the show premieres.

While my professional life is beginning to gain momentum, my private life is slowly becoming recognizable again too. My relationship with Kate has gradually thawed to the point where we've reached an amicable custody agreement for Scruff. We trade off with keeping him every two months. That arrangement was challenging in the beginning because it caused a lot of anxiety for Scruff with the stress-induced travel, but he's starting to grow accustomed to it.

He and Travis also had some growing pains in the beginning. Travis wasn't necessarily opposed to pets, but he also didn't want one either. It took him some time to get used to Scruff being underfoot as well as his constant yapping. Eventually, however, they came to tolerate one another and now they are the best of friends. So much so that when the time comes around for me to take Scruff back to Kate's, Travis gets a little downhearted about it.

Even now, he's sitting on the sofa with Scruff in his lap, scratching affectionately behind his ears while I gather up the last of the dog's things for the 16-hour car ride to New York. "Why doesn't she just move closer?" Travis gripes, "You can be a CPA anywhere."

"Yeah, I wouldn't hold my breath on Kate uprooting her entire life just so I can be closer to the dog," I snort derisively.

"Or…she could just let you keep him full time. Who shares custody of a dog anyway? That's some white people nonsense."

"As always, thank you for your candor. On the bright side, at least I don't have to listen to you complain about how he chewed up your sneakers for the next two months."

"Speaking of that, you still owe me money." He angles a glance back at me. "How long are you going to be out there?"

"A week. I don't want to spend more than half a day driving there just to turn back around. I'm gonna catch up with some friends in the city."

A 16-hour car ride confined with an irritable Yorkshire terrier is not a pleasant experience. Normally, a car trip from Atlanta to New York takes an average of 13 hours but with Scruff's high anxiety, there is no way to make the trip without frequent stops. Back when Kate and I first proposed this arrangement, I had briefly entertained the idea of flying with him to New York. I did some research on pet travel and the numerous horror stories I read on Reddit turned me off to that idea pretty fast.

Going by car is definitely the better option for him. For *me*, however, it is an ordeal. By the time I finally arrive at Kate's apartment, I am tired and slightly frazzled.

As soon as she opens the door to greet us, a trembling Scruff jumps into her arms as if he's just been through the most hellish journey of his entire dog life. She clucks and coos to him gently while I complain about the undeserved attention. "Why does he get all the sympathy? All he did was ride. I'm the one who had to maneuver the car with him in my lap most of the drive!"

She favors me with a small, grateful smile. "Thank you for bringing him home."

"Well, that's our deal, right?"

"That doesn't mean you were going to keep it."

I shake my head at her a little sadly. "You still don't trust me, do you?"

"Not entirely. But I'm getting there," she hedges almost affectionately.

Perhaps I'm expecting too much after everything I've put her through, but I really do hope that's the case. After all, almost two years have passed since everything went sideways between us. We are finally on speaking terms again. She even decided to drop the lawsuit against me and has allowed me to reimburse her for the wedding in monthly increments instead. We're not exactly friends, but I don't think we're enemies either. I'd like to think we've finally gotten back to a place of mutual respect.

But mutual respect doesn't mean we've become comfortable enough to spend time together, even casually. So, once Scruff is settled and we've completed our hand-off, I prepare to head off to my hotel room for the late afternoon check-in. The last thing I expect is for Kate to ask me if I was in a hurry to be someplace.

I freeze at the question, suspended between curiosity and wariness over the unprecedented and tacit invite. "Not really. Something on your mind?"

She reaches into her pocket and pulls out a small, black velvet box, then places it neatly in the center of the kitchen island that separates us. "I wanted to give this back to you."

There's no need to open the box. I already know what it is without looking inside or even asking the question. It's her engagement ring. What surprises me is that she still has it after all this time. I assumed it would be at the bottom of the Hudson River by now. And even though I'm sure holding on to the ring this long has probably been painful for her, I don't necessarily want her to give it back either.

"You don't have to do this," I tell her, pushing the box back towards her with an emphatic shake of my head. "It's yours. I gave it to you. I want you to keep it."

"But it doesn't mean what either of us thought it did, does it?" she counters softly.

"Point made. You don't have to keep it then. You can sell it instead. Put it towards my debt for the wedding. Do whatever you want, but I'm not taking it back."

"Why not?"

Rather than answer that question, I simply dive to the heart of the thing that's truly bothering me. "Are you really that eager to sever all ties with me, Katie?"

"It's not about severing ties, Julien. I'm trying to start over."

"Then why did you keep it all this time?"

She looks away and nibbles on her lower lip. "I don't know."

We both know that the answer is a lie. She was hoping I would change my mind. Obviously though, that hope has faded now and something critical has happened if she's ready to let it go. "Why are you giving it back?" I ask her softly.

"I've met someone."

She pauses a beat and lets the statement hang, as if she's waiting for some sort of reaction from me. I'm not sure if she's anticipating anger or disappointment or jealousy, but I don't feel any of those things. I'm happy for her. I think she must sense that because she jerks a quick nod and elaborates further.

"His name is Tom. I met him three months ago when Mom and I went to Europe together. He's British."

"Of course, he is," I joke lightly, "All Toms are British." She responds with a wobbly smile. "Do you like him?" I ask.

"I do."

"Is he good to you?"

She inclines her head in a small nod. "He's very good to me. He flew down earlier this month to spend the week with me and…I think we're starting to get serious."

"Serious like you might move across the Atlantic to be with him serious?"

"Yes…maybe…" I'm trying to absorb that news and figure out what that's going to mean as far as our arrangement for Scruff when she says, "If that happens, he should stay with you. I don't want to uproot him that way."

"Okay."

"What do you think?" she presses when I don't say anything further.

"I think you should do what is best for you."

I'm not being insincere either. I don't necessarily want her to move across an entire ocean, but I'm certainly not going to stand in her way of happiness either. For a long time, I've feared the possibility that I had broken her in some irrevocable way. Knowing that she has recovered and moved on helps to ease my guilty conscience over the terrible way we ended. I wish her nothing but eternal joy, and I tell her that.

"I want the same thing for you too."

"I'm getting there," I say with a smile, deliberately turning her earlier words to me back at her.

She surprises me when she reaches across the island to grab hold of my hand. "I really do mean that," she insists, "You deserve to be happy." When I start to dispute that declaration, she presses on. "Yes, you hurt me terribly. For a long time, I hated you for leaving me and for not loving me like I loved you. I convinced myself that you were a worthless person. And…and I think that I convinced you that you were worthless too."

As soon as I sense where the conversation is headed, I groan and try to pull my hand away, but she tightens her hold on my fingers. "I don't want to do this with you."

"We need to have the conversation. You did a bad thing, Julien, but you're not a bad person." I can't stop myself from snorting out an embittered laugh at the simplicity of that statement. "It's true. What you did to me was awful," she asserts, "You hurt me more than anyone has ever hurt me, but you shouldn't have to pay for that for the rest of your life. You've done enough penance."

"Let's not rehash this, please."

"We're not going to rehash it. But hindsight is a beautiful thing, don't you think? You could have gone through with the wedding, and it would have been a disaster for us both. We would have still ended up right here, only we might have had years of an unhappy marriage and a few kids by then too. In the end, you did us both a favor."

"What are you saying, Kate?"

"I'm saying I forgive you. And you *deserve* that. Everyone deserves a second chance."

It's not until she says the actual words that I realize how long I've been waiting to hear them. Her forgiveness has been a thing I've yearned for, but never once expected. The relief and gratitude that follows is immense.

I bob my head in response because I'm incapable of speech right then. I want to tell her what an extraordinary woman she truly is, how Tom is an extremely lucky man, how I sincerely wish I could have been all the things she needed, but all those declarations are lodged in my throat. The only thing I can manage is a barely audible "thank you" because if I attempt to say anything more, I will lose what's left of my composure.

I pull my hand free of her grasp with the full intention of beating a hasty retreat out of there when she asks me, "Are you going to see her show while you're here in New York?"

Something about the question stops me in my tracks and prompts me to slowly pivot to face her again. "See whose show?"

"Your girlfriend," she clarifies in an ironic tone, "She's starring in a musical."

"What are you talking about?"

"She's here. In New York," Kate reveals slowly, blinking at me in astonishment. "I saw her on the news some months back. She saved a woman's life. They dubbed her a local hero and everything."

Based on the way she's looking at me I'm sure my expression is nothing short of "shell-shocked." The literal wind has been knocked out of me. My chest is tight. I'm lightheaded. Blood pounds loudly in my ears, propelled by my furiously pumping heart. Yet, with all of the chaos going on inside me, I can only process one incredible thing. Iyah is here in New York. With me. *Iyah is in New York with me.*

Kate grunts a mirthless laugh over my reaction. "I guess you didn't know."

I stare at her as if she's lost her mind. "Why would I know?"

"I thought maybe you might keep in touch with her…"

"No, I don't. We're over. I haven't seen her…"

"I'm surprised to hear that."

"Why?"

"Because you were in love with her," she concludes softly. "I think you might *still* be in love with her, Julien."

If I thought I was close to tears before this moment, that is nothing compared to the agony knifing through me now. I'm seconds away from splintering. There's no way I can respond to her speculation. I can't even speak.

Kate is not discouraged by my answering silence. She pushes even further. "I don't think I'm wrong," she whispers, "And if that's true, maybe you should do something about it."

28

This is probably a bad idea.

That thought has crossed my mind numerous times since I decided to come here tonight. I'm being impulsive. I haven't even considered the consequences of what will happen if she sees me again...if *I* see her. But part of me doesn't care because I'm so desperate to be in her space again.

Besides that, it's too late to second guess myself. I've already purchased my ticket and filed in with the other patrons. I'm seated at the very back of the dark, crowded theater anxiously awaiting the curtain rise. There's no way in hell I'm leaving this place now. I'm cemented in my seat. I can't leave, not without a glimpse of her first.

My head has been buzzing continuously since I spoke with Kate. To learn that Iyah has been in New York for at least six months, that I left the city only a few short weeks before she arrived makes me crazy. If I had known she was here, I'm not sure I would have left at all. Maybe I would have taken it as a sign that I should try again. Maybe I would have gone after her then the same way I'm going after her now.

Objectively speaking, however, this isn't a good plan. It's an ambush. There are no circumstances that make dropping in on your ex-girlfriend at her place of employment to possibly declare your undying love an inherently good move. I'm probably setting myself up for failure, and I know that. But I can't and won't budge from this seat.

Iyah once confided in me that she thought I might be a masochist. At this very second, that theory has some real validity. We parted on very bad terms. I hadn't seen her in eighteen months, twenty-six days, and 20 hours. She has made it abundantly clear that she would like it to remain that way. This isn't going to be some heartwarming reunion.

At best, she'll be cold and cordial towards me. At worse, she won't acknowledge me at all, or she'll have me thrown out by security. This won't go well. I compulsively flip back and forth through the program to keep myself distracted from that knowledge.

When the curtain finally rises, I hold my breath in anticipation. There is a dizzying whirl of colorful lights, costumes and actors flitting onto the stage amid large swathes of outlandish scenery and smoke effects. But none of that confusion registers. I'm able to pick Iyah out almost immediately. Even heavily costumed and in full make-up, her tiny frame, movements, and mannerisms are easily recognizable to me.

Eighteen months hasn't dulled that familiarity. Why would it? I see her in my dreams. The moment she opens her mouth to sing, my instincts are validated. I don't take my eyes off her for a single second. It's honestly the happiest moment I've experienced since we parted.

But I don't really watch the show. I couldn't tell you the theme or premise if my life depended on it. I watch her. I listen to her, when she speaks, when she sings. I hang on every word and musical note. She is magnificent. When the musical ends and the audience rises with a standing ovation, I stand with them and clap, but my applause is for Iyah Grandberry alone.

After the curtain drops the audience begins to file out, anxious to make it back to their cars or to the subway to beat the evening traffic and congestion. I don't leave with them as was my original plan. Instead, I weave my way upstream towards the stage with the fans who are eagerly clamoring to meet the cast in person. At this point, I have no idea if I'm going to reveal myself to her or how, but I do know that I need to see her up close. Just once.

I linger with that group of intrepid fans while they chat with various cast members, snap selfies, and request autographs. From a distance of at least 15 feet, I watch Iyah interact with her own small group of admirers, smiling and laughing merrily as she poses for selfie after selfie. She is still in her costume, but her face is scrubbed clean of most of her make-up. Some smudges still linger on her cheeks and chin, and I can see the perspiration that glistens on her skin after being beneath the hot theater lights for several hours. She has never looked more breathtaking to me. I greedily drink in the sight of her.

I should leave. That was the deal I made with myself when I purchased my ticket online after all. I was going to watch her musical, allow myself a few fleeting glances of her from a safe, substantial distance, and then I would leave as quietly as I arrived. But I'm not moving. My looks are not fleeting. And this distance is hardly substantial.

It's as if my feet are bolted to the floor. They feel heavy yet disconnected from my body. I couldn't move them even if I wanted to…though a few seconds later I find myself wishing I had. Because I continue to linger, I witness the exact moment when Iyah catches sight of someone she recognizes out among the dense group of admirers and quietly excuses herself.

As soon as she approaches the tall man, I know instantly that he's not another fan. It's obvious that there is something between them. Their quiet exchange strikes me as intimate even before he gently pulls her into his arms and kisses her. And she kisses him back.

A wave of intense jealousy goes knifing through me when I see them together. My first instinct is to go charging forward to forcibly rip them apart, but mid-step I remember that she isn't mine anymore. Iyah is not my girlfriend. She's not even my lover. She hasn't been for a very long time. That's the instant when my seething jealousy is replaced with quiet anguish. The thing I wouldn't allow myself to contemplate before this moment is an undeniable reality. Iyah has moved on.

That should be enough to make me turn around and walk right out of there, but I don't. I am the masochist she said I was. Rather than leaving, I retreat into the shadows and continue to watch them like some pathetic creeper. I follow their movements and conversation as they interact with Iyah's cast members. I loiter near the stage while they discuss their plans for the evening with each other, and Iyah darts back to the dressing room to change.

Despite the directions from the ushers who are responsible for emptying the theater, I don't return to my hotel after they encourage us to leave. Instead, I sneak into the alley and find my way to the side entrance of the theater to wait for Iyah and her friends to exit. Once they do, I follow the raucous group onto the main sidewalk as they laugh and debate dinner options amongst themselves. Mostly, I watch Iyah's interactions with her boyfriend.

I take note of the way they walk arm in arm and every affectionate gesture and kiss they exchange. I see the way he smiles at her, and more painfully, the way she smiles back at him. Each look, each kiss feels like a small death to me. I should feel happy for her, like I was happy for Kate, but all I can process is jealousy and anguish.

Despite the pain, I keep following her because I also know that this will probably be the last time that I'm this close to her again. But when Iyah and her boyfriend stop in the middle of everything to kiss and nuzzle one another so he can tenderly tie his scarf around her neck, I'm physically nauseated. I can't watch anymore. That moment breaks me, and I finally have enough of torturing myself.

I turn towards the street to hail a passing taxi and, just as I do, it feels like Providence intervenes. I'm not being dramatic either. It's as if the moment had been fated to occur.

A sudden wind gust whips against me and sends a lone leather glove and an unsuspecting Iyah tumbling directly into my path. She and I make a quick dive to retrieve the glove at the same time, but I catch it before she can. She doesn't even realize it's me until she straightens, and we come face to face at last.

Though it's trite in every way, it *does* feel like time grinds to a halt as soon as we meet each other's eyes. I don't know if it's the moonlight or the way her dark eyes glitter so magnificently in the frigid air or the tendrils of wild, curly hair that whip across her beautiful mouth but, in this moment, Iyah Grandberry has never been more gorgeous to me. Even with minimal make-up, she is mesmerizing, and I want nothing more than to kiss her and never stop.

Now that I'm so close to her and able to scan every detail of this face that I have missed so much, it's impossible for me to look away. I clench down on the urge to brush her wild halo of hair back from her face. The need to feel her skin beneath my fingertips is like fire. I remind myself that touching her is a privilege that is beyond me now and wisely keep my hands to myself.

Instead, I concentrate on masking the chaotic emotion that being in her space again causes me and extend her fallen glove towards her with a wordless smile. But she is too stricken to take it right away. In fact, she doesn't move. She keeps staring at me like she's seen a ghost.

Finally, I whisper, "I think you lost this. Are you gonna take it back?"

The question seems to reanimate her because she blinks rapidly and then snatches the glove from my fingers. The shock gradually fades away. Her features become stony, and she takes a deliberate step backwards.

"Thanks."

"You're welcome." We contemplate one another in heavy silence before I whisper, "It's good to see you." What I really want to say is, "I miss you. I love you. Come home with me." What I say instead is, "I didn't know you were in New York."

Her lips compress into a tight line. "Why would you? We haven't spoken in over a year."

"Not for lack of trying on my part," I tell her wryly, "I've called you at least fifty times over the past eighteen months. I can't prove it, but I get the feeling you might have blocked my number." She doesn't deny it, and I gain a strange comfort in knowing I wasn't imagining things after all. She *had* deliberately cut me off. "You look great. How have you been?"

Her eyes shimmer at me dangerously, and I'm a little stunned to realize she's still very furious with me. This is far from the cold detachment I'd anticipated. Time has not lessened her antagonism towards me a single bit.

I can't help but be puzzled by her anger because it seems too fresh. Surely, if Kate had reached a place of forgiveness after all these months, Iyah's bitterness and resentment should have cooled by now too. But it hasn't, and I'm not sure how to react. I was prepared for her apathy but not her rage.

"Really, Julien?" she snaps, "Are you seriously asking me that after everything?"

Unfortunately, we don't have a chance to get into that even though I'm suddenly itching to have *that* conversation because her boyfriend jogs up from behind. I resent the intrusion because Iyah and I were undoubtedly on the cusp of something revealing. She tenses immediately with his arrival, and so do I. With considerable effort, I bite back the impulse to bark at him to go away.

I have to remind myself that I'm the intruder here, not him. Besides that, the man seems oblivious to the wealth of unspoken friction between us. When he approaches, his expression is open and curious.

"Did you catch it?" he asks Iyah breathlessly.

At first, I don't understand what he's asking until I realize that he is still looking around on the sidewalk for the glove. He doesn't realize that Iyah has it in her hand and she doesn't inform him either. Honestly, I don't think she registers a single word he says. Her eyes are glued on me, as if she believes she can zap me into nonexistence if she glares at me long enough.

Two minutes ago, I was ready to dive into a cab and ride back to my hotel room to lick my wounds. I was wrecked and despondent. Now, I'm curious and determined to stay exactly where I am.

Iyah knows it too, which is probably why she looks like she wants to murder me. I ignore her surly scowl for the time being and focus my attention on the boyfriend. Since she doesn't make any move to introduce us, I take matters into my own hands and make my presence known.

"I caught it actually," I tell him, "Crisis averted."

He acknowledges my existence for the first time then, and I get my first unobstructed view of the man who has now taken my place in Iyah's life. He's much better looking than I was expecting. Like model levels of gorgeous and for some inexplicable reason that bothers me. He has what could be classified as a symmetrical face, with a strong jawline and striking green eyes…the kind that would look stunning in a print ad. He's also taller than me by at least a good six inches, which I find mildly aggravating.

I'm looking at the literal embodiment of "tall, dark, and handsome." And while he's not the complete antithesis of me (because it's clear that my Iyah has an affinity for "pretty boys"), I am not exactly soothed by the knowledge that she's chosen *this* "pretty boy." I'm not soothed that she's chosen anyone at all. The thought is a selfish one, but I own it.

I don't want to feel threatened or possessive because I have no rights here. Besides, it's beyond senseless and juvenile, but at this moment, those are the two foremost emotions I can process. I feel what I feel. The Neanderthal in me wants to yank Iyah to my side and sneer, "she's mine." However, my more sensible side recognizes I'll likely get punched in the face for the attempt. And probably by Iyah herself.

Thankfully, the boyfriend is completely unaware of the wild thoughts running through my head, or he'd punch me too. I don't sense hostility from him. Instead, he is affable and polite when he thanks me. I think he might even try to offer me compensation for my trouble, but then his eyes suddenly flare wide with recognition.

"Hey! I know you! You're that guy!"

"What guy?" It's possible that he's seen me on one of New York's many billboards, but when I suggest the possibility, he shakes his head.

"No! You were in that movie with Iyah, weren't you? The one about the guy with schizophrenia."

I'm taken off guard a little by his general cheerfulness about it. I don't know many men who could react so graciously after coming face to face with their girlfriend's ex. He's either very secure, or he has no idea what Iyah and I were together.

Iyah's rather obvious panic makes me inclined to think it's the latter. She shakes her head at me imperceptibly almost like she's silently begging me to deny his assumption that she and I know each other. The idea seems ridiculous, but then she snags hold of her boyfriend's arm with the obvious intention of pulling him away and pretending she's never laid eyes on me in her life. And that's when my suspicion becomes certainty.

He doesn't know about us. Evidently, Iyah never told him. To him, I'm just some guy she made a movie with two years ago. He doesn't know that we used to be friends. He doesn't know that I've tasted every bare inch of her smooth, brown skin. What's unclear to me is if her lack of disclosure is due to shame over what happened or latent feelings that she still has for me. If the stricken expression on her face is any clue, I'm pretty sure it's a mixture of both.

She's steadily trying to pull him away, but he seems intent on arguing with her, clearly puzzled by her behavior. "Stop being weird. This is the guy, isn't it?"

On pure impulse, I thrust out my hand to introduce myself. "Yep, that's me. I'm Julien Caffrey."

If I were a piece of kindling, the withering look Iyah gives me would have incinerated me into ash. She is *not* happy with my disclosure. That much is plainly obvious. But I steadfastly ignore her death glare and shake hands with her boyfriend.

"I'm Hez Dennis," he says, "Iyah and I are dating. She *just* let me see the movie you guys did together like a month ago. She's so sensitive about that kind of stuff. It's crazy."

Iyah smiles tightly. "That was my first real job, and it was a long time ago. We've both moved on to other things since then."

331

The double meaning in that statement is unmistakable as is my response to her. "I still think it's some of your best work," I tell her softly, "We were very good together."

The insinuation that passes between us thankfully goes unnoticed by Hez. "Did you know that he was in town?" he asks Iyah.

"He lives here too, Hez. We just haven't kept in touch with one another."

"Actually, I *don't* live here anymore," I correct her, "I've been in Atlanta for the past six months."

Her eyes flash and glisten before she looks away from me. "Oh really? Atlanta? Interesting choice."

"It's for work. I'm filming a new series there. We just wrapped the first season."

"Are you down South for the foreseeable future then? You and your *wife*?" She poses the question with a definite bite.

I shake my head. "Nope. Just me. I'm not married, Iyah. I've *never* been married."

Her boyfriend regards Iyah with a quizzical grimace while she absorbs the news that I've just given her. I can tell she's stunned because she blinks at me in clear distress. She doesn't say a word. She doesn't even move until her boyfriend nudges her.

"Why would you think he was married?"

She avoids eye contact with us both when she answers. "Natural assumption. He was engaged when we were filming. I met her once."

"Oh," he says, glancing back at me, "So what happened?"

He clearly has no issues with being forward with a virtual stranger, but I'm not put off by his forthright nature. Truthfully, I'm glad he asked the question. He's inadvertently given me the opening I've been hoping for this entire time. I look over at Iyah deliberately before I answer his question.

"Turns out it's not such a good idea to get married when you're in love with someone else."

Predictably, Hez assumes that I'm referring to my fiancée and not myself because he says, "Wow. That's rough that your girl left you like that."

I flick a furtive glance at Iyah before I agree softly, "Yeah. It *is* rough."

I'm not sure what Iyah would have done next if her friends hadn't chosen to intrude with loud complaints about being hungry. But it's clear to me she's grateful for the reprieve from them. She goes through the perfunctory routine of introducing me to her castmates for the sake of being polite. Despite those actions, I suspect she's secretly hoping I will go away. I don't want to torment her, but I also don't want to leave any misconceptions between us either. So, when Hez inadvertently gives me an opening by inviting me to tag along with them for dinner, I gladly take him up on his offer.

The group decides on pizza and when we arrive at one of the more popular pizza spots it is still relatively packed. As a result, the group isn't able to sit together. Hez invites me to join him and Iyah at their table so that she and I can "catch up." He seems unaware of Iyah's less than enthused reaction over that prospect.

I also don't think he realizes that, between the three of us, he does most of the talking. Though we briefly discuss where I'm staying, how long I will be in New York and my new television series, Hez dominates most of the conversation and that is fine with me. Iyah is sullen and withdrawn and barely touches her food. She doesn't interject at all unless directly asked a question. As for me, I mostly listen to Hez while he talks.

He recounts the story of his and Iyah's unlikely meeting and how brave and confident he thought she was. He tells me how she captured his attention right from the beginning. I'm not surprised because she had a similar effect on me. I also learn from him that it took him an inordinately long time to convince Iyah to go out with him and that they've only been together for a little less than five months. He talks and talks until he abruptly gets a phone call that briefly takes him away from the table.

As soon as he steps away, Iyah hisses, "What are you doing?"

"Eating pizza. What are *you* doing?"

She would have probably ripped me to verbal shreds right then if Hez hadn't popped back over to inform us that he had to leave. Apparently, he was on call and his employer needed him to come in. Though Iyah volunteers to accompany him home, he encourages her to stay and socialize with me instead. I would probably feel guilty about how pleasantly ignorant he's being if his cluelessness wasn't working in my favor. I grit my teeth through their lingering kiss goodbye and watch Iyah as she watches him leave. Once he is completely out of sight, she whips back around to glare at me.

"You're a jackass!"

"Why didn't you tell him about us?" I counter softly.

"What us?" she snaps, "There is no us! We had sex once, Julien! That's all!"

"It was *more* than once," I remind her, "And it was *more* than sex."

Iyah flops back down into the empty seat directly across from me and crosses her arms in mutinous defiance. For the first time, I recognized that she's not just angry with me. She's on the verge of tears. Iyah is barely holding it together.

"Why are you doing this to me?"

I push my paper plate aside and stare at her squarely. "What am I doing to you?"

"You've got it all wrong! I'm over you, Julien," she says though her expression and body language totally belie that pronouncement. "I don't know what kind of game you're playing, but you are wasting your time and mine!"

"Then you should tell me your secret because I'm not over you. I have never gotten over you, Iyah."

"Stop it."

"I've thought about you every day since we've been apart. You're all I think about."

She laughs and it sounds bitter and scornful and anguished all at the same time. "Is that right? Because that's not what you told me back then. You said you wanted to try again with Kate, and that you wished you had stayed away from me! You said that we were a mistake!"

"We were never a mistake. I didn't go back to Kate. We were done after that night."

"But you told me—,"

"—I know what I told you," I interject wearily before she can finish, "and I didn't mean any of it! I was scared and stupid that night." She looks away from me, her jaw clenched tight. "I want you to forgive me."

That request triggers her. She lifts eyes filled with unshed tears and leaping fire to my own. "You...you really have a lot of nerve, don't you?" she utters, "You just drop back into my life after all this time like nothing ever happened, and I'm supposed to just fall into your arms like that!" She snaps her fingers for emphasis. "Is that what you think?"

"*You* walked away from *me*. I tried to fix it, but you wouldn't talk to me!"

"You walked away first! We're in this place because of *you*, Julien!"

"You're right. I know that. I'm sorry. I just thought you deserved someone better."

Her eyes flash again as the tears she's been holding back finally spill over, and she scoots from the booth to rise to her feet. She reaches into her pocket and tosses a handful of bills on the table with the obvious intention of leaving me there. It is an implicit declaration that our conversation is done, but she doesn't leave without a parting shot.

"Well, you got your wish. I *did* find someone better."

29

I am a little intoxicated.

So, when the first knock sounds, I'm convinced I'm hallucinating. After all, it's late, well after 10 p.m. Even in the city that never sleeps, the notion that someone would be visiting me at this time of night is ridiculous. Only a handful of people know where I'm staying anyway, and none of them would bother showing up here this late, especially unannounced. Well, except for maybe *one* person. And the chances of it being her on the other side of that door are slim to none. But when I yank the door open, I discover those chances aren't nearly as slim as I thought.

I blink at Iyah in hazy incredulity. "What are you doing here?"

"Can I come in?"

The request leaves me speechless as does her softened expression. It's doubtful I would have told her "no" even if I was capable of words right then anyway. I still can't believe she's actually standing there. When she stormed out of the pizza parlor earlier, I was pretty sure that was the last time I was ever going to see her again. I had every intention of coming back to my hotel room and raiding the mini bar. I planned to get very drunk and stay that way for the rest of the night.

Now, here we are two hours later. The mini bar is half empty and I am indeed drunk. But surprisingly Iyah is standing in the hallway just outside of my room very humbly asking to come inside. I don't even think about refusing her. I simply move aside and gesture for her to enter.

"I listened to your phone message," she says quietly when we're facing one another again.

I am the picture of nonchalance when I lean back against the door with folded arms and regard her with heavy, speculative eyes. "Which one? I left you several."

"The one about your mom."

All my indifference fizzles quickly and I become momentarily clearheaded. I straighten and close myself off a bit with the mention of my mother and that desperate voicemail I left for Iyah after her passing. It's been months but I haven't forgotten it or the visceral agony that had compelled me to leave it. Drunk or not, it's not a conversation I want to have, especially now.

"That was a while ago."

"I know." Her features suddenly crumple into an anguished mask as she takes a step closer to me. "Julien, I'm so sorry," she whispers hoarsely, "If I had known I would have answered you! I swear! I didn't mean to…"

The discovery that it is pity and not desire that has brought her to my door this late makes me inexplicably angry. I'd rather she be here because she wants me, because she needs me as much as I need her, not because she feels guilty. Or obligated. The thought that I might be an obligation to her is far worse.

"Don't you dare feel sorry for me!" I snap at her, and my vehemence stops her in her tracks. "If that's the reason you came all the way out here then you wasted a trip! I don't want your pity!"

"My God, Julien! It has nothing to do with that! I'm trying to apologize to you!" she flares.

"For what?" I flare right back.

"For ignoring you," she laments in a more softened tone, "I shouldn't have done that. I really wish I hadn't." I'm stunned to realize she's visibly close to tears, as if my perceived anguish is *her* anguish too. "I never would have done that if I had known, *never*…and I'm sorry. I'm so sorry…"

As she starts to break down with small, hiccupping sobs, I feel very helpless watching her dissolve. I've seen Iyah cry maybe a handful of times as long as I've known her, and I know that it takes a lot for her to display vulnerability in front of anyone. That knowledge makes witnessing her pain even more agonizing.

I do the only thing I can do. I take a few tentative steps towards her and gently tug her into my arms. She comes into my embrace without reserve. When her arms go around me and she buries her face in my chest, I tighten my arms around her and cradle her as closely as possible. It's almost like a dam of grief breaks open then and she sobs even harder, so much so that her tears spark my own.

Her pain is a primal thing. It shatters me. I feel it all the way down to my marrow. I wonder if she's grieving for more than just the lost opportunity to comfort me after my mother's death. I wonder if she's grieving for *us* too.

After a few minutes, her weeping finally quiets into sniffles, and she carefully extricates herself from my arms. She won't look at me as she whisks the remaining streaks of tears from her cheeks. I suppose I should feel awkward and uncomfortable too, but strangely enough I don't. Comforting her is as natural to me as breathing and just as involuntary.

"Well, that was stupid," she mutters, her words so gruff they're almost inaudible. "I was supposed to make *you* feel better."

"You're fine," I reassure her with a self-conscious smile. "And so am I. It happened months ago anyway."

At that moment, Iyah looks at me squarely and I have no doubts that she can see past my careless bravado straight down into my heart and everything I leave unsaid. Her next question to me dispels all doubt. "Does that mean you've made your peace with it?"

I duck my head when I answer her. "No."

She does something unprecedented then, something I would have never expected after how much our relationship has changed. She takes hold of my hand and leads me over to the bed. I'm a little unnerved and self-conscious about what she has in mind until she gestures for me to sit down and then sits down next to me. She gives my fingers a reassuring squeeze and then whispers, "Tell me everything."

And I do. I told her everything, beginning with the phone call from Jake. When I first begin speaking, it's as if I'm recounting someone else's story. I'm reciting facts and events. My emotions are far removed from the retelling. But the longer I talk about reconnecting with my family, the more that changes, until I reach a point where sharing the experience becomes physically and emotionally difficult, where my words become so garbled with sorrow and regret that I can barely understand myself.

"She died the day before your birthday," I tell her, "We played cards together that morning because she liked to play all kinds of games, and I wanted to tell her then that I forgave her. I wanted to say, 'I love you,' but I couldn't make myself say the words because I wasn't ready. And now I won't get the chance."

I don't even realize how freely my tears are flowing until Iyah reaches up to tenderly brush them away from my chin. But before she can open her mouth to sway me with sweet, comforting platitudes I say,

"And don't tell me that she knew how I felt! We both know that she didn't. She died thinking that I hated her. I let her die believing that, and I have to live with it now."

"Is that the reason why you said what you did in the message?" she asks me in a timid tone, "You know…about loving me? Did you mean that?"

"Yeah," I whisper, "I meant that. I love you, Iyah."

She closes her eyes briefly, as if she's letting the avowal wash over her before she raises her gaze to mine and whispers back, "I love you too."

I don't stop to contemplate the consequences of kissing her. I simply follow my instincts and do it. The contact is soft and fleeting, like the delicate beat of a butterfly's wing against a flower petal. I hold my breath when I do it. When I pull back to gauge her reaction and search her face for signs of regret or uncertainty, all I see is love and desire. Her gaze drops slowly, deliberately to my mouth and, with her tacit permission, I lean in to kiss her again. This time, she meets me halfway.

What begins as slow, tentative exploration, a sweet reacquaintance gradually spirals into something deep and hungry and primal. I'm driven by the need to kiss her as deeply as I can, to touch and taste her everywhere. I'm only vaguely aware of pulling her into my lap, but she willingly straddles me, overcome with the same need.

She kisses me again and again and I kiss her back. We're both overwhelmed by the wild desperation to rip away all barriers, to have nothing between us, physically or emotionally. There is a biological imperative to be as close to her as I can be, to explore her most intimate places with my hands and mouth and body. But once I have her beneath me, and I start to slip my fingers into the waistband of her underwear to touch her where I know she's soft and wet for me, Iyah catches hold of my hand in an agitated grip.

"Julien, wait!"

The change in her is so abrupt that I don't immediately register what is happening. I'm too clouded with passion to stop. Instead, I try to kiss her again, but she dodges my effort and rolls away from me entirely.

"I can't," she groans.

I ignore her attempt to put distance between us and shift closer. "What's wrong?" I whisper, nibbling small kisses across her shoulder. "I have protection if that's what you're worried about."

"It's not," she mutters. Before I can question her about that, she sits upright with a heavy sigh and scoots to the edge of the bed. "I'm sorry."

I stare at her naked back in hazy confusion, unable to comprehend how we've gone from being wrapped around each other so passionately to having two feet of space between us. Only a minute earlier we were tangled together, seconds from consummating our desire for one another. I don't know what changed.

While her brain and body have obviously disconnected, mine are still working in sync. I am *literally* aching for her. It's unfathomable to me after how responsive and eager she was for my touch that she doesn't want me as much as I want her. But when I reach over to caress her shoulder and coax her back down beside me, beneath me, she flinches.

"I mean it! We shouldn't have done this," she insists stridently.

The distress in her tone finally snaps me into reality. "Why not?"

The question sounds like it's being wrenched out of me. I want her so much that I'm in physical pain. It takes every ounce of self-control I have not to touch her again.

"You know why. Didn't you learn anything from the first time?"

There's no need for her to elaborate further. I'm unable to argue that point so I flop back against the mattress with an aggravated curse and drag both hands down my face in a futile effort to calm down. Every inch of my body is one pulsing, raw nerve. Everything throbs.

It takes a minute for the blood that's been shunting furiously to my groin to redirect its flow back to my brain. Of course, that doesn't happen without me expelling a string of explicit curses along the way. From the corner of my eye, I notice Iyah wince in reaction. For that reason, I mumble a sincere apology after taking a few seconds to compose myself.

"Are you mad at me?" she asks quietly when I'm calmer. "I wasn't trying to lead you on."

"I know that. And I'm not mad. I'm frustrated. I still want you."

That frustration only increases when she shifts from the bed with a resigned sigh and begins gathering her scattered clothing from the floor. I'm barely able to suppress my disappointed groan when she shrugs back into her bra and pulls her sweatshirt back down over her head. But, as much as it pains me, the finality of watching her get dressed does help to cool down my persistent lust. Reluctantly, I rise from the bed to get dressed too.

"Do you love him?" I ask her, pulling on my pants. "That paramedic?"

"I *want* to love him."

"That's not an answer."

She swivels to face me with a frustrated grimace. "I don't know what you want me to say, Julien!"

"I want you to say that you're done with him! I *want* to be in bed with you! We've been apart long enough, don't you think?"

I know it's absolutely the wrong thing to say even before she spears me with the glower of 1000 deaths but honestly, I'm too tired and too drunk to be politically correct. As far as I'm concerned, I've done my "if you love them, set them free" penance. I'm sick of being noble!

There has to be a reason we've gravitated back together after all this time. I don't know if it's God or Fate, but I do know that I'm not going to waste this second chance that we've been given. I'm especially not going to do it because she wants to use the paramedic to hide from her feelings for me. When I tell her that, her expression becomes thunderous. I know I've touched a nerve, but I refuse to back down.

"You're scared. You're making this complicated, Iyah, when it doesn't have to be!"

"Not complicated for you or not complicated for me?" she challenges stiffly, "In case you've forgotten, I'm in a relationship!"

"Maybe *you've* forgotten! Thirty seconds ago, you admitted that you don't love him! And even if you hadn't, the fact we almost had sex is proof enough!"

She jerks to attention, as if I had just physically slapped her. It's a crass thing to say, but I refuse to take it back. I won't pull my punches with her. There's too much on the line. But Iyah won't be cornered. She has that obstinate scowl on her face, the look she gets whenever she's about to come out swinging. Her dark eyes harden, she cocks her head, lifts her chin, and lets me have it.

"You really have a high opinion of yourself, don't you? There is more to a relationship than just sex! Just because I want you that doesn't mean I need you!"

"I know you love me, Iyah! Don't try to convince me that what we have is just physical! It's not! You know that, and so do I! So why the hell are we doing this?"

"Do you have any idea what you put me through?" she snaps, "You *broke* me, Julien. I was a mess after you. It took me *almost a year* to be okay again!"

"You broke me too," I whisper. But she doesn't hear me when I say that. Or she doesn't *want* to hear me.

"You don't get it, do you? Every time you and I are together we wreck everything and *everyone* in our path! That's not right! Aren't you sick of being the villain? Kate didn't deserve it, and Hez doesn't deserve it."

"Don't drag her into this!"

"Why not? You destroyed your entire relationship, Julien! And for what?"

"What are you saying? You're going to stay with him? Out of what? Obligation? Principle?"

"He loves me!"

"*I* love you!"

I realize I'm screaming at her, and that's not what I want. I don't want to fight with her at all. More than anything, I want to go back to ten minutes ago when we were the only two people who existed in the world. I slump forward in weary defeat.

"Don't do this to me. We just found each other again. Don't push me away, Iyah."

"I can't start this with you again," she mutters in clear misery, "I just can't..."

"You're the one who came to *me* tonight! *You* started this!"

"I know that! I know! And I'm sorry. It was a mistake. I wasn't trying to hurt you."

I'm ready to crumble emotionally after she says that, but then I stop myself before I go into a tormented tailspin. I suddenly remember that I've been where she is. I know the deep self-loathing and shame she's feeling because I wrestled with those same feelings the night that I ended my engagement to Kate. I'm very familiar with what it's like to devastate someone who has been nothing but good and kind to you, someone who doesn't deserve to be discarded so thoughtlessly. It caused me to question what sort of person I was and whether I even *liked* that person at all.

She doesn't want to be the girl who cheats on her loyal, unsuspecting boyfriend with the same man who, by her own account, blew her life apart. And yet, that is what she's become, and she thinks that makes her a disgraceful, worthless person. But it doesn't. It makes her flawed. It makes her human. The problem is that Iyah has never given herself any room to be either. She's her own worst critic.

This moment doesn't have to define her. She only has to find the strength to move beyond it, to make the difficult choice we both know she needs to make. But until Iyah can come to terms with that on her own and forgive herself, I know that she and I will never get anywhere. She's always going to view what we have together as something forbidden and sordid. She'll always believe she has to run from it.

She once told me that she didn't want to be my dirty secret. I don't want to be hers either. I don't want to be someone she regrets.

A charged beat of silence crackles between us. "Are you really choosing him?" I ask.

"He's good for me."

It's not an answer any more than her response to whether or not she loved him was an answer, but I accept her decision, nonetheless. "Okay."

Iyah blinks at me in disbelief. "Okay?"

"Yes, okay. I want you to be happy. And if he makes you happy…" I can't finish the statement, not only because I have my doubts about that but because it just hurts too much. "All I ask is that you consider one thing."

Her hopeful expression becomes guarded again. "And what's that?"

"You say that he's good for you, but have you asked yourself whether *you're* good for him?" Her eyes glitter with defiance and anger because she assumes I'm trying to insult her. But I quickly clarify my meaning with my next question. "Are you really going to do him any favors if you stay with him when you're in love with me?"

She doesn't reply to the question, not even a single sarcastic rejoinder and I know that's because she doesn't have an answer. At least, not one that makes sense. I take advantage of her silence to cross over to the desk and grab the complimentary notebook and pen provided by the hotel. I scribble down my address, tear off the page and then pass it to her.

Iyah barely glances at it and continues to regard me with an impatient, taut expression. "What's this?"

"My address in Atlanta," I tell her, "When you figure things out, come to me. I'll be waiting."

30

When I promised Iyah that I would wait for her, I hadn't anticipated that the wait would reach the two-month mark. Travis has no qualms about declaring me an idiot. He doesn't hesitate to remind me that while Iyah might have come close to sleeping with me in New York, that obviously doesn't translate into her wanting to take a chance on me. Hence the reason I am currently alone.

He lays it all out for me in savage detail. The paramedic is a safe, sure bet. He doesn't come with excess emotional baggage or a complicated relationship with his ex-fiancée. He doesn't have the potential to break her spirit or make her question her self-worth. He hasn't shaken her trust. When the situation is analyzed so critically, I can understand why Travis believes I'm fighting a losing battle.

I can fully admit that he's not wrong either. I shouldn't have a single shred of hope left after what happened in New York and yet…I can't let go. I almost did before and then, by some twist of Fate, she was delivered back into my life again. My chances with her now are a hell of a lot better than they were then. At least now I know she loves me. She actually said the words, and that changed *everything*.

I don't doubt at all that Iyah *will* come back to me. I don't know when, but I'm willing to wait for her as long as necessary. When I tell Travis this, he reiterates that I'm wasting my time.

"That's just sad, man," he laments, shaking his head. "You gotta let it go."

"Why do I have to? She loves me."

"She dropped you."

"She's only with that other guy because he's safe, and she's terrified of making another mistake," I tell him confidently. When he starts to argue, probably to insist that I'm being delusional and desperate, I am quick to interrupt. "You don't know her like I do! Iyah likes to be in control, and she's never more out of control than when we're together."

"Can I be honest with you?" I nod for him to speak his mind even though I know he wasn't going to wait for my permission anyway. "That's messed up."

"It all depends on your point of view."

As assured as I am, I didn't arrive at this place of hopeful serenity easily at all. I'll admit that when I first came back home, I was disheartened and frustrated. But the more I thought about the reason Iyah pushed me away, the less despondent I became. Our affair (and I hate calling it that) hadn't only caused *me* to second-guess myself, Iyah has clearly struggled with her own self-image too. She said it had taken her nearly a year to move past what happened with us.

I remember being stunned when she revealed that because, from my perspective, she had moved on from me with surprising ease. It was true that she had spent that last week of promotion with a drink in her hand constantly, but I couldn't really blame her. Having to smile and laugh and flirt my way through those endless interviews and stupid promotion stunts when I was dying inside had been agony for me. I could only imagine how Iyah felt being forced to see my face every day when she fully believed I had used and discarded her.

But she was so cold and detached afterwards that I never believed that she was anything other than done with me. When I left that morning, she didn't even say goodbye. She went to a party instead. The last time I saw her, she was laughing with her group of new friends with some other guy's hand on her ass. We left things in an awful place back then.

This time is different. This time we're different. In spite of the bitterness and pain that was still between us, Iyah had been willing to be vulnerable with me, which I know goes against every instinct she has. Even after our fight in the pizza parlor and her firm insistence that she was over me, she had still sought me out that night after listening to my voicemail because she thought I needed her. There is no way in hell that I'm giving up on her after that.

Travis shakes his head at me in disappointment before replacing his headphones and resuming his video game. I take advantage of his preoccupation to go for a run. I'm not sure he's heard me when I announce my intention until I catch the dubious glance that he throws back at me over his shoulder. His expression clearly says, "Bruh, you're crazy." Jogging remains an inexplicable pastime to Travis on a good day. Jogging in 90-degree, muggy Georgia heat, however? That's suicidal.

"Don't call me when you go down from heatstroke!" he calls out as I head out the door.

"I won't!"

When I return an hour later, I am soaked in sweat and utterly exhausted but feeling pretty good. Travis is still in the same spot I left him, currently battling his way through some kind of secret dungeon. He tips a nod of acknowledgement at me while I raid the refrigerator for several bottles of water and drain them all in rapid succession.

"Did you have fun running in the hot Georgia sun?" he wisecracks, barely splitting his attention between me and the television.

"It's doable. You just have to stay hydrated." Travis grunts his skepticism and flashes me another glance that makes it obvious that he thinks I'm "different." I laugh at his expression, having lived with him long enough to predict what he's about to say next. "Yeah, yeah, I know. That's some white people nonsense," I quote with a sarcastic roll of my eyes, "I'm gonna hit the shower now."

I linger under the lukewarm spray for much longer than I intend. Inevitably my mind wanders to memories of Iyah and the first and only time she and I showered together. I remember being appalled over how cold she liked to keep the water. When I complained about it, she'd launched into a lengthy and impassioned monologue about the benefits of cooler water and how a less scalding temperature was better for the skin. That was when I knew for sure that I loved her. I would have gladly listened to her random lectures for the rest of my life.

When I finally exit the shower, I'm still invigorated from my earlier run but a little subdued. As I shuffle through the hall, past the living room on my way to my bedroom, I catch a glimpse of Travis on the couch in my peripheral vision. "You haven't made it out of that dungeon yet?" I laugh, "Bro, you're slipping!"

"That's big talk for someone who has no gaming skills himself."

I freeze in my tracks when the reply comes, not due to the insult itself but because Travis had *not* been the one to deliver it. Instead, the voice was soft and feminine and very familiar. I slowly pivot and inch my way back to the threshold that leads off into the living room and peek around the corner. I'm almost convinced that I'm hallucinating.

Travis is nowhere to be seen, but Iyah is standing there next to the sofa and looking at me with a small, impish smile. The first thing I notice is that she's changed her hair since I last saw her. Instead of the dramatic cloud of fluffy curls that usually surrounds her face, she has it braided now. Glossy twists fall across her shoulder in a coiling side ponytail. The second thing I notice, and it is the thing that captures my attention and holds it, is the way that she's dressed. I don't think I've ever seen her display so much skin in the entire time I've known her.

She's wearing a pair of denim shorts and a red and white, striped halter top that reveals beautiful, bare swathes of her shapely body and smooth, gleaming brown skin. My mouth goes dry at the sight of her. And while it makes sense that she would be wearing minimal attire given the oppressive humidity outside, I have the irrational wish that she had chosen a turtleneck sweater and ankle length skirt to wear instead. As a result of my prolonged, self-imposed abstinence, my body's reaction to so much exposed skin is pretty much immediate.

Suddenly, I am acutely aware that I'm fresh from a shower and wearing nothing except a bath towel. Under any other circumstances, I might approach her with a warm greeting, maybe even attempt a hug, but I can't. There is no way for me to conceal the intense effect she's having on me. For that reason, I remain half hidden behind the wall.

"Hi."

"Hi," she replies as if it's not the most insane thing in the world that she's standing in the middle of my living room now without any warning whatsoever.

It's like she dropped in from out of nowhere. Not that her presence is unwelcome. Far from it. If she's here, then clearly something significant has changed. That can only mean something positive for us. I know I'm probably grinning at her rather stupidly but, given the circumstances, I can't really help it.

"Is there a reason you're hiding behind that wall?" she asks with a quizzical frown, "All I can see is your head."

I can't rightly tell her that the mere sight of her has me hard enough to drive nails, so I go with the honest and more respectable answer. "I just got out of the shower. I'm in a towel."

"Right." She appears to ponder that explanation for a moment and then she says, "You know I've seen you naked before, Julien."

"Yeah," I acknowledge, clearing my throat self-consciously. "I'm aware." But I don't dare move, not even a hair.

I dart my eyes around for Travis, desperate for some kind of lifeline or distraction, but he is nowhere to be found. My dumbfounded expression must be full of questions because Iyah quickly fills in the blanks. "If you're looking for your roommate, he left a few minutes ago. I think he said his name was Travis." She chews on the inside of her cheek. "He's…um…different."

Because I can't really refute that description, I don't even bother to try. "Did he happen to say where he was going?"

"He did not. He only said that he would be gone long enough for you to 'take care of business.' I assume you know what that means." She surveys me with a long, probing look that makes it abundantly clear that *she* knows what it means. My cheeks grow hot under her scrutiny. "I'm pretty sure he was high."

"Probably. That *is* his default setting."

She makes a breathy sound, almost like a half laugh, half groan and it stirs something primal in me. I throb. *Literally.* The surging pressure nearly triggers an audible moan. Thankfully, Iyah is oblivious.

"I didn't know you lived with someone. When I showed up, I thought maybe I had come to the wrong address."

"I figured you would call first."

Iyah looks uncertain at my reply. "Is it okay that I didn't?" she frets.

"Yes!" I shout so vehemently that she actually covers a snicker. I close my eyes and take a few seconds to collect myself. "I mean, yes. It's fine. I'm surprised. It's a good surprise."

There is a small stretch of silence that yawns between us which only heightens my awareness of my current vulnerable state. I start to excuse myself when she says, "I see that you've been painting." She nods to several bold abstracts that adorn the living room wall. She turns back to regard me with a proud smile. "They're yours, aren't they?"

"Yeah. I've really gotten back into it since my mom died."

"They're very good. I like them."

"Thanks." Another beat of silence passes, and I'm compelled to fill it. "I like your hair."

She ducks her head with a shy smile and mumbles her own "thanks," as well. "The humidity wasn't kind to me the last time I was here."

The tacit reminder of the time we spent together in Atlanta and all the unresolved sexual tension between us is not helping my present situation. I know that we need to have a serious discussion about what brought her here today and what that means for the future of our relationship, but all I can think about is sex. With her. On the floor. On the sofa. In my bed. On any available flat surface that I can find. The overwhelming need is muddling my reason. I need to get control of my surging hormones before I make a complete fool out of myself.

I hitch a nod back towards my bedroom door. "I should go and...um...get dressed now," I tell her, "We can catch up when I'm done. In the meantime, feel free to help yourself to whatever."

As soon as I reach the refuge of my bedroom, I rip off the bath towel and toss it onto my bed, but I don't get dressed right away. Instead, I use those first few minutes alone trying unsuccessfully to flatten my thumping erection into flaccid submission. I keep reminding myself that sex will come later, *after* Iyah and I have had a real discussion, but my body is not being cooperative.

Every nerve ending pulses with a continual refrain, "Sex now, please!" My self-control is hanging by a thread. I'm quietly panicking and in the middle of trying to talk myself down when my bedroom door yawns open. I whip around just as Iyah slips inside and closes the door behind her.

A mortified curse escapes me upon her entry. I snatch up the nearest item within my reach, the same perspiration-soaked t-shirt I threw aside *before* my shower, and reflexively cover my genitals. "What are you doing in here?" My distress must be obvious because I can tell she's covering an amused smile. She sweeps my body with a suggestive once-over.

"You said I should feel free to help myself to whatever," she reminds me with a feline smirk, "I'm taking you up on your offer."

"This…this is *not* what I meant!"

"Let's talk about what you *did* mean then." She advances on me slowly. "You said that if I changed my mind that you would wait for me," she considers as she purposefully closes the distance between us. "Is that still true?"

"Have you changed your mind?" I whisper.

She takes another step forward. "I have."

It takes everything I have in me not to groan aloud when I answer her. "Then you know that it's still true."

"Then we're being a little ridiculous, don't you think?" She continues to move closer and closer, matching me step for step until I'm trapped between her and the edge of my bed. And then with great deliberateness, she reaches down to tug my t-shirt from my rigid fingers and tosses it aside. When I squawk at her audacity, she bites her lip to keep from laughing at me. "Why are you acting so shy? It isn't like we've never done this before."

"We should talk first, Iyah," I remind her, but it's hard to concentrate when she's dragging her fingers down my abdomen towards my groin.

"I think we should talk later."

Her fingers close around me, and I'm convinced. "Okay. I'm good with that plan."

Coherent thought doesn't return until much later, when she's straddled over me, her hips straining urgently against mine, and I've ridden out the most intense orgasm of my entire life. But once she rolls away from me, breathless, beaded with sweat, and beautifully lethargic, I start to consider all the important things we've failed to discuss...namely where do we go from here. As exhilarating as it is to have her in my bed again, I'm not ignorant of the multiple hurdles we still have left to jump together.

I shift onto my side to face her with an ironic grunt. "Really, Grandberry?" I mumble tiredly, "It took you *two months* to leave that guy? I'm not sure how I feel about that."

"Actually, it took me two months to wrap my musical *and* to peel my dad off the ceiling after I told him that I was moving to Georgia to be with you."

For the moment, I put aside my anxiety over her father's less than enthused reaction. I blink at her in stunned delight. The possibility of relocation is nothing that we've discussed or that I even imagined she would consider, but I'm not disappointed about the possibility. Iyah seems uncertain, however.

"Is...is that okay with you?" she asks.

"Is that what *you* want?"

"I want to be where you are," she whispers, "I can figure the rest out later."

I nuzzle a grateful kiss across her lips. "Then yes," I say, answering her initial question, "It's okay with me." Later, after we've made love for a second time and she lies draped across my chest, I ask her, drifting somewhere between sleepiness and wakefulness, "What made you change your mind about us?" I'm certainly not disappointed by the outcome, but I am curious.

She traces small circles on my abdomen. "I thought about what you said that last night we were together. You were right. I wasn't doing Hez any favors by staying with him when I was in love with you."

"How'd he take your breakup?" I ask, plucking absently at one of her braids.

"He was hurt and angry at first, but he didn't seem surprised. He told me that he never felt like he had my entire heart anyway, and now he understood the reason."

"Are you okay? How do you feel?"

"Honestly? I felt awful when I did it," she confesses gruffly, "I didn't want to hurt him. But, at the same time, I know I did the right thing. It's weird. I wish I hadn't broken his heart, but I wouldn't do anything differently either. I can't regret being here with you. It feels right. It always has."

I give her a gentle squeeze. "Same."

Iyah looks up at me then, her forehead creased with a deep frown. "Why didn't you just tell me it was over with Kate?" she laments aloud, "Why did you let me think you were going back to her? We could have been together this whole time."

"It was better this way. I think I needed to grow up so I could be a better man for you."

"And do you think you grew up and became a better man?"

The question coaxes a small, self-effacing smile from me. "How about I let *you* be the judge of that one?"

She raises her eyebrows in laughing challenge. "Oh really? I'm the deciding factor on that, am I?"

"Yeah, you are. Yours is the only opinion that matters anyway."

I'm not attempting to flatter her when I say that. My emotional growth has been substantial in the past year, but if she can't see it then we're not where we need to be. Iyah has to believe I'm good for her like she's good for me, or this will never work. But when I look at her, I already know her determination even before she answers me. I release a short, trembling sigh filled with gratitude.

"Well then, in that case, sir..." she whispers, shifting over me for an affirming kiss. "...I have no complaints."

Made in the USA
Columbia, SC
14 October 2024

43530385R00202